"I'm hooked on this series!"

**Praise for the
Ladies of St. Jude's Abbey Series**

A Moonlit Knight

"Delightful . . . fabulous."   —*Midwest Book Review*

"Whether you love history, historical romances, or simply high drama, this book is made just for you!"
—Huntress Book Reviews

One Knight Stands

"A splendid read."   —Virginia Henley

"Exhilarating . . . an action-packed tale of honor, courage, and spirit that never strays from its wonderful romance."   —*Susan Grant

"The beauty of the Ladies of St. Jude's Abbey series blooms sweeter with each new novel. [Kelley] delivers a story of well-paced action, richly detailed in period lore, and caps it off with a hero worth fighting for."
—*Booklist*

continued . . .

**The Ladies of
St. Jude's Abbey Series
by Jocelyn Kelley**

*A Knight Like No Other
One Knight Stands
A Moonlit Knight
My Lady Knight*

Lost In Shadow

f

Jocelyn Kelley

A SIGNET ECLIPSE BOOK

SIGNET ECLIPSE
Published by New American Library, a division of
Penguin Group (USA) Inc., 375 Hudson Street,
New York, New York 10014, USA
Penguin Group (Canada), 90 Eglinton Avenue East, Suite 700, Toronto,
Ontario M4P 2Y3, Canada (a division of Pearson Penguin Canada Inc.)
Penguin Books Ltd., 80 Strand, London WC2R 0RL, England
Penguin Ireland, 25 St. Stephen's Green, Dublin 2,
Ireland (a division of Penguin Books Ltd.)
Penguin Group (Australia), 250 Camberwell Road, Camberwell, Victoria 3124,
Australia (a division of Pearson Australia Group Pty. Ltd.)
Penguin Books India Pvt. Ltd., 11 Community Centre, Panchsheel Park,
New Delhi - 110 017, India
Penguin Group (NZ), 67 Apollo Drive, Rosedale, North Shore 0745,
Auckland, New Zealand (a division of Pearson New Zealand Ltd.)
Penguin Books (South Africa) (Pty.) Ltd., 24 Sturdee Avenue,
Rosebank, Johannesburg 2196, South Africa

Penguin Books Ltd., Registered Offices:
80 Strand, London WC2R 0RL, England

First published by Signet Eclipse, an imprint of New American Library,
a division of Penguin Group (USA) Inc.

First Printing, July 2007
10 9 8 7 6 5 4 3 2 1

For Lucie Carley

Thanks from all of us—and the girls. . . .

Chapter 1

"It was murder. Murder most foul."

At the whisper, Jade Nethercott glanced up from the book she had taken from a shelf. Her late father had written notes in the margins and underlined sections of text. Reading his comments, which showed he had been outraged at the author's opinions, made her feel as if he were still with her. She had spent many hours in discussion with Father and her two sisters in his bookroom, where the walls were lined with shelves and chairs begged one to curl up in them.

That had ended when her father had died suddenly from a weak heart, an ailment none of them suspected he had. Neither she nor her sisters had been prepared for the loss, and a year's passage had not eased their grief.

But Father's had been a natural death, not murder. Who was talking about such a heinous crime?

"It was murder. Murder most foul," came the whisper again.

She looked around. "Who said that?"

Instead of an answer, she heard something click loudly in the corridor. As if someone had abruptly unlatched a door.

If this was one of her sisters' idea of a hoax to relieve the boredom of a stormy day, it was not an amusing one. She looked out the door and saw nobody. Maybe it was only the wind playing with ancient eaves where gargoyles spit out the rain coursing down onto the roofs.

She turned a page of the book and continued to read.

"It was murder. Murder most foul." The whisper was followed by the same noise in the hallway.

"Bother," she muttered. Who was whispering such nonsense and making that noise? Mrs. Mathers, the housekeeper, had been at Nethercott Castle for as long as Jade could remember. She oversaw the servants with a strict but fair sense of discipline. Anyone making such a to-do would be turned out by the housekeeper posthaste.

Setting the book on a table, Jade went to the door again. She looked in both directions along the narrow hall at the top of the stairs. Two lamps were lit against the twilight of day's end, creating narrow pools on the wood floor covered by a red and green runner. The paneled walls swallowed any hint of light, leaving the few paintings in shadow.

Everything looked as it should, and she heard no more clatter. She sighed. Before Father's death, the house had been filled with happy voices and laughter. No longer. It was as if after so many months of mourning, they didn't know how to be happy again.

She reached to straighten her father's portrait that hung next to his favorite room. In the painting, he looked not much older than she was now. He held a book in one hand and a quill in the other. His gaze was focused at something in the distance, and there was a hint of a smile on his lips. That smile seemed to widen as light spread across the portrait.

What light? There should not be any light coming from the far end of the hall.

But there was. Not from a lamp, for the light shone from a spot about halfway between the floor and the high ceiling. It was like a ball; then it stretched toward the floor.

"It was murder. Murder most foul." The voice seemed to be coming from the light. It was, she noticed for the first time, a deep masculine voice.

She blinked once, then another time, but the light grew stronger. What was it? It could not be anything of this world. Her gaze flicked toward her father's book-room and the book she had been holding. A book about restless spirits who walked the earth after death.

No, it was impossible. Her father had spent his life trying to prove that the old castle was haunted, but nothing he had done—séances or attempts to contact the dead directly or special candles or anything else—had turned up a single sign of a phantom clinging to the chilliest spots in the seldom used corridors and chambers. Cold spots in the rooms where the family gathered always could be explained by a drafty window or a piece of furniture blocking the heat from the hearth.

Father had been disappointed, but eventually conceded that Nethercott Castle, in spite of its location on the desolate Yorkshire Moors and its generations of inhabitants—first as a priory and then as a castle—was unhaunted.

So what was an otherworldly light doing now, lurking in the corridor outside Father's book-room? Fate was so cruel. She bit back an unseemly oath. A laugh tickled the back of her throat. Why was she worried about swearing in the presence of someone who had obviously been cursed? For what other reason would that person still be loitering in the castle?

"It was murder. Murder most foul. It was—" The bass voice in the light halted, then said, "I guess I should be grateful, Miss Nethercott, that you are not screaming or surrendering to a fit of vapors."

A ghost that spoke to her by name? She gasped and pressed her hand over her thudding heart. This was beyond extraordinary. She glanced over her shoulder. If she shouted to her sisters, would the ghost fade back into the woodwork?

Her curiosity overcame her fear. She squinted, and she could see a human shape taking form. The light was still too bright for her to discern what the ghost was wearing.

"I would appreciate the courtesy of a greeting," the male voice continued, a hint of annoyance creeping into the words. "It is the least you can offer a guest in your house."

"I am sorry. I am at a loss for words." Jade did not add that such a loss was a most unusual state for her. "You must admit that the common pleasantries are not appropriate. After all, you are a ghost!"

"Obviously." The ghost's tone suggested that he was vexed by his current state. The light around him was easing, and she could see he wore clothing of a very recent style.

But nobody had died in the past few years at Nethercott Castle other than her beloved father. This specter was not Lord Nethercott, for he did not possess the girth her father had acquired along with his many years. Nor did the voice belong to Father. He had seldom scolded her or her sisters, yet she had frequently heard him exasperated with his studies, so she would have recognized that tone.

Deciding there was no reason to waste thought in speculation, she simply asked, "Who are you?"

"I *was* Sir Mitchell Renshaw."

Jade stepped away from the door and peered at the form emerging from the light. The sensation was rather like watching a faded painting regaining its color and texture. She could now see his rust-colored waistcoat and dark breeches draped over his thin form, but his face was a glowing blob beneath his hair that was almost the same shade as his waistcoat. "Why would Sir Mitchell Renshaw haunt Nethercott Castle? He called here only a few times."

"To study with the Professor."

Her breath caught. Even though her father had rightly held the title of Lord Nethercott, twelfth baron, he had preferred to be addressed as "Professor." He had believed it more in keeping with his love for books and philosophy and science. As well, he felt it more of an honor than a title bestowed on a distant relative who had done something to gain favor with a long-dead king.

"You are, I assume, one of the Professor's daughters," the spirit said.

"I am Jade Nethercott."

"Which one are you?"

"The middle one."

The ghost's mouth twisted. Had he been wearing that expression before? His features were beginning to materialize, and they were the ones she recalled belonging to Sir Mitchell Renshaw. Even his fiery, bushy mustache was becoming visible. His waistcoat buttons appeared to be of fine gold, a surprise because burying a man with such affectations was an invitation to robbers to open his grave to relieve him of the riches.

"I thought you were the eldest," he said, drawing her attention away from his amazing metamorphosis from light to the appearance of something solid.

"That is China. And my sister Sian is younger than me by less than a year, Sir Mitchell." She might as well address him as Sir Mitchell, because that was more comfortable than the idea she was carrying on a conversation with a *ghost*.

"I guess you will have to do."

"Do? For what?" Every instinct told her that she had been want-witted to ask that question, but it was too late to retract the words.

"I cannot rest while my beloved Persis is in danger."

Jade was about to ask him to explain when footfalls came up the stairs. She glanced behind her for only a second, but when she turned back, Sir Mitchell was gone.

"To whom are you talking?" Sian asked as she walked to where Jade stood. She was carrying her sketching book. She seldom went anywhere without it.

At a cursory look, Sian appeared to be identical to her, but her sister's hair was a darker blond, and her eyes were an earth brown. Sian was a few fingers taller, just enough so she could not borrow any of Jade's clothes.

"Let me ask you a question before I answer yours," Jade said as she went back into her father's book-room. Sitting on the closest chair, she was amazed that her knees were trembling as fiercely as her hands. "Do you remember Sir Mitchell Renshaw? He studied with Father for a fortnight several years ago."

"Sir Mitchell Renshaw?" Sian frowned as she chose

the chair facing Jade's. "I thought you had heard the horrible news of his death."

"I knew he was dead." That much was obvious, for a living man did not appear in a ball of light and disappear even more swiftly. "I had not heard more."

"China told me when she came back from her visit to Scarborough last month. Sir Mitchell was found dead in a ditch not far from London. He had been . . ." She lowered her voice. "*On dits* says he was murdered."

"That makes sense."

Sian gasped. "Murder makes sense?"

"It would explain why Sir Mitchell cannot rest and why he appeared here moments ago as a ghost."

"A ghost? You are jesting!"

"No." Jade quickly explained what she had seen and heard. As she described Sir Mitchell, she was surprised to hear herself using words like "short-tempered" and "arrogant." She had learned to trust her first impressions, and her first impression of the ghostly baronet was that he was amazingly impatient. An odd trait for a ghost who had all of eternity ahead of him.

When she finished, she waited for her sister to say something. Anything. Tell her that she must have imagined the encounter; share her sadness that Father had not been present to see a *real* ghost in the castle; ask her if she had been frightened . . . anything.

Sian stared at the hearth, her face a blank. When she spoke, her voice was not much more than a whisper. "I saw an odd light several nights ago in the garden. I meant to mention it at breakfast the next morning, but I forgot about it until now." She looked back at Jade. "Do you think *that* was Sir Mitchell arriving to take up residence in the castle?"

"But why would he come here?"

"Father may have sent him."

Jade clasped her hands in her lap to still their trembling. "I had not considered that."

"He and the baronet were acquainted, and Father could have assured Sir Mitchell that we are open to the idea of phantoms in the halls of Nethercott Castle."

"I wonder what he wanted. He seemed concerned about a woman named Persis."

"He was betrothed to marry Persis Bannatyne. As for what he wants"—Sian shrugged—"we may never know if he does not reappear before we leave for London."

"Leave?"

"China believes that going to London would allow us to escape the grief of remaining here. That was what I was coming to tell you. We are departing for Town in a week's time."

"I doubt a change of scenery will give me a change of heart."

"Jade, you have spent the past year doing little but reading Father's books and correspondence, so you might inform his friends of his passing. You have done all a daughter should and much more." She smiled sadly. "You need to remember what Father wanted for us."

She sighed. "I know. For us to be carefree and enjoy a Season or two before settling down to make him a grandfather."

"So say you will come with us to Town. I could never have fun knowing you were here alone."

"I . . . I don't know."

Sian frowned. "It is unlike you to be so hesitant."

"True." Picking up the book, she paged through it until she found the spot where she had been reading. She closed the book over her finger.

"So will you come with us?"

"I don't know if I can. Now that Sir Mitchell has appeared here, I should investigate why. If I could prove Father's beliefs to be true to those who pooh-poohed him—"

"The ghost may never return."

"I think he will. I must wait and see."

"While you grow so old that you are put on the very back of the shelf?" Sian stood and went to the door. "I shall be miserable in London without you."

She did not answer, and her sister walked out. As Sian's footsteps faded down the stairs, Jade opened the book. The words blurred in front of her. If her sister did not understand her need to show the people who had laughed at her father that he was right, who would?

Jade yawned widely, her eyes squinting in the bright light. It was dawn already? She felt as if she had just fallen asleep. Or it might have been that she was exhausted from poring over her father's books for hours. Her research had gained her nothing that she did not already know.

Rolling over, she glanced at the window. Starlight fell through it. But it was light. It was . . .

With a soft cry, she pulled the covers up to her chin as she saw a man encased in light standing at the foot of her bed. "Sir Mitchell!" She groped for her robe as she stared at the phantom. Somehow, she got her arms into it. She buttoned it closed and swung her feet out of bed.

He stared at her, and she looked down to see one bare leg sticking out of her robe. She hastily flipped the robe over it and stood. When she frowned at him, he grimaced.

"Miss Nethercott," he asked in the same exasperated tone he had used in the hallway, "what do you think a ghost could do to you other than admire such a lithe limb?"

Folding her arms in front of her, she walked past the embroidered bed curtains to face him across the old chest at the foot of the tester bed. She did not retort as she would have to a living man who made such a crass comment. Rather, she said, "I had thought you would return before now."

"I returned posthaste."

"You last appeared four days ago."

He scowled. "I would vow I left only long enough for you to walk from the hall into this room."

"It would appear that time has a different course when one is no longer living." She hesitated, and then asked, "What is it like to be dead?"

Sir Mitchell chuckled, but she heard little amusement in the sound. "That question proves that you are the

Professor's daughter. He always was curious to find answers to unanswerable questions. We do not have time to discuss such issues."

"Have you seen my father?"

"No." He faltered, then said, "Oh, you mean his spirit? Yes, I did, and he suggested I come to speak with you."

"He did?"

"Yes. Don't ask me if I saw anyone else. Other than the Professor, I have not encountered any people who passed on before I did."

"Maybe because you are stuck between this world and the one where they are. Is he coming here, too?"

"Not that I know of." Again he hesitated, as if speaking of the world of the deceased were difficult. "He went somewhere else. I am unsure where, but it was not here."

"It could be that he was there to ease your transition." She sat on a chair by her writing table. "It has been suggested that those who die violently cannot find rest because they were unprepared to take the journey to whatever awaits beyond our lives."

"That is possible, but I do not have time to discuss philosophy. I had hoped your sister could see me when I first arrived at Nethercott Castle, but she apparently could not."

"But I can see you."

"Obviously." He grimaced at her. "And just as obviously she could not."

"But why can *I* see you?"

He shrugged. "Why should I know the answer to that? I cannot, it is becoming clear, decide who will see me. Just as I cannot decide when I am seen."

"Or when you disappear? You vanished when my sister came near. Do you think she caused you to disappear?"

"Again, I have no idea, and I have no interest in pursuing such useless questions. How long have I been dead?"

"I am not certain of the exact date of your death."

"I am." His mouth tightened into a straight line. "It was the sixteenth day of March."

"Not quite the Ides of March."

He sat on the chest. "If you think such words are amusing, Miss Nethercott, I may have made an error in coming to speak with you."

"Forgive me, Sir Mitchell." She came to her feet. "I am greatly unsettled by our conversations."

"As I am. How long has it been?"

"Almost two months. It is now May."

"May? So much time has passed?" His fingers constricted on the edge of the chest as if he were trying to grip it, but the wood was visible through them. "I find the whole of this situation unsettling. If it were not for my concerns for Persis—"

"Your betrothed?"

"I see you are more aware of my circumstances than you led me to believe." He eyed her up and down with a candid appraisal that would have been too bold . . . if he were still breathing.

She decided to ignore it again. "Why are you concerned about your betrothed?"

"I fear she will be the next victim of the horrific creature who ended my life."

"If that is so, why are you here? Why aren't you warning her?"

"I have tried. It seems that she can neither see nor hear me. I was unsure where to turn, but then I recalled the Professor and his interest in ghosts. I hoped one of his daughters would be able to see me." He donned a triumphant smile. "And I was right."

Jade tried to ignore the feeling that she would not have liked Sir Mitchell while he was alive. On his visits to Nethercott Castle, she had done no more than speak politely to him. Whether she found his company pleasant did not matter. He had come to her to help protect his erstwhile betrothed.

"I will be happy to send her a note—"

"No note!" he said sharply.

"Or I could arrange for the information to be taken to her when my sisters go to Town."

"No, you cannot tell her what I have told you in such a manner."

Her forehead ruffled with bafflement. "I don't understand, Sir Mitchell. You wish your betrothed to be warned, but yet you don't want me to write her or have a message taken to her."

"That is correct."

"You are making no sense."

"It is simple, Miss Nethercott. I need someone to watch that my beloved Persis does not share my fate at the hands of the one who ended my life. If you were to tell her the name of my killer, I doubt she would believe you."

"Why? Who slew you?"

"Gideon Bannatyne, third viscount. My beloved Persis's brother."

"Her brother?" She doubted if her face had any more color than the ghost's when she asked, "Your fiancée's brother killed you? Are you sure of this?"

"Do you think *I* don't know who drove that knife into me?" He stood and reached out to take her hands. He drew his own back when she shivered at the icy chill that exploded out from him. As she wrapped her arms around herself, he continued, "Miss Nethercott, I beg of you. Go to London and warn my dear Persis before it is too late. Her brother is of low reputation, and he has gotten away with murder. What is to keep him from attempting to kill again so he might have her share of the family's inheritance to replace his, which he has squandered on fast sport and faster women?"

"Tell me the facts of the murder, and I will go to the constable here in Yorkshire. He can have charges brought to the justice of the peace, who will know how to deal with such matters, and—"

"It is not that simple." He turned away. "I was not quite honest with you. I do not have irrefutable proof that Bannatyne's hand was on the blade that sliced into

me, even though he had induced me to meet him that
night. The knife was his, and he had made no secret that
he was not happy with the match. He may have hired
someone else to kill me. Either way, I need that proof,
and I cannot obtain it myself."

"So you wish me to do so?"

"Yes."

She sat again, warmer now that he was not so close.
"I still don't understand. Why me?"

"You can see and hear me, for a start." He smiled.
"In addition, I know the best way to get the proof is to
persuade Bannatyne to betray himself. If you were to
try to distract a libertine into revealing truth, what would
you use for bait?" Again he gave her a brazen appraisal.
"You are pleasing on the eye, and you have an innocence about you that will appeal to that cad."

"I am no harlot!"

"I did not mean to suggest that, Miss Nethercott. I
only suggest that you allow Bannatyne to become aware
of you. He will be unable to resist your innocence. I do
suggest you hide your intelligence. He has never shown
any interest in women who can think deeply."

"But how would I obtain such proof?"

"You will not find it in the Polite World, I must
warn you."

She clutched the front of her robe, holding it close to
her chin as another sudden chill surged down her back.
Not from the ghost, but her own uneasiness. "Are you
saying that I must go beyond the *ton*?"

"Yes, for I believe the proof waits in the demimonde.
There, in the place where I drew my last living breath,
among cyprians and concubines and others who will do
anything in exchange for a coin or two, must be someone
who conspired with him."

"More than one person attacked you?"

"Yes, and I heard a low voice of the streets as well
as a woman's voice. I was too near death to hear their
words or otherwise identify them, but I know the answer
is in the demimonde."

"But for me to go among such people would be to risk my reputation. . . ."

"And save my beloved Persis's life."

Jade sighed. No matter how much she argued, the facts came back to a young woman's life could be in danger. How many times had Father praised her for being resourceful? At this appalling time, she needed to prove that he had been right. There must be some way to find her way into the demimonde and out with the information Sir Mitchell needed without compromising herself completely. She had no idea how, but she would try because . . . She smiled and said, "All right. On one condition."

He smiled. "What condition?"

"That while I help you obtain the proof of Lord Bannatyne's part in your murder, you will help me obtain the proof that ghosts really exist."

"I stand before you, Miss Nethercott. What other proof do you need?"

"Can others see you?"

His smile became a frown. "We have already discussed that."

"While I work to obtain the information you request, I ask that you find a way to let others see you. That is my condition for helping you."

"I cannot promise that."

"You can promise to try."

"I promise to do my best, Miss Nethercott."

"As I will." It was her turn to hesitate before she said, "And if you learn the way to appear to others, maybe you can show my father how to reappear here at Nethercott Castle."

He bowed his head to her and started to fade.

"Wait!" she cried. "Do you know where the Bannatynes are now?"

"Both are at the viscount's house on Bedford Square." His voice was as wispy as his appearance. "In London."

Then he was gone.

Jade jumped up and ran across the hall to Sian's bedroom. Sian was asleep, almost hidden under the covers, but Jade was amazed to see her older sister's russet curls peeking over the back of a chair by the window. A book was on the floor, and she guessed China had fallen asleep while reading.

She shook Sian's shoulder, then China's. "Wake up, sleepyheads."

They grumbled as they opened their eyes.

"It is the middle of the night," China said with a yawn. She set herself on her feet and rubbed her eyes. "Why are you routing us up now?"

"Because we are going to London on the morrow. There is no time to waste."

"You are coming with us?" Sian asked.

"Yes."

"It will be the best trip ever."

Jade struggled to smile. "I don't know about the best, but I suspect it will be the most interesting."

Chapter 2

"You must do something to catch Bannatyne's attention at the duchess's masquerade tonight."

Jade watched the ghostly form of Sir Mitchell waft
across the foyer, his feet not quite touching the black-
and-white tiles. The house on Grosvenor Square had
been found for them by the Duchess of Northborough,
who had been a friend of Jade's mother. It was elegant
and had everything they needed. Now it even included
a ghost.

"You have," Sir Mitchell continued, "delayed too long
in speaking with him."

She did not argue, even though she had tried to arrange an introduction with the viscount since their arrival in London a fortnight before. Her attempts to call
on Lord Bannatyne's sister, Lady Persis, had come to
naught, for each time she had been told that the lady
was receiving no callers whilst in mourning. The door
was shut firmly in her face, leaving her no choice but to
go to the duchess's gathering in hopes that the viscount
might attend as well.

"I thought you said Lord Bannatyne was a rake. Such
a man is sure to take notice of any woman he has not
encountered previously." She looked down at her gown,
the best she owned. With its simple white fabric to match
the feather in her upswept hair, she had barely recognized herself in the glass upstairs.

"You are presentable, but there will be many young
women there eager to get his attention."

"If he is truly a rake—"

"His title and his family's wealth can persuade many foolish and innocent misses into believing he would change his profligate ways if wed."

"I understand," she said, even though she did not. So many of the ways of the *ton* were mysterious to her. She knew the rules Society insisted must be followed, but the logic behind them often evaded her.

"So you must do something to make him take note of you." The ghost edged closer.

She stepped back as the icy chill surged over her.

He frowned, and she could not keep from wondering if he had worn that expression so often when he was alive. "If you are skittish in his company, Miss Nethercott, you doom your hopes as well as mine."

"It is not that."

"I know what I ask is not simple, Miss Nethercott. You must accept that the search for the truth is sure to lead you into the low world where Bannatyne consorts with his courtesans."

"I know." She was lying, because she had avoided considering that fact. Murders did not occur in front of the eyes of the Polite World. She would have to seek a way into the world of the impures and, at the same time, not draw attention to her and her family.

"Good. If you can face that, then you should have no trouble confronting Bannatyne."

"I know. It is . . ." She halted herself as she heard her sisters coming toward the stairs. "Sir Mitchell, what is it you suggest I do to gain the viscount's attention?"

He glanced toward the stairs, and she guessed he had taken note of her sisters' excited voices, too. She gasped when his form started to merge back into the light.

As if from a distance, she heard him say, "Tell him he must talk to Heath, that Heath knows something about what is happening."

"Happening? With what?"

From the stairs, she heard China call, "Jade, is there someone downstairs with you?"

"No," she said honestly as the last glimmer vanished.

Sir Mitchell was gone, and she was on her own to speak to Lord Bannatyne. A shiver, even more fierce than she felt when the ghost had neared, slid down her spine. She was about to—if Sir Mitchell was correct—speak to a murderer. But if she could see her father one more time, she would risk anything.

As she stood at one side of the ballroom in the Duchess of Northborough's grand house, Jade wondered why she had been worried that she would not be able to find Lord Bannatyne in the crowd. The glances and the whispers were all aimed at one corner of the grand ballroom where a man stood by himself.

Sir Mitchell's ghost had warned her that the viscount had a dark soul, but he had said nothing about how handsome Lord Bannatyne was. His navy coat, worn over white breeches, had been cut to flatter his muscular physique, which suggested he did not solely live an idle life of afternoons at his club and evenings spent in pursuit of a willing woman. His cravat was tied at a jaunty angle. His eyes, as ebony as his hair, flanked a patrician nose. His broad shoulders would have the strength to drive a knife deep into another man.

"Is that *him*?" asked China, wafting her fan rapidly.

"Who else would be a pariah at Her Grace's masquerade?" Jade closed her own fan before she was tempted to wave it to sweep aside her unsteady emotions.

"He is not even wearing a mask."

"Maybe he wants to persuade the other guests he has nothing to hide." Jade took a deep breath and said, "I am going to speak with Lord Bannatyne."

"You are mad!" Sian whispered.

"Do you have another idea how I can get to learn more about Lord Bannatyne if I avoid him?"

"Ask anyone else."

"Gossip is always suspect." She hesitated before saying, "You should know from the irrational comments made about Father."

"Do you doubt the viscount is a prime rake?"

"No." If she had questioned it before, she would no

longer. After seeing the glares every matron aimed in his direction and the eager giggles of young misses, it was clear Lord Bannatyne was as profligate as Sir Mitchell had said. She wondered if his current mistress was here. Unlikely, for the duchess would not invite anyone from the demimonde to her home.

"And Sir Mitchell believes him to be a murderer."

"True." She gave a terse laugh. "If I went to a magistrate and told him that a ghost came to me to name his murderer, I would be labeled as mad."

Before her sister could give her more reasons not to speak with Lord Bannatyne, Jade began to cross the grand ballroom. She must make use of this chance to speak with him. Her sisters could not understand why she was willing to risk her own reputation—and her own life—attempting to prove the viscount had slain Sir Mitchell. She had not told them about the ghost's vow to try to bring Father's ghost to speak with her. With *them*. She did not want to raise her sisters' hopes. She knew how easily they could be dashed.

Her steps faltered when she saw the duchess walking toward the viscount. Lord Bannatyne gave a slight bow of his head to acknowledge his hostess. The gray-haired duchess continued past as if he did not stand there.

Jade was intrigued. Her Grace had cut him direct in front of her other guests.

Lord Bannatyne put one hand nonchalantly on a nearby table, a hint of a smile tipping his lips as his gaze shifted from the duchess to her. His dark eyes glittered as brightly as the light through the glass balls dripping from the chandelier overhead. She could not read his thoughts before his gaze moved on, dismissing her.

She faltered. He had *dismissed* her? A rake who was rumored to bed any woman who crossed his path—be she quality or not—had looked away before she could catch his eye. For the first time, she wondered if she would fail before she began. She turned and walked back to where her sisters were watching with anxiety. Maybe she should forget her vow to Sir Mitchell and her yearning to show everyone that Lord Nethercott's ideas about ghosts were not half-baked. That would be the wise thing to do.

Yet the dream of seeing her father again was impossible to set aside. She must not fail.

"Lord Bannatyne, how is your sister?"

"As well as can be expected. Thank you for asking."

"What shocking news to hear of Sir Mitchell's passing!"

"Very shocking."

"Is there anything new in the search for his murderer?"

"Nothing."

Even before he had entered the ballroom at the duchess's house, Gideon Bannatyne had repeated that conversation a half dozen times. There always was the slightest pause before the last question. The *ton* thrived on gossip, and each member wished to be the first to know the most intriguing tidbit. It was their misfortune that he had nothing else to say on the subject. What he truly knew he was keeping to himself.

The ballroom was a confection of white and gold. A pair of grand crystal chandeliers were reflected in the open windows at either end of the room. And yet the room was stuffy and hot. The music from the orchestra was battling with the many voices trying to make themselves heard. It was a cacophony better suited to a fish market.

And every eye was focused on him.

Gideon asked himself—yet again—why he had let himself be persuaded to come to a gathering that he did not want to attend in the home of a hostess who believed the basest tales about him. He knew the other guests shared the duchess's opinions, even though several young women out of view of their duennas had given him glances that suggested they would overlook his past if he would offer them a future as his wife. He was not in search of a wife to give him heirs. He had other, far more important matters on his mind.

Everyone in the room had an opinion about why he

was at the masked ball without a mask. Some whispered
that he had come to prove he did not care a rap what
the *ton* thought. Or that he wanted to prove he was
foolish enough to offer them the chance to whisper and
snicker behind his back. Or—and he suspected this
choice was the most common, for he had heard asides
as he entered the ballroom—he was really here to find
a woman who was as indifferent to the vagaries of the
beau monde as he was and was as eager as he to avoid
returning to an empty bed.

He almost laughed aloud. There was little chance of
the last when every young woman was under the scrutiny
of a chaperone or a suitor who glowered at him with a
frown as black as Newgate. How insulted the other
guests would be if they were privy to the truth of why
he was here! It was prosaic and not worthy of gossip.
For that, he was grateful. He preferred that the *ton* spent
their time focused on his past sport instead of the task
only one other person—his loyal servant Tabor—knew
obsessed him.

But that was not what had brought him here tonight.
Guilt had.

He was here because Persis could not be. His sister
had taken to her bed in the wake of Renshaw's death.
He hoped that her adoration of gossip would entice her
out of her rooms. Persis thrived on the intrigues of the
ton, so he had come tonight to collect the latest *on dits*
for her. He felt guilty that he could not share her grief.
It had taken all of his wiles to keep anyone from discovering how pleased he was that the match had not
reached the point of exchanging marriage vows. Renshaw was dead, meeting a fate he had been tempting
for years.

Gideon scanned the room. He knew almost everyone
within its gilt and white walls. Even though every face
but his was covered with a mask, he could identify most
people with ease. The few he did not know, he disre-
garded.

As he walked around the room, silence surrounded

him like an invisible soap bubble. He would not gather any news for his sister when every conversation died as he neared. Each burst back to vigorous life in his wake, and he heard his name spoken along with Renshaw's. No doubt, he had added another to his list of crimes against the *ton*. He had failed to remain secluded during the period of mourning for a man he had despised. He would not be a hypocrite.

Not about Sir Mitchell Renshaw. And not about the duchess and her guests.

His eyes narrowed as he watched Lord Derlan greet their hostess with an effusive kiss on her hand. Even with the ornate Venetian mask the earl wore, he was easily recognizable by his height, which was equal to Gideon's, and his ostentatious signet ring, which he wore as if he were a royal duke. The earl was the current darling of the *ton* because he had been the victor in a recent duel where neither man was killed. He had fought the duel to defend his mother's honor from a blackguard who had accused her of being unfaithful to her faithless late husband. Derlan now had a scar on his right hand where a ball had creased it, the very sight of which threatened to send a young miss into vapors at the thought of his heroics.

Gideon went in the opposite direction. He had not been surprised to hear of Derlan's involvement in such theatrics. Derlan had long yearned to be lauded as a hero. They had known each other since childhood. Derlan had spent several summers at the Bannatyne's family estate in Cornwall, and he never had failed to remind Gideon that he was in direct line for a title while Gideon had several relatives between him and the family's title. When Derlan found out that through the convoluted ways of succession that he was next in line *after* Gideon for the Bannatyne's title, he had stopped talking about it.

That had been years ago, long before there had been so many deaths that left both Derlan and Gideon with titles. But one thing had not changed: Derlan was

addlepated, and should never have allowed himself to
be drawn into a duel. There was no honor in dying; there
was honor in living to fight for what was important.

"Bannatyne!"

At the shout that was as out of place at the duchess's
soirée as Gideon was, he kept walking. He had no interest
in listening to Derlan's pompous self-aggrandizing . . .
again.

His arm was grabbed. He stopped, but did not turn.
With deliberate serenity, he said, "If you are fond of
that scar, Derlan, you will remove your hand from my
arm before I remove it from yours."

The hand released him instantly. He took a single step
before the earl leaped in front of him like an awkward
ballet dancer.

Derlan regarded him with that sense of arrogance that
had been the source of many jokes before that insipid
duel.

Gideon said nothing, and the earl shifted uneasily
from one foot to the other. Derlan opened his mouth
several times to speak, but no sound emerged from it.

Without a comment, Gideon moved around him.

Derlan snarled a curse.

Gideon faced him and smiled coolly. "You should
watch your language. I have learned that the *ton* is willing to forgive idiocy more quickly than someone who
bends the Polite World's rules."

It took the earl a moment to recognize the insult. By
that time, Gideon had reached the double doors to the
garden.

Derlan seized his arm again. "You cannot speak to
me like that! You are lucky the duchess asked that all
gentlemen leave their walking sticks in the foyer.
Otherwise—"

"Otherwise what?"

"Otherwise you would be sorry, you . . . murderer!"

Again Gideon measured every motion with care. He
snapped his arm out of the earl's grip, turned, and drove
his fist into Derlan's chin. It was something he had
wanted to do for years. The earl teetered on his heels,

then collapsed to the floor amid screams from the female guests. From the corner of his eye, he saw two women swoon and tumble to the floor as well.

Dash it! He had not intended to bring home gossip centering on him . . . tonight.

Derlan stood and straightened his navy coat before dabbing at his bleeding nose. "I shall gladly see you hang, Bannatyne."

"I will gladly see that you never have the chance." He was not going to argue about the accusations attached to his name since Renshaw's death.

He left the earl sputtering behind him. Again he went no more than a few paces before he heard pursuit. Vexed that Derlan refused to leave off, he did not give the earl a chance to grab him a third time. He spun and drove his fist into Derlan's chin hard enough to lift the man off his feet. The earl hit the floor again. This time he did not move or even groan.

Gideon walked out of the house and into the back garden. Rubbing his aching knuckles against his other palm, he smiled grimly. He should take his leave. He would, as soon as he regained his composure. None of the duchess's guests must suspect that Derlan's words cut more deeply than Gideon had revealed.

With a sigh, he pushed the earl out of his thoughts as he crossed the stone terrace that opened onto the upper level of the tiered garden. The quiet was wondrous. London's growth had not yet overwhelmed the duchess's townhouse, so she still had the luxury of a garden that was rumored to surpass the one at her dirty acres in the country. He heard soft voices and glanced to his right. At the edge of the shadows, in the twilight where a woman's reputation could be tempted, but not sullied, several couples stood. Each man and woman were intent only on each other. Lilting giggles and deeper voices wove together in a tapestry of flirtations.

Gideon strode in the opposite direction. The terrace was swept by the light of the waning moon. Far from its glow, the stars were sprinkled across the sky like spilled sugar. Going down the stairs lit by a single brand set between the stones, he paused next to a low wall. He leaned against it and stared up at the rooftops of the nearby buildings. Smoke trickled from chimney pots. All that heat going up into the night. If it could be captured, its power would be amazing. What size Watt engine would be necessary to consume that heat and turn it into power? How fast could it propel a boat up the Thames? Could the boat he designed sail on it along the river? On the open sea? If—

"Lord Bannatyne?"

"Yes?" He turned and swallowed his irritation at the encroachment into his thoughts. The voice belonged to a young woman. A very shapely young woman.

He eyed her up and down once, then a second time more slowly. There was enough light from the terrace for him to see that beneath tawny curls bound up on her head in the proscribed style, her green eyes regarded him coolly through the eyeholes in her white silk mask. That expression did not match her pert nose or her soft lips, which remained parted from her greeting. Her cheeks were an attractive rose beneath the lace edging of the mask, but her chin was a bit stubborn, and he could imagine it jutting toward him as her eyes flashed with fierce emotions.

He smiled. He had not expected to see *her* here, but he could not imagine a better way to set aside his dismals.

"Gwendolyn," he said with a chuckle, "tell me how you persuaded that old tough to let you into her house."

"I am not—"

"Interested in talking? Neither am I." He grasped her shoulders and pulled her to him. Her pliant body brushed his as he bent to claim the mouth that he had not tasted in far too many nights.

His nose bumped into the gloved hand she raised between them. He frowned. It was not like Gwendolyn to be coy.

"You are mistaking me for another, my lord," the woman said in the prim tone he despised among the misses of the Polite World. "I am not your *friend* Gwendolyn."

He released her, vexed as much by her reprimand as his mistake. He did not make mistakes often, but he had now. Her voice was more educated than Gwendolyn's, and there was a hint of northern accent.

She sure as hell *looked* like Gwendolyn would while wearing a mask. Or did she? Her hair curled about her face while Gwendolyn's was very straight. So who was she? Letting his gaze wander over her necklace, which had an odd pendant in a design he did not recognize, he suspected the curves visible beneath her chaste gown would elicit fiery passions in a man. Over a dark green ribbon, her breasts pressed against her gown with each quick breath that revealed she was not as well versed in sangfroid as she must wish him to believe. She was neither tall nor short, but just the right height for him to tip her chin up while he bent forward to taste her lips.

Gideon recalled himself as he realized he was raising his hand toward her to put his thoughts into action. He would not give any passing guest the pleasure of watching this young woman slap his face for his impertinence. He had already provided too much fodder for the *ton*'s enjoyment tonight.

"Yes," he said in a less impatient voice, "I am Gideon Bannatyne." He tilted his head toward her in a polite bow. "But you have the advantage of me, miss, for you know my name when I don't know yours. All you have told me so far is that you are not Gwendolyn."

"I am Jade Nethercott."

"Nethercott?"

Her chin rose as her shoulders squared like a soldier about to embark onto the battlefield. "Does the name mean something to you, my lord?"

"I have heard of the title recently passing to a distant cousin."

"My father died last year."

"Belated condolences." Again he bowed his head.

"Thank you." In the faint light, her long lashes

brushed against the mask as she blinked rapidly. Trying to hold back tears? Or a blatant attempt to flirt with him?

He chided himself. When had he become so cynical? Miss Nethercott had just spoken of her father's passing. That was a worthy time for tears to form. He simply had not expected any woman to shed quiet tears. His sister's idea of mourning consisted of keening and tearing apart her private chambers.

Reaching behind him, he plucked a flower from a bush. He held it out to Miss Nethercott.

She looked from it to him with astonishment in her expressive eyes. "My lord?"

"I regret bringing sorrow to you with my unthinking comments and my untoward actions, Miss Nethercott. Will you forgive me?"

"There is no need for an apology, save on my part for intruding on your obvious interest in being alone. I heard the comments inside about the recent loss your family has suffered."

He wanted to tell her that Renshaw's death was no loss to his family, but refrained. "If you can forgive me, I daresay I can be as benevolent to you. I trust you *will* be forgiving and not as much of a block as Derlan."

A hint of a smile danced across her lips, and he felt his body react. If he had spent half the time the *ton* believed he had in one woman or another's bed, he might be able to stop thinking about taking this blonde to his. Then again, maybe not. Even though he could not see her whole face because of her mask, his imagination suggested it was as lovely as the rest of her. He was curious to discover if he was right.

"I do not fault you for being irked at Lord Derlan's rudeness, my lord," she said, her smile broadening. "I daresay I would not have been as indulgent of his comments for as long as you were."

"He says only what others think."

"Do you care what others think?"

Gideon was taken aback again by her question. Miss

Nethercott was most definitely not like Gwendolyn, who thrilled in gossip as much as his sister.

When he did not give her a quick answer, she continued. "I would like to speak to you of a matter of some importance. My lord, if you would grant me a few moments of your time . . ."

Knowing he had to regain control of the conversation—and himself—he set the flower on her palm and closed her fingers around its stem. His wrapped around hers, and her smile faltered as her hand quivered within his. He drew up his elbow, bringing her a single step nearer. "You did not answer my question, Miss Nethercott. Will you forgive me?"

"I would rather that you answer one of my questions."

"The answer is yes."

Her eyes widened, and he wondered if he could have ever envisioned such a green anywhere beyond his dreams. Not even Gwendolyn's eyes had such color. Jade Nethercott was a woman who invited a man to think of finding any possible way to bed her. She possessed an undeniable innocence, for a more sophisticated woman would never have come out to the very edge of the light to speak with him. In spite of that, her words suggested she was quite intelligent. A combination, despite gossip's assumptions that only a stupid woman would share his bed, that he had never been able to resist.

Her voice quavered like her hand when she asked, "How can you say that when you do not know what I intend to ask you?"

"What man with a bit of life within him could say no to a beautiful woman like you?"

A soft pink colored her cheeks. He was not sure if she was embarrassed or pleased. He hoped it was the latter, because he could think of many other ways he would be glad to please her, if she was willing. Dash it! Why was he letting his thoughts wander *again* in that direction? If his enemies suspected he was seeking them,

Jade Nethercott could have been sent to distract him. That was absurd, for his enemies dealt with their foes themselves, relishing every minute of another's torment. He could not blame Miss Nethercott—or those who were trying to destroy him and his family—for his own thoughts.

But what other reason could there be for a young woman to seek him out when she risked damaging her reputation in front of the pink of the *ton*? He glanced toward the terrace and saw two women watching them closely. Her chaperones?

"I am serious, my lord," she said.

"So am I!"

"Really? I suspect you are seldom serious about anything except what concerns you alone." She drew her hand out of his, but did not release the flower.

"You might be surprised how serious I can be about others' concerns." He ran his finger along the white silk covering her arm. He drew back his hand, wondering if his finger had a mind of its own. If so, it clearly had lost all good sense. Trifling with this young miss was a diversion he could ill afford. One minute, he had been thinking about steam power, and the next, she was making him hiss like an escape valve. "What is your question, Miss Nethercott?"

For a moment, he thought she would not answer his sharp demand, but then she said, "In light of Lord Derlan's comments, I believe I have some information you might find intriguing. I would gladly exchange it for your help in a private matter."

"Intriguing? Private matter?" He chuckled. "Miss Nethercott, you have a most enticing way with words." When he saw her color rise, he added, "What information?"

"First, it would behoove me to insure myself that you will help me before I blurt out the information that may assist *you* in dealing with what has happened to your family, my lord."

Gideon's breath caught. Her careful words suggested she was speaking of something beyond what a young woman should know of his business. He quickly searched his mind for what he knew of the Nethercott family. An eccentric father who held the title, had sired no male heir, an estate in the near wilderness of Yorkshire . . . nothing more. There was no reason she should know anything to help him. She might be lying so he would do as she asked.

He hoped she had not heard his reaction, and he kept his voice even when he asked, "What is it that you want help with, Miss Nethercott?"

"To gain entrance into the demimonde."

Chapter 3

The demimonde? This proper woman who had bristled when Gideon had almost kissed her wanted to enter the world of mistresses and cyprians?

Again Gideon was shocked. Again he hid it as he said coolly, "Why do you need my help, Miss Nethercott? The duchess's name can open any doors you wish, even in the demimonde."

"But she cannot help me in other ways."

"And in what other ways do you need to be helped?" He let his finger drift across her cheek, seeing how unsettled she was by his touch. She had said she had information. Was it possible she knew something about whoever was preying on what remained of his family? Could he unnerve her enough to cause her to reveal the very truth he sought? Forcing a rakish smile, he asked, "In a way that only a man could help you?"

"Yes."

Gideon was shocked anew by her forthright answer, even though he had been sure nothing in Town could ever amaze him again. "I am listening."

"So are the duchess's guests." She glanced toward another couple who had come down the steps.

Seeing the man pointing toward them and the woman fanning herself in agitation, Gideon's smile broadened as his gaze slipped along Miss Nethercott again. What a beef-head he was! She was the distraction *he* needed. He only had to focus his attentions on her, and the gossip of the viscount and the miss from daisyville would keep the

Polite World so busy prattling they would not note what he was seeking until he found the key to unlocking the truth of his enemy's secrets.

It would require him to take extra care in what he did or said, and it would require him, as well, to keep Miss Nethercott from guessing that his attentions toward her were simply because she was his way to obtain the information he needed. He found the idea of using her distasteful, but listening to his conscience could mean passing up the best—and perhaps only—chance he had to gain vengeance on his enemies.

"Come with me, Miss Nethercott. I believe the upper garden is growing crowded."

Without giving her a chance to reply, he took her hand and settled it on his bent arm. He steered her toward a set of steps leading into the lower section. When she faltered at the uppermost step, he gave her arm a gentle tug. She glanced back toward the terrace and then went with him down the six steps to the knot garden.

"I think we can speak more plainly here, Miss Nethercott."

Again she looked up at the house. She drew her hand out of his arm and edged a step away. She slanted back against the wall as if she wanted to put as much space between them as possible.

Or, he thought with a tightening along him, was the motion meant to show off how her firm breasts pressed against the fine white fabric of her gown? He imagined sweeping her away from the gathering and into the closest bed. Making love to her while she wore the mask was the most erotic thought he had had in months. When his tongue explored her breast, her eyes would close behind the mask as a soft moan slipped past her lips. He almost moaned himself.

"I hope you will be honest with me," she said, drawing his gaze back to her masked face.

"And you with me."

"There is no reason for you to question my honesty."

"Why not? I don't know you."

"True, but I can assure you that I find being less than honest most troublesome, my lord. I suspect you revel in it."

"You are insightful, Miss Nethercott, but you are also hiding too much."

"Pardon me?" She stood straighter, her hands clasped in front of her. "I am not sure what you mean."

"It is easier to speak when there are no masks."

"I forgot I was wearing it."

He halted her from reaching for the ribbons holding the mask in place. "Allow me, Miss Nethercott."

She hastily undid the ribbons. "I think any woman would be want-witted to say yes to you, my lord, without realizing where such an answer might lead."

"You accuse me of crimes I have not committed."

"With me."

"Yes. With you." He could not keep from grinning, and he was surprised that he was unable to recall the last time he had worn any expression beyond cool indifference in public.

"You appear overly satisfied with the tawdry state of your reputation, Lord Bannatyne."

"It is what others have deemed it to be."

He was going to add more, but she lowered her mask, and he realized his imagination had been a weak imitation of the truth. He could not have guessed a face could appear so delicate and strong at the same time. Her nose was straight and dusted with freckles that spread lightly across her high cheekbones. If she had tried to hide them beneath rice powder, the lace on her mask had swept it away. He thought they fit her pert face perfectly.

Her eyes shifted away as she said, "My lord, I wish to speak to you of an important matter."

"You wish to speak of a private matter that will lead you to the rougher parts of London where a young miss should not want to go." He laughed tightly. "It is to be supposed that a proper miss does not even know such places exist."

"I am not oblivious to the ways of the world."

Gideon knew she had no idea that her statement

proved her naïveté. Lifting her hand, he folded it between his. Her fingers quivered as they had when he
handed her the flower. If she was afraid of him, she
might not become his unwitting ally. He could not allow
her to guess even a portion of the truth, but he must be
certain she was aware of certain aspects of life among
the *ton*. Otherwise, she might betray him inadvertently.

"What is this private matter that would lead you into
the demimonde, Miss Nethercott? And you said you had
some information I might find interesting. Can I hope
what you have to say to me includes an offer to return
with me to my house and let me show you what honest
pleasures we could find together?"

"I don't understand what you are talking about,
but—"

"You don't understand?" He laughed as he pulled on
her hand, bringing her up against him. When she started
to move away, he caught her face between his hands.
Her gasp of astonishment warmed him as he moved to
slant his mouth across hers.

She kicked him in the shin, and he yelped.

"What was *that* for?" he asked.

"For thinking you could kiss me!" Jade clutched the
wall beside her. She did not want Lord Bannatyne to
see her shaking fingers, for then he might notice how
every inch of her was quivering with the sensations that
had erupted through her at the moment his fingers
touched her cheeks. Never had she imagined her first
kiss might have been from a dark-haired profligate in
the duchess's garden. Nor had she imagined how she
wished—in spite of her protests—that it had been.

Was she out of her mind? She should walk away, but,
in the narrow space between the wall and the knot garden, she could not edge past without touching him. She
had been foolish not to see before now how easily he
had cornered her.

Refusing to let him suspect that he daunted her with
his candid gaze, she raised her chin and said in a prim
voice she copied liberally from the duchess, "If that is
all that is on your mind, this conversation is over."

"It was not *all* that is on my mind." He stepped forward to lessen the distance between them. "Forgive me, Miss Nethercott. I thought it was on your mind as well. *You* approached me. *You* initiated the conversation."

"I did, didn't I?" She was making a muddle of the whole of this discussion. No wonder her sisters were watching from the terrace. Lord Bannatyne had not seemed aware of them, but she knew her sisters were worried while she spoke with a man accused of murder. What else could she do? She had promised Sir Mitchell to unravel the tapestry of lies surrounding his death.

"Did I misread your intentions?"

"Yes, most assuredly." She did not want to admit how enticing she found him. Yes, he had been accused of being a murderer by his victim's ghost as well as Lord Derlan, but he was undeniably charming. She knew the risks of lowering her guard with him . . . even for a moment. "My lord, I have one thing on my mind."

"As I said—"

"And it is not that."

"A shame." His finger trailed along her jaw again, and the yearning to soften in his arms teased her anew. "Is it possible I could change your mind?"

She did not answer his question, for she was afraid that if she did, she might say he could change her mind easily. Instead, she said, "I have a question to ask you."

"Speak it."

"No." She slipped the mask into her bodice and looked up to find his gaze directly on the spot between her breasts. "My lord, I would appreciate having your attention focused on what I have to say."

"Then you should stop being so damned provocative." He scowled fiercely.

She almost took a step back, but she steadied herself. The brutal deed Sir Mitchell had suffered occurred along a lonely road. Lord Bannatyne would not slay her in the duchess's garden. Looking at him coolly, she said, "I believe you are a man who is easily provoked in such matters."

He rested one hand on the wall beside her, and his

smile returned. She suspected it could melt a glacier, but she did not trust its warmth.

"You have an unquestionable ability to see the truth about me."

"I doubt I am the first."

"You are the first *tonight*."

Bother! Did he have to turn every word into a suggestion that this conversation should be taking place with her lying beside him? If he thought he could bamboozle her, he needed to learn she was not a shrinking miss who would swoon at his double entendres. The Nethercott women were made of sterner stuff.

His intensity revealed that the titillating words were an attempt to conceal what he was thinking. But what was that?

"Yes, it is plain that you see almost as much of me as I do of you, Miss Nethercott."

"It does not take great sensitivity to read your thoughts."

"And what am I thinking now?"

"I would rather not say."

When his hand swept up her back, pressing her to his hard chest, she was shocked. Not at his action, for he had been forward from the beginning of their conversation. She was shocked by how the fierceness in his eyes did not match his teasing words. For the first time, she truly believed she was standing in a murderer's embrace. She had never been so frightened in her life. If she tried to call for help, would he slay her before she could make a sound?

Yet there was a gentleness in his forceful embrace she would not have suspected a cold-blooded murderer would show. She could not befool herself because she enjoyed trading words with him.

Jade heard a laugh from the upper garden. Looking up, she saw a pair of men pointing at her and Lord Bannatyne.

"Please let me go!" she ordered in a sibilant whisper. "They are watching."

"Ignore them." His voice was oddly strained.

"Why? You are not."

"No, I am not."

She was surprised at his straightforward answer. Or what appeared to be a straightforward answer. Every warning she had heard about the viscount rippled through her head. To let him convince her that his lies were the truth could destroy any chance to discover the real truth and the proof of his crimes.

She eased out of his arms. "I think it would be wise to bring this conversation to an end."

"You have yet to explain what you wanted to tell me or why you wish to be given carte blanche to the demimonde. You are every inch a lady, and I cannot imagine a reason you would want to go into such a world where you would stand out like a saddle on a sow."

"Good evening, my lord."

"It is not evening."

"Then good *night*, my lord."

He smiled.

She looked away before he could guess how his smile in response to commonplace words threatened to undo her composure, which had withstood his candid appraisal. She would be wise to take her leave before she allowed him to draw her into another duel of words, where she seemed to be—astoundingly—losing.

As she stepped past him, he caught her arm. She stiffened as he brought her hand to his mouth. It was a proper way to bid her adieu, but his smile suggested the most improper fantasies. At the last moment, he flipped her hand over. His lips pressed to the bare skin just above her glove.

She gasped. His lips were more heated than she had guessed human flesh could be. She expected kisses on the lips to light up her soul, but a kiss on her wrist? It seemed to sear into her skin. Knowing she should pull away before his mesmerism betrayed her as it must have other women, she could not move her feet. Her fingers rose toward the dark hair falling forward on his forehead as he slowly lifted his head. His eyes shifted toward them, and she forced her hand back to her side. Amusement tilted his mouth.

He was about to laugh at her! In Yorkshire, she had endured too many hidden chuckles at her expense and at her father's. She was not going to suffer the same in London.

Yanking her hand out of his, she turned on her heel and walked back to the ballroom. This had been a mistake. She would have to find another way to prove what Sir Mitchell's ghost had told her. Some way that did not include Lord Bannatyne and his too enticing kiss.

Before she could give the troublesome idea of how to do that any thought, Jade heard screams. From inside the house. Women's screams and men's. Shouts for the watch and for a doctor. Shrieks of terror.

Lord Bannatyne raced past her, taking the steps two at a time. Lifting the hem of her skirt, she ran after him. People were rushing out of the ballroom. One woman reeled and would have fallen if a man had not grabbed her. Lord Bannatyne, she realized. He handed her to another man and pushed through the crowd to enter the house.

Jade went in his wake, determined to find her sisters. They were not on the terrace. She guessed they had hurried inside at the first sign of trouble.

Lord Bannatyne halted in front of her and refused to move. She tried to elbow him aside. He growled something. She would not be halted. China and Sian could be in danger.

As if she had spoken aloud, he said, "You don't need to see this, Miss Nethercott."

"See what?"

He did not answer.

She had her chance when a man to his right shifted slightly. She pushed between them and looked at an open expanse of floor in front of them. Everyone was staring at a blanket by one of the doors. She did, too, and saw the bloody body of Lord Derlan. He had been beaten to death.

Chapter 4

Jade handed cups of warm punch to her sisters. They sat on one side of the ballroom, not far from where two men from the watch talked to several guests. In another corner, the duchess was being fanned with the feathers she had worn in her hair. The odor of sal volatile clung in the air, because a trio of women still suffered from vapors a few chairs away.

"Who could have done such an atrocious thing?" China whispered, even though nobody was taking note of their conversation.

"We have to hope the watch will discover the truth." Jade bit her lower lip as she watched a stout man drape a blanket over the battered corpse.

Then she looked, as she had often in the past hour, at Lord Bannatyne. He had talked with the two men from the watch, and he remained near them, listening to the answers the other men were giving.

She had been listening, too. Closely. The facts were simple. A man named Stinmore had found Lord Derlan's corpse in the shadows of the front staircase. Either the earl had sought a futile haven under a table, or the body had been hidden there. A handful of guests owned to having walked past without noticing the body, but nobody admitted to seeing anything out of the ordinary.

"Excuse me," she murmured to her sisters before going to a door near where the orchestra members were packing up their instruments. She half expected China to call her back or Sian to come after her, but neither tried to halt her as she went out into the hallway.

Like the rest of the duchess's home, the corridor was magnificent. As wide as the sitting room in the house on Grosvenor Square, its floor was covered with gold-streaked marble tiles that matched the gilt decorating the Grecian columns and intricately carved newel posts of the staircase that arced up and away from the front door. Plaster carvings of vines and fruit had been delicately painted on the ceiling, and the walls had a mural of a bucolic outing with figures draped in togas.

Jade went to the long table half hidden by the curve of the stairs. Her stomach threatened to revolt when she saw a rug had been shifted aside to reveal rusty specks that must be dried blood. She looked away, and an indentation in the wall beyond the table caught her eye. Going to it, she ran her fingers along the depression, which was almost concealed by the grass painted in the mural.

"I did not guess you would be bloodthirsty," she heard Lord Bannatyne say.

She faced him. "Simply curious how a man could be killed within earshot of scores of people and nobody saw or heard anything."

"They *say* that they saw or heard nothing. A very different thing."

"Quite true." Reaching up, she ran her fingers along the damaged wall. "Did you see this?"

He edged closer. She realized she was trapped between him and the wall. A scent of cool night air drifted from his sleeve as he stretched out his hand to touch the dent in the wall. She suddenly could not draw in another breath. He was not touching her, but his nearness was sweeping every bit of air away.

"There are actually two places where the wall was struck," he said.

"Two?" She was proud that she could manage even that single word.

"Whatever was knocked against the wall before it

struck Derlan did not have sharp edges. If it had, it would have broken the wall instead of denting it."

Jade put her hand against his chest and pushed. He gave a startled gasp but stepped aside. Going to the stand by the front door, she pawed through the walking sticks left by the duchess's guests. She examined one, then another.

Lord Bannatyne's shadow cast from the brass chandelier overhead climbed up and over her as she lifted out two more walking sticks. One she set back into the stand, but she held out the other. Beneath its ivory handle shaped like a knob, it was splattered with rusty specks like those on the hall floor.

"The men from the watch will want to see this." Her stomach cramped again when she examined the dried blood beneath a zigzag pattern of gold painted below the ivory.

"Not that the Charleys will do anything with it but turn it over to the coroner for his investigation."

"Maybe it will help someone get an answer."

"Only if the person who wielded it steps forward and owns to the truth." He took the walking stick. Holding it in one hand, he put the fingers of his other beneath her chin and tipped it toward him. "Quite impressive, nonetheless. Your curiosity serves you well, Miss Nethercott."

"My father taught me that there is an answer to every puzzle." She gazed into his dark eyes and could not help wondering what mysteries hid in their depths. Recalling Sir Mitchell's warning not to be tempted by the undeniably tempting viscount, she started to look away. But she did not want to. She wanted to explore those mysteries and discover the truth.

"He should have taught you as well how dangerous it is to risk a murderer's wrath by unraveling the clues left by his crime. That is why I would ask that you let it be believed that I found the walking stick." His mouth tilted at an angle. "I have no wish to detract from your wise appraisal of the facts and your discovery, but Derlan is dead. You cannot do anything more for him, and endangering yourself will gain you nothing."

His words made sense. She was about to reply when his thumb grazed her lower lip. A thousand sensations, each one indescribable and luscious, surged through her.

"Be careful where your curiosity leads you, Jade Nethercott," he whispered.

He lowered his hand, and she backed away, still held by his gaze. She bumped into a table. Not the table where Lord Derlan had been found, but a smaller one topped by a plant. The impact of her hip against the table broke the connection between her and Lord Bannatyne. She turned and hurried through the door into the ballroom.

Nothing had changed. The men from the watch were still discussing what to do and how long it would take the coroner to come and if they should remove the body to a church before his arrival.

"Where did you go?" asked China as she held out Jade's cup of punch.

"Into the hall. I wanted to see the scene for myself."

Sian's nose wrinkled. "I don't want to see where that poor man died."

"But aren't you curious about what happened?"

"Yes, I *am* curious." Sian glanced at her older sister. "And so are you, China. You said as much just a few minutes ago."

China nodded. "Yes, I am curious, but—"

The quiet of the room was broken by a shriek from a white-haired woman. She jumped up from one of the chairs and ran across the room. Raising her fists, she began to pummel Lord Bannatyne, who once again stood near the corpse. He handed the blood-spattered walking stick to a man and tried to hold the woman off without hurting her.

Jade shoved her cup into Sian's hand and sprinted toward the maddened woman. Ducking under the woman's wild blows, she grasped her arms and forced them to her side. The woman had a strength that surprised Jade. The woman broke away and whirled.

"Don't stop me! He killed my son!" the woman shrieked.

Jumping back from her swinging fist, Jade called, "Someone grab her arms!"

Everyone seemed frozen except for Lord Bannatyne. He wrapped his arms around the woman, locking his hands together under her breasts. Her arms were clamped against her sides. She struggled to escape, then deflated. She sagged against Lord Bannatyne.

"If you will calm down, madam," Jade said quietly, "we will listen to what you have to say."

The woman nodded, her head lowered.

"Can you be calm?"

Again she nodded.

Jade looked past the woman and motioned to Lord Bannatyne to release her. He shook his head, frowning. She gave him a scowl as fierce as his own and said, "Please release her, Lord Bannatyne."

"Miss Nethercott, you have no idea—"

"Please release her! She needs comfort, not to be imprisoned."

She thought he would argue further, but he dropped his arms. For a moment, the woman wove on her feet. Jade stepped forward to steady her.

The woman's arm struck out at her. She would have hit Jade if Lord Bannatyne had reacted a second more slowly. He caught the woman's arm and steered her to a chair close to the duchess's. Sitting her there, he walked back to where Jade was staring, wide-eyed.

"Next time, listen to advice from those who know more than you do," he said without a bit of emotion.

Jade looked from his tightly restrained fury to the white-haired woman who was now keening hysterically. "Thank you," she whispered.

He said nothing, drawing her aside as the body was lifted to be carried out of the house and put in a cart to take it to the family's church.

The older watchman, a stubby man who smelled of ale and sweat, said in a rough accent, "We could use a few strong men. Sometimes the resurrectionists don't wait for the bodies to get in the ground."

Nobody moved. She was unsure if they were more

uneasy at the thought of the dead body or the resurrectionists, the disgusting creatures who harvested bodies from graveyards and sold them to surgeon-anatomists for dissection.

" 'Tain't like a ghost'll join us," the watchman said with obvious impatience. "The man's dead. Spirit's gone. Ain't no ghosts anyhow."

Jade clamped her teeth over her lower lip so she did not speak out. She knew all too well that ghosts were real.

Lord Bannatyne stepped forward and motioned to the man who now held the walking stick. "Come along, Gibbs. The two of us should be the match of any body-snatchers."

Lady Derlan cried, "Stop him! How can you let him just walk out? He murdered my son as he did Sir Mitchell Renshaw."

There were sharp intakes of breaths, and Lord Bannatyne remained as still as if he were the corpse.

"Why are you all standing there?" the white-haired woman moaned. "You heard him. He said my son would not live to see him hang."

Jade looked at Lord Bannatyne. Why wasn't he defending himself from these accusations? Did he want people to believe he had beaten the earl to death? Why?

As the earl's mother went on, her voice rising more with every word, Jade asked the viscount that in a whisper.

He glanced toward her and asked as quietly, "Who would believe me if I protest?"

"I would. I know you could not have killed him."

"Yes, *you* do." His dark eyes drilled her. "You alone."

She swallowed her retort as she understood what he meant. Was he mad? Did he think she believed her reputation was more important than the truth?

Before she could ask, the duchess charged up like a furious watch-dog. Her dark curls and all three of her chins bounced with her indignation. "Miss Nethercott, you should come with me. You are newly down from

Yorkshire, so you may not know a young woman must be on her guard in situations like this."

"She knows." Lord Bannatyne offered the duchess a smile, although he clearly felt no desire to.

Jade frowned again. He was the most bothersome man! Trying to play the hero when there was no need, and playing the rake when she had tried to talk seriously with him.

"I do know," she said, squaring her shoulders. "I know the truth."

"Miss Nethercott, don't," he said, his smile vanishing.

She ignored him. "I know that Lord Bannatyne could not have murdered Lord Derlan because he was with me in the garden."

"With you?" gasped the duchess. Her face flushed red, then became icy pale. "You were with him in the garden? How could you? I have welcomed you to London and was ready to sponsor your entry to Almack's, and you—you—you—" She seemed unable to go on.

"I was in the garden with him at the time of Lord Derlan's death." She looked from face to face and noticed how eyes quickly averted.

"As I was," came China's voice from behind her.

"And I," Sian quickly added as she came to stand on Jade's right.

The Duchess of Northborough gave a relieved sigh. "I am pleased to hear that the three of you were together."

"You should know that we would never do anything to cause you grief or shame," Sian said with a smile that grew stiff when she glanced at Jade.

Instead of answering her sister, she watched Lord Bannatyne leave with the man who was obviously his friend. She was more confused than before. He had been ready to accept the label of suspected murderer— again—to protect her. Was it because nothing more could blacken his name? Or had he allowed himself to be stigmatized falsely for Sir Mitchell's death as well?

Nothing about Lord Bannatyne made sense, and her curiosity demanded to be appeased.

* * *

"I promise," Jade said for the third time.

Her older sister stared at her for a long minute. China had dressed her down last night on the ride back to Grosvenor Square. Her sister had been furious that Jade had spent time alone with Lord Bannatyne. The scold had begun anew at breakfast and continued during the midday meal.

"I promise," Jade repeated yet again. "I will not do anything as want-witted as wandering off to speak with an accused murderer again."

China shook her head and sighed. "Jade, I know how desperately you wish to prove that Father's research was right. I wish that was possible, too. However, you know that he would not wish you to endanger yourself."

"I considered it unlikely that the viscount would try to slay me with so many witnesses in the garden and ballroom."

"Maybe," China said, "you should take last night's horrible circumstances as a sign you have been given a reprieve by the Polite World. You saw how the duchess was looking daggers at Lord Bannatyne before he took his leave."

"I do believe the duchess was already eager for any excuse to hang him from the gallery, not waiting for proof that he was guilty of any crime."

Wagging a finger, China chided, "That is no way to speak of the Duchess of Northborough. Without her help in finding Mrs. Willow to stay with us here, we could not have remained in London."

"If you were a mere six months older, China, we would not need to worry about such things."

"Yes, I would be twenty-five and assumed to be permanently on the shelf." China smiled in spite of her attempt to remain serious. "I do not feel old. Nor do I believe in six months, I will have become a crone."

"You could have accepted the new Lord Nethercott's offer of marriage."

Wrinkling her nose, she gave a shiver. "I know he is a relative, but he is odious and older than Father."

"But you are about to become *old*."

China laughed as she took a last sip from her cup of hot chocolate and stood. "Remind me to remind you that you are not much younger than I am."

"And Sian right behind me. I wonder if there is room on the shelf for all of us."

"Just be certain you don't do something untoward and leave Sian and me alone on that shelf mourning you."

Jade came to her feet and gave her older sister a hug. "I promise."

"No more talking to Lord Bannatyne alone."

"I promise."

"Sir Mitchell's spirit must find someone else to discover the proof he seeks."

She nodded, but did not reply. Her promise to China was one she wanted to keep, but she had also vowed to help Sir Mitchell. The idea of breaking either pledge was repugnant.

Jade sat on the settee again as her sister left the room. Resting her head back against the ivory brocade, she stared at the ceiling. It was simple, not ornate with plaster moldings like in the duchess's house. The tall windows that overlooked Grosvenor Square allowed in the day's gray light. Along with the fire on the hearth, the pot of hot chocolate kept away the day's dampness.

Unable to sit still, she picked up her cup and went to look at the square. Nobody was walking in the rain, but she saw, through the trees, a pair of carriages on the far side.

She turned away, bothered by the sight of people going about their lives. Hers had been simple, too, before a phantom had asked her to bring his murderer to justice. Before a man had been discovered dead during an evening's entertainment. Now nothing seemed simple. There had to be some way to do as Sir Mitchell's ghost asked and still keep herself from danger . . . and from wanting another of the viscount's delicious kisses.

"Bother!" she muttered under her breath. Lord Bannatyne had kissed only her wrist. She should be thankful that she had stopped him before his lips caressed hers.

But she was not.

Hearing footsteps, she glanced toward the door. Smithson, the butler who oversaw the rented house, was as thin as a cadaver and had as little sense of humor. He took his duties—and himself—very seriously. He had tried to hide that he was distressed to have three young women living in the house. That they were from North Yorkshire seemed a huge burden for him, because he was constantly offering "suggestions" on how to behave amidst the *ton*. If he had any idea how amusing Jade found him, he would be abashed, so she concealed that.

"A gentleman is calling, Miss Nethercott. He is asking to speak with you."

She smiled. She had not expected Mr. Robertson to be so quick to reply to her message that she had sent this morning. Mr. Robertson had been a devoted student of her father's. During his visits to Nethercott Castle, he had been absentminded while caught up in his studies. Once, he had missed several meals in a row until he had been found sprawled on the floor, faint with hunger. Even then, while he had been placed in bed and offered tea and toast, he had refused to set aside the book he was reading.

"Please bring him in," she said. "He is a friend of my father's." That relationship would give their conversation countenance.

Smithson's gray brows shot up, but he quickly regained his placid expression. "As you wish, Miss Nethercott. Shall I have more chocolate brought?"

"Yes, that would be lovely."

As Smithson left, she set down her cup and smoothed her dress. She need not worry about her appearance. Mr. Robertson was never interested in anything but books. Even so, she wanted to look her best when she asked him to assist her on a task she could not fully explain. She hoped his discussions with Father had taught him that what she was about to tell him was, indeed, possible.

Jade walked about the room, adjusting a statue of some Greek goddess on one table, restacking a trio of books on another. She must be calm when Mr. Robertson arrived. She must not blurt out her request in one great blast. If she overwhelmed him, he might excuse himself and return to his studies without helping her.

"Bother!" she said under her breath again. "I need the assistance of someone more assertive."

"Miss Nethercott," intoned Smithson from the doorway. "Lord Bannatyne."

She whirled, bumping into the table. The books bounced to the floor with a crash. She bent to pick up the topmost one, her father's favorite, which she had brought from Yorkshire. The motion gave her time to try to regain her composure, but it was impossible.

What was *Lord Bannatyne* doing here? And why was she acting like an accursed stupe?

The butler stepped back as Lord Bannatyne entered the room. She had heard of a chamber seeming smaller when someone powerful entered it. She had considered that a cliché . . . until now.

Lord Bannatyne said nothing as she continued to stare. She had persuaded herself that she had been so overmastered by his bold ways last night that she had failed to see any fault with him. Surely no man could be as handsome and have eyes that twinkled so merrily as he did. But he was every bit as handsome as she recalled, and while his dark eyes were not aglitter now, she could easily imagine them sparkling as he used words to joust with her.

"Good afternoon, Miss Nethercott," he said, breaking the silence that might have gone on the rest of the day if he had not spoken.

"What are you doing here?" she blurted out, then hastily said, "Forgive me, my lord. I should not have spoken so. I should have welcomed you to our house."

"You have every right to be on edge. The whole of the Polite World is in shock at the events we witnessed last night." He took a step toward her. "How are you?"

"I am fine. And you?"

"Taking a dead body to a church has unfortunately been a task I have handled too often of late."

"I am sorry."

"Thank you."

"And the walking stick?"

"The coroner took it. He doubts it will be of any value. Without witnesses, nobody can tell from the stick who used it to batter Derlan." He gestured toward the chair as if he were the host and she the guest. "May I speak with you of another matter, Miss Nethercott?"

"If you will wait a moment, I shall ring for—"

He stepped between her and the table where a bell waited. "May we speak privately?"

"My lord, that would not be proper." She did not add that she had promised her sister minutes before not to speak with him alone again. "After last night, I think we both need to be especially cautious about how we are perceived."

His mouth worked. She was unsure if he were about to smile or to scowl. "I doubt you wish to have anyone overhear us discuss your request last evening and the information you said you had for me."

Ignoring her instinct to call a footman to show the viscount the door posthaste, Jade nodded. She motioned for him to follow her to where they could sit and talk. She wished she had stepped back to allow the viscount to precede her, for she had not guessed how unsettling it would be to have him follow her and know that his gaze was fixed firmly on the sway of her hips beneath her simple gown. Too late now. She perched on the settee, edging to its center so he did not think she had chosen that place as an invitation for him to sit beside her. When he sat on one of the chairs facing her, she let her breath sift out slowly through her clenched teeth.

It was time for her to be a suitable hostess. In Nethercott Castle, they had grown accustomed to the relative informality of the countryside. Now she was in London, and she needed to act in a manner that would not shame her or her sisters.

"Would you like some hot chocolate, my lord?" she asked as she lifted the pot decorated with bas relief figures of fauns playing flutes.

"May I hope it contains a touch of brandy?"

"Simply chocolate with some cream." She poured steaming chocolate into a cup and held it out to him.

He took it and smiled. "Are you completely without vices, Miss Nethercott?"

"I doubt anyone is completely without vices."

"I did not ask about anyone. I asked about you." Taking a sip of the chocolate, he smiled at her over the cup.

Bother! He was exasperating when he used words as if they were a saber, parrying and seeking out any weakness.

"I have vices," she said.

"Such as? You speak prettily, and you seem to feel everyone—even a man with a reputation such as mine—is to be trusted. Maybe that is a vice, even though I have never heard a lack of wisdom derided as a vice. Simply as a misfortune, unless one is of the highest birth and the greatest wealth. I would suggest that your curiosity is troublesome and may prove disastrous for you, but that is no vice either."

"Do you truly enjoy the sound of your own prattle?"

He smiled, but coolly. "One of my vices is the vain assumption that others will appreciate what I have to say. Or at least be amused by it." Without a pause, he asked, "What information do you have for me?"

Jade blinked, shocked at how abruptly he changed the subject. Gathering herself, she put her cup on the tray. "As I told you last evening, I will share that when you have agreed to help me."

"And no one else can?"

"As far as I know, no. I wish to keep my actions clandestine."

"Clandestine? If that was your intention, you picked the wrong man to ask for assistance. Don't you realize that everything I—and now, by extension, you—do is being closely watched by those who wish to accuse me of further crimes? Everyone is eager to be the one to label me pounded."

"Excuse me?"

"Guilty of some misconduct."

"Why would anyone else care?"

He laughed. Hard and with genuine amusement. "My dear Miss Nethercott, it would appear you have no idea that the Polite World needs gossip to thrive. And if you embark on whatever you are scheming, you invite everyone to speak about your antics and banish you and your family from the Polite World forever."

"I understand that, which is why I am asking for your help so I may do what I must and still protect my family's reputation."

"I don't understand why you wish to go into the demimonde. Why would a young miss want to enter such a realm where she risks ending up with a reputation like—"

"Yours?"

Another smile slid along his lips. "You *are* plainspoken, Miss Nethercott. That suggests you appreciate those around you being equally blunt."

"Yes." What else could she say? She needed to learn to curb her impatience. How many times had Father or her sisters chided her for failing to wait until someone was finished speaking before interjecting her own comments? If she had learned to heed to their advice, she would not find herself in such an untenable situation now.

"Good." Clasping his hands between his knees, he leaned toward her. "You want me to escort you, offering you entrée into the demimonde. Tell me why."

"My father's last request."

His brows rose toward his dark hair. "Your father requested that his daughter ruin her reputation? Forgive me, Miss Nethercott, but I find that unbelievable."

Standing, she walked around the settee, giving herself some time to steady her expression. He was right. Such a tale was ludicrous. If she had been better prepared for his call . . . No, she must not start lying to herself. No matter how much time she had had to ready herself for a conversation with Lord Bannatyne, she would be at a disadvantage. She must not become lost in his eyes once more. She must prevent herself from thinking—for even a second—about how wondrous his chaste kiss had been.

"Lord Bannatyne," she said, congratulating herself for putting exactly the correct tone of condescension into her words, "I trust you will remember that my father was renowned for his eccentricity."

"A trait inherited by his daughter?"

"That, my lord, is none of your bread and butter. All that should concern you is my yearning to fulfill a promise I made to my father on his deathbed."

Setting himself on his feet, he put one hand on the settee's arm. "And your other yearnings?"

"We are speaking of only one."

"Of yours. What of mine?"

"A matter I have no interest in discussing."

He slid his hand up the settee's wooden arm and along the back as he came toward her. With each step he took, with each inch of the settee he touched, she could not keep from imagining his fingers gliding along her with such a slow, intriguing caress. She tried to cast the thought out of her mind, but she stared at his fingers edging along the settee.

His crooked finger beneath her chin tilted her face toward his. She was amazed to see that his smile had vanished. There was an intensity in his eyes that startled her. Gone was the raucous rake, whose only care was finding another woman to bed while he satisfied every sense's demands. Instead, she saw honest curiosity. Or was it honest? She would be a beef-head to accept anything about the viscount at face value.

"What was your father's dying request?" he asked.

"To find his mistress and give her a gift that he wanted her to have."

"You expect me to swallow such a tale?"

"If you choose not to believe me, you are welcome to leave with my gratitude that you took the time to call, my lord."

"You know I cannot go when you have yet to share the information you say you have."

"Your choice, my lord. Help me in fulfilling my father's last request, and I shall divulge the information that may in turn help you." She did not let her gaze waver. If she gave any sign that she was lying, he would denounce her before he left along with her best chance to see her father again.

His smile remained icy. "You are quite the she-lion when backed into a corner, aren't you? I shall need to remember that while I help you with your ridiculous errand. All right. What is his mistress's name?"

"Her name is Violet."

"Violet what?"

She faltered, trying to think of a surname that would sound right, but would be rare enough so there was no harlot with the same name.

"You don't know her whole name?" he asked with a derisive frown. "How do you expect to find his mistress when you don't know her full name?"

"I am certain I know it, but have forgotten it."

"Did she ever write him a letter? Her name would be on that."

She was losing control of the plan that she should have fleshed out before approaching Lord Bannatyne. Standing face-to-face with him when she was too aware of where his hands were and how small the space was between them was not conducive to thinking rationally.

So all she could say was, "Such letters would be at Nethercott Castle, my lord."

"In Yorkshire?"

"Yes."

He arched a dark brow. "That will make our task a bit more difficult, but nothing is impossible, so we might as well jump in. The first thing to do is to make you appear to belong to the demimonde. You need some lessons on how to behave properly." He smiled coolly. "Or maybe I should say *improperly*. With your daisyville appearance and your polished manners, you will be in the wrong box."

"Excuse me? 'In the wrong box?' "

"It means only that you will be out of your comfortable, normal world, Miss Nethercott. That you do not understand such simple cant reveals you for who you truly are. However, with the right tuition, it is possible you might slip in and out of the cyprian's world without anyone—save you and me—being the wiser."

"You would do that for me?"

"I would do that for you, Miss Nethercott, but you must be equally willing to do something for me, too." His smile warmed as he eyed her boldly.

"I have already said I will offer you the information I have."

"True, but those are your terms for my assistance. You have yet to hear my terms."

"Terms?" She took a half step back, but froze when his hand slid over hers on the settee.

Lord Bannatyne's eyes became ebony slits. "Did you think I would ask for no reward in exchange for helping you?"

Although she feared she already knew the answer, she whispered, "What do you want?"

"That is the critical question, isn't it?" His voice became low and rumbling. "The *ton* has expectations it does not wish to have altered. No woman has ever been seen on my arm for more than a week without her sharing my bed."

"Seven days?" She calculated quickly. Seven days should be enough time to obtain the truth about the murder.

"Seven *nights*." His voice became velvety warm. "Unless you wish to accede to the inevitable sooner."

She folded her arms in front of her, clasping them tightly, so she was not tempted to reach out to him. "Your offer is that, if I am still on your arm at the end of a week, on the seventh night, I will share your bed."

"Or yours. It does not matter which to me."

How could he act as if he were negotiating for nothing more important than the services of a tailor? Was he so sated by the pleasures of the city that he considered making love with her of as little significance? She had saved his life last night by offering him an alibi, and now he was acting as if she were as low as a harlot. Had she been wrong when she believed he had a sense of honor?

She had no answers for those questions. She was not

even sure why she was thinking of them other than they kept her from facing the truth. She was negotiating for her virginity with a man who, it was said, had taken the same from many foolish women and left them with ruined reputations and broken hearts. At least she would not have to worry about the latter. She had no interest in offering her heart to a rake. And it was absurd to think anyone could feel anything but lust in such a short time.

Knowing she might be speaking the words that damned her, but hoping instead they would lead her to find the proof that would bring her father to speak with her, she said, "Very well, I will agree to your terms." She held up a single finger between them. "But only if you agree that in addition to helping me, you vow to stay out of my bed until that seventh night."

He wrapped his fingers around hers. "My dear Miss Nethercott, there is no need for me to make such a vow. *You* will invite me to join you there before the seventh night has passed."

"Don't be so sure of that."

"I have seldom been so sure of anything."

Chapter 5

At Lord Bannatyne's outrageous statement, Jade tried to pull out of his grip. He drew back his fingers, one at a time. She barely noticed because at the same time he bent to run his tongue along her finger. He ceased doing so and searched her face, looking for something she suddenly wanted to give him. She brushed her hand across his cheek. Glorious sensations leaped along her palm, urging her closer.

"And there is one more thing I want in exchange for helping you," he said.

"One more?" She yanked herself away. "What more could you ask of me?"

His smile suggested he had many answers to that question, and she would be foolish to ask to hear any of them. "Actually it is nothing more than a refinement of my initial offer. If I assist you in finding this woman named Violet, you agree that once those seven nights are passed, you will reward me by becoming mine for a month."

She dampened her lips. "Yours for a month?"

"Thirty nights. Surely the offer of seven days and nights of my time are worth thirty of your nights."

"We are not speaking of a loan of money. We are talking about . . ."

"Something far more delightful. What say you, Miss Nethercott? You have agreed to accept my help. Now you need only accept my terms."

"I thought you meant a single night."

"Why only one night when we could enjoy each other for a full month?"

She drew back a step farther. "How can you speak of such matters with no hint of emotion? You make it sound like a business deal."

"It is." His eyes narrowed. "A very common business deal among the demimondaines. It was your request that inspired my terms."

Turning away before she could let his shockingly logical comments persuade her, she asked, "Are you mad?"

"Maybe, for I have not done this." He grasped her arms and whirled her back to face him. He released her only for a moment before his fingers burrowed into her hair as his other arm slipped around her to become an embrace. Then he was kissing her. With a mastery that overwhelmed her, he teased her lips into surrendering to him. When her hands slid, as if they would no longer heed her, about his shoulders, he urged her mouth to soften and offer him a welcome within. She forgot everyone and everything but the delight of his breath mingling with hers while he caressed her back. When his tongue brushed hers, she clenched his coat, overwhelmed by sensations she had not guessed existed—delicious and dangerous.

A sigh of regret flowed past her lips when he raised his head. His fingers remained tangled in her hair. When he spoke her name softly, she opened her eyes to discover his face near hers. Her lips parted when his arm slipped around her shoulders, tilting her back against its iron strength.

Good sense burst back into her mind. What was she doing welcoming the touch of a man whose hands had been stained with another man's blood? She stiffened and tried to draw away. His face hardened, but his smile returned when he tightened his arm around her.

"No, no, Miss Nethercott," he murmured. "We are not done with our negotiations. I have agreed to help you in exchange for the information you say you have, but you have not yet given me your answer."

She fought not to become lost within his dark eyes. "You will help me if . . ."

"If you are mine for a month at the quest's end."

"You want me to be your mistress for a month if I accept your help for a week? Is that what you mean?"

"Yes." His gaze locked with hers. "I thought I was quite clear in my request. You agreed to accept my terms."

"Before I understood them completely."

"Now you do. I have explained them, answering all your questions. Will you be as straightforward with your answer?"

She wanted to tell him that she would never agree to such an unseemly bargain, no matter how much his kiss had thrilled her. She wanted to tell him that she knew the truth of what he had done to Sir Mitchell. The words burned on her tongue, but she swallowed them. She eased out of his arms, grateful he released her. Her fingers tingled as she recalled his muscles beneath them. He might wear a gentleman's clothes, but there was nothing gentle about his passions. He had the powerful, sleek build of a man who would be able to handle himself well in fisticuffs and to handle her well in a far more intimate battle.

She must not think of that. She must keep her mind on the search for the truth.

"Will you give me an answer, Miss Nethercott?" Lord Bannatyne asked, his hushed voice as enchanting as his touch. "Will you agree to the reward I wish in exchange for my help in your quest?"

Raising her head, she met his eyes squarely. "Yes."

She thought she saw amazement in his eyes, but she could not tell because they closed as his mouth slanted across hers again, daring her to release the passion rippling through her. A thousand thoughts fled through her mind. Only one remained. She liked kissing him. She liked it a lot.

His lips coursed across her face and trailed fire along her neck. When his tongue teased her earlobe, his breath pulsed, slow and deep, into her ear. She quivered. Her own breath erupted out of her in a gasp when he ran his tongue up along her ear.

"What do you know?" he whispered.

"What?" She could not think. She could only feel, only exult in the sensations rippling along her like a breeze over a still pond.

"What information do you have for me?"

Again Jade tried to pull away, but his arm was an iron band behind her. He was working his sensual magic on her to persuade her to give him what he wanted. And it was not her. It was the tidbit that Sir Mitchell had told her to reveal to him.

Hoping he would not renege on his offer, even though she intended to bring their odd partnership to an end before the seventh day, she said, "I have heard that you should speak to someone named Heath."

His eyes narrowed. "Heath? Are you sure that is the name?"

"Very sure."

"Who told you this?"

"Revealing that was not part of our agreement."

His mouth straightened. "This is no game! Tell me, or—"

When Lord Bannatyne released her and stepped away before finishing his threat, Jade was amazed. Then she heard what she had not before because her heart was thudding madly in her ears. A footman entered the room carrying a tray topped with small cakes. He set it on the table beside the pot of hot chocolate.

Her sister Sian was following him. A leaf stuck out of one side of Sian's straw bonnet, and smudges of dirt on her light green gown showed where she had been kneeling on the ground. A matching spot darkened her cheek. She must have wiped her hand against her face.

As if the viscount called at the house every day, Sian walked over to them and said, "I was so pleased when I heard you were here, my lord." She glanced down at her sketchbook and rumpled gown. She smiled. "I was in the garden drawing, and I fear the time got away from me."

"This is my sister, Miss Sian Nethercott," Jade said. "You left the duchess's house before I could introduce you."

"Miss Sian, I thank you for your generous support of your sister and me last evening." The viscount took her hand and bowed over it. He did not bring it to his lips, which remained rigid. It was the only sign of his fury that Jade had not given him the answer he wanted. "If I may be so bold, may I say it is a lovely name for a lovely lady?"

"Our father was interested in many exotic parts of the world," Sian replied, blushing. "He named us for his love of the Far East. Sian and Jade, and our older sister is China."

"So there are three Nethercott sisters?" He looked back at Jade. "So that was your other sister who spoke up as well?"

"Yes." She added nothing more as Sian, prompted by the viscount, began to talk about the sketches she had made in the garden.

When her sister opened her sketchbook, Jade watched without comment. The viscount was engaging and asked intelligent questions and made comments that usually would have brought a smile to Sian's face. But Sian's lips were stiff as she answered his questions about her drawings.

Jade quietly said, "I am sure Lord Bannatyne will excuse our inhospitality, but we must get ready for our afternoon walk. We never miss it, rain or sunshine, do we, Sian?"

Her sister gave her a puzzled look, then hurried to answer, "Never. We never miss it."

"Then I shall leave you ladies to your promenade. I hope I receive as warm a welcome at my next call upon you." Ignoring Sian's gasp—quickly smothered—he looked at Jade. His practiced smile did not reach his cold eyes.

She was amazed. Moments ago, he had sounded sincere when he was talking with her sister. Now he wore the calculated expression that warned he would not allow them to be interrupted next time. He would want to know how she had obtained the information. What could she tell him?

When she heard Sian bid him adieu before she carried her sketchbook to her favorite chair by the windows, Jade was caught anew by the viscount's gaze. There was nothing chill about his eyes now. They were fiery hot with emotions he did not try to hide. She fought the shiver edging up her back because she suspected he was imagining how it would be when he claimed his reward.

When he claimed *her.*

And just the thought of what he must be envisaging created the most amazing erotic thoughts in her head. She was no protected, coddled young woman without any idea about what males and females shared. The many animals, both wild and domesticated, roaming the North York Moors mated as the seasons dictated. Would he be as feral as a beast? The shiver exploded through her again, only this time as hot as an oven.

He lifted her hand and bowed over it. He did not kiss it. If he had, she was unsure if she could have remained on her feet. Just the thought of his mouth on her weakened her knees. His thumb caressed her palm, a slow, sensuous motion that sent a pulse of heat stabbing deep within her to places she had never been so vividly aware of before.

His eye closed in a slow wink as he murmured, "Our week begins right now, sweetling."

She flinched as the endearment shattered the fantasy. She had promised herself to a man who was accused of slaying his sister's betrothed.

"Tomorrow," she said as quietly.

"At midnight?" he asked with a smile that suggested they would watch the clock's hands go straight up together.

"At midday."

"You know how to put one in the dismals, don't you?" He gave her no chance to reply. "Very well. Tomorrow at noon exactly, our time begins." His gaze swept over her, and she abruptly felt as naked as Eve. "Better that you should come to me first in the afternoon when I can enjoy your beauty unhidden by the night's shadows."

She gasped, unable to halt herself. As she watched him cross the room to bid her sister a pleasant afternoon, she put a hand on the settee to steady herself. His steps were jaunty as he walked out of the sitting room. Why shouldn't he be in a good mood? He had persuaded her to trade her body to him in exchange for his help.

But all she needed to do was obtain the proof in less than seven days.

Jade realized she had reacted to that thought when her sister said, "I don't know why you are smiling. Just as I don't know how you could allow *that man* to come into our house."

"It was a mistake." It was wonderful to be honest. "Smithson announced that a gentleman was calling, and I assumed it was someone else."

"I shall speak with Smithson immediately." Sian stormed out of the room.

Jade came around the settee and sat. Had she made the right choice? If there was any chance—any chance at all—that she could see her father one more time, she would do everything to make it possible. But what had Lord Bannatyne meant by "a proper tuition"? What sort of lessons did he expect her to learn before he would escort her into the low world where she could find someone who would share the facts of Sir Mitchell's murder in exchange for a handful of coins? And how long would those lessons take? She could not allow them to consume too much of the short time she had before he would insist on his *reward*. She should have asked the viscount more about his plans, but she had been in such a flutter at his offer and his bold, delicious kiss that she had forgotten everything else until now.

A flash of light caught her eyes. She looked toward the back corner and swallowed her groan. This was the absolutely worst time for Sir Mitchell to make an appearance. Had he been listening to her conversation with Lord Bannatyne? Had he *seen* how seductive the viscount had been? Had he sensed how she had been tempted by Lord Bannatyne's touch?

Rising as Sir Mitchell's form appeared out of the light,

she waited for him to dress her down for speaking with the viscount. For *kissing* him.

All he said was, "Miss Nethercott, we need to talk further."

"And we shall," she said, her vexation filling her voice, "if you would stop popping in and out of existence."

"I told you I could not control it."

"Then you need to figure out a way to do so. You vanish in the middle of a conversation, leaving me with unanswered questions."

He eyed her as if she were a recalcitrant child who understood nothing. "I am doing my best, Miss Nethercott. I did promise that, as you recall."

"I do."

"Then believe that I am doing so."

"Forgive me for doubting you," Jade said, chagrined. Sir Mitchell had not scolded her for failing to obtain the information he needed. She needed to be as patient with him.

"Certainly. As I said, I wish to speak further with you."

"About Lord Derlan's murder?"

He frowned. "Derlan is dead?"

"Murdered. Beaten to death with a walking stick."

He tapped one finger against his chin. "I should have guessed the killing would continue. Bannatyne—"

"Is innocent of the crime."

"Of *that* crime maybe."

"He has an irrefutable alibi that places him somewhere else." She was surprised at her hesitation to reveal more to the ghost. "And he had no reason to slay the earl."

"No, it would be the other way around. Derlan would have been happy to see Bannatyne hang because then the title would be his."

Jade was shocked. "I had no idea they were related."

"Not closely, but Derlan was the next male in line. Fortunately for my beloved Persis, her childhood home in Cornwall is not entailed." He sighed, the light fluttering around him as if he still possessed some breath. "She need not worry about that. However, you should be worried. Before you meet again with Bannatyne, there are some things you need to know."

"I am forewarned, Sir Mitchell, of the viscount's ways and habits."

"And of the danger to you?"

"I am aware of that as well."

The ghost surged toward her, and she backed away as the cold threatened to envelope her. He paused, hastily apologizing and putting more space between them before adding, "My thoughts are for your safety, Miss Nethercott. We cannot be certain I am his only victim. There were tales of several young women who worked for the family. They were seen in the viscount's company, then they vanished."

"Why didn't you tell me this before?"

He rubbed his forehead and scowled. "I thought I had. My mind seems to be functioning more and more slowly as the days pass since my death. I must endeavor to share with you all I know about Bannatyne. I trust you have a plan to speak with him after your encounter at the duchess's house."

Jade did not bother to try to hide her shock this time as she asked, "Didn't you see him here?"

"Bannatyne was here?"

She could not doubt Sir Mitchell's astonishment. The light around him dimmed as if battered down by his strong reaction.

"He called here and spoke with both me and my sister. I gave him the information about Heath."

"Good. What else?"

"Nothing." She was not going to share the details of what she had agreed to do in exchange for obtaining the information Sir Mitchell required. "I had hoped you would be nearby to confirm he was telling me the truth."

"What has he been telling you?"

"Nothing of import at this point." She hesitated, then

asked, "Are you certain it was Lord Bannatyne's hand holding the knife that slew you?"

"Do not be taken in by his charm, Miss Nethercott. He is a vile man with thoughts of nothing but his own pleasure. When do you expect to see him next?"

"I am not sure, but it will be soon."

"Good. I shall try to watch for his return."

"I would appreciate that. It would ease my disquiet to have someone else here when I am speaking to him." *And to act as a chaperone.* The thought vexed her, but she needed a watch-dog. When the viscount had touched her, she had been eager to melt into his arms. She had to regain control of her emotions before she spoke with him again, or . . .

She did not want to think of what the consequences could be.

Chapter 6

The rain pelted against the room's only window. The door was closed, and hushed footsteps went past. Gideon did not look up from the drawing on his large desk. It appeared that the builders had followed the exact dimensions on the blueprint for the small boat named *Perdition's Folly*. This time, the steamboat *should* work. If it did not, he could try . . . That would have to wait until after he escorted Miss Jade Nethercott to Sharla's house for lessons on how to act among the demimonde.

No, he needed to check on the boat before he made some important calls this afternoon. If he went to the assembly being hostessed by Sharla Maguire . . . Perhaps there, while Miss Nethercott was being introduced to a world he doubted she could imagine, he might discover the very facts he needed.

With a curse, he let the plans for *Perdition's Folly* roll shut. He walked to the window and stared out at the narrow garden at the back of the house on Bedford Square. He did not want to let Jade Nethercott intrude on his thoughts.

Whatever she was planning could not be as important as his work. Not only the steamboat he was hoping would be able to sail beyond the mouth of the Thames in an upcoming race, but the real reason he was in London.

Someone was decimating his family, one member at a time. In the past four years, there had been more deaths than he wanted to count. He had accompanied Persis for her first Season, but her Season—and his renewed pursuit of pleasure—had been cut short by their grandfather's death. That had been the first of eight deaths. None of them appeared suspicious. The coroner had deemed all to be the result of natural causes or accident, but Gideon was not convinced. The family's title had come to him about eighteen months ago. At first, he considered the title a burden even though Persis immediately insisted on being addressed as "lady"; then he realized it would open doors and get him answers from people impressed by it.

Even so, he still had not found what he sought. The proof that someone was preying on his family. Had the tree branch that fell just when his third cousin passed under it really been an accident? Or were the poisonous mushrooms mixed in—by accident it had been decided when the cook was questioned—with his great-uncle's favorite sauce only a sad, tragic occurrence? There had been other incidents. None were in the same parish, so nobody—not even Gideon at first—had seen any pattern. In spite of his efforts, he had been unable to get anyone to listen to him until he inherited the title from a cousin who had inherited it from another cousin who had inherited it from his older brother, all within the period of less than two years.

The killing went on. Derlan had been part of the family. If his death was related to the others, the murderer— or murderers—had made a mistake with a killing that could not be deemed an unfortunate accident.

Now a young woman from Yorkshire was suggesting she had information to help him uncover the truth. Heath was involved? It was possible, but unlikely. The solicitor had had the opportunity to visit all the victims. Yet why would he slay those who paid him, losing their business? Gideon would have to wait until the morrow to learn more from that quarter. A message he had sent to the solicitor's office had brought a reply that Heath was returning to Town late tonight or on the morrow.

So all he could do was wait.

And he did not do that well.

With a curse, Gideon opened his door and smiled when he saw his valet Tabor in the hallway. Tabor did more than oversee the care of Gideon's clothes and bedchamber. He was one of the few servants in the house whom Gideon had brought from the family's estate in Cornwall. The rest had come from his sister's household, which she kept separate in a wing of the rambling house there. When any of them saw him here on Bedford Square, they scurried in the opposite direction as if they believed he would kill them on the spot.

"Yes, my lord?" asked Tabor, his West Country accent a reminder of the estate where both of them had grown up. Tabor was a squat man with a wrinkled face and graying hair, weathered by the harsh sea edging the lands of Bannatyne Hall, even though he was only a few years older than Gideon. He wore his dark green livery with pride.

"Have my closed carriage brought around immediately."

"Of course, my lord." Tabor went toward the stairs that connected the floors of the townhouse. "You should find her at home on such an inclement day."

"Her?" He clasped his hands behind his back and regarded his valet sternly. Tabor had the uncanny ability to be privy to thoughts that Gideon had not spoken.

"Miss Nethercott . . . I presume."

"You presume mistakenly, Tabor."

"My error. As much as you have spoken of the young lady, I assumed . . ." He cleared his throat, obviously embarrassed. "I will see that your carriage is waiting, my lord."

Gideon smiled as soon as his valet was out of view down the stairs. Tabor was seldom wrong, and it riled Tabor when he was caught in a misconception. Gideon had always been amused the few times it happened, but took care never to let Tabor discover that.

As he started down the stairs in the valet's wake, Gideon's smile faded. His sister's private chambers were the next floor down, and, as it had been since the news of

Renshaw's death, her door was closed. He sighed, his spirits again as low as the clouds melding with the fog that hid the buildings across the square.

It was not a long drive to his destination. The carriage slowed in front of the house that was outwardly identical to the others on the street. He had been within most of them during his years in Town, and he knew the interiors were as unique as the women living there. The decor depended on each woman's taste, sense of style, and how plump the pockets were of the man who paid her invoices.

As he stepped out of the carriage into rain, Gideon's eye caught a motion. He glanced to his left, even though he could not see much through the fog. For the past year, he had felt he was being watched. He wished he knew by whom. If he had that information, he might have the key to the answer of who had murdered his family.

The door opened at his knock, and he was ushered in. The footman, who was no taller than Tabor, glanced again and again at Gideon. Uneasiness stiffened every step the footman took up the stairs, which followed one wall of the light blue foyer. Niches along the stairwell contained Wedgwood vases of the same hue.

At the top of the stairs, a broad arch led into a sitting room that never changed. Sharla knew what she liked, and once she obtained it, she would not let it go. Only with men did she relinquish her claim without argument. The men who had played a part in her life, including Gideon, appreciated that, as she knew quite well.

He lingered in the shadows, letting water drip from his cloak onto the brightly patterned rug, while the footman went in to announce him. He could not keep from remembering when he had not needed to wait on such formalities. When he had been as at home here as in his own house.

"Lord Bannatyne, madam," the footman announced with as much pomp as if they stood in a grand ballroom.

Sharla looked up from where she had been reading.

Her hair, as black as his, was drawn back beneath a cap edged by a full ruffle in the same sprigged linen as her gown. With a smile, she motioned for him to enter.

"Gideon! What a pleasant surprise!" Sharla came to her feet and held out her hands to him. As he took them and bowed over them, lifting one, then the other to his mouth for a quick kiss, she said, "I was unsure if you were in Town now. There have been so many tragedies for you and Lady Persis that I thought you might have retired to the country."

"Did you really think I would hie back to Cornwall and conceal myself in a cupboard until everyone else is dead by this murderer's hand?"

Sorrow added lines to her face, and he wondered how old she was. She had to be at least ten years his senior, but she had a beauty that did not dim with the passage of years.

"I had hoped you would consider leaving." She sat and motioned for him to do the same in a chair across from her. "At least until the true murderer is found."

He chuckled, hoping the sound covered his pleasure that she was not accepting gossip as gospel, as too many others had. "If I go, who will find the murderer?"

"If you stay, who will keep the murderer from finding *you*?"

"The murderer seems to have other prey in mind."

She wrung her hands. "I heard of poor Derlan. What a shock! You should take it as a sign to leave Town posthaste."

"Sharla, we could continue all day with this brangle, but I did not give you a look-in to argue."

"Why are you calling, Gideon?"

"To beg a favor of you."

"You know I would do anything for you."

He laughed again. "You should ask what the favor is first."

"I know you to be a sensible man, in spite of what the *ton* believes."

"My low reputation is not altogether without a basis in truth."

"Now you are trying to make me upset with you again when I know it would be impossible for you to slay anyone."

"If I were to chance upon the one killing my family, I would be hard-pressed to hold my hand."

She gave him a sympathetic smile. "Say what you will, but you are a man of honor who would not let the hunger for vengeance overcome his good sense."

"Even a man of honor will endure only so much without putting aside the law to protect what he holds dear."

"True, but you did not call to discuss such matters with me. So tell me what is bothering you, Gideon."

"Rather you should ask who."

"Very well. *Who* is bothering you?"

"Jade Nethercott." He had always been honest with Sharla, and he would continue to be as long as he could. "She is newly arrived in London from Yorkshire."

"A young miss?" Her brows lowered. "It is not like you to become involved with an inexperienced woman."

"Jade Nethercott is not like other young misses. She approached *me*."

Sharla waved his words aside. "Do not try to make me think that she is the first young miss to do that in hopes of capturing you in the parson's mousetrap."

"She is the first young miss who has ever tried to obtain my help in fulfilling a deathbed promise to her late father."

"Her father wanted his daughter to seek out *you*?"

He smiled. Sharla spoke plainly, and he appreciated her candor. "It goes beyond that. Her father asked her to find his mistress."

"Who was Lord Nethercott's mistress? I never heard of him having a lover here in Town."

"All Miss Nethercott has told me is that his mistress's given name is Violet."

"Without more information, your Miss Nethercott might as well try to number the waves, Gideon."

"True. It sounds quite impossible."

"Yet, you intend to help her." Sharla's eyes narrowed. "How lovely is she?"

"Lovely enough that having her on my arm at events among the *ton* in the coming week will create talk."

"And distract the Polite World from what she—and you—are seeking in the demimonde."

"You understand."

"I understand that you are continuing on your quest to find whoever is trying to destroy your family, but how does Miss Nethercott's search for her late father's mistress help *you*?"

He gave her the sardonic smile that even she would expect from him. "I could use some distraction for myself as well."

"There are others who would be willing to distract you. Women who do not believe that a single kiss leads to the altar."

"Miss Nethercott suits me at the moment." He wished he could spill the whole truth to Sharla. "But she is too prettily mannered, and, I daresay, she would be greatly shocked by what passes for sport among the demimonde. That is why I am asking this favor of having you teach her enough so she causes only a distraction and not a debacle."

"Teach her?" She laughed. "My dear Gideon, teaching a young lady to fit into the demimonde is about as possible as teaching the stars to swim."

"I have seen the stars afloat in the Thames when I check on the progress of *Perdition's Folly*."

"Only a reflection."

"And that is all I want you to do with Miss Nethercott. Help her create an image—a reflection of the demimondaines around her, if you will—that would serve her when I take her to your gathering at week's end."

"You are bringing her to my gala?"

He leaned back in the chair and folded his arms over his chest. "Where better? You know who is on your guest list, and you can prepare her how to act while she asks the questions she believes she must."

"And?"

"She goes back to Bedford Square with me for a month."

Sharla's eyes widened with astonishment. "A month? You have never spent a month with any one woman, not even me."

"I realize that, but that is what she has agreed to, so I cannot renege now." He gave a wicked laugh that always brought a smile from her.

It did now, but expression quickly sobered, as she replied, "Take care, Gideon, or she may persuade you to spend more than a month with her."

"If she is intriguing in bed—"

"You know that is not what I mean. Innocent misses have ways of inducing men to offer them a lifetime in their beds."

As she had before with him, he waved aside her concerns. "Will you help me by tutoring Miss Nethercott?"

"You know I cannot say no to you, my dear Gideon. If your Miss Nethercott is willing to be taught what a demimondaine needs to know, tell her that I will teach her."

"It may be the start of a new career for you."

"Opening a school for young ladies who want to push beyond the boundaries of the *ton*?" She laughed. "I doubt there would be many interested."

"You might be surprised. If they thought they could slip into the demimonde for some fun and an adventure and then return to the *ton* . . ."

"Is that what Miss Nethercott expects to do? Gideon, that may be impossible. You have to be certain that she understands the ramifications of the course she is about to embark upon."

"She knows." He stood and smiled at her. "And she will be here tomorrow for her first lesson."

Chapter 7

"I am sorry, Miss Nethercott," the butler said without meeting Jade's eyes. They stood in the simple foyer of the Bannatyne house on Bedford Square. "Lady Persis is receiving no one now."

Folding her hands together over the strings on her reticule, Jade tried to appear calm. A felon on his way to meet the hangman could not have been any more uneasy than she was to be standing inside Lord Bannatyne's house the day after she had agreed to his outrageous offer.

The quest Sir Mitchell's ghost had set her upon was no longer a game. It was real, and she was embarking on it with a man she would be a fool to trust.

Quietly, Jade said, "Please let Lady Persis know that I have called."

"Of course, Miss Nethercott."

"I see from the pots on her window that she enjoys flowers. May I send her one?"

"That is not necessary, Miss Nethercott." He put his hand on the door in an obvious hint for her to go. Suddenly he drew his fingers back and said, "Good afternoon, my lord."

Jade turned with what she hoped would appear to be serenity. She smiled and offered her hand to the silhouette in the doorway. "Good afternoon, my lord," she echoed.

"It is after noon, isn't it?" With the words that told her that the viscount was determined to hold her to the agreement they made, Lord Bannatyne stepped into the foyer, and a gasp bubbled in her throat. The wind had sculpted his hair with invisible fingers and tossed his rain-dampened dark cloak back to reveal the stylish black coat he wore over buckskin breeches. In the time it took her frantic heart to make a single beat, her gaze was captured by his ebony eyes.

"It is." She could manage no more than a whisper.

A smile warmed his mouth, and she recalled how it had heated hers when he kissed her with such unexpected passion. She had thought of little else since he had left yesterday. Every effort to put him out of her head had been futile. His image—his smile, his laugh, the way his eyes twinkled as he captured her mouth—flooded her mind the moment she let down her guard.

"What are you doing here?" he asked.

The ordinary question released her from the exciting memory of his kisses. Praying her voice would remain steady, she replied, "I had hoped to express my condolences to your sister on the death of Sir Mitchell."

"You knew the baronet?" he asked as he closed the door and motioned to the butler to leave.

Opening her reticule as the butler vanished through a door beyond the stairs, Jade drew out a calling card and set it on the silver tray. She needed to give her hands something to do to hide how they trembled. "He studied with my father for a short time."

"The Far East?"

"My father's interest in science was varied." She hesitated, then asked, "Has anything been learned about Lord Derlan's attacker?"

"No."

His terse answer warned her not to ask another question. The fury in his eyes burned with a strength that astounded her when she thought of the sharp words that the earl had fired at him. Because of that, she said only, "I have been informed that your sister is not at home to visitors now, so I should take my leave, my lord." She reached for the door's latch and faltered when she stared at walking sticks set in a wicker basket.

Going to the basket, Jade lifted out one almost identical to the bloody cane she had discovered at the duchess's house. Only a thin band of gold beneath the ivory knob was different. It was straight where the other one had been crooked. Two others with similar knobs were set in the basket. One had a checkered pattern painted beneath the ivory; the other had four gold dots.

"Is it a set of three?" she asked.

"No, it was a set of four." His voice was taut. "I had not noticed the other one was missing until you lifted it out from among the others at the duchess's house."

"Why didn't you say anything?" She set the walking sticks back into the basket.

"That would have been foolish. I knew suspicions would focus on me because Derlan and I exchanged very heated and very public words before I went into the garden."

"But you had someone who would offer you an alibi."

"I could not be sure of that . . . then."

She nodded, as unsettled by the gratitude in his words as by the sight of the three walking sticks. "You have no idea when the other walking stick disappeared."

"None, and there have been many visitors eager to call on Persis in hopes of offering her sympathy and learn more details of Renshaw's death."

"How horrible!"

"So many callers that I cannot guess who took the walking stick or—"

"No! That people would use her grief as an opportunity to fill their need for gossip." Her eyes widened. "You don't believe that I came here for that reason, do you?"

"No."

"I am relieved to hear that." Again she turned to reach for the door. "I should take my leave now."

"Don't you wish to know what I learned about Heath?"

At the name Sir Mitchell's ghost had spoken to her, she halted, her hand outstretched. She lowered it as she faced Lord Bannatyne again. "What did you learn?"

"The most amazing tidings."

"What is that?" She hoped he would not say that Heath had been found dead, too. No matter how she tried, she could not erase from her mind the image of Lord Derlan's battered corpse.

"I learned that he will not be returning to London until tomorrow. Amazing tidings, no?" He grinned.

She did, too. It felt surprisingly good to smile, and she realized how taut her shoulders were. "Truly amazing."

"Sometimes no news is good news."

"Yes. Thank you for trying to lighten my spirits."

"And my own."

Jade felt sudden tears flooding her eyes. In the midst of the to-do, she had allowed herself to forget that he must be deeply distressed at his sister's grief. She was intruding into their lives, and maybe she should not be, despite the pleas of Sir Mitchell's ghost.

"I should go," she said again.

"I would be glad to offer you a ride to your house."

"Thank you, but I am sure you wish to spend the afternoon with your sister."

"My sister is seeing no one."

"Not even her own brother?" She tried to imagine any reason she would refuse to receive her sisters. The lady's grief must be more overpowering than she had guessed. Her own sisters had been a source of comfort after Father's death.

"No one is what she requested, and I am honoring that wish. I have sent her notes about the doings in the *ton* in an effort to draw her out of her pain, but I have not spoken to her since she retired to her room before Renshaw's funeral."

"You are a good brother."

"It would appear so. Now allow me to be a good host and escort you home."

Jade shook her head. "Thank you, my lord, but you must realize that I cannot accept your invitation to ride with you in your carriage."

"Dash it! If you intend to find your father's mistress, you need to be ready to flout the absurd dictates of the Polite World."

"I am not ready to do that, as you well know. Otherwise . . ."

"You would not need my help." He grumbled something under his breath, then called up the stairs, "Tabor! Where are you, man?"

Jade heard quick steps from overhead, and then a short man rushed down the stairs. He was not as tall as she, but twice as round. He wore the same livery as the servant who had opened the door.

Not once did he glance in her direction as he asked, "Yes, my lord?"

"Miss Nethercott reminded me of the need for a watch-dog when I offered her the use of my carriage and my company while she returned to her house," Lord Bannatyne replied. "Miss Jade Nethercott, this is my valet, Tabor."

Only then did the man named Tabor look at her. She saw something flicker through his eyes, but it was gone before she could decide which emotion it had been. Lord Bannatyne gave her no time to reply as his hand at the back of her waist steered her out of the house.

The carriage was elegant and dark. The interior seemed even darker with the deep brown leather cushions and draperies drawn over the windows to keep out rain. As she sat on the forward-facing cushion, she drew aside the draperies. Several drops of rain struck her hand. Even so, she wanted the draperies open to keep all suggestions of impropriety at bay.

The thought of the weather vanished from her mind when Lord Bannatyne stepped in and sat facing her. She glanced toward the door, but no one else entered before it was closed. She had not guessed such a grand carriage could feel so small once they both were inside it. Yet Lord Bannatyne did not touch her, except where the hem of his cloak brushed her gown. He did nothing to ease her discomfort as he rested his arm on the back of his seat.

"Tabor will be riding above with the coachee," he said as if she had voiced her unsettled thoughts. "A single scream of dismay will invite him to open the door in the roof." He reached up to tap a small trapdoor. "I hope that meets your approval."

"I hope it meets the *ton*'s approval."

He chuckled and leaned back on his seat as the carriage edged away from the curb. "The *ton* would greatly approve of us giving them something to chatter about and allowing them to look at us askance."

"Is it for the *ton*'s sake that you have amassed your reputation?"

Again he laughed. "The concerns of the Polite World never entered my mind at times when I was breaking its rules."

"I find it interesting how a man can exult in his tarnished reputation but a woman must be on alert never to do anything that would suggest hers is less than pristine."

"A man is concerned that his heirs are of his own siring."

"I understand that, but I still find the disparity amazing." Jade allowed herself to sink back into the seat. Odd how once he entered the carriage that it and the day no longer seemed dreary and dank. There was a warmth in his laugh that seeped into her and swept away grim thoughts.

"I suspect you find much about Town and the Polite World amazing."

"Yes."

"The demimonde will astonish you further." He slanted toward her, his hands clasped between his knees. "Tell me what you know of your father's mistress, Viola."

"Violet."

"I stand corrected. Tell me about your father's mistress, Violet."

She did not believe—not even for a moment—that he had made the mistake unintentionally. Did he still believe that she was making up the story? She must not give him any further suggestion that she had fed him a banquet of lies.

"I honestly have little to tell you," she said, knowing

any *fact* she spoke could be the very one that tripped her the double and collapsed the whole tale she had created. "My sisters and I did not learn of her existence until Father mentioned her just before his death. At the time, we were too distraught to pose the questions I know in retrospect we should have."

"So you have no idea if she is alive or dead?"

"No."

"Or of her age?"

"Nothing. I hope that by quietly spreading the word of my search through the demimonde, Violet herself would hear that I am looking for her and find us. It is an air-dream, I know, but I know of no other way, short of knocking on every door in London, to find her."

"You may have chosen the best route. Gossip flies through Town more swiftly than a boat driven by storm winds." He sat back again. "For example, I trust you have heard the rumors that you and I are of a long and very intimate acquaintance."

Her eyes widened. "I had not heard that. Are the rumors based on my defense of you at the duchess's house?"

"You are learning quickly. That you offered an alibi, so quickly confirmed by your sisters, suggests that you had a cause to do so."

"I did. The truth."

"But truth is boring. Conjecture and conspiracy offer much more enjoyment to those who talk about the deeds of others."

She sagged against the seat and sighed. "I see this will be far more complex than I had imagined."

"That is the way of the Polite World." He gave her a lopsided grin as he rested one hand on one of the carriage's windows.

"Something else I am learning."

"You seem to be an eager student." His smile became sultry, sending a swirl of heat through her. That smile suggested he would like to teach her some very private lessons. His hand was stroking the carriage window in a slow motion that drew out the memory of his fingers doing the same along her. He had touched her and then he had kissed her, sending that luscious ripple of delight along her. Now he was talking of teaching her . . . and she was eager to learn.

The carriage bounced in a chuckhole on the street, jolting her back to reality. What was she thinking? She was letting nothing more than his motions create fantasies that could destroy everything she had come to London to do.

"Yes, I do think you would be a good student," he said, his voice becoming a cat's low purr. "That is why I want you to meet Sharla Maguire."

"Who is Mrs. Maguire?"

"*Miss* Maguire."

She grimaced and folded her arms in front of herself. "Who is Miss Maguire?"

"A good friend."

"How good a friend?"

He frowned. "That sounds like jealousy."

"How can I be jealous of a woman I have never met?" She regarded him with genuine puzzlement. "You seem to be hearing a meaning in my words that I have not put in them."

"Maybe I was hoping you would be jealous of a woman who once shared my bed."

Jade flinched. She could not halt herself. The contradictions in the Polite World astounded her. It was proper to speak of a love affair but one must never discuss topics that were commonplace in the countryside, such as a good day's labor in the garden or the pleasure of kneading bread dough and savoring its scent while it baked.

"Maybe you were," she said, not sure how else to reply. "If so, you must be disappointed." Not giving him a chance to make another absurd remark, she continued, "Why do you wish me to meet Miss Maguire?"

"She can teach you to be a part of the demimonde. There are many things you must learn before you can wander about without drawing undue attention that would damage your reputation and your sisters'. I doubt your father intended that with his deathbed request."

"No, he did not. But I think I am perfectly capable of handling myself during a short visit or two to the demimonde."

"Are you?" He balanced the heel of one boot on the seat next to her. With a smile, he pointed at his boot. "From your face, my dear Miss Nethercott, I can see you are disturbed by the thought of the seat being dirtied by my gauche motion. That is a reaction from a woman of the Polite World. A mistress of the demimonde would be accepting of the idiosyncrasies of her protector."

"May I remind you that I do not have any interest in a protector?"

"Or a lover?"

"A topic you promised not to discuss for the next seven days."

He wagged a finger at her. "I promised not to make love with you. I never promised not to talk about sex." His eyes widened. "You didn't blush at the word that usually brings embarrassed titters from young women who spend the Season trying to put a besotted man on a leash."

"Have you always been so cynical?"

"No."

Jade blinked at the abrupt change in his voice. Gone was the teasing tone. In its place was the regret of a man who had been forced to change by events beyond his control.

The door in the carriage roof opened, and a voice called down, "My lord, the street ahead is clogged. It looks as if a cart overturned."

Lord Bannatyne looked at her for a long moment before asking, "Can we get to Grosvenor Square another way, Crawley?"

"We could cut through Hyde Park," came back the answer.

"Do so."

The trapdoor closed. The carriage bounced again as

they left the road, and she looked out at trees and grass. Fitful rain splattered into the carriage. She jerked back when she saw a flash of lightning.

There was a pause before the distant thunder was followed by Lord Bannatyne saying, "You should be cozy in your house before the heart of the storm arrives in Town."

"I appreciate your kindness even more."

"I told you that I would help you. I always keep my word."

She nodded. "I have not heard anything to suggest otherwise."

"You do heed gossip a lot, Miss Nethercott."

"When one has been the focus of it, one learns to listen to it simply to know what others think."

"Even when they are wrong?"

"Especially when they are wrong." She smiled. "My father taught me that knowledge in any form is a superior weapon."

"I think I would have liked your father."

Jade was startled by the comment, for she had never imagined Father and the viscount discussing one of the scientific puzzles that enthralled her father. Yet now she could easily envision the two of them enjoying raising a cloud of pipe smoke while they debated possible answers to the unanswerable. Quietly, she said, "I think you would have, too. He enjoyed talking with those who agreed with him and even more with those who did not."

"He sounds like a man of rare intelligence . . . even though he has sent his daughter on a want-witted errand." This time when he leaned forward, his gaze held hers. "Are you certain you want to continue on this path?"

"Yes, I am certain. I will allow Miss Maguire to teach me what I need to know at her mistress school."

He laughed, but humor left his voice. "Mistress school? That is the perfect name for it. You grow more intriguing all the time, Miss Nethercott." He began a slow scrutiny that slid along her like a caress, even as it tried to ferret out every secret she had not divulged.

His gaze reached her feet and began back up her again, and she had to fight to keep her mind focused on what she should tell him. While he enjoyed this easy perusal of her, his eyes glittered as brightly as the jewels the duchess wore. His perusal teased her to do the same to him, and her gaze traced his aquiline nose and the firm line of his lips. She looked away. She was risking enough by asking him to help her; she could not let herself conjecture how wondrous it would be to welcome his kisses in the carriage while he held her against his hard, virile form.

"Jade . . . ," he breathed.

Unsure if she had heard him correctly, for he had never used her given name, she asked, "What?"

"Jade . . ."

"Yes?"

He smiled, and she realized she had let her own longing ensnare her once more. Even as she thought that, he shifted to sit beside her, and, in one smooth motion, twisted his fingers through the hair at her nape. He pressed his mouth to hers. She stiffened, then her lips softened against his, as the succulent heat of his breath swirled into her mouth. Her breathing became staccato, her breasts pushing against his chest, as he stroked her tongue with his. Boldly seeking every silken pleasure within her mouth, he dared her to be as brazen. Her hand slipped up along his back, her tentative touch growing more eager as he drew her close.

There was a loud clap.

"Thunder," he whispered against her lips. "Just thunder."

The sound came again followed by a shriek. Something struck the carriage.

Jade bumped back against the carriage wall when Lord Bannatyne abruptly released her. She stared at a hole in the side of the carriage. It was small and matched one on the opposite side where a projectile had cut through it.

A ball!

Someone was shooting at the carriage.

Lord Bannatyne threw open the door.

"Are you mad?" she cried, grasping his coat sleeve. "If you go out, you could be shot."

"It will take some time to reload. If I—"

She pushed him to the floor as she heard another shot. The ball struck the open door, slamming it into the carriage. Something whistled over her head. The ball hit something. She did not dare to look up to discover what.

"Let me up!" growled Lord Bannatyne.

"Stay where you are. The shooter must have more than one gun."

"I will be damned if I let *you* protect *me*." With a quick motion in the narrow space, he twisted out from beneath her.

Again she grabbed for his sleeve, but he shoved her down roughly. She winced when her elbow twinged with pain. Regret flickered through his eyes, but he said, "Stay here until the carriage is on the road, Jade. Don't move until then."

"But . . ."

He was gone.

Jade cursed under her breath, then more loudly. Rising as far as her knees, she looked out. Lord Bannatyne was racing across the open grass toward some trees. Someone was following him. His man Tabor. Lightning sliced across the sky, and she ducked. She was silly. She was safe from the storm. In the carriage, the lightning could not touch her.

But the coachman . . .

Another shot was fired. Her heart cramped as it halted with fear in midbeat. Lord Bannatyne! Then the ball struck the carriage again, with a second following in quick succession.

Now might be her chance. She stretched up and opened the door in the roof. "Come inside! Now!"

All she heard was a moan.

Jumping out on the side opposite from the shots, she pressed against the carriage. It would not offer her much of a shield, because the balls had gone through both walls.

"Miss Nethercott, I think we need to talk," said a calm voice from behind her.

Jade looked over her shoulder and groaned as a glow like lightning coalesced into the ghost's form. "Not now, Sir Mitchell!"

"I know you think I have an eternity to wait."

"Not now!" She put her foot on a spoke of the front wheel to climb up to where she could reach the coachman. She had to get him out of the line of fire.

"Miss Nethercott, I do believe you could do me the courtesy of listening to me."

"Not now! Go away and come back later!" She scrambled up long enough to draw the unconscious coachman off the seat in the box. She could not get him into the carriage by herself.

Hearing a shot, she jumped to the ground and flattened herself. The hiss of the ball flying over her head told her how close it had come. Sharp fire seared her right shoulder, and she shrieked. She had been hit. She glanced at her shoulder. It was encased in the cold light that surrounded the ghost. She had not been shot. The fire came from Sir Mitchell's icy touch. Reaching up, she pushed his hand off her, and her fingers were burned with the agonizing cold.

"Go away!" she cried as tears ran down her face.

"I didn't mean to hurt you." He stared at her in dismay. "You must realize I am sorry. I need your help. I would not have hurt you intentionally."

"Go away!" she shouted. "Go away *now*. If you don't leave *now,* my offer to help you is over."

"And you will never see your father."

She faltered, then turned her back on the ghost. "Meet me at the house on Grosvenor Square."

"Aren't we there?" He looked around himself, squinting as if all he could see was the bright light around him.

Jade did not pause to answer. Clambering back up into the box, she gathered the reins that had been dropped by the senseless coachman. Her left hand felt as if it were on fire. She paid it no mind. Rain burst from the sky as she looked toward where Lord Bannatyne and his man had gone. She saw so sign of them.

She had never driven more than a pony cart, but she slapped the reins and shouted to the horses. The carriage rocked wildly as she gave them their heads once they were going toward where the shots had come from.

Lightning crackled overhead, and thunder boomed before the flash had left the sky. It must have touched down on the Serpentine. She hunched into herself, trying to be as small a target as possible.

Suddenly out of the rain, a form appeared. Tabor! He was chasing someone. The shooter?

She tried to turn the carriage to cut off the fleeing man. It was impossible. The angle was too tight. The horses whinnied a warning, then one rose on its hind legs. She pulled back on the reins before they could panic and hurt themselves. Renewed pain sliced through her right shoulder and across her left palm.

The horses slowed, then stopped. She bent over to check the coachman. She saw no sign of blood on him, but he remained senseless.

Hating to leave him yet unsure what she could do to awaken him, she lashed the reins around the dash and jumped down. She had to find Lord Bannatyne. She ran into the needle-sharp rain striking her face. Ahead of her she saw a form on the ground. It was Lord Bannatyne! If he had been killed . . . Her stomach threatened to erupt, but she ignored it as she knelt beside him. A red mark on his left cheek suggested the shape of a fist. That would not have been enough to leave him senseless. What had happened? She saw no sign of where a ball had pierced him. Hoping she would not do him further damage, she put her hands on his shoulders and struggled to push him onto his back. Her left hand burned anew as it brushed his rough cloak, but she kept pushing until he was sprawled on the grass.

"Lord Bannatyne!" she called softly. She must take care not to alert the shooter that they were still beneath the trees.

He did not open his eyes.

"Lord . . . Gideon!" She tapped his right cheek lightly. He groaned, but his eyes remained shut.

Flipping his cloak aside, she tore open his coat and waistcoat. Buttons scattered through the grass. The fine linen of his shirt was soaked with rain, but she saw no sign of blood. Had he been shot in the back? No, that would mean he had been running away, and she could not imagine that. Had he been injured in another way?

She ran her hands along his left side. Everything felt intact. Leaning across him, she did the same on his right. Again she discovered no broken bones. She stretched to check his legs.

His arm shot up, and his fingers closed around her wrist. "Enough," he said with a laugh. "A man can enjoy only so much and recall that he is a gentleman."

Jade stared at him. She was relieved and vexed at the same time. "You are unhurt?"

"Mostly."

"How long have you been conscious?"

"Since you tumbled me over onto my back and rammed my aching skull into the ground." He ran a finger along her cheek. "I thought I would be the one to tumble you first, but you proved me wrong again." He drew her down so she slanted across his chest as she had when she checked his ribs. His other arm came up to encircle her.

His mouth was damp beneath hers, but the raindrops sizzled away as heat grew between them. He rolled her beneath him. She heard her bonnet crack at the same time his thick cloak enclosed them in a dark wonderland. When he deepened the kiss, stroking her lips with his tongue before slipping it between them, she gasped at his intensity. His tongue boldly explored each hidden delight of her mouth. She curved her arms up around his back and felt his eager reaction all along him. That she—a novice in the arts of seduction—could thrill him was thrilling. Rapture overwhelmed her, and the ache of longing seared through her, demanding satiation. As his tongue flicked along her cheek and sought the curves of her ear, she tightened her arms around him, not wanting to be swept away from him in the tempest of passion.

When he whispered for her to open her eyes, she gazed up at him. A hint of a smile tilted his lips as he bent forward to kiss the sensitive skin along her neck. She arched her neck to offer him every inch to delight. Her fingers clenched on his back, and she pressed closer to the hard lines of his body.

A throat was cleared once, then again more loudly.

Lord Bannatyne looked up, his motion shifting his cloak so she could see a pair of legs just beyond it.

"I am sorry to report that the shooter eluded me. Shall I bandage the wound on your head, my lord?" Tabor asked with a serenity that suggested he often found his lord in such a position with a woman.

With a curse she had never before spoken aloud, Jade tried to shove out from beneath Lord Bannatyne. She halted when he said, "Keep doing that, and you will push my self-control past its limits."

"I believe that has already happened!" she fired back.

He laughed. "You have no idea how much I am controlling myself."

"That is true. I have no idea because I have seen no sign of it." She pushed him off her. Standing, she thought she heard a chuckle from his valet, but Tabor's face was blank of any emotion when she glanced at him.

She strode toward the carriage. She heard Lord Bannatyne stand and follow, despite his valet's call for caution. She did not look back until Lord Bannatyne put out a hand to block her way back into the carriage.

"Is everything a joke to you, my lord?" she asked, still not looking at him.

"No."

"Just everything about me? Is that it? You seem to take special delight in bamboozling me."

He turned her to face him again and cupped her face in his hands. "You know that teasing you is not what truly delights me."

She raised her foot and slammed her heel into his instep. When he released her with a startled shout of pain, she started to climb into the carriage. He put his hand on her shoulder to halt her.

She screamed as agony exploded through her. Dropping to her knees in the carriage, she clutched the edge of the seat with her right hand. She drew in deep breaths as she waited for the pain to diminish. When she heard Lord Bannatyne asking what was wrong, she wondered how she could explain her injury to him. He would not likely believe the truth, and her mind was so filled with anguish that she could not think of any lies.

Tabor's shout was followed by the carriage bouncing. She guessed he was climbing up to check on the coachman. Leaning her head on the seat, she struggled to regain her breath. She did not resist when, stepping over her, Lord Bannatyne sat on the seat. He gathered her up in his arms and settled her across his lap. She watched his eyes close, and the lines of pain etch more deeply into his face.

The carriage began moving, but she did not. She stayed within the cocoon of his arms. When they curved around her, not holding her against her will, but holding her against him with gentle compassion, she leaned her head against his shoulder. She was in too much pain to fight him . . . to fight *herself.* She closed her own eyes, knowing the respite would be all too brief.

Chapter 8

"That was careless of you."

Ignoring Sir Mitchell's ghost, Jade placed another compress on her shoulder and leaned back on the chaise longue in her bedchamber. She had boiled ivy leaves and combined them with wine. Poured on the compress, the mixture eased the pain of the burns on her shoulder and hand.

"I would say that *this* was careless of you," she replied tersely. She did not appreciate that the ghost had come into her private room again, but at least she was dressed decently in a morning dress with the top buttons along the back undone to allow her to keep the compress in place.

She stared at the simple ceiling that was crisscrossed by narrow slats of wood painted the same white as the plaster. The walls were a pale pink that gave the cherry furniture in the room a rather bilious appearance. Even so, the tester bed, the cupboard, dressing table, and cheval glass were lovely pieces. The coverlet was a deeper shade of rose and of the same brocade as on the longue where she could look past the dark green draperies to the square.

The street was empty. Lord Bannatyne had refused to come in and allow her sisters to tend to his injuries. Thanking them graciously, he had reeled back to the carriage after being reassured that her sisters would guard over her and guarantee that she spent the rest of the afternoon quietly.

And she had . . . until Sir Mitchell's ghost made another appearance. She could not help wondering if the man had been so bothersome before his death.

"How was I to know that touching you would cause such damage?" demanded Sir Mitchell in a petulant tone. His face was edged by the glow that always announced his arrival.

"That is true. You still are learning about what it means to be a ghost."

"I would not have to learn more if you would obtain the proof to send Bannatyne to hang. Surely then I would go on to where I shall spend eternity."

"Are you *sure* he was the one who slew you?"

He scowled. "You must not let him persuade you to believe him innocent."

"Innocent?" She laughed coldly. "I do not believe that, but it is clear that someone intended to kill *him* this afternoon. He does not know who would be trying to kill him or why."

"It might have been a random attack. Some low creature saw a fine carriage coming into the Park. He took the opportunity to call for Bannatyne to stand and deliver."

"Highwaymen are seldom seen within London's borders. I suspect that it was not random. I suspect the attack is related to Lord Derlan's murder."

"Why?" His voice rumbled through the room like distant thunder. "I say. I had no idea that my question would sound like that."

She started to shrug, then thought better of it. "I have no reasons for my suspicions, but two attacks in such a short period of time suggest—"

"Nothing!" He strode across the room, the glow from the light around him flowing like fog. "You are allowing yourself to be distracted from your true task by unrelated events."

"Maybe so." Jade found it difficult to own that Sir Mitchell could be correct. Perhaps she was letting herself look for someone else to blame for the baronet's death. Yet, she had begun to have doubts about Lord Bannatyne's guilt in the baronet's murder from the first time she spoke with him. Her first impressions had always been ones she could trust. So why wasn't she trusting them now? Could it be as simple as a ghost was telling her that her instincts were wrong, or was it even more prosaic—that she did not trust herself near Lord Bannatyne?

"You must be more careful." Sir Mitchell wagged a finger at her. "What will happen to me if something happens to you?"

"I am pleased to hear how concerned you are for *me*."

"You misunderstand me. I . . . By old Harry!" He started to fade. "I will be back as soon as I can."

Don't hurry. She dared not speak the words aloud because she was unsure if the ghost could hear her even when he was not visible.

Jade was not surprised at a knock on her door. The ghost always vanished before someone else came near. When it opened to reveal Sian, she motioned for her sister to enter.

Saying nothing, Sian sat in a chair that offered her a view of the square. She opened her sketchbook and began to work, but Jade noticed how her sister's eyes flicked toward her as well as toward the rain-soaked square.

"You might as well scold me," Jade said when she could not stand the silence any longer.

"What do you expect me to say? That you broke a promise to China by allowing Lord Bannatyne to bring you home in his carriage?"

"We were not alone. His valet rode with us."

Sian set her book on the dressing table and moved to sit at Jade's feet on the chaise longue. "No, you were not alone. You were ambushed. He has been labeled a murderer, and he has enemies who must be furious that he has not paid for his crime."

"What if he is not guilty of that crime?"

Sian's dark brown eyes widened. "You are being taken in by his fascinating arts!"

"Nonsense." She looked up at the ceiling again, not

able to meet her sister's eyes while so uncertain about the viscount. "I am looking at the facts and considering what I am learning and trying to piece it together like a puzzle where there are too many blank spots. Lord Bannatyne has offered to help me for the rest of the week."

"To do what?"

Jade quickly explained the tapestry of lies she had woven for Lord Bannatyne. When she was finished, Sian slowly rose and sighed.

"Who would believe such a tale?"

"He did."

"Did he, or does he have reasons of his own for agreeing? What does he expect to get in return?"

"A gentleman assists a lady without expectation of a reward," Jade said, raising her gaze once more toward the ceiling. "The proof of Sir Mitchell's murderer is in the demimonde, and I cannot go there by myself."

"Maybe you need to rethink your offer to help Sir Mitchell, Jade."

"I promised."

Sian sighed. "I know, but I hope your promise will not bring you to grief or worse."

"So do I!"

Gideon walked into the office, which smelled of decaying books and rampant dust. Someone had recently cleaned one of the windows overlooking the street, but the other was opaque with dirt.

At a desk facing away from the windows, a man was bent over an open book, writing with the scratchy sound of a quill. Bookshelves behind him were stacked with more papers and books. The single lamp gave off very little light.

The man had an athletic build that belied his work in the filthy office. Thick, dark hair curled around his ears and dropped over his collar. A black coat that had been out of fashion two years ago was draped over his chair, and his gray waistcoat was devoid of any design.

Gideon cleared his throat.

The man looked up, peered over his quizzing glass, and gasped, "My lord! I did not expect to see you today." He jumped to his feet.

"All the more reason for me to pay you a call, Heath."

"I don't understand." Without a pause, he asked, "How do you fare, my lord? I heard there was an incident in Hyde Park."

Resisting the temptation to reach up to where a small bandage still was visible through his hair, Gideon smiled coolly. The motion hurt his left cheekbone. The bruise there was turning a deeper shade of navy with every passing hour. He knew he had been both lucky and careless. Lucky that the shooter had been hurrying to reload when Gideon discovered him crouching in the grass. Careless that he had given the shooter a chance to strike him first in the face with the butt of the pistol and then, while Gideon was distracted by Jade's scream, hit in the back of the head. Only Tabor's arrival had kept the shooter from firing into him.

"I am fine. A bit marred, but nothing that will not heal." Gideon drew off his right glove, one finger at a time. He watched how Heath's eyes focused on the motion. The solicitor's Adam's apple bobbed like a boat on stormy waters.

"I have heard whispers that include your name," Gideon said as he sat. Settling his right boot on his left knee, he leaned back in the straight chair. "Disturbing whispers from an unlikely source."

The solicitor's face grew wan. "Will you enlighten me, my lord? What is being whispered about me?"

"That you are in a position to have the opportunity to know more than anyone else about the recent deaths of my family."

"Me?" He choked. Pressing his hand to his chest, he staggered back against the wall.

Dash it! He had not intended to give the man heart palpitations. Coming to his feet, he guided Heath to his chair. He opened a drawer in the desk. Lifting out a bottle, he poured the solicitor a cup of comfort. Gin, he suspected, but he doubted if the solicitor would care which spirit it was. He held it out to the solicitor.

"Thank you," Heath muttered as he took a sip, then a gulp. Raising his head, he said, "My lord, it is true that I had the opportunity, for I have called often upon each of those who died." He shuddered. "But I swear on my own late mother's soul that I had no hand in the tragedies that have inflicted your family."

"You misunderstand me, Heath. I am not *accusing* you of murdering them. I—"

"Murder?"

Gideon thought the solicitor was going to swoon. Taking the glass, he poured more gin into it.

"Drink this," he said as if he were a doctor and the solicitor his patient.

Heath grasped the glass in both hands and slurped down the gin with fervor.

Gideon sighed. If he had known the solicitor would drink it so rapidly, he would not have put more gin in the glass. He reached out and put a single finger on the bottom of the glass, tilting it away from Heath's mouth.

"Slowly," he said.

Heath nodded. "Of course."

"Let's start anew. I came to ask you if—upon your many visits to my relatives' houses—had seen anything amiss. Anything that would offer a clue to why they died in such quick succession."

"I don't know. I never considered looking for any such things. The deaths were deemed accidental or from natural causes."

"I know that. I simply don't believe it."

Raising the glass, Heath took a more temperate sip. He put the glass on his desk and said, "There is one thing." He added nothing more as he stared across the room.

"Don't leave me in suspense. What is it?"

"All of them talked about a recent call from someone in your family."

"Who?"

"Actually several people. You were one." He looked hastily away.

"I realize that. Who else?"

"Your sister, Lady Persis."

"Who traveled with me. Who else?"

He faltered, then shook his head. "No one else called at all the houses. I do remember several talking about having the chance to meet Lady Persis's betrothed, and they thought him quite arrogant." Color flashed up his sallow cheeks. "Forgive me, my lord. I should not have spoken so of a man who is now dead."

"No need to ask forgiveness, Heath. Anyone who knew Renshaw would recognize that as an accurate description."

Gideon asked a few more questions, but it was clear that the solicitor had no further information. It was, without a question, a dead end, as dead as those who had held the title before him. And it was just as clear what he needed to do next.

Find out what else Jade Nethercott knew and how she had learned it.

Chapter 9

Jade was not surprised that Lord Bannatyne arrived at the door of the Grosvenor Square house exactly at the hour he had told her he would when they parted the previous afternoon. Nor was she surprised when he was gracious to Mrs. Willow, the companion found by the duchess to give countenance to three young women living alone. The rotund woman seldom smiled, but the very edges of her lips curved when Lord Bannatyne greeted her as warmly as if he had called to speak solely with her. As they drove away from the square through the spring sunshine, he spoke more to Mrs. Willow than he did to Jade, asking the older woman's opinion on various matters of interest to the *ton*. Jade's attempts to discover if he had spoken with Mr. Heath were either too veiled for Lord Bannatyne to guess what she truly wanted to know, or he was evading her questions.

She guessed it was the latter, but she could not accuse him without revealing in Mrs. Willow's hearing what she wanted to know. It was not a good beginning to the second day of her search for what Sir Mitchell hoped she would find.

Did she hope to find it as well? As she looked across the carriage to where Lord Bannatyne politely was, once again, riding backwards, she knew nothing was as simple as the baronet's ghost had led her to believe. Was he capable of murder? After seeing him race to stop the shooter in the park and, just as important, after savoring his kisses, she knew he was a man of very potent passions. He had been ready to sacrifice his life to protect her and his servants. Would a man willing to do that kill another by driving a knife into him from behind? She could not reconcile what Sir Mitchell had told her with what she was witnessing herself.

So who was right—Sir Mitchell's foggy memory of his death or her own observations of Lord Bannatyne?

Jade watched in awe as he entranced the usually dour Mrs. Willow without any apparent effort or hypocrisy. He seemed truly interested in what Mrs. Willow thought about a new bookstore and several recently published authors. The gray-haired woman almost preened as he began discussing music with her.

When the carriage slowed to a stop in front of an elegant townhouse on a square Jade did not recognize, Lord Bannatyne handed Mrs. Willow out first. He turned back to hold out his hand to Jade. He started to wink, then grimaced. She knew the simple motion had strained his bruised cheek.

"Are you sure you are well enough to do this today?" Jade asked.

"I promised you that I would help you, and I will not allow my own stupidity to cause me to renege on that promise." He arched a brow as his thumb traced the lines of her palm out of sight of their chaperone. "Or are you hoping that I would break my pledge to you so you could break yours to me?"

"I am hoping to find the answers I am seeking."

"And I am hoping the search will take the full seven days." His smile glittered in his eyes.

Her breath caught. He was doing no more than holding her hand, but every motion he made suggested the intimacy that he wanted to share with her. Could she believe what seemed so genuine, but might be just another aspect of the easy charm he spread about like jam on bread?

Jade drew her hand out of his. "It will take far longer than that if we remain on the walkway instead of letting me begin the lessons at your *friend's* school."

"The mistress school," he said with a laugh as he offered his arm.

"Shhh!"

He glanced as she did at Mrs. Willow who was waiting by the steps to the front door of the house that looked exactly like all its neighbors set around the small patch of greenery. "I will endeavor to leave Mrs. Willow's sensibilities unruffled."

And mine, she wanted to add, but she doubted that was possible.

When he took her hand and settled it in the crook of his arm, she wondered how a lovely house on a pleasant square could be the beginning of her risking everything on the slight chance that she would obtain the information Sir Mitchell needed in exchange for bringing Father to see her one more time. She swallowed roughly. Finding the proof could mean publicly accusing Lord Bannatyne of murdering his sister's fiancé.

She would do what she must to get that chance to see her father. Nothing must sway her from that path, not even Lord Bannatyne's brown eyes that promised thrills she guessed were beyond her maidenly imagination.

The door opened as they climbed the stairs. They were ushered in by a footman in simple black livery. He took their names and then Mrs. Willow was shown to a small room on the ground floor where she could enjoy tea while she waited for Jade to complete her call.

"You were very kind to Mrs. Willow," Jade said as they climbed the staircase hugging the left-hand wall. Landscapes were hung on the silk wall covering. "Thank you."

"You are welcome. I assumed you would be so unsettled by meeting Sharla that you would prefer not to stammer in front of your *duenna*."

"I would not . . . I mean, I don't . . . Oh, bother!"

"I did not mean to put you to the blush now."

"I am not blushing."

He ran his rough fingertip along her cheek. "I beg to differ. Even in the faint light here, I can see your face is a lovely shade of rose."

"You should be a gentleman and not mention that, Lord Bannatyne."

"You must address me as Gideon."

"That would be untoward."

He laughed, the sound surrounding her like an embrace. "My dear Miss Nethercott, you are entering a realm where the untoward is commonplace. For you to call me by my title will draw unwanted attention to you." He tapped the brim of her bonnet. "You are going to be the focus of every eye when you walk into Sharla's gathering at week's end. The women will regard you with jealousy and the men with lust."

She met his eyes evenly. If he thought he could succeed where her sisters had failed and persuade her to give up her quest, she must show him how mistaken he was.

"I am aware of that, my—Gideon."

Again he laughed. "Gideon will do, but that is a good address to save for the proper moment."

"What address?" she asked, baffled.

He leaned toward her, and his other hand slid up the banister to brush against hers. "I doubt you meant the endearment, but if you call me in such a breathless tone 'my Gideon,' you may give everyone the very right opinion of the circumstances between us. Shall I call you 'my sweetling'?"

"I would prefer you did not."

"There must be some term I may use to show that you are, indeed, a very special friend."

"Jade will suffice."

Leaning back away from her, he smiled. "You were named rightly. You possess a heart as hard as stone."

She blinked back unexpected tears. She had been unprepared for such a smiling insult. Wondering why she cared what he thought, she continued up the stairs.

A footman was waiting at the top. "This way," he said quietly as he led them toward a door near the front of the house. "Miss Maguire, Lord Bannatyne and Miss Nethercott."

From what she could see through the doorway, the room was gloriously and tastefully decorated in pale shades of blue. A flowered rug was set beneath a settee with pale gold upholstery. Two chairs faced it across a low table. On the mantel were several small statues of figures dressed in flowing skirts. The draperies over the pair of windows were a darker blue with flecks of gold sprinkled across the fabric.

"Thank you, Bowden," came a woman's voice. "Do come in."

Gideon's hand in the small of her back urged Jade forward a half step. She did not need to be prompted further. Walking into the room, she saw a woman sitting at another settee, identical to the one she had seen, near shelves of books at the back of the room. A twinge of nostalgia pinched her as she was reminded of Nethercott Castle's book-room and the time she had spent there with her father and sisters.

But she needed to focus on her present circumstances if there was to be any hope of seeing Father again. She affixed her best smile in place and looked at the woman on the settee.

Sharla Maguire was nothing as she had imagined. There was an elegance and grace in every motion as the dark-haired woman rose to greet them. Tall and slender, she wore a blue gown that was the perfect complement for her sitting room. She offered her cheek for Gideon's kiss as if she were a beloved aunt, but her eyes were focused on Jade.

"You two look far better than I had feared after hearing of the excitement in Hyde Park," Miss Maguire said. "That bruise makes you look like a ruffian, Gideon."

"I thought it made me look like a hero."

"From what I have heard, Miss Nethercott saved the day." She held out her hand to Jade. "It is an honor to meet such a brave woman. Do recall your manners, Gideon, and introduce us."

He laughed. "You are not supposed to lecture me on remembering my manners, but Jade on forgetting hers." When her breath caught, he asked, "Is something amiss, Jade?"

She shook her head. How could she explain that when

he spoke her name she thought of the first time he had used it as he drew her into his arms?

"Enough of your moonshine," Miss Maguire said. "If you please, Gideon . . ."

With a grin, Gideon did the introductions.

Jade felt unworthy of any of the lauds Miss Maguire offered her. Her own dress was unable to measure up to Miss Maguire's splendor, and she knew her bonnet was outmoded. But no, her clothes were not what she feared would fail to obtain Miss Maguire's approval. It was herself. She was unsure why she wanted the approval of a woman of the demimonde, other than Gideon had spoken highly of her.

"Do come in and sit with me, Miss Nethercott," the older woman said, motioning toward the settee where she had been sitting. On a table beside it were the makings for tea. "We should begin by getting to know one another better. Gideon, you can take a cake or two to enjoy while you wait in the small salon."

"Can or must?" he asked.

"*Can* take a cake. *Must* wait in the small salon."

He laughed. "I see you are taking to your position as taskmistress with eager delight."

She motioned him out of the room with her hands. "Begone, and do not try to eavesdrop. I shall send for you when Miss Nethercott and I are done with our discussion."

"Do not forget to ask Jade what she has deemed the proper—or should I say improper?—name for your lessons." He lifted two small cakes from the tray and, with a wink, walked out of the room.

Jade was astonished at how alone she felt. She had been accustomed to meeting and speaking with many sorts of people in Yorkshire. The carefully separated strata of society in Town were unheard of in the countryside. So why did she yearn to run after Gideon and plea with him to stay?

"Please sit down, Miss Nethercott." Miss Maguire gave her a warm smile. "And tell me what this name is that you have given to our lessons?"

"It was a jest only. I did not mean for it to be more than that."

"Come now, Miss Nethercott. If you cannot trust me with such simple information, how will you trust me to teach you what you need to know?"

Embarrassed to repeat the foolish words, she nevertheless said, "I called it 'mistress school.'"

"Mistress school?" Miss Maguire smiled. "A fitting name. And if it makes you feel any better, I know how you must be feeling right now."

"You do?" she blurted, then put her fingers to her lips. It was too late. The words had already escaped.

"Yes, for I was once where you are now, a young woman poised between the *ton* and the demimonde. I know how steep the fall appears from where you are standing."

Jade lowered herself cautiously to the very edge of a chair. "And how impossible it is to climb out once one has slid down from the peak."

"True." She sat and folded her hands on her lap. "If you would like my advice, Miss Nethercott, I would suggest that you rethink your plan. The demimonde has rules as stringent and unforgiving as the Polite World's. A single mistake will bring unwanted attention to you. Such attention is guaranteed to leave you and your family shunned by the *ton*."

"Your advice is wise, but I made a promise, and I cannot break it."

Miss Maguire sighed. "I expected that would be your response. No wonder you have caught Gideon's attention. You two are much the same." She raised her hand to halt Jade's retort. "And he is right when he says that you need my assistance to slip into the demimonde and out without damaging your reputation. You have very pretty manners, and no one would mistake you for a demimondaine."

"But your manners are as fine as mine."

"Because I am the mistress of a man of high standing, so I keep a household that would not be out of place on Berkeley Square. Yet, what you see here is nothing like what you will witness if you attend any assembly beyond the *ton*."

"I don't understand."

"I realize that. Your first lesson is to remember that while a woman among the Polite World seeks to maintain a pristine reputation in order to win a titled and rich husband, in the demimonde, women vie for the attention of those men who have seen much and experienced much."

"So they must be jarred out of their ennui?"

"You comprehended that with ease."

"It seemed logical." She met Miss Maguire's eyes for the first time. "My father considered logic a virtue without peer, so he insisted that his daughters be well familiar with it."

"But logic differs from place to place. You will discover that when you venture into this world where you do not belong."

"That is why I am grateful for your assistance."

Miss Maguire picked up a teacup and glanced at Jade. "Sugar? Cream?"

"Both please." She took the cup, watching while Miss Maguire poured a second for herself.

"I understand your father had many students among the Polite World."

Startled by the sudden change of subject, Jade managed to keep from spilling the tea. "Not many. A few people came to study with him."

"Including Lady Persis's late betrothed?"

"Yes. Did you know Sir Mitchell?"

Her nose wrinkled. "He was very high in the instep."

"Excuse me?"

She chuckled and added, "It means he was disagreeably arrogant. My dear Miss Nethercott, you have much to learn and such a short time to study. Do not fret about a man who will be of no further bother to anyone."

"The man is dead! You should speak of him with more respect." She felt color flash up her face. "Forgive me. I should not be lecturing you."

"You are right to be shocked by my comments. However, what you do not know is that I offer him the same respect in death that I did while he was living. I never could understand what Lady Persis saw in him. I swear Gideon had not been in receipt of his title more than three seconds before the baronet was pressing him to accept his suit for Lady Persis."

"I did not realize that."

Sir Mitchell had suggested that he had had a *tendre* for Gideon's sister for a long time, and that he had worked hard to win her heart and her brother's permission for them to wed. Had she misunderstood him, or had he lied to her?

"Let us speak of your lessons." Miss Maguire set her cup on the tray and smiled. "Tell me how you address Gideon."

"By his given name . . . now. He told me that it would be the right way to address him."

"Not only must you allow him to use your given name and you use his, but you must be comfortable with him touching you openly."

"Touching? What do you mean?" Her face was growing hotter, and she guessed it was now a brilliant shade of red.

"Miss Nethercott, if you cannot discuss such things, you will certainly be unable to pass among the demimonde. I urge you again to reconsider your plan."

"I will try to contain my disquiet."

"Good." Miss Maguire folded her hands on her lap. "Now, let us get the first lesson under way. The first thing you must know is . . ."

Gideon paged through the book on the table in the small pink salon. He despised the color of the room, and the book was poetry by a poet he had never heard of and whose work was almost as distasteful as the room's paint. The newspapers stacked neatly beside it were ones he had already read. Clasping his hands behind his back, he walked to the window and looked out at the drizzle that had begun anew.

Dash it! Everything depended on Jade now. If she was so aghast at what Sharla had to teach her that she refused to go on with their plan, he would lose his chance to discover more about the mysterious deaths.

And I will not have her in my bed.

No, he would not think of that now. He needed to keep his focus on what he had been pursuing before Jade entered his life. Would his plan work? Would an obviously out of place Jade Nethercott create the distraction that he needed, the distraction that would lead to the truth of who had slain most of his family and why?

He heard soft slippers on the carpet outside the room. Turning, he saw Sharla in the doorway.

"Are you finished already?" he asked.

"No, although I must say that Miss Nethercott is a very eager student." She smiled. "And a very good one. If we continue the lessons the rest of the week, she will be prepared for what she will encounter at my soirée. And whom."

"I am not as sure as you are," he replied.

"You underestimate her."

"I know she is not being honest with me."

"Or you with her, I would guess."

"Did she speak of any matter beyond your lessons?"

Sharla hesitated, then said, "Yes. One."

"Which was?"

"She asked about Sir Mitchell Renshaw. She seems very curious about the circumstances of his death."

"More curious than anyone else in Town?"

Again Sharla did not answer quickly as she pondered the question. Finally she said, "Her questions suggest she has only recently been informed of his death, but she seems to know more about the man than I would have guessed possible for a young woman from Yorkshire."

"Gossip travels on winged feet, as you know all too well."

"I know." She held out her hand. "Gideon, do come and assist us."

"Help you?"

"With the lessons."

"I thought you said she had done well."

Taking his hand, she drew him out into the hallway. "She has, but she has so much to learn, and she needs your help to learn it."

Gideon considered protesting further, but knew it was hopeless. Sharla had a heart of gold, but a spine of steel. Much as Jade did. He dared not think what the two women had devised that would include him.

Jade put down her cup as he entered the room. He noticed how she winced when using her left hand. Not once had she complained about the injuries she had suffered yesterday. His brow rutted, sending pain across his face anew, when he realized she had never explained how she had been hurt. He had assumed she damaged her shoulder while clambering up into the box to drive the carriage. Had she injured her hand at the same time?

She did not meet his eyes, but came to her feet when Sharla spoke her name. Sharla glanced at him and raised her eyebrows. He was unsure what she intended him to understand from that silent message, and she pushed past him to stand beside Jade.

"Miss Nethercott," Sharla said quietly, "please allow me to introduce Lord Bannatyne. Gideon, Miss Jade Nethercott." She motioned for him to step forward.

He did, bowing over the hand that Jade held up to him. "Miss Nethercott . . ."

"Good afternoon, Lord Bannatyne." Jade's voice trembled.

Because he was touching her or because of something else? He rather hoped it was the former.

Sharla smiled. "That is how you are accustomed to a gentleman greeting you. It may not be the same when you are among those in the demimonde. Now, Gideon, if you would be so kind . . ."

He smiled as he took Jade's hand again. He could not keep from noticing how her breasts rose and fell with her swift breaths. How much more quickly would her breath flow if he pressed his mouth in the downy valley between them?

"Must you stare so?" Jade whispered.

For a moment, he was confused. Then he realized she thought he was gaping at her in his role as a man seeking his pleasures in the demimonde. He would be wise to let her continue thinking that.

"What is your name, young woman?" he asked.

She glanced at Sharla who motioned for her to reply. "My name is Jade Nethercott."

"Jade? Ah, a woman who knows exactly what she is."

Sharla laughed. "Oh, dear me! I did not think how your lovely name could be construed as an insult to your virtue."

Color flashed up Jade's face. Jerking her hand out of his, she gasped, "How could you say such a thing?"

"To prepare you for what you may face at Sharla's gathering," he answered coolly. "Did you give no thought at all to what 'jade' might mean and how a common term for a harlot might be taken by the men who will find you intriguing?"

"I had not intended to use my real name." She raised her chin and regarded him with icy disdain, her green eyes snapping with fury. "I planned to create one that would not connect me in any way with my family."

"An excellent idea," Sharla said into the silence that fell on the room. "Now, Gideon, please continue with the lesson."

He took Jade's hand in his again. She stared at his chin, not raising her eyes higher. "Miss Alias—"

Her head tilted back as she stared at him in amazement. When he saw the hint of a smile on her lips, he gave her a slow wink. It was worth suffering the pang across his cheek when her smile slowly broadened.

"Yes?" she asked in a breathy tone that took his own away.

He had to regain control of himself and the situation, or he might not be able to resist pulling her into his arms and kissing her as he had imagined doing again and again since she had appeared out of the darkness in the duchess's garden. He jutted his chin toward her and said in a self-important tone he stole from his sister's late fiancé, "It is our mutual good fortune to have met tonight, Miss Alias."

"So I would say, Lord High-and-Mighty." Her eyes twinkled, but the sparks strengthened into a flame when he lifted her hand.

The flavor of her hand, silken soft beneath his lips, created a hunger in him that he knew no one else could sate. He had felt a craving for other women, but never had it been so powerful, blasting him as he had been hit by steam from the engine on his boat. Was it her sweet innocence or was it her sharp wit or was it how her eyes softened—just a bit—when he gazed into them?

"Gideon?" prompted Sharla quietly.

Recalling the role he was to play, he tightened his grip on Jade's hand and pulled her a step closer. "You are beautiful. Your hair glitters like pure gold spun from sunshine."

She giggled.

"Miss Nethercott!" chided Sharla, but her lips were twitching as well. "Do not forget where you are and what is expected of you."

"I will not, but how can I be expected to remain serious when someone says something so absurd to me?"

Gideon made sure his face revealed nothing of his astonishment at her reaction to the type of compliment that had always brought him the reward of sweet smiles. He had not intended to be absurd. He had, he was startled to realize, been honest.

"Begin again," Sharla ordered as she handed Jade a fan and sat on the settee to watch.

"Good evening," he said bowing his head toward Jade.

She gave a half curtsy. "Good evening, my lord. Isn't this a wondrous gathering?"

"Maybe not the exact word I would have used up until this moment, but I would say that the gathering has now become wonderful with this opportunity to speak with you."

"You flatter me, my lord." She wafted the fan in front of her face, her bright green eyes twinkling over it.

"Only if you believe that the truth is flattery."

She laughed again and, snapping the fan closed, shook her head. "I am sorry, Miss Maguire, but I cannot take such silly flirtations seriously. Maybe it is hopeless. Maybe *I* am hopeless trying to be something I am not."

"Nonsense. Begin again." Sharla motioned for them to take their places.

Gideon half expected Jade to rebel against the order, but she obeyed. Why was it so important for her to find her late father's mistress that she was acquiescing to Sharla's commands? He suspected that Jade was hiding her dismay at the brazen coquetry between men and the demimondaines behind her nervous laughter. If he truly wished to help her, he should persuade her that she was want-witted to continue with her scheme to find the woman named Violet. There were other ways for her to discover the truth and for her to help him distract the *ton*.

Even as he thought that, he was taking her hand she held out to him and bowing over it. They went through the vapid exercise of introductions, and again she began to laugh when he offered her a compliment.

"Dash it!" he snarled as Sharla motioned for them to begin over. "Let's make this realistic. Do you want to know what a man would do if he saw a beautiful woman like you alone?"

"Yes."

"As you wish." Taking care he did not touch her right shoulder, he seized her arms and tugged her against him. He captured her mouth that was open with shock.

The heat of her startled gasp swirled through him, sending his senses careening out of control. He wanted to taste more than her fragrant lips. He ached to discover every inch of the soft curves pressed against him without her prim gown in the way. When her tongue boldly stroked his, he knew he had been a fool to agree to wait a week to bring her into his bed. He wanted her now.

Her hand slid up his back, and his senses raced like runaway horses. But he was not fleeing something; he was rushing toward something. This woman who enthralled him with her questing touch and eager response to his kisses.

His own fingers edged up along her toward the soft fullness of her breasts, but he halted himself when he heard an unsteady laugh. Sharla! He had become so immersed in Jade's kisses that he had forgotten they were not alone.

Gideon was not surprised when Jade pulled back, her face's color deepening. He was pleased at the thought that she had been so rapt by their kisses, too, that she had become lost in the delight. As he withdrew his arm from around her, she wobbled slightly. He held her again, glad for the excuse to keep her close.

"Well," Sharla said with another laugh, "there is also that possibility. I think Miss Nethercott should sit down until she regains her usual color."

"I am fine," Jade answered. Slipping out of his embrace, she added, "And I thank you, Gideon, for showing me what I might experience at Miss Maguire's gathering."

"My pleasure," he replied. He regretted the sharp answer when she glanced at him and away, her cheeks growing ashen.

He cursed under his breath. Did she think he was callously playing with her emotions? The question halted him from saying more, because he was unsure of the answer. *Was* he toying with her in the hopes that she could help him find the truth that had evaded him?

What a muddle this was becoming! If he had any sense, he would put an end to the whole agreement posthaste. How could he when Jade might have information that proved more valuable than her suggestion that Heath was involved? Someone had told her about the solicitor. What else did she know? *That* he needed to discover.

With a smile, he wondered if he knew exactly the way. Even if he was wrong, holding Jade again would be delicious. It was a treat he wanted to sample soon, and he knew just the place.

Chapter 10

Jade was relieved when Miss Maguire said, as gracious as the finest lady in the *ton*, "I will see you tomorrow at the same time, Miss Nethercott. You still have a lot to learn at my mistress school." She chuckled. "I do have an affinity for that name. I wonder if Rudy would mind me opening a true mistress school here."

"Rudy pays for everything you see," Gideon said under his breath.

"Oh." Jade appreciated his quiet explanation, but did not look at him as she added, "Miss Maguire, thank you for your help. I will endeavor to return tomorrow to continue my lessons."

"Gideon, make sure Miss Nethercott has directions to reach my door."

"Of course," he replied, but she could hear he was as perplexed as she was at Miss Maguire's unspoken suggestion that his presence was not wanted tomorrow.

Even though she was curious what Miss Maguire planned to teach her without him to serve as a substitute for the men who lived partly in the Polite World and partly in the demimonde, she simply bid Miss Maguire a farewell until the next day. She watched as Gideon gave Miss Maguire a brotherly buss on the cheek; then she went to rouse Mrs. Willow, who was asleep in a comfortable chair in the room on the ground floor. Gideon escorted both of them to his waiting carriage and handed them in.

"I had no idea you would be so long in your call,"

Mrs. Willow said as she sat on the seat facing forward. She yawned delicately.

Jade tried to hear what Gideon was saying to Reeves, who was driving the carriage while his usual coachee recovered from his thankfully minor injuries received during the attack in the park, but the words were muffled by the carriage walls. Before she had a chance to reply to Mrs. Willow, Gideon climbed in and sat facing her.

"I trust you found your call satisfactory," he said.

"It was interesting."

"I have found that calls on Sharla Maguire usually are."

She looked hastily away. Why did he have to make everything more uncomfortable by reminding her that Miss Maguire had once been his mistress?

"You are reading an inaccurate meaning into my words," he said, warning her that his keen eyes had taken note of her reaction. "As I told you before, she is now a very dear friend. Nothing more."

"I understand that." Her gaze came back to meet his, and she discovered his eyes still were afire with the yearning she had seen in them just before hers closed as his lips found hers.

"Sharla said you were curious about Sir Mitchell Renshaw," he said.

She tried to conceal the flinch rippling up her back. "I suppose I am. An unsolved murder is a nine days wonder."

"Allow me to give you some advice, Jade."

Her breath came out in a soft gasp as he spoke her name. No matter how she tried, she could not hide her reaction to her delight each time he used it. "Of course."

"Don't speak of Renshaw. He had few friends and many enemies."

"Which were you?"

"I was no friend of his, but he never gave me cause to be his enemy."

"Probably wise of you when he was going to be your brother-in-law. How does your sister fare today? I still wish to call, but know too well how difficult it is to pretend to be getting over grief when it remains a constant companion."

"She remains in seclusion."

"I hope she has been spared the tale of the ambush in the Park, because that would upset her further."

He gave her a wry smile. "I have no doubts she has heard all about it. She has the servants well trained to bring her any hint of poker-talk."

"What?"

"Gossip," Mrs. Willow said quietly.

"Thank you, Mrs. Willow." Looking back at Gideon, she realized he was staring out the window. His face in profile was enticing. There was a strength in his features that urged her to believe he could be trusted, that he had been falsely accused. Yet, from her memory came Sir Mitchell's warning to take care she did not succumb to Gideon's captivating ways, for such foolishness could lead her to the same fate the baronet had suffered.

"May I ask you a favor, Jade?"

She blinked and refocused her eyes on his face to discover he was regarding her with a smile. Bother! She had let herself get too caught up in her thoughts and failed to notice that he was now looking at her.

"Certainly. I do owe you a favor for helping me."

"It is not *that* favor."

Heat scored her cheeks. When was she going to think before blurting out the first thing that came into her head? She did not look at Mrs. Willow, not wanting the older woman to have any hint of why she was blushing.

Gideon's smile broadened, but his voice remained serene as he continued, "I need to check on one matter, which, if I could do so before I return you to Grosvenor Square, would save me quite a bit of time."

She nodded, unwilling to speak when she did not trust her voice. To own the truth, she did not trust an inch of herself because every bit of her was reacting to the thought of what she had offered Gideon in exchange for his help. Maybe if he had never kissed her, she would be able to talk of their agreement without her face burning. As it was, she must prevent everyone—most of all, Gideon—from guessing that the fire on her cheeks was only a reflection of the flames searing her deep within places she had barely been aware of before he burst into her life.

"Where do you wish to go, my lord?" asked Mrs. Willow, again yawning behind her hand.

"To the Thames."

"The Thames?"

"It will be only a short distance out of our way, and I need to check one thing on my boat."

Jade's curiosity shoved aside her embarrassment. "Your boat? You have a boat?"

"I have a *steam*boat." He gave a quick laugh. "I had no idea when I decided on the name *Perdition's Folly* that she might prove to be just that. I had hoped to have her ready earlier this spring for a trial to prove she would be seaworthy as well as capable of being used on the river, but . . . the situation did not allow it."

Jade sighed silently. She knew he had been distracted by tragedy. Trying to force a cheerful tone, she said, "I have read about boats powered by steam, but I have never seen one. Would it be possible for me to go aboard while you are there?"

"It would seem, Jade, that you inherited your father's interest in science."

"He was a good teacher, always urging us to ask questions."

Jade noticed how Mrs. Willow's head nodded forward, then suddenly straightened. Holding her finger to her lips, Jade motioned with her head toward Mrs. Willow. Gideon opened his mouth, and she leaned forward to put her finger to his lips. When his fingers curled around her wrist, she knew he had worked his enticing arts on her once more. And she did not want to resist any longer. His other hand cupped her cheek. His fingers sought across her face for . . . she was not sure what, but she wanted to offer him whatever it was.

His thumb tilted her mouth toward his. Closing her eyes, she awaited the thrill of his kiss. Mrs. Willow stirred beside her, and he released her. She saw his frustration as he settled back against his own seat. She shared it. His kisses were magnificent, but too quickly interrupted.

Jade hoped Mrs. Willow would speak, but the older woman was as silent as Gideon. Noise came from beyond the carriage along with disgusting smells of open sewers and rotting food. Drawing out a handkerchief, Mrs. Willow covered her nose and mouth.

The noise became more raucous, but the odors eased when they reached the river. The breeze now was redolent with mud and low water and tar.

When the carriage halted on a street where the buildings looked as if a light breeze would send them tumbling into the river, Gideon opened the door. He stepped out and turned back with a smile. "Would you like to satisfy your curiosity on my boat?"

A dozen answers swirled through her mind—answers to questions of how she ached to discover how his hands would feel as they swept along her, what her fingers would discover when she explored his hard chest, how much pleasure was waiting for her in his arms—but she only nodded, aware of Mrs. Willow listening to each word. She knew that was an excuse, because sometimes curiosity should not be eased. Not when the man she longed to be with was an accused murderer.

No! Impossible!

But Sir Mitchell seems very sure. . . .

No!

Silencing the quarrel in her mind, Jade held out her hand to Gideon and let him help her out of the carriage. She released his fingers slowly. He smiled, and she feared she would melt into a puddle right there by the Thames.

"No, thank you," she heard Mrs. Willow say primly. "I have no interest in visiting any sort of boat. If you would be so kind as to instruct your coachman to move the carriage so I might have Miss Nethercott always in sight, I shall remain here."

"That may be difficult," he answered.

"Then I must request that Miss Nethercott return here to sit with me while you complete your errand."

Gideon chuckled under his breath and muttered, "Old tough!" Raising his voice, he called, "Reeves, Mrs. Willow needs to see the boat from the carriage window while I give Miss Nethercott a tour of it."

"My lord, that will be—"

"Thank you, Reeves," he interrupted as he offered his arm to Jade.

She saw the coachee roll his eyes before he snapped the reins and clucked an order to the horses. The carriage continued up the narrow street to where it could find a place to turn around. As it moved away, she became aware of being watched. On the steps of the decrepit buildings or in open doorways, people were sitting and staring at her and Gideon.

"Stay close," he cautioned as a rat skittered past them, scolding them for wandering into its domain. "Not all vermin scurry about on four feet here."

She nodded. Putting her hand on his arm, she matched his steps as they walked between two tumbledown buildings and out onto a wharf jutting into the Thames. The water was high, but she had read how the river's tide dropped many feet over the course of a day.

"These boards are uneven," he said, his steps making a hollow sound. "It is easy to trip."

The sun seared her eyes as it reflected off the river, turning the dirty water into a richer shade. Watching her feet, she kept up with him without tumbling on her nose. She heard the carriage return and match their pace.

"Here we are." Pride filled Gideon's voice as if he were talking about an eldest son.

But Jade knew he was talking of a *she,* his boat. She raised her head, shadowed her eyes beneath her bonnet, and looked down a pier to where he was pointing.

The bright red and green boat was the oddest she had ever seen. Without the majestic sails and sheets she was accustomed to seeing, it seemed puny as it rocked with the gentle rhythms of the Thames. On its sides were what looked like two spoked wheels without rims. They were freshly painted as well in the same bright colors. In the center, coming up the roof of a chamber that took up most of the deck, a chimney rose high.

Gideon led her to a plank connecting the pier to the boat. When he walked across it, she hesitated. The board bounced with every step he took.

"What are you waiting for?" he called from the deck. "Have you changed your mind, or do you still want to come aboard?"

"You know I cannot resist satisfying my curiosity." Jade laughed. She put one foot on the plank. With much slower steps, it did not move as much as she had feared.

He offered his arm when she stood beside him on the gently rocking deck. "Still five more days before I can satisfy mine."

"Not now. Don't ruin this exciting moment with such talk."

"If you had any idea what true excitement is." His finger rose to stroke her cheek. "You have no idea, Jade."

She could not argue with that. Just his touch set off pulses of delight bouncing through her as wildly as the plank had beneath his feet.

"Let's start the tour of your boat," she said before the need for him overmastered her. "It is so very small." She watched a majestic ship pass, its sails filled with the breeze. "I hope when you cast off, someone makes sure you do not come too close to any other ships."

"My pilot has learned to be skilled. He has had no other choice, because I no longer have as much time as I would like to spend here."

"Where does he stand when the boat is under way?"

"I will answer your questions later, because our tour will need to wait." His smile faded.

"Why?"

He led her along the narrow deck past the row of windows on the long, low room that took up so much of the space. A glance at them gained her no insight into what was beyond them. They were covered with dirt and grease. When they reached a small open space

near the bow, he stepped away. He looked back toward
the shore where the carriage sat like a sentry keeping
watch.

"What I am about to tell you," he said, "is not yet
widely known. The duchess has hired some Robin Red-
breasts from Bow Street to discover the truth about Derlan's death."

"But what could a Bow Street Runner see that the
watch did not?"

"Anything. Everything. The watchmen were interested only in getting the corpse to the church and col-
lecting their fee for transporting it safely." He frowned
as he folded his arms on the rail. "Rather you should
ask what they might learn that *we* missed."

She watched the water brushing against the boat.
"They will want to talk to us."

"Yes, because you and I could not restrain our curiosity at the Duchess of Northborough's house and re-
ported our findings to the Charleys. If you wish, I will
speak with them alone. There is no need for you to
be there."

"So you can continue to take credit for what I discovered?" She tried to make her question a joke, but it was
useless. There was nothing amusing about murder.

"I thought you would feel that way, so I said he could
speak to us here." He gave her a wry smile. "I assumed
you would not wish for anyone from Bow Street to give
you a look-in on Grosvenor Square."

"You assumed correctly. When will they be coming
here to speak with us?"

He pointed along the wharf. "I would say very soon.
Here he comes now."

Watching a man with one of the bright red waistcoats
that had given the investigators from Bow Street their
"Robin Redbreast" nickname, Jade gripped the rail so
hard that pain sliced across her burned palm. She yelped
and jerked it back.

" 'Tis nothing," she hurried to say.

"I had not realized," he said, cupping her hand in his
much broader one, "that you had injured it so griev-

ously. Such a friction burn from you sliding it against the carriage should not still be so painful."

"It is much better." She lifted it away. "Much better. Do not fret about it, Gideon."

"If I had remained at your side instead of dashing off like some slowtop determined to be a hero . . ."

"It is much better, and we have other more important matters to concern us."

Jade thought he might argue, but he nodded as the sound of boots came along the deck. When he turned to look toward the stern, she did as well.

The short, stocky man in the brilliant waistcoat had one hand on the rail and the other on the windows as he fought to keep his balance. She was astonished because the deck barely moved beneath her feet. He wore a dusty black hat on his hair that was several shades lighter than Gideon's. His coat and breeches appeared as if they had endured many cleanings. His shoes were scuffed, but the white shirt he wore beneath his bright waistcoat was neatly pressed.

"My lord, forgive me for being late," he said as he reached out to shake Gideon's hand.

"We arrived ourselves only minutes ago," Gideon replied with a studied smile. "Miss Nethercott, allow me to introduce Mr. Ward of Bow Street. Ward, this is the young woman I mentioned to you. The one with the extraordinary eyesight that allowed her to see what no one else had."

"Miss Nethercott." He touched the brim of his hat.

"Mr. Ward," she replied. "I am pleased that the duchess has arranged for professional assistance to learn the truth about poor Lord Derlan's murder."

"Thank you. First of all, I want to express my thanks for agreeing to speak with me." His voice suggested he had been well educated, quite the opposite of what she had expected from the stories of Bow Street Runners. Those tales suggested the Runners were hardly better than the criminals they pursued. "I know this appalling situation must have left you with every decent feeling offended."

"True."

"If you are willing, Miss Nethercott, would you relate how you came to be in the passage in the duchess's house and everything that you saw?"

"Of course." As she began to explain, he interrupted—always with a polite apology—to ask questions. She realized how little she had to describe when Mr. Ward mentioned he had seen the dents in the wall and that the walking stick had been given to Bow Street. It was her turn to apologize. "I have nothing more to share with you, Mr. Ward."

"I am pleased that you have confirmed what I surmised." A smile crept across his face, and she guessed he was a man who smiled often because there were many lines left by past laughter. "Her Grace was not as succinct or as logical in her explanation as you." He glanced at Gideon. "I understand you came upon Miss Nethercott when she was examining the wall."

"At the time, she had found only one dent," Gideon answered with a smile at her. He grew somber again when he added, "But we discovered the other quickly."

"And did you see anything else unusual?"

"Unfortunately no."

Mr. Ward was clearly disappointed, but, after a few more questions for which they had no answers, he thanked them and asked if he could return to speak with them again if the need arose.

Before Jade could reply, Gideon said, "You are welcome to call here any time, Ward. If I am not here, a message will be relayed to my house and I will arrange to meet you at a time convenient to both of us. However, I must ask that you call neither at Bedford Square nor at the house where Miss Nethercott is staying. Such a call would be unsettling for both my sister and hers."

"I understand." He did not seem insulted. Instead he thanked them again and, with another tip of his hat in her direction, walked back toward the plank connecting the boat to the pier.

As soon as Mr. Ward was out of earshot, Jade asked,

"Do you think he will find anything to pinpoint the murderer?"

"Bow Street is better known as thief-takers than for solving murders." Again he looked across the river as if seeking something important. "If you are still curious about my call on Heath . . ."

"I am!" Anticipation leaped inside her like a fox with the hounds on its tail. "What did he tell you?"

"Nothing."

"Oh."

"Is that all you have to say?"

She edged along the railing toward the bow. "I have no idea what you expect me to say. I was told he might have information that would be of interest to you, and I shared that fact with you."

"Who told you?"

"A gentleman who said he thought you should know."

"At the duchess's party?"

"Yes, it was that evening." As he had, she looked out at the river. She did not want to risk him seeing her disgust at lying to him. She was not being completely false, but she was evading the most important truth—the tidbit had come from the ghost of Sir Mitchell Renshaw.

"What else did he tell you?"

"Nothing."

He put his hand on her arm. "Answer a question that has taunted me, because I cannot begin to imagine what its answer might be. Why did he tell *you* when we had yet to speak a single word?"

"You thought I was someone else that night." She did not want to tell him an out-and-outer, so she would give him half answers for as long as she could.

"So he might have mistaken you for someone else as well." With a sigh, he shook his head. "Dash it, Jade! I had dared to hope you might have the answers to what I sought."

"What are you seeking?"

"The truth to how I came to possess this title." He released her and fisted his fingers on the railing. "I do not believe in coincidence, and, even if I did, having eight members of my family die in the past four years cannot be coincidental. So many accidents simply cannot be by chance."

She was so shocked she could not speak. She had not guessed that Gideon was chasing the faint clues of a murderer, too. For a moment, she almost revealed how she had been sent to speak to him by a ghost accusing him of murder. She silenced the words she must not speak. Bother! She had made too many promises to too many people . . . and one vexing ghost.

"Gideon, I am so sorry at your loss. I—"

"No!" he growled under his breath before adding, "Do not be like everyone else and try to soothe me with platitudes. Be honest with me, Jade, as you are with everything else."

Not wanting to tell him that she was not plainspoken with him about *everything,* she asked quietly, "So you believe without doubt the deaths were intentional?"

"Without doubt? There is always doubt, but I believe that it is possible they were murdered." Pushing away from the rail, he locked his hands behind his back as he walked past her to the bow. He put his foot on the ridge above the deck. "One death is a tragedy. Two are a great tragedy, and three may be a coincidence. But eight goes far beyond coincidence."

"Does that include Sir Mitchell?"

His lip curled with derision. "No, for he was never an official member of the Bannatyne family. I speak of those who were in line for the title I now hold and those who held the purse strings in the family. In four short years, I went from being the son of a younger son's younger son to the holder of my family's title. I was accustomed to a simple life on our family's small estate in Cornwall, but now I am responsible for lands throughout England." He folded his arms again on the railing, but she was not fooled by his pose. Tension creased his forehead and stiffened his shoulders. "And a man responsible for so much cannot act on any whimsy that fills his mind."

"I never imagined that inheriting a title would proscribe you from doing what you had hoped to do."

"It was nothing that I wanted. I was very happy to let my various uncles and cousins have its obligations while I worked on this ship and tended to my own family's business concerns."

"So now you do not have the time to test a boat that you have worked so long to build."

He faced her, his expression grim. "You are quickwitted, Jade. As I told you, I had hoped to test *Perdition's Folly* before this. I want to prove that steam-powered ships are viable in journeys between ports. Now . . ."

"You have other matters on your mind."

"You see what others, including my sister, have failed to see."

"Or refused to see." When she saw his eyes widen, she hurried to say, "Forgive me for judging your sister when I have yet to meet her."

"No apologies are necessary because you are right. Shall I show you around the boat?"

"Yes, but tell me why you named her as you did."

"I named her *Perdition's Folly* because I hoped she would prove to be the bane of the smugglers and shipwreckers who do their dirty deeds all along the shore of Cornwall."

"Where you lived before coming to London."

"Yes. I thought Persis might wish to return there after Renshaw's death, but she announced she would not leave her rooms until she was done with her mourning."

"Not even for Sir Mitchell's funeral?"

"Not even for that."

"Did you go?"

He gave her a crooked grin as he leaned on the railing. "You never ask the simple questions, do you, Jade?"

"It is not a very complicated question. Did you go or not?"

"I went. Sometimes I do what is expected of me."

Putting her hand on his arm, she said, "I think you often do what is expected of you. More often than you

wish to own to. Such as when you did not deny your
sister's request to marry Sir Mitchell, even though you
clearly despised the man."

"I thought she would come to her senses and see him
for the fortune-hunter he truly was. She had pined for
him before the family's title came to me, but he had
paid her little attention. I think I saw them dance only
once or twice before then. I heard they had spoken a
few times in the park, but I saw him often with other
women who had greater dowries than I was able to
offer Persis."

"Until you gained your title."

"Yes." He held out his hands. "Enough talk of that.
Let me show you my steamboat."

Jade put hers on his and let him draw her away from
the rail. When he glanced toward the carriage, she lifted
her hands away and put one on his arm. "That is a good
idea, Gideon. I doubt Mrs. Willow will wait too patiently
for too long."

"Then shall we begin?" He smiled. "This is the front
of the boat. The bow."

She chuckled. "I know something of boats because the
port of Whitby is not far from Nethercott Castle. Father
took us there to enjoy the sight of the boats embarking
for distant ports. He even arranged for us to go aboard
one of the great ships like the one Captain Cook sailed
to the distant southern Pacific."

"I had no idea you had such experience with ships."

"As I told you, my father had many interests." She
motioned toward the structure in the middle of the boat.
"What is that? The cabin?"

"Partly, but mostly it protects the steam engine from
the elements." He led her to a door on the far side.
Opening it, he said, "Be careful. I have banged my head
on that low door more times than I wish to own to."

Jade ducked as she stepped down into the dim cabin.
Very little light came through the soot-covered windows
that ran along the walls. Other than benches running
beneath the windows, the room was empty. Two large,
closed cupboards were set into the wall opposite the win-

dows. A door at the far end was open, and she went with him toward it. The motion of the boat seemed stronger here, and she wobbled slightly.

He put his hand over hers on his arm. "All right?"

"I need to get my sea legs. Or should I say river legs?"

"Either way, you will become accustomed to the motion quickly, I suspect. You are a very determined woman and do what you set your mind on."

Except find the proof that you did not kill Sir Mitchell. She could not speak that thought aloud, but she was not surprised at its course. The ghost would be furious that she was following her instincts instead of his instructions. And her instincts were telling her that Gideon had not slain Sir Mitchell. She must find the truth so she could persuade the phantom he had made a mistake and still bring Father from the realm beyond death to speak with her one more time.

As Gideon opened the door more widely, she tried to envision how she would tell her father about Gideon Bannatyne. Father would not be pleased that she had entwined her life—even so briefly—with a man of such a reputation. Yet how many times had Father urged her to think for herself instead of heeding the opinions of others, even himself?

"Here is the engine that moves the paddles on the side of the boat, sending it through the water," Gideon said.

"Like powerful rowers?"

"Yes." He stepped aside to allow her to peek inside the chamber.

Heat slapped her in the face, a blow that almost sent her reeling back. She gripped the edges of the doorway and stared at the great boiler where water was turned into steam. Pipes were connected to it along with two arms that reached through the sides of the boat. She guessed each arm was hooked to a spoked wheel.

As he explained, showing her how steam moved past a piston, giving power to the arms that turned the wheels, Jade watched his face as much as his fingers that pointed out one aspect after another. She had seen so many expressions on his face, but never such an honest excitement. While he talked about improvements he and his assistants had made to the basic Watt engine, she heard how proud he was of each tiny step forward. He squatted to show her the gauge on the front of the steam chamber, and she had to resist reaching to brush his hair back out of his eyes. He reminded her of a small lad with a new toy.

Then he glanced over his shoulder, his gaze capturing hers, and she realized he was every bit a man. The hunger in his eyes was a mixture of his yearning to prove his boat was worthy to sail beyond the Thames and his craving to show her that he was more than worthy of being her lover.

Her fingertips lightly brushed his forehead as she gave in to the temptation to push back his hair. As he had before, he grasped her wrist. He slowly stood, edging toward her. His other hand slid around her waist as he backed her out into the cooler room. Shoving the door closed with his foot, he tugged her to him.

"Gideon . . . ," she whispered in the moment before his mouth found hers.

His lips were as heated as the steam within the engine, and she let that warmth seep through her. When he pressed her back against the door, her straw bonnet protested. She whipped it off and tossed it onto the bench to her right, then wrapped her arms around him, drawing him even closer. He drew her lower lip into his mouth, suckling on it before he gently nibbled along her jaw. Each touch of his teeth, each brush of his tongue, each pulse of his breath evoked more craving from deep within her.

She heard her own moan escape when he toyed with her earlobe before tracing the whorls of her ear with his tongue. Her body refused to remain still. She pressed to him, needing what she could not explain. All that mattered was her craving and how he could satisfy it.

"Jade," he murmured in her ear.

"Hmmm . . ." She slipped her hands beneath his coat and explored the strong, firm muscles of his back.

"Jade, look at me."

She opened her eyes to find his so close that bare inches separated their lips. "Yes?"

An eager smile spread across his lips as his hand came up to cup her breast. Her fingers tightened on his shirt as his hand slowly, slowly, so agonizingly slowly slipped up along her breast to tease the very tip. One of his fingers sought up over the top of her bodice, inching beneath it to stroke down while his other hand lowered her sleeve over her shoulder.

"Beautiful," he whispered as he freed her breast. "You are as beautiful as I dreamed."

"You dreamed of me?"

"Even before I met you." He bent and drew her breast into his mouth. His tongue teased it as he had her earlobe, daring her to surrender to the need aching deep between her legs.

When his leg pushed hers apart, so his thigh was up against the source of her craving, she yanked on his shirt. She had to touch him, to give him a share of this rapture that was too wondrous to savor alone, to give release to the yearning that she could no longer control.

"That is it," he whispered against her skin. "Just like that, sweetling." He hooked his finger in the other side of her bodice and drew it down to allow her other breast to flow out onto his eager fingers. Again he was in no hurry as he traced a fiery path up along her breast's curve with his tongue. He put his hands on her hips, holding her even closer.

She gasped as she felt the hard line of him against her. As he shifted her hips, against him and away, while he continued to stroke her breast, the need for him overwhelmed her. She must give him what he wanted because it was what she wanted.

Suddenly he released her, swiftly pulling her dress back into place. He stepped away from her as if she had become something distasteful. She opened her mouth to ask what was wrong. He put his finger to her lips as she had his in the carriage. Stretching, he picked up her bonnet and held it out to her.

Only then did Jade hear the footfalls that Gideon

must have already noted. How could he have heard
above the throb of their bodies' mutual desire?

As if she had asked the question aloud, he said, "After
all the hours I have spent on this boat, I know every
sound it makes. When there is a different one . . ." He
turned as she hastily drew the bonnet over her mussed
hair. He smiled and called, "We are in here, Mrs.
Willow."

Mrs. Willow?

Jade brushed her hands against her gown, making sure
there were no signs of Gideon's bold caresses. She struggled to smile, but it was impossible when her body was
racked with the sweet longings that had become excruci-
atingly unfulfilled.

Mrs. Willow's silhouette filled the doorway. "Lord
Bannatyne," she said in a scolding tone, "I had understood that you and Miss Nethercott would remain in
sight of the carriage."

"I offered her a tour of the boat, which she accepted
with your approval." He offered his arm to Jade as they
stepped back out on deck. When she put her fingers on it,
she was relieved he had offered her that way to hide how
they trembled. "How could I give a tour without showing
her the steam engine that makes the ship move?"

"Miss Nethercott should be returning home now."
Mrs. Willow's pursed lips strained out every word, making each sound like a separate reprimand.

"You are correct." Gideon stepped onto the plank
connecting the boat to the pier. Holding up his hand, he
said, "Allow me to help you, Mrs. Willow."

"Thank you." She accepted his assistance and stepped
hastily back in an obvious order for him to guide Jade
over the plank.

Jade did not want to let Gideon's hand go as she
stepped onto the pier, but she knew the danger of infuri-
ating Mrs. Willow further. As it was, she guessed the
older woman would waste no time in going to China
with complaints about Gideon's untoward behavior and
Jade's questionable demeanor.

"Don't fret," Gideon said, drawing her hand within

his arm again. She wondered as she had before if he had some special ability that allowed him to be privy to her thoughts. "She could not have seen anything through the blackened cabin windows. I had intended to clean them, but I am glad now that I did not."

"Me, too." She would not be coy and pretend she was shocked with the liberties he had seduced her into offering him. She had been very aware of what she had allowed him to do and how much more she wished they had had time to do.

He gave her a grin as he handed her into the carriage. This time, he did not pause, but followed her in to sit beside her on the forward facing seat. The coachman assisted Mrs. Willow, who made no effort to hide her irritation.

Is she irritated at having Gideon sitting next to her charge, or having to ride facing backward? Jade did not ask, knowing that the answer—whichever it was—would be certain to add to the tension. Instead, she relaxed back against the seat. She pretended she was unaware of Gideon's arm along its top, but she had never been unaware of him. From the moment she first spoke to him in the Duchess of Northborough's garden, she had been conscious of his every motion as if he had become an extension of her own body.

Another moan bubbled up in her throat at the thought of them being two parts of a whole, together in the sweetest intimacy. She swallowed it before it could escape to betray her.

Jade was astonished when Mrs. Willow said, "You were very kind to show Miss Nethercott around your boat, Lord Bannatyne."

"I was glad to have the opportunity." His fingers twisted in the hair that was falling out from beneath her bonnet, out of sight of their chaperone. "She was very interested in the steam engine. Such a lively curiosity should be given a chance to express itself."

She smiled, lowering her eyes so Mrs. Willow could not see the joy that still must be visible in them. If she looked at Gideon, she doubted she could keep from flinging herself into his arms again. She kept her hands folded in her lap. Mrs. Willow would be scandalized if Jade slipped her hand into Gideon's while they rode in the carriage.

If Mrs. Willow had any idea . . .

She kept her laugh to herself. It was good that Mrs. Willow had no idea. Her yearning to laugh faded as she realized she must keep Sir Mitchell from discovering the truth, too. If he learned she had been in Gideon's arms, he might be so furious that he refused to bring Father to speak with her. She glanced at Gideon again, hoping she would never have to choose between him and her father. Even a day ago, she would have had no trouble selecting. Now she was far less sure.

Of everything.

Could Gideon be right that someone had slain his relatives? But why? For the titles and the lands? No one else but he would have had the motive to do that, for now he possessed both. There must be some other connection between the dead people, something that had nothing to do with the title and property, but what could it be?

Suddenly the carriage turned at a sharp angle. Mrs. Willow screamed. Gideon cursed. She grabbed the window. Beyond it, the street seemed to be rocking even more wildly than the boat. Shouts came from every direction. Horses shrieked. The door popped open. Gideon reached out to keep Mrs. Willow from sliding out of the carriage.

Then it struck something hard. Wood shattered. She was flung forward, hitting the seat where Mrs. Willow sat. Pain scored her forehead. Gideon shouted something. She heard her name but nothing more.

Then only silence. Dark silence.

Chapter 11

"What have you done now?"

At Sir Mitchell's vexed question, Jade opened her eyes. She blinked because she was standing in an open field with sunshine so bright she could not see much farther than she could stretch her fingers in any direction.

"Sir Mitchell?" she asked, unsure where he was.

"Here," came the answer from her left.

She turned and saw him stepping out of the brilliant light that spewed him forth and swallowed him again each time he appeared. "Where are we?"

He shrugged. "Why are you asking me? You know I have a difficult time discerning where we stand when we speak."

"But I was riding in a carriage with . . . Lord Bannatyne." She hoped he did not hear her slight hesitation. To use Gideon's given name would send Sir Mitchell into a pelter.

"And where are you now?"

"That was what I was asking you."

He glanced around himself and gasped. "You cannot be here!"

"Why? What is here?" She started to take a step to her left, but he put a hand out to halt her. She jumped back, not wanting to be seared again by the cold that was worse than anything in the grave. Stumbling, she looked down to see what she had first thought was a grassy meadow was a stone-strewn expanse like the most desolate moors beyond Nethercott Castle. "Sir Mitchell, where are we? What is this place?"

"It was where I found myself when I opened my eyes after I was stabbed."

"Are you saying I am dead?" She put her hand over her heart. It was beating, but faintly. "I am still alive."

"Then you should not be here."

"I know that!"

"What happened just before you discovered yourself here?"

"I was riding—"

His mouth twisted as he spat out, "You said that already. I want to know what happened *just* before you discovered yourself here?"

Jade sought through the barrage of images in her mind. "The carriage turned sharply. Then I heard shouts and screams. It rocked. I hit the other seat hard, then I was here."

"You must return."

"To the carriage?"

"Where else? I thought you had a brain. It would behoove you to use it now."

Jade flung out her hands. "Sir Mitchell, we would get much further if you did not take that patronizing tone with me."

He grumbled something, but repeated, "You must return."

"I know that, but how?"

"You must take yourself back. If you are still alive, you should be able to take yourself to the moment when you left your corporeal being to come here."

"Are you saying *I* am a ghost?"

"I am saying you do not belong here." He waved his hands at her as if shooing away a goose. "Go back to where you belong. I need you there to help me."

She forced down her annoyance at his selfish comments. If he were not depending on her to help him, he would not have cared if she stayed here or returned to the world of the living. She considered telling him that she tired of him focusing only on what *he* wanted.

But she wanted to escape this place where she should not be.

"Go back to where you were," Sir Mitchell ordered. "To the time and place you were. Go back there. Now!"

She closed her eyes, trying to recall the exact moment before she found herself in this odd place. She had been thinking about Gideon's amazing tale of the tragedy that had stalked his family.

Suddenly the carriage turned at a sharp angle. Mrs. Willow screamed. Gideon cursed. She grabbed the window. Beyond it, the street seemed to be rocking even more wildly than the boat. Shouts came from every direction. Horses shrieked. The door popped open. Gideon reached out to keep Mrs. Willow from sliding out of the carriage.

Then it struck something hard. Wood shattered. She was flung forward, hitting the seat where Mrs. Willow sat. Pain scored her forehead. Gideon shouted something. She heard her name, but nothing more.

Then only silence. Dark silence.

She shrieked, but no sound emerged from her lips. She was lost in the darkness once more.

Jade opened her eyes and winced. Every inch of her hurt. Around her were the cacophony of shouts from many voices. Beneath her cheek, the seat was rough. Something reeked. Everything surged over her at once. She moaned when arms lifted her from where she was sprawled on the carriage seat.

"Hand her here," she heard Gideon call.

She was placed in his arms. She leaned her aching head on his strong shoulder. For just a moment, as she savored being again among the living. She shut out the chaos and drew in the fresh scent of his skin so close to her face. When she ran her hand across his chest and up under his coat, she felt his heartbeat pound even more wildly.

"This may not be the best time," he whispered against her bonnet. He laughed lowly.

The sound startled her, and she opened her eyes to

discover his searching her face. For what? To see if she was unhurt, or to find out if she was surrendering to him as he had vowed she would?

" 'Tis you!" she cried.

"I would hope so, for I dislike the idea that you would be stroking anyone else so enticingly."

"We are alive!"

His smile became a frown. "Why would you think otherwise? The accident was not that dreadful."

"No, it was not." She could not tell him about her experiences with Sir Mitchell. Or had that really occurred? She had hit her head hard, so it might have been nothing but imagination. "Mrs. Willow?"

"She is shaken, but no serious damage." He set her on her feet and kept his arm around her waist. "What of you?"

"I am standing and I am talking and I am able to think—slowly—so it would appear I have suffered no serious damage either. What happened?"

"A cart pulled out of the side street right in front of us. Reeves tried to avoid it, but we hit it and a lamppost."

She turned to see the carriage. A moan escaped her lips when she saw how it had been mangled by the lamppost. The horses were cut loose. As Reeves led them away, the carriage shuddered and collapsed into itself further.

"A total loss," Gideon said with a shake of his head. "I had it only for a few months."

"Not a total loss." She put her hand over his heart, which was still beating wildly. It seemed to leap to an even more incredible speed, and her own did the same as she gazed up into his eyes. "We were not seriously hurt." Her eyes widened. "What about the other vehicle?"

"Destroyed." He bent to pick up a chirping chick and set it on the walkway. "His siblings are everywhere."

"And the driver?"

"Nowhere to be seen." He laughed tersely. "He must have run away when he saw the damage he wrought. By this time, he is probably halfway to Covent Garden."

As if to contradict his words, someone yelled, "Here he is! The lad who caused the accident."

Gideon paused long enough to seat Jade beside Mrs. Willow on steps that had been hastily brushed off. When Jade put her arm around the older woman's shoulders, Mrs. Willow began to prattle about the crash as if Jade had not been there. He gave Jade a sympathetic glance before going to where raised voices were getting louder.

Reeves rushed up to him. "That is the lad, my lord. They caught him hiding behind a barrel."

"Who caught him?"

He pointed to a trio of men who looked as if they had rolled in the offal and mud in the street. "That lot."

"Thank them." Dropping some coins into his coachman's hand, he said, "This should show my appreciation more than mere words. Divide the reward between them, and let them do with it as they wish."

"That I will, my lord." He took a step, then paused. "And the lad?"

"Have him brought to the carriage. I will talk with him. Alone."

Reeves nodded and ran to do Gideon's bidding.

With a deep sigh, Gideon walked around what was left of the carriage. Persis was going to be furious over its loss. She had insisted he buy a new carriage for her wedding. Now it was gone, just as her dreams were of marrying Renshaw.

He threaded a path among the frightened chicks, picking up a few to keep them from skittering out among the vehicles trying to drive around the mess. He stopped beside an overturned box. Righting it, he set the chicks inside, where they chirped in terror. He called to some urchins to collect the rest.

"A crown for the one of you who saves the most and brings them to me alive," he added when they regarded him with disinterest. The offer of such a grand reward spurred them into motion. Each grabbed another empty box and began chasing the frightened chicks.

Only then did Gideon go to where a lad, not much older than those gathering the chicks, was wringing his hands as he stood between the ruined carriage and the broken cart. His clothes were worn, but recently cleaned. A bruise under one eye probably would give him a black eye.

"You were the one driving the cart?" Gideon asked.

" 'Twas an accident, milord." He glanced at where his cart was slanting at the rear where the axle had broken. "Sometimes Daisy gets it in 'er 'ead t' stop in the middle of the street. Nothin' moves 'er then."

"But your cart *drove* in front of mine."

The lad recoiled and stared at him in horror. "Milord—"

"Do not ply me with moonshine. It is a waste of your breath and my time. Why not be honest and tell me the truth? I would be willing to speak to the watch about not dragging you off to prison for causing this accident where two ladies could have been killed."

He gulped, rocking from foot to foot. "I should not say anythin', milord."

"Then you will have to explain to the magistrate at Bow Street."

"What crime 'ave I committed?"

"That will be for the magistrate to decide." He smiled coolly, then said, "However, if you are willing to tell me the truth of why you arranged for my carriage to run into your cart, then it is likely I would be persuaded by one of the ladies, who have more forgiving natures than I, to release you from further questions."

He was bluffing. He hoped the lad would not guess. There might be some law the lad had broken, but he had no idea what one. The magistrate would be too busy with true criminals to deal with such small matters. He had learned that when he approached one to get his help in investigating his great-uncle's death. The magistrate had told him quite bluntly that the coroner had made his report and nothing more was necessary. It was at that point that he had known he must depend on himself to obtain the truth.

"Well?" he prompted when the lad continued to shift from one foot to other.

"Was not quite an accident," the lad mumbled.

"Excuse me?"

He repeated the words only a bit louder, glancing around as if he expected some avenging angel to swoop down and smite him. "I was paid two guineas to . . . arrange it."

Gideon hid his astonishment. Two guineas would seem like a fortune to a young teamster. No wonder, the lad had been willing to risk his cart and others' lives to obtain such a windfall.

"Who?" he asked quietly.

"A fine gentleman named 'Eath."

"Heath?" He was sure he had heard the lad wrong. "Are you certain?"

"Yes. Told me 'is name was 'Eath."

A slender hand on his arm halted his next question, and he heard Jade ask, "Can you describe Mr. Heath, young man?"

"Tall with thick, rusty 'air. Skinny as an anatomy. Mustache as thick as your finger."

Gideon cursed. If the lad was telling the truth now, the description did not fit the solicitor. Behind him, he heard a soft gasp. He looked back and saw Jade's face was even more ashen than it had been when she was lifted from the carriage, when, for a horrifying moment, he had feared she was dead.

As gently as he had with the chicks, he bent and lifted her into his arms. At her soft cry of astonishment, he smiled. "You look as if you are about to faint—quite understandable after what you have endured. However, I think you have spent more time than you wish senseless on this street. Pride is fine, but good sense is even better at times like this."

"I am being sensible."

"No, being sensible would have required you to remain seated on the steps while I arrange for another way to get you and Mrs. Willow back to Grosvenor Square."

"Gideon—"

He silenced her with his mouth over hers. Every sound, every scent, everything on the street vanished but the two of them. To speak of how he had been as frightened as one of the witless chicks when he feared she had been killed was impossible. The words would reveal what he was not ready to . . . not even to himself.

Her mouth was soft and quivering beneath his. With her breasts close to his chest, he could feel every unsteady breath she drew in. His own was far from even, too. If Mrs. Willow had not come seeking her on *Perdition's Folly,* would he have seduced sweet Jade into becoming his?

When he raised his head, he looked down into her glowing eyes. That green fire was a danger to any man who enjoyed his freedom to savor other women and live without commitments. No matter how well she learned her lessons from Sharla at the "mistress school," Jade was still a lady who would offer her heart along with her luscious body. And expect the same in return.

He should set her on her feet, and then he should head in the opposite direction.

Yet, when her hand curved up along his cheek, he smiled and continued to lose himself in her amazing eyes.

"Gideon," she whispered.

"Yes?" He could not imagine any other answer he would give her now.

"Does Mr. Heath look like what that driver described?"

Her words jolted him back into the street with the noise and the stench and the hard cobbles under his feet. "No."

"From your face, I thought not."

"But you gasped. Do you know who he described?"

"Yes."

He set her on the steps again. Mrs. Willow had moved, but he did not look to see where. He was focused entirely on Jade. "Who?"

"Sir Mitchell Renshaw."

"But he is dead!"

"I know, which is why you did not make the connection." An odd expression crossed her face. "I think it is obvious what is happening, Gideon. Someone else has used Mr. Heath's name and disguised himself as your sister's late betrothed while arranging such a nefarious crime against you."

He did not want to agree, but he had to own that she was right. There was no other plausible explanation. He still did not understand why someone would do such a thing, but he vowed to find out as soon as possible.

Clouds allowed only a bit of sunshine into the sitting room at the back of the house on Grosvenor Square. Sian sat by the window, trying to capture as much light as possible while she drew with a piece of charcoal. Facing her on another straight-back chair, China was working on a leaf for a flower she had already finished embroidering. Neither of them spoke, but Jade saw the uneasy glances they aimed at her as she paced from one end of the long narrow room to the other.

"You should sit and rest," Sian said, breaking the silence. "Mrs. Willow took to her bed as soon as you returned. You were as bounced about as she was."

"I cannot sit still." Jade gave her younger sister a smile. "I tried, but it is impossible. I keep thinking about the disasters that have surrounded the Bannatyne family in recent years. There have have been many deaths with a mysterious aura."

China jabbed her needle through the fabric. "You know such things are always whispered when a family has bad fortune."

"But that is just it," she argued. "Nobody is whispering about the Bannatynes' bad luck. The deaths were quickly deemed accidents, and everyone put them out of their minds."

Sian lowered her sketchbook, her eyes widening. "Like the accidents that have chased you and Lord Bannatyne the past few days? Either incident with the carriage could have had deadly results. 'Twas only good fortune yesterday and the skill of his coachee today that allowed you to escape with your lives."

"I believe they are connected, but I have no idea how."

"Who are his enemies?" Sian leaned toward her. "That would be an excellent place to start."

"I don't know. He had no love for Sir Mitchell or Lord Derlan."

"Both of whom are now dead."

"Yes, and the question is, why?"

China set her needlework on the windowsill and stood. "You could ask Sir Mitchell."

"He becomes agitated when he speaks of his last moments." Jade clasped her hands in front of her, kneading her fingers together. "I have resisted speaking to him of them after I realized he has only the sketchiest memories of what happened."

"No clarity in death?" Sian sighed, but a grin tipped her lips. "A quite literal dead end."

Wagging her finger at her younger sisters, China said, "You two are making light of something . . . serious."

"Were you about to say 'deadly serious'?" Sian's laugh burst from her. "You are as guilty of being irreverent as we are."

Jade sat on the edge of the settee in the middle of the room. Listening to China scold Sian again, she stared at the hearth where the fire was unlit. She understood why her younger sister was jesting. It was too horrible to think about someone wishing to slay Gideon and having failed twice in two days.

When the settee shifted, she looked up to see Sian had come to sit beside her. "You did not tell us where you went with Lord Bannatyne."

"To obtain some information I need to help Sir Mitchell."

Sian rested one elbow on the arm of the settee and propped her chin on her hand. "If you want to be mysterious, then I shall have to ask Mrs. Willow. She will tell me, I have no doubts."

"She will." Knowing she must satisfy her sister's curiosity without revealing the whole truth, she explained how Gideon had taken her to see a friend to learn more about the demimonde. "After all, it is there among the lower parts of society where I will have my best chance of learning the truth."

"Why?" asked China. "The baronet's murderer may not even be in London."

"But someone will know the truth," Sian interjected before Jade could devise a reply. "And you know how impossible it is to keep the truth hidden when someone is half in his cups."

"Sian!" China shook her head. "Trust you to learn the basest cant."

"You need not try to act as if you are our mother." Sian stood and glared at her sister. "I know when it is appropriate to use such words and when to keep them unsaid. And it is proper now when Jade has a face as long as a fiddle. I hoped to make her smile."

Taking her sister's hand, Jade said, "I appreciate the concerns both of you are showing me. And I assure you that I am fine. A bit bumped, but otherwise fine."

"What have you discovered?"

She gave her sisters a quick overview, including the questions from the Bow Street Runner and her call on Miss Maguire. She did not add that Miss Maguire had once been Gideon's lover and was now giving Jade lessons to allow her to pass herself off as a cyprian.

"It sounds so exciting!" gasped Sian.

Again China shook her head. "Listen to the two of you acting as if you were eager to be a part of such a low life."

"Oh, China, we are teasing." Rising, Jade gave her older sister a hug. "In many ways it was ghastly being on that street. I am glad that I was with Gideon—"

"You should not speak of him so!"

"I must use his given name when we are among the demimondaines as we will be at the week's end."

China clenched her hands on her lap. "This was a mistake right from the beginning. You need to tell Sir Mitchell's ghost that you are very sorry, but you cannot help him further."

"I promised him."

"But he could not have known what the cost of such a vow might be. He is—*was*—a man! His reputation was not so easily tarnished as yours. He was Father's friend, so he will understand why you have to step aside. Let him find someone else to help him."

"Who?"

"Any of his friends he had while he was alive."

"But nobody else will be hoping to show the world that Father was right in his research."

China deflated and nodded. "That is true, but, Jade, Father would not wish you to ruin your life to prove that his was not ill spent. He knew the truth, and *we* know it."

Wanting to be completely honest, Jade refrained. Sir Mitchell had said nothing more about being able to bring Father with him once she had found the proof that pointed to his murderer.

Gideon . . . She was finding it difficult to believe that his hand had been the one that had driven the knife into the baronet. Yet, when she thought of the obsession in his voice when he spoke about his work on *Perdition's Folly,* she could imagine him doing whatever he must to get what he had worked so hard to obtain. He would allow no one to halt him.

Neither must she.

"I think I shall get some air before I retire," Jade said.

"Do you want company?" China asked.

"No, I think I need to gather my thoughts."

China stood and put her hands on Jade's arm. "Sister dear, I know you hold every promise you make sacred, but the Bow Street Runners are now involved."

"In the investigation of Lord Derlan's death."

"But what they find while investigating that may reveal the very answers Sir Mitchell has asked you to learn."

"I will keep that in mind."

Her sister smiled. "I know you will."

Bidding her sisters to have a good evening, Jade walked out of the sitting room. The back garden would be quiet at this hour. Her thoughts trailed her down the stairs.

Gideon was a man with a clear view of what he must

do. He burned with the need to avenge the deaths of his family members. He would gladly see the murderer hang and smile as the man danced in midair.

Over that image came the memory of him scooping up the downy yellow chicks in the middle of the road. While others had driven by, uncaring as the terrified chicks tried to avoid hooves and wheels, his first concern had been those helpless little creatures. Only when he had persuaded others to take over the task, paying them out of his own purse, had he turned his attention back on what could never have been far from his mind.

The garden was misnamed. There were no plants growing in the narrow space between the brick walls separating the area from the neighboring houses' gardens. Stone covered the earth. A tree growing by the wall was the only hint of greenery. Beneath it had been built an arbor, but no vines upholstered it in shades of green. It might once have been painted white, but the wood was weathered and gray.

She sat and stared at the pattern of bricks in the wall. Slowly her fingers rose to touch her lips. Could anyone who had kissed her with such delicious fire be a murderer? She had always considered herself a good judge of character. Now she was not sure. Either Sir Mitchell or she was wrong.

A glow appeared in one corner of the garden, and Jade grimaced. Why did Sir Mitchell have to pay her a visit whenever she had a moment alone? His visits were becoming more bothersome with each passing day.

"You look pensive," he said without so much as a greeting, and she wondered if he was aware that time had passed since they last spoke.

"Sir Mitchell, my sisters fret about my reputation."

"When you unmask that murderer and provide incontestable proof, you will be lauded as a heroine. Even the Prince Regent himself will be impressed." He rested an elbow against the wall. Not exactly *against* it, because, as always, she could see the wall through his ghostly image. "And you will have brought your father the proper respect he deserves. You must not listen to them when they tell you that Bow Street will solve the mystery of my untimely demise."

Jade jumped to her feet. "Sir Mitchell, you were listening to our conversation!"

"How is a man to learn anything when he is in my state if he does not listen in on others' conversations?"

"There can be no more eavesdropping. If you are nearby, you must make yourself known to me as if you were paying an ordinary call."

"Bothersome rituals."

"I must have your word on this, Sir Mitchell. We all are disconcerted at the idea of where you might appear and when. The others are bothered more than I, because they cannot see you even when you materialize."

"You should assure them that I would never enter their private chambers." He straightened, looking like a soldier on parade. "I am too much of a gentleman for that."

"You have entered mine."

"Not by intention. And, you know, the only woman in my thoughts is my beloved Persis."

Jade tilted her head as if she could discern more about him from another angle. "You never appear when Gid— when Lord Bannatyne is present."

"Speak his name if you wish, Miss Nethercott. I am well aware of the ways of the low world he inhabits." He sighed. "I have been unable to coordinate my appearances with his visits. I am not sure why."

"There seem to be many things you do not understand."

"True."

"Could you have misunderstood the identity of the person you believe slew you?"

He frowned. "I had thought you more intelligent than this, Miss Nethercott! Already you are succumbing to Bannatyne's fascinating arts! I should have waited for the chance to speak to your older sister. She seems to be far wiser."

"But she cannot see you."

"There is that." He deflated slightly. "Forgive me, but I am discomposed that you would continue to ask such a question. It is true that I find my current circumstances baffling in many ways, but I do not need to remind you that I was very much alive when I caught sight of that knife coming down toward me."

"True, but how did you know it was being held by Gideon? Weren't you struck from behind?"

"I saw him fleeing after he had done the loathsome deed. Imagine my shock that the brother of my beloved Persis would lie in wait and ambush me."

"What do you know of these other deaths in their family?"

"Very sad circumstances. Accidents and foolishness."

"Foolishness?"

"Any person who has been raised near the sea should know the dangers of going out alone in a small boat when storm clouds are on the horizon."

"What relative was that?"

He hesitated, then said, "I do not remember exactly. My memory seems cloudy at times."

Jade nodded, even though she wanted to say those uncertain memories disappeared at the most convenient times. She sighed. She could not be cruel to a man who was already suffering a horrible fate.

Sir Mitchell clearly did not share her compunctions because he said, "You are wasting your time on deaths that have been well investigated. Don't you see the truth? Bannatyne is trying to mask his filthy deed with coincidence." His brows shot up. "Or maybe he intends to create so many questions that my death is considered just one of those within the Bannatyne family."

"I doubt that is his intention." She thought of how Gideon had reacted on *Perdition's Folly*'s deck when she asked if he counted Sir Mitchell's death among those in his family. He had been both horrified at the idea and relieved that the baronet had never become a part of his family.

"I know well what his intentions are where you are concerned," Sir Mitchell said.

"Do you?"

"Yes, and you know them, too. As a man of honor, I have done my best to warn you."

"As a man of honor, you should not have put me into any situation where I could be compromised. Good day, Sir Mitchell."

She left him blustering behind her. She never knew how long he lingered in the garden, because she did not look back.

Chapter 12

Gideon stepped out of his carriage. Shrugging off his coat, he tossed it back on the seat. "Reeves, I will walk from here." He loosened his cravat and threw it on top of his coat.

"Yes, my lord." He touched the brim of his black cap. "The usual place at the usual time, I assume."

"No." He drew out a slip of paper and held it up to his coachman. "Follow these instructions."

Reeves read it, and his brows rose nearly to his cap.

"Do you understand?" Gideon asked.

"Yes, my lord."

"Then go."

While the carriage continued down the street before turning to vanish into traffic, Gideon did not move except to rub first one foot, then the other against a lamppost. That took off the polish Tabor had worked hard to place on his boots. Nothing must suggest, on a quick glance, that he did not belong on this street frequented by cutpurses and pickpockets and whores.

A young lad inched toward him, but Gideon's scowl sent him scurrying. Not that the urchin could have stolen anything, because Gideon would not be foolish enough to come to such a low part of London with anything worth stealing. Letting himself be complacent would be stupid, because there were those hidden behind the broken windows and doors who would gladly slay him for the clothes he wore.

Or simply because I am a Bannatyne.

He walked toward the appointed meeting place. No one approached him, but he was aware of many eyes watching him. A daylight attack was too risky for most thieves. Even so, he was on alert with each step.

When he paused by a murky space between the row houses, he took care not to look into it. Not truly an alley, the space once must have been occupied by another house. Any sign of it had vanished, and the space had become filled with trash and filth. Instead, he stared at the tavern on the other side of the street. Even though the hour had not reached midday, it was busy.

"You are late." The man who had spoken stepped out of the shadows between the row houses. Like Gideon, he had rid himself of anything that would identify him. Without his red waistcoat, Ward would not be recognized as a Bow Street Runner.

"I am grateful you waited," Gideon replied.

"I thought you might have given up on your quest."

"Unlikely." Gideon let no emotion sift into his voice. "You sent a message that said you had further information."

"I don't rightly know if it is further information, but it confirms what you have already discovered, my lord."

"Why do you think you know what *I* have discovered?"

Ward laughed in the same scolding tone. "My lord, there are several of us who will profit if you find what you seek. Think of the prestige it will bring my employer if the truth is discovered. And," he added, his smile growing cold, "if I discover the answer before you do, I can offer you that information."

"For a high price. That is not Bow Street's usual way of doing business."

"It is mine. After all, wouldn't such information be worth any price?"

Gideon curled his fingers into fists at his sides. If he took a step closer, Ward would flee and never return. He needed to pay no attention to Ward's taunting arrogance. How easy it would be to ignore it as he ignored the prattlings of the Polite World . . . if he did not need the information so desperately.

"What have you discovered?" he asked in lieu of what he really wanted to say.

"You are the next target."

"I already guessed that from what has happened in the past few days. Two failed attempts on my life."

"Three."

"Three?" he repeated in surprise. "You are mistaken. There have been two in the past three days."

"There have been *three* in the past *five* days."

Gideon started to retort, but clamped his mouth shut. The duchess's gathering had been five days ago. That had been brought to an abrupt end with the discovery of Derlan's corpse. He cursed under his breath, then more loudly.

"I see you understand," Ward said.

"*I* was the target, but Derlan was mistaken for me."

"It was a masked ball, so I heard."

He did not bother to explain that he had not worn a mask. Quibbling about such details was a waste of time, especially when he guessed the Bow Street Runner was right. If Gideon had not been distracted by Jade and her discovery of the cane, he might have realized that himself. No, he could not blame her for his own inability to see the facts in front of him. Derlan was the only other man of his height at the party, and they both had been wearing navy coats and white breeches. If the initial attack had been from behind or beyond lamplight, the murderer could have mistaken Derlan for him. Yet, if that were true, why had the walking stick been stolen from his own foyer to be used as a murder weapon?

He asked that question aloud, but received no answer. He repeated the curse he had spoken before. Ward had vanished back into the shadows, leaving once he had delivered his message.

And Gideon was alone with his unanswered questions.

*　　*　　*

"Miss Nethercott, if you keep blushing, you will attract more attention than you wish." Miss Maguire shook her head. "Maybe it is impossible to turn a silk purse into a sow's ear."

"I will endeavor to restrain my reactions," Jade said, watching Miss Maguire pace back and forth in front of her. They were, once more, in Miss Maguire's elegant sitting room. "I am trying my best."

"And that may be the problem." She tapped her chin with one finger. "You are trying. You need to assume this new life as if it is your own, not as if it were a role you are playing. Have you decided on a name for yourself?"

"I thought I would use the name Miss Netter. It is close enough to my own name that I shall not miss noticing when someone speaks it."

"You are not going to be among the *ton*. You need a given name that you will answer to."

"Jasmine. It was my mother's name. She has been dead for a long time, but my father spoke of her constantly so I still react when I hear someone speak the name."

Miss Maguire smiled. "That is all to the good then. I will use that name with you, so you can become more accustomed to it."

She did not give Jade a chance to reply. Instead she launched into an explanation of what liberties a man would take with a demimondaine. Jade tried to pay attention to Miss Maguire's words and keep her blush under control. It was difficult when the description of a man's bold caresses created pictures in her mind of Gideon touching her so. Not just pictures, but the memory of the luscious sensations he had evoked in the cabin of his steamboat. With every touch, he had made her more aware of her own body than she had ever been. And she had only begun to explore his masculine angles. While she had tried to fall to sleep last night, she had ached with the craving for his touch again. At last, she had found sleep, but her dreams had been filled with the same desires.

"Jasmine!"

At Miss Maguire's sharp tone, Jade opened her eyes that she had not realized she had closed while lost in her fantasies. She guessed that the older woman had spoken the name more than once.

"Forgive me," she said. "My thoughts were wandering."

"Something you must not allow." Miss Maguire stood in front of her, then drew up a chair to sit facing her. "You must be careful at all times, or you may find yourself in a situation that will ruin more than your reputation. The men coming to my gala will expect the women here to be looking for the chance to advance themselves. Gideon is a viscount, so it will be assumed that you, while on his arm, will be eager to garner the attention of a higher ranking peer."

"If I remain in his company . . ."

"But you cannot. Such an action belongs to a member of the *ton,* not my world. You will be expected to flirt and try to engage the attentions of an earl or marquess." With a wave of her hand, she said, "Show me with the fan how you would ask a man to wait for you."

Jade picked up the folded fan from the table. Snapping it open, she held it up in front of her. She felt silly smiling, but did as Miss Maguire had instructed earlier. Shifting her eyes toward the corner, she pretended she was asking an invisible man to wait for her there.

"Good," Miss Maguire said. "Now show me how you would ask a man to follow you."

Closing the fan, she held it in her right hand and drew it up so it was in front of her face.

"Go on," ordered Miss Maguire.

Jade stood and, still holding the fan in front of her face and facing the invisible man, walked toward the door. When she bumped into a chair, she lowered the fan. "How is one supposed to see where one is going while doing such silent flirtations?"

"I know it is not simple, but you will learn if you keep practicing."

"In two days?" She shook her head. "I doubt I can

learn enough to persuade anyone that I am of the demimonde."

Miss Maguire sighed and set herself on her feet. "I felt that way when Gideon first approached me about teaching you, but then I reminded myself that your mistakes will be overlooked because you are lovely and new and every man will be eager to win you away from Gideon."

"Why?"

"I thought it was obvious. He has won the attentions of so many women from other men."

"But I thought you said the women would be interested in finding a man of higher rank."

"That is what men believe we want." A smile drifted across her lips. "However, we women think differently. We want a man who will be as generous as a lover as a protector. As Gideon has proven that he is."

With every passing minute, Jade wished she had devised another set of lies for Gideon. She was in too deep to turn back now, because she was constantly aware of how few days were left before he would demand that she pay him what she had agreed to in their bargain. And she was just as aware how impossible it would be for her to deny him—and herself—that pleasure. The samples she had savored in his arms had whetted her yearning for more and more and more until she was sated.

"So you must be extra careful," Miss Maguire continued.

"I understand." She tapped the fan against her lips. "If I find any man too interested, I—"

"Not give him that signal with your fan, I hope," came Gideon's voice from behind her.

She whirled. "Signal? What signal?"

He took her hand that was holding the fan and tapped its end gently against her lips. "*That* signal."

"That is a signal?"

"Yes. For this." He drew her hand aside as his lips caressed hers with a slow, deep kiss that threatened to turn her knees into jam.

As soon as he raised his head, Miss Maguire asked, "What are you doing here? I thought you understood that your presence was not required today."

He kissed Miss Maguire on the cheek and chuckled. "When did I ever heed you, Sharla?"

"True. You have always sought your own path, even when it set you on the road to ruin."

"Best when it did so." His smile broadened when he looked at Jade. "Now I have a travel companion on that delightful road."

"You know that is not her intention, which is why I have been teaching her how her fan can be used to her advantage."

"Using it to beat some would-be suitor over the skull?" He winced, and she knew he had not meant to remind them of Lord Derlan's tragic death. "She does not need to learn such things. I don't intend to abandon her to the attentions of rogues who would treat her so lowly."

"Give me credit for knowing that." She wagged a finger at him. "But you know as well as I what she may encounter, and she must be prepared to be approached by those who seek new entertainments to ease their boredom."

Jade interjected, "Why don't you ask *me* if I think I can play the role you have selected for me?"

"Because you still have no idea what you will face here." Gideon's frown refocused on her.

"Nonsense," she retorted, even as she was wondering why he looked so grim. She wanted to ask him what was wrong, but if he had wished to discuss it in Miss Maguire's hearing, he would have spoken of it before now. "I may come from Yorkshire, but do you think I have failed to notice since I was a child how some of the young men and women vanish during parish celebrations? They disappear into the night and return some time later with mussed hair and clothes. I recall my father shielding my eyes during one drive when we passed a ditch where a man and a woman were so involved with each other that they had not taken notice of our approach. **In the country, beyond the Polite World, rules of decorum are bent as often as they are followed.**" Folding her arms in front of her, she said, "I may be new to Town and its ways, but some aspects of human ways are as old as the Garden of Eden."

Gideon roared with abrupt laughter as Miss Maguire stared at her in astonishment.

Picking up her bonnet, Jade walked out of the room. She had not intended her words to be amusing. She had wanted to show them that she was not as innocent as they believed her to be. Bother! She should have taken Miss Maguire's advice and put an end to the lessons right at the beginning.

She tied her bonnet under her chin as she hurried down the stairs. Hearing heavier footfalls behind her, she paused. She would not run away like a frightened child.

Turning, she said, "Gideon, if you are giving chase in order to fill my head with more warnings, do not bother. *I* have heard too many already."

"I have no intention of offering you more warnings, although Sharla may when you come back for your next lesson later this afternoon." He edged past her, continuing down until he stood on a riser exactly where their eyes were level.

"Nor will I be scolded for speaking out of hand."

"You have to agree that your outburst was surprising." He cupped her elbow and tilted her toward him.

"No, I don't have to agree to that or anything else." She shrugged his hand off his arm. When he touched her, she found it difficult to think clearly. Grasping the banister, she frowned at him.

"You are right yet again, Jade."

"I am?" She was startled by his sudden about-face.

"Yes. From what I have learned about you, I am more surprised that you did not explode before this. You are a strong-willed woman, and you have been very docile in accepting the lessons at Sharla's mistress school."

"What is wrong?" she asked. "Even when you are

teasing me, there is an undercurrent of something amiss in your voice."

"I cannot tell you here." He held out his hand. "Come with me."

She wanted to ask where, but she said nothing as she put her hand in his. Trusting him might lead to her downfall. Even so, she doubted anything had ever felt so right as his strong fingers cradling hers.

Because she had expected him to open the door to the street, she was astonished when he guided her into the room where Mrs. Willow had sat during her first call at this house. It was a simple room with two chairs that looked as if they had been seldom used and a single window overlooking the street. The three paintings on the wall were of the same subject: a manor house that had been crenelated at some point in its history.

"Sharla uses this room to store items that Rudolph Stommel has given her, items she does not like, but does not want to hurt his feelings," Gideon said with a taut smile.

He closed the double doors, then twisted the key that locked them in place. Setting the key on a table, he crossed the room in a pair of long steps. He swept her into his arms as his mouth reclaimed hers.

Every instinct urged her to soften against him, but she put up her hands as she turned her head away. "Not here."

"Why not? This is a house made for lovemaking," he whispered.

"Not ours."

"Sharla would not be averse to allowing us to use one of the bedrooms here."

"You said you would wait for seven days."

"I said," he retorted with a laugh, "that you would come to me before those seven days have passed."

"So far, you are wrong." She eased out of his arms, despite her craving to remain there. "Will you tell me what is upsetting you?"

"I should have known I could not distract you."

She curved her hand along his cheek. "That is not quite true. I find you very distracting."

"As I do you, and if you keep touching me, I doubt I can resist the temptation to break my vow to wait seven days for you."

When she lowered her hand reluctantly, he caught it and pressed his lips to her wrist as he had at the duchess's. A longing, even more powerful than she had discovered that night, surged though her. She gazed up into his eyes and saw her craving mirrored back at her. But she also noted the lines of strain along his face.

"What is it?" she whispered. "What is wrong?"

"You should sit while I tell you."

Jade stared at him in dismay as she lowered herself slowly onto the closer chair. "What is it, Gideon?"

"I have heard suspicions that Derlan was not the true target of the murderer at the duchess's party."

A tremor of icy cold—as frigid as when Sir Mitchell's ghost had touched her—clawed its way down her spine. She wrapped her arms around herself as she asked, "And you were the true target?"

His eyes widened. "You suspected that, too?"

"Not until just now, but it should have been obvious before. Your family has been slain so the title moves from one to the next. Lord Derlan would not have received the title while you live." A horrible thought filled her mind. So appalling that she did not want to utter it, but she could not allow her distress to endanger Gideon further. "Who is next in line after Lord Derlan for the Bannatyne title and lands?"

"The next in line is . . ." He pondered for a moment, before saying, "I am not certain who is next. Derlan was an only son, and there are no other possible heirs after him. None of the female cousins has wed yet, so they could not be producing an heir soon."

"You know that conception doesn't always wait until after marriage vows are spoken."

"But the child would need to be born within legal wedlock, and the oldest of the lot has yet to have her first Season."

She sighed. "I am glad to hear that my horrific thought has no basis in truth."

"Horrific?"

"That your family has been slain one after the other in order to get the title and the lands attached to it in the hands of one person."

"I am that person, Jade." He knelt by her chair. "Whose machinations have led to me having a title I never wanted and left so many dead?"

She drew his head down onto her lap. Brushing his hair back from his eyes, she whispered, "I don't know, but I fear if we do not find out the truth quickly, Lord Derlan's death will not be the last."

Chapter 13

Jade hummed to herself as she brushed her hair. Every note was an effort, but she was trying to make herself feel optimistic. Her conversation with Gideon at Miss Maguire's house that morning echoed through her head, repeating over and over. How had they failed to see the truth before this? Why would someone be so evil that they would slay member after member of a family to manipulate the succession of the titles and the lands?

And, most important, was the person who murdered Gideon's relatives the same one who had driven the knife into Sir Mitchell?

She wished she had thought of that question when she was talking to Gideon, but she had been so distraught at the information. She tried to make the new facts fit with the ones Sir Mitchell had revealed to her. Something simply did not fit together. She was missing one—or more—tidbits of information that would make the whole puzzle clear.

A knock sounded on her bedroom door. Setting down her brush, she called, "Come in."

Smithson opened the door and walked in a single step. "This was delivered for you, Miss Jade," the butler said in his pompous tone. If he thought to impress her, he failed.

She knew it was important to him that he was viewed as a vital asset, so she thanked him graciously for taking time from his other duties to bring the folded slip of paper to her. He bowed his head tersely and left, closing the door in his wake.

Jade looked at the sheet where her name and the house's address had been written in a precise, spidery hand. Breaking the seal that held the folds together, she read:

> *Dear Miss Nethercott,*
>   *I have been informed that you have called at the house on numerous occasions to express your sympathy at the great loss I have suffered. I deeply regret I was unable to receive you during those calls.*
>   *If you would call this afternoon at one, I shall be at home for you. I understand that you are recently out of mourning yourself. Perhaps speaking with you will ease my own grief.*

The letter was signed *Persis Bannatyne*.

With a gasp, Jade quickly reread the letter. "Persis Bannatyne," she whispered.

"Persis? My beloved?"

She swallowed her groan as she looked over the top of the page to discover Sir Mitchell near her bed. Coming to her feet, she said, "I thought we had agreed you would not come into my private rooms."

"You worry about unimportant matters." He strode toward her, but halted when she backed up hastily. "You need not worry about your maidenhead with me, Miss Nethercott."

"I am not." She copied Smithson's rigidly correct tone. If Sir Mitchell had been so coarse speaking in life, she could comprehend how he had gained his reputation for being crude. "But I have learned that your touch is very painful."

He waved aside her protests as he had so many others. "You spoke my beloved Persis's name. Is she here?"

"No." She set the page on the table. "I received a note that she would like me to call."

"My beloved Persis—"

"Sir Mitchell, I must ask you something." She was not going to listen to another soliloquy about Lady Persis. "You know of the other deaths in the Bannatyne family."

"Yes, yes, very tragic. My Persis is—"

"What is your opinion of those deaths?"

"Tragic accidents." His nose wrinkled. "Why are you asking me?"

"Let's just assume for a moment that they were not accidents, but murders."

His eyes widened. "Murders? What makes you say that?"

"You knew my father, Sir Mitchell. You knew his devotion to solving problems by reviewing the facts and focusing on them to draw a logical conclusion. He taught me well, and I can tell you that *my* logical conclusion is that yours was not the sole murder."

His scowl was a dark spot in the light glowing around him. "I see that Bannatyne has persuaded you to heed him in playing hide and seek with the facts. If he can convince everyone that those tragedies were part of a greater scheme, he can pretend that he had no hand in my death."

"So we do agree on one matter, Sir Mitchell."

"We do?" His shock seemed genuine.

"We agree that whoever is to blame for the deaths in the Bannatyne family had something to do with your murder, too."

He laughed, the sound as icy as his touch. "Whose side are you on? You are accusing Bannatyne of far more than I ever have."

"I did not say I believed Gideon slew anyone. I said—"

He gave a roar that seemed to shake the whole room. She cringed back, terrified at the fury she had not expected. Then he was gone.

Jade straightened slowly and groped for her chair. She gripped the edge of the table as she sat, for she did not trust her knees. Sir Mitchell's ghost had been pompous and condescending, but she had not seen signs of such rage before. It scared her. Had he been so volatile in life?

She looked down at the page on the table. The person who would best know the answer to that was Persis Bannatyne. Folding the page, she rang for a footman. She sent him to have the small cart ready at the front door. It was already past noon, and she did not want to be late calling on the lady. After that call, she would go directly to Miss Maguire's for her next lesson.

"Are you going out already?" asked Sian as she peeked in.

"I have some errands to run this afternoon." She wished she could be honest with her sisters about what she was learning, but that would upset them more. "I am leaving early because Lady Persis wishes to see me."

Her sister gasped. "Really? Why now?"

Jade shrugged as she reached for a lacy shawl. "I think she wants to speak with someone else who has been in mourning."

"Why not her brother? Didn't you say that there had been many deaths in the family?"

Putting the shawl over her shoulders, Jade looked at her sister. "Maybe she wants to speak to another woman. Or it may be as simple as she wants to speak to someone beyond her family."

"I cannot imagine doing that."

Jade gave her younger sister a quick hug. "That is because we three have each other to depend on."

Sian stiffened and drew away. "What happened there?" She pointed toward the bed.

In amazement, she saw one long section of the bed curtains had been wrapped tightly around the tester pole. Another section hung from just two rings. The covers were tossed about as if the bed had been through a wild windstorm.

"Sir Mitchell was angry," she replied.

"*He* did that?"

"He flew into a rage. Quite literally, it appears, even though I did not realize it at the time."

Sian's face grew taut with concern. "China is going to be deeply distressed that he was in your room."

"He is a ghost, Sian!"

"Even so, he is obviously not a congenial one."

"No, not any longer." She hooked her arm through her sister's and steered Sian out into the hallway. "Say nothing to China about this."

"But, Jade—"

"Give me a few more days to get some answers, and then Sir Mitchell will bother me no more."

Sian nodded with a sigh. "A few more days."

Jade kissed her sister's cheek. "Thank you. I have to hurry so I am on time for my call on Lady Persis."

"Good luck."

"Thank you," she said sincerely, before she rushed down the stairs.

Jade gave her name to the footman at Gideon's house on Bedford Square. She resisted looking around. Her composure was tattered, and she was unsure if she wanted to see Gideon now or avoid him until she had a chance to speak with his sister.

She hardly dared to breathe as the footman told her to follow him. After so many calls, she found it difficult to believe that—finally—she was being taken to speak with Lady Persis.

Fearing that anything she said or did could be the reason the invitation was rescinded, she followed the footman in silence up the stairs. She glanced at the portraits hanging along the stairwell, but did not pause to admire them or try to note which ones resembled Gideon.

Jade was astonished when she was led up a second set of stairs to the private regions of the house. She had not expected Lady Persis to receive her in the lady's bedchamber, but that was where she was led.

The room was at the front of the house. A grand bed with ornate carving on the headboard had been set so its occupant could look out the window at the garden in the center of the square. Several pots of flowers were on the sill. Elegant furniture, most pieces accented with gilt, filled the room so very little of the white rug was visible. The walls were covered with painted silk the same shade as the rug. It was the most glorious room she had ever seen.

But where was Lady Persis?

As if she had spoken that question aloud, the covers on the bed rippled. She realized Lady Persis was still abed. She waited for the lady to speak, but there was only silence. Looking over her shoulder, she gave the footman a questioning glance.

The footman said as formally as if they stood in the Prince Regent's reception room, "My lady, Miss Jade Nethercott as you requested." He must have seen some signal because he added in a near whisper, "You may go over to the bed."

Jade nodded. What an odd way to conduct a call!

As she walked toward the bed, she saw a woman propped amidst a stack of pillows. There was no question that the lady was Gideon's sister. Her hair that fell over the shoulders of her bed jacket was ebony, and she had the same patrician nose. Jade guessed that, if Lady Persis was standing, she would be almost as tall as Gideon. But her face was pale as if she had been recently ill.

"Why are you gawking?" demanded Lady Persis in a tone Jade had never heard Gideon use. It was petulant and sharp. It brought Sir Mitchell to mind.

Quickly Jade reminded herself of the tremendous loss the lady had suffered. Whetted words had come too easily in the wake of Father's death until she and her sisters had promised not to let their pain overwhelm their love for each other.

"I appreciate you seeing me today, Lady Persis," she said with an unsteady smile.

"I have been told that you have called on several occasions, even though I have no idea who you are."

"My name is—"

"Yes, yes, I know your name. The footman told me, so I could send you an invitation to call." She shifted impatiently on the bed, then winced as if in pain.

Gideon had said nothing about his sister being ill or

suffering from anything other than grief. Maybe he did not know, for Lady Persis had refused to receive him since her fiancé's death. Why was the lady trying to hide the truth from him?

Jade warned herself not to look for conspiracies everywhere. It could be as simple as Gideon was not good in a sickroom or that the lady did not want to burden her brother more.

"I simply," Lady Persis continued in the same dismissive tone, "have no idea *who* you are."

"My father was acquainted with Sir Mitchell Renshaw." Jade held her breath, unsure what the lady's reaction would be to the baronet's name.

The lady's face flushed, then grew ashen again so quickly that Jade feared she would be ill anew. Before Jade could ask if she was all right, the lady ordered, "Do sit down. I have no interest in staring up at you."

"Thank you." She was unsure what else to say. Sitting on a nearby chair, she made sure she could see the lady past the brim of her bonnet. Lady Persis had not invited her to remove it, and to do so without invitation would be rude.

"Have you been calling in hopes of speaking to me about my betrothed?"

"Yes."

"Why?"

"First of all, I want to express my sorrow at your loss."

Lady Persis gave a sharp laugh. "Loss? What an absurd term! Mitchell is not lost. We know exactly where he is. In a grave in an empty churchyard."

Jade bit her lower lip to keep from correcting the lady. Sir Mitchell was *not* solely in that grave. Stuck in that odd place where brilliant light baffled the mind and played tricks on eyes, he was seeking the answer to the one thing that was unfinished in his life—bringing his murderer to justice.

"So, as you can see," Lady Persis continued, "he is far from lost. Just as he is far from me." Tears coursed down her face along the reddened paths left by ones she must have cried before.

"He may be closer than you think," she said, wanting to offer the weeping woman some comfort. "There are those who believe that the spirit may linger, especially when the death was unexpected."

"Linger?"

"Yes."

"Are you suggesting he is a ghost?"

Jade chose her words with care. She had promised not to reveal the truth to Lady Persis. "As I said, there are those who believe that is possible."

"Like your father? I have heard about his bird-witted beliefs about all sorts of ludicrous things."

"There are many, in addition to my father, who believe that spirits are near us." She forced her vexation down. Lady Persis was overwrought, so should not be held accountable for her comments.

"I don't want to be haunted by Mitchell. There is no warmth in a ghost. I want a husband, not a phantom."

"Tell me about him."

"What?" The lady seemed honestly astonished.

"Tell me about him. I have heard many comments from those who knew him slightly."

She sniffed. "They were jealous of my dear Mitchell. They spoke ill of him when he would not fawn over them as they wished."

"So he was a man who did as he thought was right?"

"Yes. He knew what he wanted, and he would not be denied it." A faint hint of color returned to her face. "And he wanted me, lucky woman that I was. I had no idea how lucky."

"So he was a man of strong passions."

"Very." The pink brightened on her cheeks, but her lips began to tremble. "Oh, how I miss him!" Turning her head away, she said, "You have come here to do your duty. You need not linger."

Jade thought quickly. After waiting so long to speak with Gideon's sister, she was not going to squander it by allowing herself to be shown to the door before she had a chance to ask even one of the questions battering at her lips.

"That is not the only reason I hoped to speak with you," she said quietly.

"What other reason could you have?" She glanced back at Jade.

"I . . ." She cleared her throat as she tried to recall exactly what she had promised Sir Mitchell *not* to say to his betrothed. "I have heard there are questions why his murderer has not been found."

"Because the person who killed him has found a way to hide the truth." She shivered, looking suddenly very fragile.

"I understand the coroner came to you with information about Sir Mitchell's passing."

"You understand?" Lady Persis sat straighter and scowled again. "What could you understand? You cannot imagine what it is like to lose a betrothed as I have."

Tears flooded into Jade's eyes, but she refused to let them fall. If Lady Persis was not so prickly, Jade might have said that she did understand losing someone dear. She guessed anything she said would vex the lady more, so she remained silent.

Dropping back into the pillows, Lady Persis put a hand over her forehead and gave a soft moan. "It was the worst moment of my life. I never imagined our courtship would come to such an end."

"You are fortunate that your brother has been here with you."

The wrong thing to say, she realized, when Lady Persis looked daggers at her. "My brother always was finding fault with Mitchell. We would have married if Gideon had not kept finding excuses to force us to delay."

"He must have loved you very much," she said when she could not think of anything else.

"He? Gideon?"

"No, Sir Mitchell," she answered, not wanting to set the lady off on another tirade. In truth, Gideon cared deeply for his sister, and it was a shame Lady Persis did not recognize that fact.

"My sweet Mitchell was growing very impatient with Gideon, and I heard them come to cuffs the last time they were together."

"Fisticuffs?"

"No, *come to cuffs*. Argue." Her brows lowered. "You are not long in Town, are you?"

"No."

"I thought you must be recently arrived, for you seem to find it difficult to understand even the simplest cant of the *ton*."

"I am endeavoring to learn as quickly as possible."

"And who is teaching you?"

Jade faltered. Had word of Miss Maguire's "mistress school" reached Lady Persis? If so, then the tale of it would have been spread by now across the *ton*. Such knowledge of what she was attempting would render her plan useless.

"My sisters and I are guests of the Duchess of Northborough," she answered.

"Is that so?" Lady Persis appraised her anew. "I had not heard *that*."

"The duchess has long urged my sisters and me to come to Town for a Season."

"When you return, you should bring your sisters with you." Lady Persis's smile grew warmer. "I would enjoy meeting them. I understand the duchess recently had a gathering that began wondrously."

Jade nodded, again at a loss for how to reply. The mere mention of the duchess's name had changed Lady Persis. Recalling how Gideon had spoken of his sister's delight in the Polite World and all its intricate interactions, Jade spoke of the masked party that had ended in tragedy. Not that she had to say much. Lady Persis interrupted her, over and over, with questions about what the other women had been wearing and which men were paying attention to which young misses.

While she answered the lady's questions to the best

of her ability, which was quite inadequate as Lady Persis made clear, Jade tried to sort out what she had learned during this odd conversation. Nothing Lady Persis had said helped to solve the mystery of the Bannatyne family deaths. But her comments about Sir Mitchell were intriguing. A man of great passions who did as he pleased would garner many enemies. One of them might be determined—even eager—to see him dead.

She sighed silently. A man of great passions who did as he pleased was a description that fit Gideon as well as Sir Mitchell.

"What a shame," Lady Persis said, drawing Jade's attention back to her, "that the duchess's party was brought to an end because someone wanted to repay my brother for Mitchell's murder!"

"Are you suggesting—?"

"That Lord Derlan was killed in error? It is a possibility, even though the man was loathsome in his own right. Still, I suspect the true target was Gideon, and the motive was vengeance for my beloved's death."

"Your brother? *You* believe he murdered your fiancé?" she asked. Surely she had misheard Lady Persis.

"How it is that you are aware of certain details of Sir Mitchell's death that have been kept from the *ton,* but you fail to have heard the rumors circulating about my brother?"

"I have heard," she said, again selecting her words cautiously, "that Lord Bannatyne has preferred certain activities in Town to other pursuits."

Lady Persis lifted a quizzing glass from among the pillows and peered through it at her. "Miss . . . Nethercott, is it?"

"Yes."

"Miss Nethercott, you seem to have a skill with words worthy of a member of Parliament. You say nothing, but suggest much."

"One can never be certain which rumors one hears are true and which are embellishments."

"Again the pretty language. Why not call an embellishment what it is? A lie, and I can assure you, Miss

Nethercott, that if the rumors you have heard tarnish my brother's once pristine reputation, they are not simply poker-talk."

"But being accused of a fast life is far different from an accusation of murder."

"I agree." She lowered the quizzing glass. "But I know what my brother is truly capable of. The question, Miss Nethercott, is what you believe."

Chapter 14

Gideon took the steps to the front door two at a time. It opened as he approached, and he did not slow. When he bumped into someone coming out, he put out his hands to steady the person. His fingers told him immediately whom he was holding.

"Jade!" he gasped. "I thought you were going to Sharla's house this afternoon. I did not expect you here." For a moment, his body reacted to the thought that she had done as he had predicted, that she was here to join him in his bed. In that moment, he forgot everything about his frustration with learning nothing more about the deaths surrounding his family. He thought only of how wondrous it would be to hold her for the rest of the afternoon . . . and the evening . . . and the night . . . and the one after that . . . and . . .

Then he noticed the tears making her eyes a richer green. "What is wrong?"

"Not here." She walked past him and down the steps toward a simple wicker cart.

"Where would you prefer this to take place then?"

She whirled to face him. Her eyes snapped with fury. Above her taut shoulders, her chin tilted at him in a pose that, if she had been a man, would have been an invitation to hit it. But she was not a man. She was an amazing, desirable woman.

"I am not speaking of *that*," she snapped.

"Who said you were?" He was glad she could not have heard his thoughts. Had something in his own face betrayed the hunger clawing inside him when he had touched her, even chastely?

Looking hastily away, she said, "I am sorry, Gideon. I am all on end at the moment." She put her hand on the side of the wicker cart.

He lifted her hand off the cart and folded it between his broader ones. "What has you all on end, sweet Jade?"

"I cannot talk of it here." Her gaze flicked past him and up over his head.

He did not need to look at the house. He guessed she was looking at the window of his sister's room. She must have come to see Persis. Even the most outrageous harlot would not come uninvited and alone to a man's house, and Jade was every inch a lady no matter how hard she tried to learn otherwise at Sharla's mistress school.

If that was so, why was Jade upset? Because she had been turned away from his sister's door again? No, she had not acted unduly troubled when last she had called in an attempt to offer her condolences. That left only one alternative. She must have spoken with his sister. Something about that call had left her wretched. But what could it be?

He could not guess, but he knew one thing without doubt. When Jade had said she would not discuss whatever it was in front of his house, she had meant it and would not have her mind changed.

Without another word, Gideon handed her into the cart. She regarded him with astonishment when he said, "Wait here while I saddle my horse. I will escort you to Sharla's house."

"You need not do that."

"I want to."

"All right."

When he returned several minutes later, Gideon was not surprised to find that she had done as he asked. Her distress was visible in each stiff motion. He rode beside her as they left Bedford Square and threaded their way along the busy London streets. The journey was not long, but it seemed an eternity when Jade said nothing. The silence was unpleasant, and he wished to break it. He could not think of anything save for silly platitudes about the weather and gossip.

Even when he helped her alight from the cart, she was mum. She did put her hand on his arm when he offered it. He thought he heard her whisper a nearly soundless "Thank you," but could not be sure. Her gentle touch sent fireworks off in his skull, and he was unsure if he would have heard her even if she had shouted.

Seven days? How stupid could he have been to make the term of their agreement so long? He should have made it far less time. Either she would have laughed in his face and denounced him as a cad and a rake and a roué, or, by now, he would have enjoyed her lovely body. He would not be racked with a craving for her that distracted him from finding answers. He would be able to sleep without having her come to him in his dreams and slip away just before he satisfied his intense need.

If Sharla's footman was astonished to see Gideon with Jade, the man gave no sign. He announced them at the door of the sitting room.

Sharla was not so quick to conceal her surprise. As she came to her feet, she said, "Gideon, I thought I made it clear that this afternoon's lessons did not require your help."

Jade glanced at him and quickly away. Were those recriminations he had seen in her eyes? As she lifted her hand off his arm, she edged away. Dash it! Whatever Persis had said must have been more distressing than he had imagined.

"Why didn't you tell me that Miss Maguire had asked you not to come with me this afternoon?" she asked sharply. "Why did you lie to me when you knew your deception would be uncovered as soon as we arrived here?"

Hearing Sharla draw in a sharp breath, he said in his calmest voice, "Jade, I did not lie to you." He wanted to ask why she was overreacting. What *had* happened during her call on Persis? "I simply forgot."

"A convenient answer."

"The truth."

"Which you must own to when you have no other choice."

Vexed when she continued to scowl at him, he tossed aside his composure and snapped, "Why are you dressing me down for something so insignificant? What did my sister say to you?"

Jade recoiled as if he had struck her. "I . . . She . . ." Walking to the settee, she sat and, with her hands folded in her lap, stared at the floor.

"If you would like me to leave," Sharla began.

"Thank you," Jade said softly before he could answer.

Sharla glanced at him, raised a single eyebrow, then went out, closing the double doors behind her.

Gideon went to where Jade sat. Even though he wanted to sit beside her, he selected a chair facing her. He waited for her to speak, but silence once again enfolded them in its smothering embrace.

"Jade," he whispered, "it cannot be as appalling as you are acting. Nothing could."

"No?" Her eyes rose to meet his as she undid her bonnet and set it on the table. "Do you know that your sister believes that you murdered Sir Mitchell?"

He flinched at her blunt question, but he answered as curtly, "I had my suspicions that might be the reason she refuses to see me." He set himself on his feet and walked to the window, clasping his hands behind his back. "However, there is a great chasm between having suspicions and having confirmation that those suspicions are true. Did she give you a reason for her assumption of my guilt?"

"Not in so many words, but she seems to believe that you have always despised the baronet."

"That is true, as you know." He stared out at the brisk traffic on the street below and did not look at Jade as he asked quietly, "And you? Do *you* believe I killed Sir Mitchell?"

"Your sister became vexed with me when I said I doubted you would commit such a crime."

It was not the enthusiastic denial he had hoped for, but upsetting Jade further by asking her to give him a more specific answer would be cruel. "What did you think of my sister?"

"I think she looked drawn as if she had been ill or injured. I think she is suffering a great deal of grief. I think—"

He cut her off as he looked over his shoulder at her. "No, that is not what I meant. What did you think of *her*? How did she treat you?"

"Gideon, she has suffered a great loss," she said so slowly that he knew she was trying to choose words that would not offend him. "I should not judge her now."

"You suffered a great loss when your father died, and you are warmhearted. I cannot imagine you screeching at your servants or acting as if you were better than the royal family."

"Gideon! You should not speak so of your own sister!"

"Don't waste your breath chiding me." He focused his gaze on the traffic below again. "I know you think I am a beast to deride Persis, but you did not know her before Renshaw forced his way into our lives. She was always smiling and seldom said a cross word to anyone. In many ways, she remained the innocent, endearing child who followed me around our estate, always wanting to do what I did.

"Then she met Renshaw, and she changed so much that I hardly recognize her. Her smile vanished, except when he was nearby. She became secretive and demanding and would fly into a pelter at the slightest provocation. At first, I believed she was suffering from unrequited love. While I did not want her to suffer, I was relieved that Renshaw had no interest in her."

"But that changed after you came into your title," she said softly.

"Renshaw changed, but she did not. She remained as difficult as she had become. If I said the sky was blue, she would insist it was red. Renshaw readily sided with her."

"Just sided?" she asked, her voice closer now. "Or did he press for her to be at outs with you?"

He turned and discovered she was standing right behind him, as he had guessed. What he had not anticipated was how his whole soul leaped with joy at the genuine compassion in her eyes. Rather than answer her question, he cradled her face as he tilted her mouth beneath his. She leaned into his kiss, her hands sliding up his arms. Her gentle touch undid his frayed self-control. He wanted her. To perdition with bargains and time frames and anything but the flavor of her sweet lips.

Bending, he scooped her up in his arms. Her gasp swirled into his mouth, sweeping aside every thought but pleasure. Lifting his mouth from hers only long enough to gauge his route across the sitting room, he carried her to the settee. He sat slowly, holding her on his lap. Her soft breasts pressed against him as he captured her mouth again. Sliding one hand up to caress her beguiling curves, he smiled when she gasped with eagerness.

He leaned her back on the settee. Her arms swept up his back, keeping him close. Pressing his mouth between her breasts, he felt her arch up to be even nearer him. She shifted to run her tongue along his ear, and he gasped, shocked at the power of his craving for her. Reaching down, he slid his fingers up beneath her skirt. She drew her leg up along his as he stroked her silken skin.

"That tickles," she said with a giggle, when he caressed the back of her knee.

"What about this?" He ran his fingers higher along the inside of her thigh.

She breathed out a soft sigh, her head falling back to offer him the curve of her neck. He pressed his mouth to that arch, and she trembled beneath him. He thought he heard her whisper his name, but his pulse was pounding through his skull, drowning out everything but his need. The very thought of him pushing inside her, letting her surround him as they found ecstasy together was so strong that he reached beneath her and began to unhook her gown. He could not wait. She was in his arms. To hell with their bargain. As he gazed down into her glazed eyes, he knew she had forgotten it, too. It was time for them to be together. Completely together as he had imagined since he saw her in the duchess's garden. With a groan, he slanted his mouth over hers again and hooked a finger in her bodice to draw it aside.

"Who are you and what are you doing with her?"

The back of his coat was seized, and he was jerked away from Jade and to his feet. In astonishment, he stared at the furious face and thick, gray hair of Rudolph Stommel. Sharla's protector's full lips twisted.

"Bannatyne, how dare you come here!" He ripped off his glove.

"Stommel—"

The glove smacked Gideon's cheek as the older man snarled, "I will have my satisfaction."

"Stommel—"

"Enough!" Again he was interrupted, but this time by a lighter voice. When Jade stepped between him and Stommel, holding her dress to her firm breasts, Stommel's eyes widened in puzzlement.

"Who are you?" he demanded.

Gideon did not give her a chance to answer, because the truth could destroy her reputation. Hooking up her gown was one of the most difficult things he had ever done because he wanted to loosen the rest of the hooks. But, for now, he had to protect her. "This is my friend."

"And mine," Sharla said as she walked into the room. Shock tightened her face, but she quickly recovered herself. Slipping her arm through Stommel's, she smiled. "Why are you here when I was waiting for you . . . elsewhere?"

The older man cleared his throat before saying, "I do believe I owe you and your companion an apology, Bannatyne. I assumed . . . That is . . ." He glanced at Jade, hurrumphed again, then said, "If you will accept my apology and allow me to withdraw my challenge, Bannatyne, I would be grateful."

"Most certainly, Stommel."

Sharla smiled. "Now that honor has been served, do excuse us, Gideon and Jasmine."

"Jasmine?" Gideon repeated, baffled.

"Oh, Gideon," Jade said, slapping his arm playfully. "You could vex a girl with your sense of humor. Pretending you don't even know my name." She laughed.

When Sharla did as well, he forced a smile. He intended to ask Jade to explain as soon as Stommel and Sharla took their leave . . . and he finished what he had started with Jade. He never had the chance because Stommel asked him about his opinions of Derlan's death. By the time he could graciously extricate himself and Jade from the conversation, the hour was growing late. Jade's comments about joining her sisters for tea were meant for him as much as their hostess and her paramour.

Their trip back to Grosvenor Square was as silent as the one to Sharla's house. He sensed Jade glancing at him again and again, but each time he looked in her direction, she was concentrating on steering the cart through the crowded streets. Fitful gusts of wind sprayed dust over them as clouds thickened overhead.

At her door, he swung off his horse as a young stableboy appeared to get the cart. Clearly, someone was watching for Jade to return home.

His restraint was challenged anew as he bid her a good evening and reminded her that he would speak with her again before escorting her to the gala at Sharla's house in two days. He bowed over her hand, grimacing at the hypocrisy forced upon him by the canons of Society. Raising his head, he saw the longing in her eloquent, deep green eyes.

"Why did Sharla call you Jasmine?" he whispered.

"It is the name I am using while in the demimonde." She put her hand to her bonnet as the wind threatened to tear it off.

"It does not suit you."

"No?"

He smiled. "No, because while you are sweet as jasmine, you are more like jade."

"Hard and heartless?"

"I should not have said that. I meant rather that you are glorious and unique and a sensual joy."

Color flashed up her face, and he smiled. He was coming to see that all her blushes were not because she was embarrassed or shy. Some—and he hoped this was one—were because she was pleased. She tilted her head to look up at him.

He silenced his groan of overwhelming need as her motion put her mouth directly beneath his. She seemed to realize that, too, because she edged back one pace, then another before whirling to go up the steps and into the house.

He considered, for a moment, following and sweeping her up into his arms again. He did not care about her sisters or her chaperone Mrs. Willow or her reputation or anything but giving her the rapture she craved as much as he did.

He turned and swung into the saddle, riding at top speed out of the square while his good sense still could mute his need for her.

"Jade, come in and speak with us," China said in the tone that suggested arguing would gain Jade nothing. She motioned toward the sitting room. The windows were rattling with the winds that had grown even stronger as twilight deepened.

Sian put her arm around Jade's waist and smiled. "We have seen so little of you lately. You have become caught up in a swirl of calls like the pink of the *ton*."

"We are interested in sharing what you have been enjoying," China added.

"She means we want to know why Lady Persis asked you to call this afternoon." Sian laughed when their older sister made a face at her. "Oh, China, you know you are as curious as I am. You may as well own to it."

"Very well. I *am* curious why the lady asked you to call, Jade. What did she have to share with you that she has avoided sharing with anyone else?"

"Nothing," Jade said as she dropped with an unlady-like lack of grace on the settee. It creaked, bringing a dismayed frown to her sisters' faces. "Don't dress me down for my poor manners. There is no need to fear I am being influenced by the people I have encountered in the low sections of London."

Her sisters exchanged an uneasy look before China said, "We are not worried about that."

"But we are worried about the amount of time you are spending with Lord Bannatyne," Sian added, sitting next to Jade. "He is a man with a questionable reputation, and we cannot help fretting about your safety when you are with him."

"He has not murdered me, if that is your fear."

Again her sisters glanced at each other.

Jade sat straighter. "Forgive me. I am tired of the chase, which is leading nowhere. I have seen no signs that lead me to believe he truly murdered Sir Mitchell."

"Did you believe he would own up to such a crime?"

"You misunderstand me." She leaned forward to pick a sweetmeat out of the bowl, but paused. Standing, she went to the window that overlooked the square. "What I mean is that he seems honestly dismayed at the turn of events that kept his sister from marrying Sir Mitchell."

"Could it be a ploy?" asked China, as always anxious to watch out for the family's well-being.

"I thought that at first, but I do not any longer." She folded her arms in front of her. "Maybe he is acting and betwattling me with every word, but I just don't sense that. He seems as honest about Sir Mitchell as he does about his yearning to discover the truths about the others in his family who have died."

"And his sister?"

Jade recoiled from the question she had not expected China to ask. "What about her?"

"You did not explain why she asked you to call."

"She was curious why I had come to the house several

times." Jade shrugged, then wished she had not. Her shoulder still burned from Sir Mitchell's inadvertent touch. And the rest of her burned with the memory of Gideon's intentional touch.

"Does she know that her brother has been calling on you?" China asked.

"I don't know. She did not mention anything about that and neither did I."

"Odd."

"What is odd about it? It is not as if she is expecting him to come here to ask you for my hand, China." She tried to laugh, but the sound was uneven.

Her sisters exchanged another uneasy glance.

"Please don't do that!" Jade begged.

"Do what?" her younger sister asked.

Shaking her head, she stood and turned to look out at the trees swaying in the strong wind as the windows rattled wildly again. "I was making an absurd jest, and you two are looking as if you think I was being honest."

Sian rose and put her hand on Jade's shoulder. "We are worried about you. If you truly do not believe that Lord Bannatyne was the murderer, you should cease in your investigation of the baronet's death."

"I don't know what I believe any longer."

"I believe you are falling in love with him."

"Didn't you hear me? I said it was an absurd jest."

Coming to her feet, China said, "You need not raise your voice, Jade. We are not the focus of your frustration."

"No, you are not." She walked away from her sisters and—she wished—all her dilemmas. Pausing by the hearth where the flames danced wildly in tempo with the trees in front of the house, she faced them. "Forgive me. I fear I have lost every bit of ability to think rationally."

"But we have not," her older sister said gently. "It is time for you to bring this to an end. Father would not want you to risk so much when it no longer matters to him."

"It matters to me! I would do anything to see him again!"

Her sisters stared at her, astonished.

Sian whispered with breathless hope, "See Father again? Is that possible?"

"I don't know, but I agreed to help Sir Mitchell in exchange for him trying to find a way to show himself to you and to bring Father to speak with us as Sir Mitchell has."

"He has failed with both," China said. "Maybe he has been as stymied in his efforts as you have. It is time to let this madness come to an end, Jade."

"I wish I could. I cannot." She looked down at the fire on the hearth. "I—"

"What did Persis say to you?"

Jade started to turn to answer her sisters, then realized the voice was deep and came from the other side of the room. She glanced toward the back wall and saw the light that always appeared just before Sir Mitchell.

Instead of answering, she went back to her sisters, gave them each a kiss on the cheek, and ignored Sir Mitchell's voice calling her as she left the sitting room. She climbed the stairs and went into her bedchamber. Closing the door, she twisted the key in the lock. It would not keep the ghost out, but the motion made her feel as if she were in control of a single aspect of her life.

She leaned against the door and sighed. Could her sisters be right? Was she in love with Gideon? How sure she had been that nobody could fall in love in less than a week. The jest was on her, because she had been ready to cede herself to him in Miss Maguire's sitting room.

A tremble coursed through her at the thought, and she closed her eyes to savor the memory of his astonishing touch. If Miss Maguire's lover had not intruded . . . She sighed with the longing that sent quivers along her. She *was* falling in love with Gideon, a man accused by his own sister of being a murderer.

Was her nascent love for him blinding her to the truth? No! The attempts on his life suggested he was the prey rather than the hunter. But had those incidents been in an effort to gain revenge for deaths he had caused? That made no sense. If someone had proof Gideon had slain Sir Mitchell, then the hangman could obtain the ultimate vengeance on him.

Yet if he were innocent of murder, she should put an end to her search for the truth. That idea saddened her more than anything had since Father's death. It was impossible to imagine going to him and telling him that she was giving up her search for *Violet,* and that she no longer needed his help. To thank him and walk away . . . No, she did not want to think of that, for the very thought sent pain lashing at her.

"Miss Nethercott!"

Jade opened her eyes to see Sir Mitchell's furious face. She had known he would be annoyed because she had pretended not to see him downstairs.

"You need not use your voice to shake the whole house," she said calmly.

"I did not shake the house." He glanced around him. "Are we in the midst of a storm?"

"Yes, it is very windy." She did not add that the gusts beyond the house were minor compared to the tempest swirling through her. "What do you want, Sir Mitchell?"

"How does my beloved Persis fare?"

"She looks pale."

"She has been closeted in mourning."

"No, more than that." She sat at her dressing table. "I would say she has been ill, very seriously ill. She was as wan as someone who has suffered an injury and lost a lot of blood."

He did not reply quickly, surprising her because he usually snapped back a retort or a demand. His voice was little more than a whisper when he asked, "How could that be? She has been within the walls of her room since my death. What could injure her there?" His lips tightened. "Bannatyne!"

"Don't be ludicrous. She will not even see her brother, and he has not spoken with her since before your funeral." Coming to her feet, she said, "Sir Mitchell, I tire of your inability to discuss anything without trying to place blame on Gideon."

"He is a murderous criminal."

"You have asked me to find proof of that, and I have found nothing to support your contention."

"Then you have not been looking in the correct places."

"And where would that be?"

The only answer she got was a half-spoken curse before the ghost faded. His spells of being visible seemed to be getting shorter and shorter. She would have to ask him about that when—or if—he returned. And she would have to ask him why he had failed before to give her information that would allow her to discover the truth.

As the light surrounding Sir Mitchell vanished, Jade readied herself for bed. What information could the ghost give her that would persuade her to change her mind? She did not want to hear that Gideon had any part in the baronet's death, but she must listen. It was the only way she had a chance to see her father again.

Her thoughts went round and round, blown in every direction as if on the wind whistling under the eaves. It was hours before she could sleep, long after she heard her sisters and the other residents of the house go to their rooms.

Jade had no idea how long she had been asleep when she was routed awake by the inhuman shriek of the wind. Or was it someone human crying out?

The house shook again. Overhead, the crack of wood was matched by more screams.

Throwing her robe over her shoulders as she ran out into the hallway, she saw light coming from the uppermost floor. Not candlelight, but a cooler light. Then wind lashed her face.

She looked up and out into the sky visible through the leaves and branches of the tree that had come through the roof. Whirling, she saw the front part of the house was lost in more debris. She cried out her sisters' names and heard soft sobs as she began to tear at the debris. Someone was alive within the twisted branches, but could be seriously hurt.

"China! Sian!" she shouted, running up the stairs. "Answer me!"

"Here," came China's reply, tight with pain.

"Sian?"

"I don't know." China's voice broke. "The tree came right into our rooms."

Jade shrieked her younger sister's name.

There was no answer.

Chapter 15

"**M**y lord! My lord!"

Gideon rolled over, shoved his pillow aside, and opened his eyes. He recognized who stood in his bedchamber doorway. "Tabor, if you don't have the best damn reason in the world for waking me when I just found sleep, I shall give you your congé at dawn." He yawned. "Or whenever I wake again."

"My lord, I must speak with you posthaste."

Hearing the distress in his usually calm valet's voice, he muttered, "All right. What is it?" He sat and swung his legs over the side of the bed.

"Miss Jade and—"

"Jade? What has happened to her?" Something he could not describe, a sensation more powerful than a ball piercing his flesh, propelled pain through him.

"First, I want to reassure you, my lord, that I am told they are alive."

"What has happened? Tabor, spit it out!"

As his valet began to explain the damage done by a toppled tree to the house on Grosvenor Square where the Nethercott sisters had taken up residence, Gideon halted him with orders to bring some clothes.

Tabor complied, then went to have Gideon's horse saddled and brought around to the front of the house.

Gideon threw on his clothes, not bothering with a cravat. He shoved his arms into his coat as he rushed down the stairs. He faltered when he thought he heard his sister's door open, torn between seeing how she fared and his worries for Jade. There was no need to choose because it quickly shut again.

Continuing down the stairs at a breakneck pace, he pushed his sister out of his mind. He gave the footmen more orders, ending with, "Don't dawdle a moment!" He did not wait for a footman to open the door, throwing it aside so hard that it crashed into the wall. Porcelain rattled, and he heard something fall and shatter. He did not wait to see what.

Wind lashed at him, and needles of rain scratched his skin. He threw himself in the saddle and rode neck-or-nothing south toward Grosvenor Square. By perdition's wicked light! If he had enticed Jade to come back to his house with him, she would not have been endangered.

Lanterns lit the macabre scene as Gideon turned his horse into Grosvenor Square. He could see the massive tree that had collapsed on three houses. The one in the middle was where the Nethercott sisters lived, and it had borne the brunt of the tree's fall. Broken glass glittered on the wet walkway, and bricks, roof tiles, and shattered boards were strewn among leaves and bark. Dozens of people had gathered, not daunted by the high wind and the rain, to survey the damage.

He saw Mrs. Willow sitting on nearby steps, a blanket over her shoulders and something in her hand. When someone urged her to take a drink, he hoped it was stronger than tea or cocoa. He swung out of the saddle, handed the reins to a lad who was staring in awe at the fine horse, and then hurried to her side.

"Mrs. Willow, I am pleased to see you are unhurt," he said.

The older woman squinted. "Thank you . . . Lord Bannatyne! Thank heavens you are here!"

"Why?" He felt something plummet into his gut. Hard. That the companion of the Nethercott sisters wanted to see him suggested matters might be far worse than Tabor had heard.

"Maybe you can talk some sense into Miss Jade's head. She refuses to let anyone tend to her."

He breathed a deep sigh of relief. If Jade could argue

that she needed no help, that meant she was relatively uninjured. "Where is she?"

"Over there." Mrs. Willow waved toward where the crowd had gathered around the roots of the tree.

Gideon thanked her, but he doubted Mrs. Willow heard. A group of ladies appeared out of the darkness to offer her sympathy and to praise her courage. Mrs. Willow, who had been relegated to the corners as a companion, was abruptly the center of attention, and he could see she intended to relish every moment.

Lanterns rocked in the wind, and he was astonished to see some hung from the lower branches of the toppled tree. Were they out of their minds? A tipped lantern could set the whole tree and the houses on fire.

He scanned the square. People walked in and out of the pools of light from the lanterns, but he did not see the one he sought. Where was Jade?

He elbowed his way past the inquisitive onlookers. Curses and disgusted sniffs followed in his wake, but he ignored both. When he pushed beyond the ones closest to the tree, he still saw no sign of Jade. Then he noticed people pointing at the house.

"She would not be so foolish," he said under his breath, but knew he could be wrong.

No one tried to halt him when he ran around the broken branches and climbed the steps. The door was ajar, and he stepped inside. Twigs and leaves were scattered across the foyer floor.

"Jade!" he shouted. "Are you in here?"

"Gideon?" came back a shocked voice from above him.

Racing up the stairs, he saw light at the far end of the hall. It moved, and he knew it must be from lanterns outside the house. He paused when he heard her shout to wait.

"Where are you?" he yelled.

"The sitting room." Her words sounded as if she were speaking past gritted teeth.

"Are you hurt?"

"Just stay there, Gideon. Please!"

He had never felt so helpless. He heard her gasp, then mutter a curse she had never spoken in his company. Unable to stand and do nothing, he edged closer to the front of the house. Glass crunched under his feet. His foot hit something, and he heard it crash past the railing and down onto the foyer floor.

"Gideon, don't come any closer!"

"Jade—"

"It is too dangerous."

"Do you need help?"

She did not answer right away. As he was about to repeat his question, he heard, "I am fine, but the floor is not. I don't think it can hold both of us."

He edged closer to the door and the light. In spite of himself, he gasped when he saw a gaping hole where the front of the house had been battered away.

"What are you doing?" he shouted when he saw her inching across the floor, not toward the door, but away from it.

"Gideon, please! Stay where you are." She took another cautious step. The floor creaked ominously beneath her.

"Jade!"

"I am all right."

"Come back here."

"Not yet." She stretched toward a table that remarkably was still upright. Picking up two flat items, she held them tightly before she turned and moved slowly toward him.

The creak became a high pitched squeak and a deep rumble. The boards and the joists under them must be damaged.

He stretched out his arm. "Take my hand, Jade!"

"I—"

The floor seemed to come alive beneath her feet like a boat fighting waves. He jumped forward, grabbed her arm, and shoved her into the corridor. Beneath him, the floor started to fall into the room below. He threw himself toward her. She dropped what she held and clasped his arms. Pulling him toward her, she careened into the railing. It made a sound too much like the floor had before the boards had given way. He snatched her away from it, holding her to him.

"Thank you," she whispered, her voice warm against his neck.

He kissed her as if he would never again have a chance. She pressed even closer to him, and he realized she was wearing only a thin nightdress beneath her half-opened robe. The thought of ridding her of those clothes sent his head reeling, but they had to get out of the house before it collapsed.

Releasing her, he said, "We must go. Now!"

"Yes." She sounded more breathless than she had when she had been crossing the disintegrating floor.

He ran his thumb across her lower lip that was swollen from his desperate kiss. "Now, Jade."

"Yes."

As she turned slightly to collect the two items she had rescued, he wondered if she had any idea how that single word had exploded within him, honing his need. He said nothing as she hurried with him toward the stairs.

Only when they reached the outside steps did he ask, "What do you have there?"

"My father's favorite book and my sister's sketch-book." She hid both beneath her robe as they stepped out into the rain. "I could not leave either behind."

"I should have guessed." He guided her down the steps, glad to see she was wearing shoes that were thick enough to protect her feet from glass shards. "Your family matters more to you than anything else."

"Them and a few others." She glanced at him and quickly away.

He did not reply as she was surrounded by her neighbors who had dozens of questions about the condition of the house. Dash it! Into his mind echoed Sharla's warning: *There are others who would be willing to distract you. Women who do not believe that a single kiss leads to the altar.* He had come to believe that Jade was of that sort, that she truly was focused on finding her late father's mistress. She never had denied him a kiss

or a caress, suggesting that they should wait until they
had a parson's blessing. She had learned the lessons
Sharla had taught her, lessons that had taught that a
woman should consider other situations than marriage
when men admired them.

In spite of that, she might be falling in love with him.
Dash it! That emotion could complicate everything.
They had been having such adventures together, and he
had more planned. Why did she have to become doe-
eyed when she glanced at him?

Maybe he was the one overreacting now. She had not
said she loved him, just suggested he was important in
her life. She was important in his as well. At Sharla's
gala, if all went as he hoped, she would be the way to
help him discover more about his family's deaths. He
was jumping to conclusions, propelled by exhaustion and
too many knocks to his skull in the past week.

No matter, now was not the time to brood. A catastro-
phe had happened to the Nethercott house, and he must
help Jade deal with that. Going to where she stood, he
put his hand on her arm.

"How are you?" he asked, as she turned. "How are
your sisters?"

"I am fine, Gideon," she said, pushing her wet hair
back from her face. "We all are. Everyone is accounted
for, and the only damages to the household members
are a bump on Sian's head when she was knocked out
of bed by the concussion and a twisted ankle suffered
by one of the maids who rushed too quickly down the
stairs. We are fortunate."

"If you call a tree in the middle of your roof lucky."

She smiled, and he wondered if stars had descended
to glitter in her eyes. "At least, this is truly an accident.
Nobody can assert that someone *tried* to do us injury."

"Do you always see the most positive side of any
situation?"

"It is either that or sit and cry."

Mindful of the crowd gathered in the square, he did
no more than run the back of his fingers against her

cheek. Her skin was chilled. He shrugged off his coat and set it over her shoulders.

"Where are your sisters?" he asked when she slanted toward him. If he took her into his arms, he doubted he could let her go.

"At a house on the other side of the square. The one with the open door. I don't even know who lives there, but they insisted we come inside and out of the storm."

"But you could not resist coming back out?"

"I had to retrieve the books, and then I wanted to look for Mrs. Willow. She went only as far as nearby steps before telling us to go without her."

"She is being properly pampered as a heroine for escaping the clutches of the tree. You should go inside yourself."

"All right." As she reached to lift off his coat, he halted her. "But, Gideon, you are soaked, too."

"Let us get out of the rain."

He put his arm around her shoulders and started to guide her toward the far side of the square. She kept pausing and looking back. He thought he heard a sob break in her throat, but she did not say anything. He would not embarrass her when she was struggling to be the strength her family would need during the days to come.

The house with the open door was a mirror image of the house where the Nethercott sisters had lived. As they were led up the stairs to the sitting room, he noticed how Jade glanced about her. Her eyes glistened with tears, but none fell.

China Nethercott surged to her feet when they reached the sitting room door. She clasped her sister to her, chiding her for being so reckless, but becoming silent when Jade withdrew the book and handed it to her. Holding the book to her chest as Jade had, she began to cry.

Jade went past her older sister to where her younger one was lying on a settee. Kneeling, she held out the other book to Miss Sian, whose hands shook. Jade did not release the book until she was certain her sister could hold it. Running gentle fingers along her sister's forehead, she whispered something too low for him to hear.

When Jade rose and came back to him, she said, "Thank you, Gideon. I would not have been able to retrieve the books without your help."

"I suspect Jade Nethercott can do anything she sets her mind to."

"I might have thought so before tonight, but now . . ." She shuddered. "I am not sure what we will do now."

Miss China raised her head. "If the duchess did not have a full house of guests, we could go there."

"You must come and be my guests." Gideon saw the shock on the Nethercott women's faces, but he continued, "It will take at least a month, probably longer, to repair the house to make it fit for you to return beneath its roof."

"My lord," Miss China said with a strained smile, "your kindness goes beyond any expectations, but we do not want to impose on you."

"Where do you expect to lease another house when the Season is at its peak? Any decent house has been let and is filled to overflowing with distant cousins and hangers-on. It is amazing that the duchess was able to find you the house here."

"Thank you, but you must understand that it would be untoward to accept your generous offer. I . . .." She glanced over her shoulder. "Excuse me, my lord. I should be sitting with Sian."

As China hurried toward the settee, Jade sighed. China could be unbending at times, even when the situation demanded other considerations.

"Jade," he said as if she had spoken aloud, "persuade your sisters that even the most judgmental among the Polite World will not believe I am bedding you one at a time." A wry smile settled on his lips. "Or all at once."

"You should not say such things." Her tone was chiding, but her mouth worked as she tried to restrain her laugh.

"Why not? They make you smile."

"Do not be absurd."

"No?" He bent. His gaze held hers, not letting her escape.

"What of *your* reputation, Gideon? Such an act of kindness is sure to force those who speak poorly of you to reconsider."

"Silly question. I have given none of the gossips any credence before now. Why would I at this point?" He stroked her chin with his curved finger. "Jade, you know my offer is probably the best you will get. To find a *suitable* place for your household and your sisters would be nigh onto impossible. And when will you have time to find such a place? Sharla's party is tomorrow night."

She stared at him, shocked that she had forgotten that important matter. "Let me talk to my sisters and see if I can convince them."

"You must, or you will have no choice other than a place where none of you would want to stay."

"So it is a choice between a place where none of us would be willing to stay and a place where one of us would be?"

His smile was warm, but not as heated as his eyes when he replied, "I suspect your younger sister could be easily persuaded. Why don't you do that while I arrange to have a doctor meet us at my house?"

As she had before, she said softly, "Thank you, Gideon. You have saved me more than once from my own want-wittedness. Now you are doing the same for my sisters."

"Go," he ordered, rather roughly.

She guessed she had overmastered him with her praise, so she nodded. While he hurried down the stairs, she went to speak with her sisters. China remained resistant until Sian pleaded with her to agree. Sian's head was aching too much to endure their quarrel.

"Not that I need to see a doctor," Sian added when China concurred. "There is nothing a doctor can do for me other than to order warm compresses, and you are doing that already."

It did not take long, with the help of their neighbors

who could not hide their relief that the three sisters had found a place elsewhere to spend the night, for Sian to be wrapped in blankets and taken downstairs to sit on a bench. The neighbors were kind, but a newlywed couple who clearly wished to have their house to themselves. Jade noticed that they did not ask once where the sisters were staying. They were so engrossed in each other that they had no thoughts for anyone else. She could not help being envious of how open and simple their love appeared.

Nothing seemed simple for her now.

The door opened, and Gideon rushed in along with a curtain of rain. Shaking his head to get some of the water out of his eyes, he said, "You may find this difficult to believe, but I think the storm is lessening."

"That is good news," Jade said, hoping her cheerful tone would ease her sisters' disquiet.

"Let's go."

"How?"

"I have Stommel's carriage waiting outside. Before I left Bedford Square, I sent for it because I wanted to have it ready in case it was needed." He chuckled. "One learns to be ready for any contingency when aboard a boat."

She watched as he effortlessly lifted Sian and carried her to the carriage. Setting her inside, he assisted her to sit before offering his hand to China to help her inside. She heard her sister thank him quietly. Even from where she stood, Jade could sense China's dismay; yet her older sister was too practical to turn down such a generous offer. Gideon had been right. They could not return to the house until the damage was repaired.

"Jade?" he prompted. "You are getting soaked again."

Letting him help her in, she was astonished when he shut the door. "Gideon, aren't you coming with us?"

"I have my horse, and I shall speed home to alert the household to have hot baths waiting for you."

She did not care that her sisters—and half the residents of the square—were watching. Stretching up to the window, she put her hand on the back of his head and slanted her mouth across his. He seemed shocked at her boldness, then she felt his lips curl in a smile.

Drawing back, he said, "I will see you on Bedford Square." He vanished into the storm.

Jade sat as the carriage lurched into motion. She was relieved it was too dark to see her sister's expressions. As they traveled on the streets, she drew Sian's head down into her lap and stroked her sister's arm.

"I wonder," China said into the darkness, "if Sir Mitchell's ghost will follow us to Lord Bannatyne's house."

"I don't know." Jade had not considered that. She had been too concerned about the living to worry about Sir Mitchell. "He loathes Gideon, and the antipathy was mutual." She did not add that Sir Mitchell never seemed to be certain where he was materializing. It would be better to let China believe that problem had been left behind them.

When the carriage stopped in front of Gideon's house, it appeared as if every lamp was lit. A glance toward Lady Persis's room revealed someone peeking past the drawn draperies, but Jade doubted the lady herself was at the window. She probably had sent a maid to discover what the hullabaloo was.

Servants poured from the house to assist them inside. Gideon stepped forward to carry Sian into the house rather than allow a footman to lift her from the carriage.

In the house, it was as busy as morning. Maids were rushing up and down the stairs carrying buckets. The housekeeper, a spare woman with silvery hair, stood overseeing everything.

"Oh, my!" gasped Jade.

"What is it?" China asked.

"We left Mrs. Willow behind."

From the stairs, Gideon called, "Josephs, have the carriage return and retrieve Mrs. Willow." He added a quick description. "It might be better if you mention

only that you are bringing her to where the Nethercott
ladies are rather than mentioning the actual destination."

The footman looked puzzled but rushed to obey.

Jade laughed, and even China smiled weakly.

An hour later, Sian had enjoyed a steaming bath and
was in bed two doors from Lady Persis's room. The
housekeeper, Mrs. Arnold, had escorted China to a room
across the hall where her sister was now luxuriating in
a bath of her own. Clean, dry clothes were found from
storage cupboards in the house.

When Jade stepped out of her younger sister's room,
she saw Gideon speaking in hushed tones to his valet.
She walked toward them, and Gideon's arm settled
lightly on her shoulders. She wanted to lean her head
against him, close her eyes, and stay like that until the
craziness of the past month disappeared. Maybe some-
day she would have that wondrous moment with him,
but, for now, she needed to make sure her sisters were
taken care of and comfortable.

"How is Miss Sian?" Gideon asked.

"Other than her aching head, she is doing fine."

Tabor said quietly, "I will have some lavender mixed
with wine for Miss Sian. That will ease the pain of her
head."

"Thank you, Tabor," Gideon replied. "You might
offer the same to Miss China Nethercott, because I suspect she is suffering a headache as well. I have seen that
these Nethercott women are unlikely to complain on
their own behalf."

Tabor bowed his head. "And for you, Miss Jade? Can
I have you brought a posset too?"

"That will not be necessary," she said. "I think I will
go to sleep now, so I can get a few minutes of rest
before dawn."

"There is no need for you to rise early." Gideon's
face was drawn with fatigue. He motioned toward the
front of the house. "Let me show you to where you
can sleep."

She started to follow him, then paused. "What about Mrs. Willow?"

"She is already asleep upstairs. Your housekeeper and several other maids are there, too." He gave a weary chuckle. "You will find the household is very efficient."

"And quiet." She glanced at the door that had not opened once during their arrival.

"That was how Persis trained them." He put his hand on the newel post of the staircase leading up to the next floor. "I trust you will not mind climbing another set of stairs. There is no other bedchamber on this floor."

"I can share a room with Sian or China."

"Nonsense." Taking her hand, he led her up the stairs. "There is plenty of space here for the three of you, and you all need a good night's sleep. So why not have your own bed?" He gave her a leering grin. "Unless you want to share it and not sleep."

"Do you never think of anything else?"

"Not when you are standing close to me with nothing but my coat and a few layers of linen separating us."

"It has not been seven days yet."

"Almost." He ran his finger along her shoulder and up to the sensitive skin behind her ear. There it uncurled in a simple caress.

But it was enough to send an explosion of delight through her. She was abruptly aware of the shadows at the top of the stairs and how that darkness enclosed them in a private space separated from the rest of the world. And she was aware, too, of every breath he drew in, because she suddenly seemed unable to breathe on her own. It was as if she needed every part of her to match his rhythms.

She was unsure what she might have done if he had put his arm around her instead of opening a door behind her. As it was, she could not find any words to reply when he motioned for her to enter. She wished she felt less like she was fleeing as she turned and went into the chamber.

There was nothing feminine about the room. The fur-

niture was dark and simply carved. The walls were a red
that would be a brilliant shade in the sunshine. At night,
with only a pair of lamps lit, the color seemed to turn
the large chamber into a comfortable cave. She looked
at the bed, half hidden by shadows. She wanted to climb
in, draw the covers up, and forget about everything.

Everything but Gideon.

"Will you be comfortable here?" he asked as he had
Sian when her sister was settled in downstairs.

"Yes."

"You should get some sleep. You are weaving on
your feet."

"I am exhausted, but I don't know if I can sleep." She
clasped her arms across her. "I feel as if that steam
engine on your boat is pumping through me."

He smiled gently. "You must have been very frightened by the tree crashing through your roof. Then you
went back to rescue two precious items."

"And succeeded, thanks to you."

"You would have succeeded with or without me. You
are a resourceful woman, Jade. I am sure you were fearful of the fate of everyone else in the house and were
ready to go to battle with all those branches to save
them. Now that everyone is safe, you are left with the
remnants of your own courage and outrage."

"That is exactly it. Outrage." She shook her head.
"Do you know how useless it is to be angry at a tree?"

"You would have fought it bravely if you had had a
chance." He chuckled. "I have seen you in action. You
were willing to risk yourself to protect me—a man you
barely knew—from an assassin's shots."

"I don't want to recall that tonight. I prefer to take
my challenges one at a time." She started to add more,
but a knock was set on the half-open door.

Gideon's valet came in, carrying a tray. "I brought
you some mint tea, Miss Jade." Tabor set the tray on
the table.

"Thank you, but you should not have bothered."

"It was no bother. Cook keeps water hot in the
kitchen at all hours." He drew a nightdress from over

his arm and placed it on the bed. "I trust this will serve, Miss Jade."

"It seems you have thought of everything." She drew off Gideon's damp coat. Carrying it to a chair where it could finish drying, she was shocked when something brushed her foot. Bending down, she picked up a long strip of linen. She stared at it, astonished, then asked herself why she should be surprised by another example of Gideon's kindness.

Walking back to where Gideon was giving Tabor additional instructions to share with the household, she said, "It might be simpler if you allow me to retire elsewhere, so you have the use of your own room, Gideon."

"How do you know?" he asked.

She handed him the cravat. "Your valet did a heroic job to clear the chamber of your personal belongings on such short notice."

"Tabor is a treasure."

The valet rolled his eyes before leaving the room.

"I suppose I should take my leave as well now," Gideon said. "Polite society would be aghast at the idea of me standing in the middle of my own room while you are my guest. Let me wish you a good night's sleep. Or what remains of it. Do not be in a rush to rise. Sharla's gathering will go very late."

"Thank you. If you continue being so kindhearted, even China may come to see that you are not an unredeemable rake."

"I rather like that reputation."

She shook her head. "I would think that you would tire of being treated like a pariah when you enter a room."

"If I am shunned by everyone else, then I can spend more time alone with you."

"You can be very charming, you know."

"I know." He gave her the smile that set every inch of her aflutter. He closed the door and walked slowly toward her. She leaned back against the bedpost as he closed the distance between them. Her breathing became the tempo of his steps. Was he a sorcerer? He invoked

his enchantment upon her with no more than a seductive
smile. Caught by it, she could give him no answer. She
could only stare into his sparkling eyes and imagine
them closing in the moment before his lips found hers
again.

"You should go," she forced herself to say.

"I know." He kept walking.

"You could ruin *my* reputation."

"I know."

"If I scream—"

He gripped a handful of her hair and tilted her face
up toward him. In a husky whisper, he said, "If you
scream, let it be with pleasure at my touch, sweetling."

His lips found hers with the ease of the longing she
knew too well. When his fingers combed through her
hair, she raised her hands to push him away. He lifted
his head enough to laugh, before he caught her wrists
and pinned them to the bedpost. His mouth pressed over
hers again, stealing her breath from her.

Slowly she became aware of the teasing massage of
his fingers against the sensitive skin on the inside of her
wrists. Some scent from him, musky and bewitching, fla-
vored every breath she took. When he released her
wrists, his hand curved along her cheek, the rough texture of his palm raking her skin with the flames she had
seen in his eyes. Through her thin nightclothes, she felt
his firm, muscular lines.

He drew his mouth away from hers and ran his finger
along her palm, making her conscious of each inch of
her skin touching his. He smiled as he brought her hand
toward him. His eyes were luminous, inflaming the tempest whirling through her. Settling her fingers on his
shoulder, he slipped his other arm around her, cradling
her between him and the unyielding post.

She reached to touch his cheek, which was as sharply
carved as a polished gem, and then slid her hand up his
hard arm. As her fingertip grazed his nape, he captured
her lips anew. Demanding, yet gentle, his lips caressed
hers, eagerly inviting her to partake of the pleasure she

wanted to share with him. Her fingers sifted upward through his black hair, keeping his mouth against her.

His breath brushed her skin, setting it afire with scintillating sparks, as he tasted her cheek, the curve of her jaw, and along her neck. All of her being converged on the moist heat of his mouth as he blazed rapture into her. Hearing a soft moan, she realized it came from her only when he gave a hushed laugh in the moment before he claimed her lips anew.

Then Gideon heard an unmistakable sound. Dash it! Footsteps. Someone was walking up the stairs and toward the bedroom door. He abruptly released Jade who regarded him with a diffused gaze. He moved more than an arm's length away. How many more interruptions must they suffer before they had the opportunity to become one?

As the door was pushed open, he asked, "Is there something wrong, Miss Nethercott?"

China Nethercott came into the room.

Jade's older sister surveyed the room quickly before her gaze settled on Jade. "How kind of you to check personally that each of us is settled well for the night, my lord."

"Gideon, if you would, Miss Nethercott. As your host, I beg you to indulge my preference for informality."

She bowed her head toward him, looking at him at last. "As you wish, Gideon. And, of course, you must address us by our given names. With three Miss Nethercotts in one house, it can become quite confusing."

As he continued making silly conversation with China, acting as if they were standing in the park by the Serpentine and had chanced to meet, he listened to Jade trying to slow her breath without drawing her sister's attention to herself. Each quick, low gasp sent another thud of need through him.

He realized China would not leave before he did, and she was fighting to stay awake. Dash it! It was a curse to be a gentleman, which was why he had gladly set aside such a reputation. As a rake, he could say and do as he wished. Now, with three young unwed women beneath his roof, he had to act as if he were as constrained as a young miss greeting the patronesses at Almack's. He fought his own grin as he thought of how he had shocked them himself, but then he had risked only his own standing in the Polite World. As Jade had reminded him, a man could be far more careless about such matters than a woman.

"If you need anything, do not hesitate to ring," he said, accepting defeat in the silent battle of wills. "My household is ready to serve in any way they can."

"Thank you, Gideon." Jade took a step toward him, then halted as if a wall had been raised between them. It had, when her sister entered the room.

"Breakfast will be ready when you are in the morning." He forced a smile. "Or later. I suspect we will sleep very late after our adventurous night. If you prefer breakfast in your chambers, ring, and it will be brought to you."

"Thank you, Gideon," China said with a cool finality that suggested he had overstayed his welcome.

"Good night, ladies." He went to the door. When he glanced back, he saw Jade sitting on the bed.

His bed.

Then Jade met his gaze, and he was suffused by the longing again. He hurried out, knowing that if he stayed any longer, not even China's presence in the room might keep him from surrendering to his longing to hold Jade.

He heard China say, "And, Jade, I am sure you would not be upset to have me stay with you tonight. I am greatly distressed by what has happened."

"Yes," Jade replied, "that bed has plenty of room for two."

With a groan of unsated need, he stumbled along the hall toward his office. The accursed chair would be an uncomfortable perch for a bed.

If only she was not so devilishly beautiful and if only her hands that emphasized every word she spoke did not make him ache for them sliding sinuously along him . . . How many more days left in their week? He should have walked away from her at the duchess's party, leaving her to find some other man to serve as her escort into the dens of easy sensuality.

Now she was in his bed, and he was banished from his private chambers. So many people had damned him to perdition for his antics. It would seem that they had gotten their wish, because he was truly in hell.

Chapter 16

Jade opened her eyes. Something was not right. The sunlight was crossing the bed at the wrong angle. The color of the bed curtains seemed different. She reached out to touch the fabric. It was thicker and stiffer than the curtains on her bed.

Where was she?

The answer popped into her head, and she rolled over to stare up at the carved top of Gideon's bed. The woodland pattern had been created by a master craftsman. She glanced to her left and saw the bed was empty. China must have arisen already.

Wondering what hour it was, she sat and stretched. She swung her feet over the side of the bed and slid off, not bothering with the steps. She pulled on a dressing gown and walked with care across the room. She had not been surprised last night to note that on every flat surface were drawings of ships. Not just steamships, but sailing ships and canal boats and every other sort of vessel that could float. The walls were covered with paintings of great ships, their sails filled with the wind. She had not noticed last night when the walls were shadowed, but the room suited Gideon perfectly.

She went to the closer window and shouldered aside the heavy draperies. Sunlight burst around her, outlining every raindrop clinging to the glass. She could see twigs and shredded leaves littering the square, but all other signs of the storm were gone.

"It is about time you woke up," came a vexed voice from behind her.

In the reflection of the glass, she could see the bright glow of light that announced Sir Mitchell's arrival. She let the draperies fall into place as she faced him.

"I thought," she said, crossing her arms in front of her, glad she had drawn on her dressing gown before rising, "that you had difficulty with the passage of time among the living."

"Everyone else in the house is awake and at their tasks while you linger in bed. That tells me that you are late abed."

"Do you often spy on everyone?"

He gave her a scowl as his fingers clenched and unclenched at his sides. She could not help recalling Miss Maguire's comments about Sir Mitchell's violent temper. "I was looking for you, Miss Nethercott. The house seems odd today."

"Because we are not in the house on Grosvenor Square. It was damaged in last night's storm. We are staying at the Bannatyne house on Bedford Square."

"Bannatyne?" He flinched, then squinted as if trying to make out what was beyond the light surrounding him. Crossing the room, he paused by the door. "My beloved Persis . . ."

"Maybe if you were to go to her now, she could see you."

"Even if she could, what would the sight do but bring her more misery?" He put a glowing hand on the door. "I would do anything to make her happy again. When I think of the tears she has shed and all she has suffered, I . . ."

Jade turned away, unable to offer him comfort, not even a pat on the arm. Seeing his grief was as potent as Lady Persis's, she whispered, "She believes, as you do, that her brother slew you."

"She does?" His eyes filled with hope as he faced her. "Surely she persuaded you to heed her opinions."

"I think you are both wrong. I don't think Gideon killed you."

"He has betwattled you. He—"

"I am not speaking of anything but the facts." She would not be drawn into another brangle with him. "In the past week, I have seen him risk his life for others, and I have seen the pain he suffers from not discovering the truth about those who murdered his family." She held up her hand. "You need not repeat yourself and say that those deaths were accidents while yours was not. I might have believed that before several apparent *accidents* have occurred. I think you are completely wrong, Sir Mitchell. I think there is a murderer, but I fear whoever it is wants to slay Gideon, too."

He stamped toward her. When she held up her hands, a cold gust struck her. "You speak of the facts, Miss Nethercott, but you refuse to see them."

"I would gladly see them if you would tell me where to look. I have found nothing to suggest Gideon had any hand in your death."

"Have you looked through the house? The knife that was driven into me—" He flinched again as if pain surged through him anew. "It may be here."

"I doubt it was returned to him after the coroner's investigation."

He opened his mouth to reply, but she did not hear his words. His face screwed up with frustration. He seemed to be shouting. She heard nothing, and he began to dissolve into the light.

Jade was not surprised when someone knocked at the door. Nor was she surprised to open the door to find Gideon standing in the hallway. For some reason that the ghost did not know—or refused to explain—he could not be in the same room with Gideon.

"Good afternoon, stay abed," he said with a grin as his gaze moved along her with slow, deliberate appreciation. "I am sorry to bother you, but I need to go out to arrange a few last matters for our evening at Sharla's. It would appear that Tabor left more than my cravat behind." He gestured beyond her. "May I?"

"Yes." She remained where she was as he walked into the room. Her fingers tightened on the door while she fought her craving to close it, lock it, and throw herself into his arms.

He went to a table and picked up a comb.

"Did Tabor forget on your orders?"

He laughed and bent to peer into the mirror as he combed his hair. "You can accuse me of ulterior motives, but not Tabor. He will be chagrined to know he missed another item."

When a maid walked in, setting a breakfast tray on a table in front of the window, she gave Jade a curious glance, then scurried out.

"Don't mind Rose's gawking," Gideon said. "I fear you put her quite to the stare. She is not accustomed to me allowing a beautiful woman I have brought home to sleep alone." Gideon gave her a wink that sent quivers through her center.

She should order him to leave, but the words did not come as she perused him as he had her last night. His pale green waistcoat was embroidered with darker green vines that were the exact color of the breeches that adhered to his legs, outlining every masculine angle. She watched the teeth of the comb sifting through his hair, as she wished her fingers were doing. When her gaze was captured by his reflected in the mirror, he set down the comb, then picked it up once more before he walked back to where she stood.

"Gideon . . ."

"Don't say anything," he murmured. "Don't say anything unless you are willing to close that door now and come to bed with me."

Her body begged her to say yes, but she could not forget that her sisters—and his—were under the roof, too. She could not ruin them by succumbing to her needs. Stepping aside, she opened the door farther. She continued to lean against it, clutching it so she did not reach out to him.

As he walked past her, he said, "I wish you had said something."

She closed her eyes and whispered too low for him to hear, "So do I."

*   *   *

"How do I look?" Jade gave a half-turn in front of the cheval glass that had been brought to Gideon's room along with several boxes from the house on Grosvenor Square. She had not guessed his errands before the gathering at Miss Maguire's house would be supervising servants—from his household and theirs—to collect undamaged items from the house.

At the top of the first box delivered to her had been the gown she planned to wear to Miss Maguire's gala. It was the same one she had worn to the duchess's house the night she met Gideon. She had spent the afternoon raising the hem to a height considered indecorous by the *ton*.

China shook her head as she paced the room behind her. "No matter what you do, Jade, you still appear too much a lady to enter the demimonde. I don't understand why you are continuing on this course. The answers you seek are in the crime against Sir Mitchell, not among courtesans."

"But his ghost has been emphatic that the crime took place when he was to meet Gideon at an event where cyprians were participating. How can I prove anything if I am not a witness to the viscount among these low creatures?"

"You want to spend more time with him." Sian sat on the chaise longue.

"Do not be absurd. We are living beneath his roof. I am going to the gathering tonight with him. How much *more* time could I spend with him?"

"True, but you did not deny it."

"Do not be absurd," she repeated. "Why do you expect him to be guilty of such a crime? He has been nothing but charitable to us."

"So you are now trying to prove he was not involved?" China shuddered. "Jade, you are too deeply involved. It is clear that he has dangerous enemies. Helping him is putting you in peril."

"Would you have me step aside now and do nothing?"

Sian sighed. "She is right, China. We would be poor

guests to repay our host's hospitality in such a way."
She sat straighter. "And how otherwise can she discover
the truth and persuade Sir Mitchell's ghost to help us
prove to the whole world that Father was right about
ghosts being able to contact us?"

Jade smiled at her younger sister. "I am pleased that
you see my dilemma."

"It is *our* dilemma." China tucked a piece of loose
hair up into the curls drawn to the back of Jade's head.
Picking up a silk flower, she wove it through Jade's hair.
Stepping back, she said, "You look lovely."

Jade picked up her fan and noticed her fingers were
trembling. "I hope tonight provides an answer one way
or the other about the mystery surrounding Sir Mitchell's death."

"So do we." China said as she gathered up her
brushes and walked to the door. "Be careful, Jade."

"I will." She struggled to smile. "I intend to remain
near Gideon throughout the evening."

"Be careful, Jade," she repeated. "Coming, Sian?"

"Just a moment," her younger sister said. As soon as
China had left the room, Sian asked in a conspiratorial
whisper, "Jade, can I ask you a very personal question?"

"You know you can ask me anything."

"Is it as fun as it looks?"

"It?"

"Having a man kiss you with longing."

Squeezing her younger sister's shoulders, she said,
"Even more fun than it looks."

Sian giggled again. "I cannot wait until it is my turn
to be kissed by a dashedly handsome man."

"Be careful what you say when China is near. She
would be distressed."

"China thinks I am an infant. She would say, 'You
are using too many cant terms of late. Continue with
such language, and no man will consider you worthy of
kissing.' " She giggled and added in her own voice. "Or
all of them will."

A knock on the door silenced Jade's answer, which
was good because she was unsure what she would have

said. She appreciated Sian's silly attempts to make her smile. She was aware of the dangers she faced tonight—from the demimonde, from whoever wanted to see Gideon dead, and from Gideon himself. When the door opened and he took her hand, his touch almost undid her.

The sight of him in a spotless navy coat and white breeches, just as he had worn to the duchess's house, flooded her with emotions—longing and admiration and longing and trepidation . . . and longing.

"Beautiful," he whispered. "I will be the envy of every other man there tonight."

"Please don't compliment me. I am nervous enough already, trying to recall all Miss Maguire taught me."

He laughed as he drew her out into the hallway. There, Tabor waited with a cape. Gideon released her long enough to pull it on and then offered his arm again.

If she ran back into the room—*his* room—she could admit defeat and good sense. Even as she thought that, she settled her hand on his arm. He smiled broadly as he swept her down the upper stairs and along the lower hallway to the next set.

She faltered at a soft sound.

"Did you forget something?" he asked.

"Did you hear that?"

"Hear what?"

"It sounded like a door opening."

Hope burst into his eyes as he glanced toward his sister's door. It remained firmly closed. His sigh was so quiet she could hardly hear it; yet when he looked back at her, his smile had returned. It was taut.

"I am sorry," she whispered as they went down the stairs. "She will come out eventually."

For once, he did not give her a glib answer as he led her out of the house. It was, she thought with a shiver, not a good omen for the evening to come.

The carriage borrowed from Stommel was not as elegant as Gideon's had been, but he doubted Jade noticed the difference. She was so unsettled by what awaited her

that she said scarcely a dozen words on the journey from
Bedford Square to Sharla's street. She sat as rigid as a
soldier on parade. When they reached the brightly lit
house, she did not move while he stepped out.

He waved away the tiger who had come to hold the
door. Leaning back inside, he said, "If you sit here all
night, Jade, you will have no luck at finding the person
you seek."

"That is true." She rubbed her gloved hands together,
but otherwise stayed still.

"If you have changed your mind, you only need to
say so. I will have the coachee drive you back to Bedford Square."

"But you are going to stay?"

"You know my reasons for being here tonight, Jade."
His smile faded. "As much as I would prefer to spend
the evening in your company, I cannot set aside my
search for the truth."

"Nor can I." She put her fingers on his outstretched
palm. Her movements were stiff as he handed her out.

He drew her hand within his arm. "I hope both of us
have found what we need to discover before the dawn
sends the last of the guests home."

When she gave him no answer, he did not press her.
He watched her survey the street and the guests entering
Sharla's house. More than once as he led her to the
door, he heard her draw in a sharp breath at the sight
of a supposedly happily married man with his mistress
on his arm.

"Jade, remember where we are," he said quietly.

"I am trying. You must, too. Here I am Jasmine."

"I will make every effort to recall that. This may make
you feel better." He drew out a black mask edged with
lace from beneath his cloak.

"Miss Maguire said nothing about it being a masked
ball."

"I asked her if she would arrange it to be so." He
settled the mask on her face and reached to tie it behind
her. "To make you as comfortable as possible."

As he started to draw his hands away, she clasped his

arms and kept him close. She raised herself up to meet his lips with a kiss that was filled with gratitude and other far more fiery passions. He lowered his arms to curve around her waist and pulled her even more tightly to him. The lace on the mask tickled his face, but he thought only of the sweet invitation on her lips, an invitation to explore every facet of pleasure with her.

But did she mean it, or was he reading meaning into what she might have considered a simple thank you?

He could not tell as they drew back when a carriage rolled to a stop close to where they were standing. With the mask, her face was too shadowed for him to read her expression. Maybe he had been a beef-head to ask Sharla to have her guests come disguised.

"What about a mask for you?" she asked.

"I have not decided if I will wear one."

"Gideon, I know that you think the mask you normally wear will conceal your true thoughts."

"Mask? What mask?"

She took his hand and folded it between her own. "The one you wear with a studied smile and a pose of nonchalance. It has fooled many people, but it has not fooled everyone. Whoever is stalking you, wishing to do you more damage, sees through it."

"And so do you."

"Yes." She laughed softly, startling him. "And so does Miss Maguire."

"Dash it! Why do you have to be so logical?"

"It is easier to think of your concerns than my own tonight."

Gideon was astonished anew. After months of trying to understand why his sister was acting as she did, hiding away from the world where she could nurse her grief and keep it close as if it had replaced Renshaw as her lover, he was unaccustomed to any woman being so forthright. Even Sharla had plied him with fibs when she thought he did not want to be burdened with the truth.

"Maybe you are right." He pulled out another mask he had brought, just in case. This one was stark black with no lace to soften its edges. He settled it in place. "Better?"

"You look the perfect rake now."

"And you my newest bit of muslin."

Again she lapsed into silence while he was greeted by men he called friend and by others who believed the rumors that had sprung seemingly from nowhere about Renshaw's death. Each man craned his neck to get a better look at Jade. He knew everyone would be curious about Lord Bannatyne's latest conquest, who she was and how long she had been in his bed and how long she was likely to stay.

He did not satisfy anyone's curiosity as he led Jade into the house and up the stairs to the grand room Sharla had had constructed on an upper floor. It was less than a quarter of the size of the ballroom at the Duchess of Northborough's house. Already, it was crowded and hot and loud.

In so many ways, the gathering looked like the one at the duchess's house. The women's clothing was glorious; the men's coats and breeches were of the most recent style; the setting glittered like the jewelry worn by both sexes. He noticed how Jade was glancing around, appraising.

"You should fit in here indiscreetly," he murmured.

"I will do my best."

"When have you done anything less?"

When he heard a woman's laugh followed by the cheers of several men, he glanced to his right, then back at Jade. Her eyes widened when she saw a woman lifting the hem of her gown to reveal her leg most of the way to her knee. The men were bending toward it to look at the woman's stockings more closely.

"Oh, my!" Jade gasped.

Gideon chuckled. "If you are shocked by *that*, there is no hope of you hiding your identity through the whole evening. Where would you like to begin your discreet inquiries about the lady you hope to find?"

"I am not sure."

"Gideon! Jasmine!" Sharla rushed up to them, gave them both a hug, and said, "I have some friends whom Jasmine must meet right now."

"Lead on."

"This will be talk among women, Gideon. Why don't you get some champagne and join Rudy and some of the other gentlemen by the large window? I will return Jasmine to you in short order, none the worst for her experiences."

He smiled and nodded, giving Jade's hand a squeeze before releasing it. She would be as safe in Sharla's company as she would with the dour Mrs. Willow watching over her.

Walking to a nearby hearth, Gideon lit a cheroot. A woman waved aside the smoke and turned to chide him. When her eyes met his, she looked hastily away. He smiled coolly. Did she think he would regale her recently acquired husband with the details of the night she had hoped to compromise herself in an effort to force Gideon into marriage? Good luck and the help of his man, Tabor, had foiled the young woman's plans to have her father discover her in Gideon's private chambers. All apparently had ended well, because she had convinced a baron to marry up. He wondered why she was at Sharla's party. Maybe she had tired of her husband and was looking for adventure elsewhere.

As a trio of musicians began to play a cheerful tune, a motion in a shadowed corner caught Gideon's eye. He smiled as he walked to where Stommel was watching Jade and Sharla. He was not surprised at Stommel's interest, and his perusal allowed Gideon to do the same without anyone suspecting the true reason he wanted to keep a close watch on Jade.

"Is that the same young woman," the older man asked, "who was with you when I interrupted you and— that is—?"

"One and the same."

"Sharla seems to have taken that young woman under her wing."

"Sharla has been very generous with instructing . . .

Jasmine." He hoped Stommel did not notice the slight hesitation. He sent another cloud of smoke billowing around them and tapped ashes into a dish on a nearby table.

"Where did you find such an innocent young thing?"

"She actually found me. In a garden, if you can believe that."

"No, but it is a good story." Stommel laughed and took a deep drink of his wine. "Be careful who you lather with your lies, Bannatyne. If others believe you in the habit of telling out-and-outers, they may not accept your protestations of innocence about certain crimes that have been connected to your name."

"Speak plainly."

"Are you expecting me to believe that you have not heard the rumors that your hand brought Sir Mitchell Renshaw's miserable life to an end?" Stommel's deep voice rumbled like a distant storm, even when he spoke barely louder than a whisper.

"Listening to gossip is a waste of time."

"I agree, but there are others who don't. They are speaking of an investigation by Bow Street into Renshaw's death."

Gideon laughed. He ignored the heads that turned to regard the two of them with curiosity. "You are getting your stories mixed up, Stommel. Bow Street is already involved, but in the investigation of Derlan's appalling murder."

Stommel took another sip as he turned to watch his mistress introducing Jade to several of her friends. "Your young woman truly is quite lovely."

"I noticed that."

"I thought you might have." He smiled swiftly, then grew somber again. "You may want to take her home posthaste. To have her connected with you now could be perilous for her."

Gideon scowled as he set the cigar in the bowl. "Something we have already discovered. Have you heard among the rumors floating through Town that there is another attack aimed at me?"

"Yes." Again Stommel tore his gaze from the women and met Gideon's eyes. He wore an expression Gideon had never seen before, an intensity that was almost frightening on such a customarily placid face. "Nothing definite. Otherwise, I would have sent you word immediately, for Sharla considers you a good friend. I would allow nothing to transpire that would make her unhappy, and she would be unhappy to see you dead—either in a so-called accident or on the gallows."

"What have you heard?"

"Only that there have been rumbles that you have escaped justice."

"Who has been saying this?" A single name could be the clue that led him to the truth.

Stommel gave an indifferent shrug. "I have heard it spoken of in many places. I simply wanted to warn you, so that you can take precautions."

"I appreciate your concern."

"I do not wish to see Sharla mourning your death."

"Good of you. I—"

A scream ricocheted through the room. Not just one scream, but several. All in female voices in the back corner of the room. The music ended in a squawk.

Dash it! He had let Stommel's warnings distract him. Where was Jade?

He heard a man's curse come from the same direction of the screams, then the unmistakable thud of a body hitting the floor. He pushed his way through the gathering crowd. Where was Jade?

He got his answer when he stepped past the inner ring of onlookers to see her standing, the lace on her mask torn, beside the prone body of a man. He could not identify the man who was facedown on the floor, with shards of glass surrounding him. He did not care about the man. He ran to Jade and pulled her into his arms. Murmurs surrounded them, but he ignored them as he asked her if she was all right.

"I am fine." Fury punctured each word. "You should see if he is."

Reluctantly he released her to squat on the floor next

to the senseless man. When he rolled him onto his back, he recognized the presumptuous puppy he had seen once or twice before. A younger son, Cummings was enjoying the entertainments of the city with an enthusiasm that dwarfed even Gideon's own first year in London.

"Is he awake?" asked Jade as she bent toward him.

"Not yet."

"Oh, dear. I did not mean to hit him that hard."

"You hit . . . ?"

"He was being overly bold." She touched the ripped lace on her mask.

"So you hit him?"

"Hard." She pointed toward the pieces of glass. "That was a decanter." She shivered, but he suspected it was more with anger than fear. "I made a muddle of the whole evening, didn't I?"

"A muddle sometimes is necessary." Standing, he went to where two women held glasses of wine. He bowed toward them, plucked the glasses from their hands, and walked back to where Cummings still had not moved. He tilted one glass so the wine splattered across the senseless's man's face.

Cummings sputtered, but did not wake.

With a smile, Gideon tipped out the contents of the other glass.

Coughing and wheezing, Cummings opened his eyes and pushed himself up. "Who dares to—"

"I do." Gideon grasped him by the lapels and yanked him to his feet with the sound of snapping threads. "You are fortunate that I am not going to try to knock some sense into your head as this young woman had to."

The man eyed Jade with rage. She clasped her hands in front of her and returned his stare coolly, hoping nobody would notice how her fingers quivered.

"I do believe you owe her an apology," Gideon continued. His voice was so bereft of emotion that she knew he was even more furious than the young man was.

"She—"

"An apology, Cummings." He shook the younger man like a dog with a rat.

Wincing and putting his hand to his head, Mr. Cummings said, "I am sorry, miss."

"Thank you," she replied.

Gideon shoved the other man away a few steps and held out his hand to her. She gladly put hers on it, letting him draw her through the crowd, which opened to let them pass. Behind them, the music began again.

Sharla appeared out of the crowd. "Dear me! Are you all right? I had no idea he would be so outrageous. Otherwise, I would not have allowed him to speak to you."

"I am fine," Jade assured both of them. "Mr. Cummings may have a headache for a few days."

"It is good that she knows how to defend herself," Gideon said, his rage creeping into his voice. "You should choose your guests with more care, Sharla."

"I did not invite him. He came as someone's guest."

Jade put her hand on Gideon's arm. "Do not fault her. She was the one who shoved the decanter into my hand." With a smile as she pulled the loosened lace off her mask, she added, "Thank you, Miss Maguire."

"You are welcome." Her eyes still snapped with annoyance. "And you, Gideon, are welcome to remain at her side to prevent further interruptions to the evening."

"Perhaps we should leave," he said.

"Don't be silly!" Miss Maguire's smile returned as she looked at Jade. Taking the ruined lace, she said, "She has only begun asking about Violet. Give her a chance to be rewarded for the hard work that has brought her to this point."

Gideon was silent as Miss Maguire went to calm her other guests who were buzzing like a swarm of bees at what they had witnessed. Jade was not sure what to say when she had done the very thing she had asked him not to—put her at the center of attention. As the music flowed around them and the guests began to dance in the middle of the floor while a serving maid cleaned up the shattered glass, a pool of silence surrounded them.

Abruptly Gideon cleared his throat and said, "Dance with me."

"I don't know how to waltz."

"You need to learn quickly." He caught her around the waist and tugged her into the pattern of the dance. When she stumbled as she tried to move with him, he said, "Relax and follow my lead. It is simple. One-two-three, one-two-three, one-two-three . . ."

He continued as she matched her steps to his, watching each one. Her skirt swirled around her ankles, and she hoped it still covered her modestly. Why was she worried? All the other guests believed her to be Gideon's doxy, and she would not be out of place flashing an ankle to attract a richer, more powerful man even while she was dancing with him.

"Much better," he murmured.

She looked up and saw he was staring at someone beyond her left shoulder. Each time he turned her, his eyes focused on the same spot. "What is it?"

"Don't ask questions when you will not like the answers."

"A strange request when I have no idea what you are speaking of."

He smiled. "You learn quickly, Jade."

As if on cue, she missed a step. He swept her along, and she struggled to keep up with the tempo.

"Is it Mr. Cummings you are looking at?" she asked.

"You did deny me the chance to avenge your honor by letting me knock Cummings senseless."

"I am sorry."

"So what *did* he say to you?"

She stumbled once more. His arm around her kept her from falling.

"You don't want to know the answer to that," she said.

"Don't be coy, Jade."

"Watch what you call me."

He smiled icily. "I should have said, 'Don't be coy, *Jasmine*.' Why did you knock Cummings senseless?"

"I did not like what he said."

"About me."

She nodded. "He pretended he wanted to warn me

about you, but he had intentions of his own." She glided through several steps without stepping on his toes, then asked, "How did you know?"

"It would appear I owe you thanks for defending my badly blemished honor." He stroked her back in tempo with the music.

"Don't do that," she said, staggering forward to keep up with him.

"Don't do what?"

"Don't intrude on my concentration when I am trying to count my steps."

"Let me help." He drew her closer as he whispered against her hair, "One-two-three, one-two-three . . ."

Her fingers tightened in his when his heated breath coursed along her ear and down her neck. When his thighs brushed hers with each motion, she gazed up into his eyes and surrendered to the music and his touch. He kept repeating the count in a succulent whisper, and she moved with him in perfect unison. Nothing had ever been as sensual as this rhythm; they might as well have been alone on the floor.

Then the song ended.

A sigh escaped her lips, for the ephemeral moment was gone. Or was it? As he murmured her name, she met his eyes once more. What she saw there was the longing within her.

"It is time to leave," she whispered.

"But—"

"Now, Gideon. Before I change my mind and regret that we have lost this night together."

A slow smile edged across his lips before climbing up to crinkle the skin around his eyes. Putting his arm around her waist once more, he steered her through the guests toward the door. He turned to the left when they reached the top of the stairs.

"Where are you going?" she asked.

"There is a very private chamber along this hallway." He stroked her face his fingertips. "We will not be disturbed."

"Not here," she whispered. "You and Miss Maguire were lovers in this house."

"That is over, sweetling. Years ago."

She ran her hands across his chest and heard his breath catch. "I know that, Gideon. But I want our first time to be a first for both of us."

"I know just the place."

"Where?"

He smiled. "Trust me, Jade. You will like it."

While he ushered her down the stairs, out of the house, and into his carriage, he refused to answer her questions about where they were bound. She had no interest in asking questions when he sat beside her in the carriage and thrilled her with kisses that told her that he was as eager as she was to share the passions ready to explode within them. Even when the carriage slowed, he insisted that she put on his cloak and draw the hood up, so she could not see where they were.

Jade let herself get caught up in the game as well as his delight in trying to make every minute exciting for her. Even so, she was shocked when, instead of handing her out of the carriage, he swept her up in his arms. She realized he was holding her so that the cloak blocked any chance she would have to guess where they were.

She smelled water. She heard creaking boards and the gentle slap of water against a shore. Smiling, because she was certain she knew where he had brought her, she relaxed in his arms, letting his hard muscles cradle her.

Then he set her on her feet. She threw back the hood as she felt motion beneath her. "*Perdition's Folly*!" She smiled as she undid her mask and looked around the steamboat's cabin. "Here?"

"Where better, sweetling?" He laughed as he took her mask and set it with his on one of the benches. Lighting a single lamp, he added, "I have been waiting with very little patience to bring you back to finish what Mrs. Willow interrupted."

The thought of those sensual kisses threatened the stability of her knees. She glanced around the cabin again. "But . . . the benches?"

"I think not." He reached for the doors of what she had assumed were cupboards. Swinging a pair open, he revealed a bed built into the boat's wall. It was not very broad, but it had room for two lying very close together. "Will this do?"

"Perfectly." She slipped her hands up under the shoulders of his coat and slid it off his arms. As it fell to the deck, his lips covered hers, coaxing and teasing. Then the gentle, lingering kiss disappeared as his mouth pressed deeply into hers. As his breath grew uneven against her, she sensed his desire inflaming him . . . and her.

When his mouth drifted to the vale between her breasts, amazing sensations roiled within her. She swept her arms around him, bringing him closer. She could not deny him—or herself—any longer. She needed to sate this craving that came from deep within her most intimate recesses.

Her own frayed breaths brushed her against him until she wanted to feel him all along her. His arm curved around her, and his hand cupped her breast. Excitement rippled along her when his fingers—so strong, yet so tender—caressed her. She ached for him.

She met his mouth with her own. She wanted all the ecstasy they could share. No, it was more than a want. She *needed* the satiation only he could give her.

His tongue tasted the corners of her mouth, and she smiled. Her lips softened, and his tongue teased hers. She giggled, even as liquid fire flooded her body.

"What is so funny?" he asked in a gruff voice.

"I never imagined I would be ticklish here." She stuck out her tongue.

"Let's discover where else you are ticklish, shall we?" He stroked her sides as his tongue slipped along her ear.

She moaned, unable to halt the sound. Each touch incited the fervor more. When he sat on the bed, he brought her down beside him. The motion of the boat swayed her against him.

"Now I know," she said, "why you brought me here."

"I thought that was obvious." He ran his finger along the deep neckline of her gown.

She caught his finger, halting him, because she could not think clearly when he touched her. "You brought me here, because this is a very special place for you. You designed *Perdition's Folly,* and you savor every minute you can be here."

"Never more than now when you are with me, sweetling."

"And we can rock with the soft waves, letting the boat be a part of our rapture."

He drew back and regarded her with astonishment. "I did not think of that, I must own." His smile returned. "But I do like how you think."

"I don't want to think. I want to feel." She wrapped her arms around his shoulders and leaned back on the blanket that smelled of dampness and mold, but it was the sweetest perfume she could imagine.

His hand curved over her breast, toying with it. She loosened his shirt from his breeches, slipping her hands beneath it. His skin was deliciously warm. Touching him would not be enough. She wanted to taste him.

He sat up and undid his waistcoat, shrugging it off. Rising to her knees, she halted him from unbuttoning his shirt.

She smiled and whispered, "Let me."

"I will let you do whatever you want, except leave."

"I am not leaving. Not now." *Not ever,* she wanted to add, but she did not want to talk. She wanted to discover every inch of his male body as he taught her about her feminine one.

He scattered kisses across her cheek before trailing moist warmth along her neck. When his lips reached the top of her gown, he reached behind her and unhooked it with a speed that told her he had imagined doing this with her often. Just as she had dreamed of the thrill of his touch.

She gasped as his fervid kisses blazed along her, demanding her surrender to passion. It took all her strength to pull away from him long enough to lift her gown over her head. She tossed it out of the bed, not caring where it went or if she ever redressed. She wanted to stay here with him. She undid the rest of her clothes, and his eyes followed each motion, the flame in them growing even more fierce. When she sat again on the edge of the bed to take off her stockings, he pulled her back down onto the pillows.

"Save some of the fun for me, sweetling," he said with a ragged laugh.

He held her gaze as he drew up her right leg and slowly slipped a single finger under the top of her stockings. He did not look away as he rolled her stocking down. She struggled to breathe and to hold still. She never had guessed such a commonplace action as removing her stockings could be erotic. After drawing off that one, he lifted her left ankle and set it on his shoulder. Now he was looking *over* her leg at her. She gasped when he used his teeth, their smoothness grazing her leg to pull it off the last few inches. Her fingers clenched on the blanket, as her body was riveted with a tempest of sensations, each one new and exciting and more powerful than the one before it.

Sitting up, she drew her leg down and reached to open his shirt the rest of the way. She ran her fingers across his brawny chest. She could imagine him working, sweaty and tanned, on the boat. Just as she could imagine her beside him as they sailed off to spend days exploring the sea and nights exploring each other.

When he leaned her back on the bed, she entwined her legs with his. He laved the skin across the top of her chemise, and she moaned with the longing.

It took him only moments to divest her of the rest of her smallclothes. He drew her hand to the buttons on his breeches. She did not hesitate. She wanted to give herself completely to the wanton she had tried to portray tonight.

His male body fascinated her. She stroked his chest, then as he pressed her back into the bed, grew more bold. When she curled her fingers around the silken shaft between his legs, she knew it soon would be between hers. His groan of need throbbed through her with a sultry fire as he cried out her name.

He set her skin ablaze with his kisses and caresses. She was sure she was about to dissolve in his arms when his hand slipped up her inner leg. Now she gasped in astonishment as he slid one finger deep within her. She clutched onto his shoulders as she had the bed.

In her ear, he whispered, "Another dance for you to learn tonight, sweetling. This one has a slightly different tempo. One and two, in and out, together and away, ebb and flow, deep and recede, you and me. Yes, you and me." He repeated the words over and over as he had when they waltzed.

She became the words. Then she became the rhythm as she writhed beneath him. With a shudder, she was overwhelmed by sensation. It consumed her, sweeping her into ultimate pleasure.

When she opened her eyes again, the sound of her own panting loud in her ears, she gazed at him. She wanted to say something, but no words seemed sufficient. Reaching up both hands, she drew his mouth down over hers.

He rose over her and, with his lips still on hers, drove deep within her. She choked out another gasp at a twinge of pain, but the need muted it as her body demanded more ecstasy. Moving with him, she recalled the tempo he had whispered in her ear. He drew his mouth away from hers as he gasped with the escalating need. She sensed his explosion moments before she vanished once more into rapture. A rapture she wanted with only him tonight and forever.

Jade opened her eyes as shouts came from beyond *Perdition's Folly*.

"Pay no attention," came Gideon's whisper. "Just some drunken sailors."

"I want the world to stay away a while longer."

"It will stay away as long as we both wish it to." He leaned on his elbow and smiled down at her. "You are a tigress, sweetling. Such passion!"

"Inspired by you." She tapped his nose. "What other dances do you have to teach me tonight?"

"I am sure there are one or two that I could help you learn." He pressed his mouth to where her neck met her shoulder.

She quivered as her body was buffeted with the craving that had not lessened. She had been sure it would after they became lovers, but he had shown her that not even a second time was enough to ease the need completely. In fact, it seemed even stronger now.

"I am ready to learn whatever you have to teach me."

"So I have seen."

She laughed. "Do not sound too proud of yourself, Gideon."

"Why not? I told you that you would succumb to me before seven days had passed, and you have."

"What?" She pulled back and stared at him, her happiness extinguished. "Is that all I am to you? An easy victory?"

"Jade, you know that is not true."

"No? Then why did you mention it?"

"I was only teasing." He sat when she did.

"Were you? Is this only for tonight, Gideon?"

He shook his head. "No! I told you that I wanted you for more than a single night."

"That is right!" Swinging her legs over the side of the bed, she stood. She picked up her chemise and slipped it on. "You wanted me for a whole month before you moved on to your next conquest. How stupid could I be! I thought you might love me, too."

"Love?" His eyes widened. "Jade, what made you think that?"

"There is no need to answer when it is clear that I have been only bamboozling myself." She would have felt even worse to list the reasons she had dared to trust him: his kindness to her sisters; his insistence right here on his boat that the Bow Street Runner do nothing to taint her reputation; and how he had made her smile as she had not since her father died.

Standing, he caught her by the shoulders. "Jade, don't

leave in a pelter. We do not need to set a limit on our nights together."

"So I can stay with you as long as we both want."

"Yes!" He smiled.

"What if I want it to be for the rest of our lives?"

When he did not answer, she moved away from him. It was the most difficult thing she had ever done. She pulled on her dress, then tossed his cloak over it, not waiting to hook herself up and not willing to ask his help. She jammed her feet into her slippers. Paying no attention to her stockings on the deck, she walked toward the door. She hoped, on every step, that he would tell her to stop, to come back to him, to be his forever.

He said nothing, and she hurried out into the darkness. She had never felt so alone.

Chapter 17

The room Mrs. Atkinson led them to on the third floor of the duchess's house was as luxurious as any in Gideon's home. It contained two large beds, a marble hearth, a small mahogany table, and a pair of overstuffed chairs in front of a window offering a view of the garden.

"I hope you do not mind sharing this room, Miss Nethercott," the buxom housekeeper said with an uneasy smile at China. "The duchess has many guests now, so we cannot offer you each a room."

"It is fine," Jade hurried to reply when China said nothing. She set her bag on the closer bed. "We are grateful that Her Grace was able to find any place for us on such short notice."

With a sigh, Sian sat on the room's sole chair. China perched on the edge of the bed. Both looked exhausted. And why not? Jade had wakened them in the middle of the night and insisted that they leave Gideon's house immediately. They had asked questions, but when Jade avoided answering them, they seemed to understand that she was not ready to talk about what had happened.

How could she explain to her sisters? She had allowed herself to be taken in by a rake's smooth patter and had even dared to believe he might be falling in love with her as she had with him. At what point had she lost her perspective? Had it been the moment he mistook her for one of his convenients in the duchess's garden? His touch, his smile, his easy laugh . . . She had been gulled by his practiced skills until she invited herself into his bed.

Exactly as he had said she would.

She should have seen right from the onset that the chase was the sport he truly enjoyed. Once he had bedded her, he was glad to stay until the hunger for new prey drew him away. He had been honest with her right from the beginning. She had refused to believe him, instead creating the man she wanted him to be.

That was why she was no longer furious with him. He had done exactly as he had said he would. What irked her was that *she* had done exactly as he had said she would.

Bother! It should be easy to turn her back on Gideon and his philandering bachelor fare, but her heart refused to see sense even now.

A knock was set on the door, and Jade went to open it. Tabor stood in the hall with the larger of the two bags they had packed at Gideon's house. Everything else could wait until later.

The valet set the large bag just inside the room and turned to leave. He paused and faced her. "May I have a word with you, Miss Jade?"

"Yes." She stepped into the hallway and closed the door.

She waited for him to speak, but he acted as if he had no more voice than the portraits lining the walls. In the twilight of the half-lit corridor, she tried to stifle a yawn . . . and the tears that oozed up into her eyes whenever she let her guard down, even for a second.

"Thank you, Tabor, for coming to help us tonight," said Jade softly to fill the void of uncomfortable silence. "Gideon is fortunate to have you serving him with such devotion."

"Devotion? If I were as devoted to him as you suggest, do you think I would have helped you and your sisters sneak out of the house in the middle of the night?" His usually calm countenance altered with the anger that she could tell he was struggling to restrain.

"Miss Jade, I implore you to give Lord Bannatyne another chance. With a bit more time, you will see he meant you no dishonor."

"My time with him is over. Nothing will change Gideon. He exults in his ravaged reputation. You know that."

"No, I don't," he insisted, taking her arm as she turned to go back into the room.

She was shocked at his untoward action. He had always displayed perfect manners in her presence. "Tabor, I don't think there is anything more to say."

"Yes, there is!" he asserted. "I know Lord Bannatyne better than you do. He cares more for you than he has any woman. Whether he will own to it or not, he needs you now. You have brought a joy back to his life that disappeared when tragedy descended on his family."

"He does not need me." *Not the way you mean,* she added silently. Gideon did want her in his bed, but once the thrill of the pursuit was over, he would be gone. She preferred to walk away from him before he could leave her. "Good-bye, Tabor." She went into the bedchamber and did not look back. That part of her life must now be over.

"Jade, are you still abed?" came a call from the hallway. Sian peeked into the room.

Her sisters were thrilled to be in the duchess's fine house. The duchess was so distressed by their misadventures, first with the tree falling through the roof of the house she had found for them, and then having to accept Gideon's hospitality that she insisted that they must be made to feel at home.

Jade pushed herself up against the pillow. Her eyes were burning from lack of sleep, and her mind seemed encased in honey, because every thought was an effort. In the near week since they had left Gideon's house, she had gotten about eight hours of sleep . . . total. She had stared at the ceiling while her sisters slept. When they woke, she pretended to be lost in dreams so she did not have to see the sympathy . . . no, the pity in their eyes that reminded her how much of an air-dreamer she had been.

"I am getting up," she said when Sian bounced into the room, acting as excited as a child with a new hair ribbon.

"Then hurry and get dressed. Breakfast is being served, and there is a very, very handsome gentleman the duchess wishes to introduce me to. Do come with me and keep me from saying something·silly."

"You may be asking the wrong person."

Sian laughed and, sitting on the edge of the bed, linked her arm through Jade's. "You are the most sensible woman I know, and you will keep me from saying something skimble-skamble."

Realizing that her sister would not accept any answer but an agreement, Jade quickly dressed and went with Sian to the elegant room where breakfast was being served. The room seemed too bright to her aching eyes, and a multitude of voices added to the pain arcing across her skull. She wondered how long a person could go without sleep.

A very tall ginger-hackled man, whom the duchess hurried across the room to meet Sian, seemed as dubious about what to say or do as her younger sister.

"Constantine Lassiter, eighth Earl Lastingham," the duchess announced as if she were a footman at one of her own gatherings, "allow me to present Miss Sian Nethercott."

"Lastingham?" Sian asked. "We have a town by that name not far from Nethercott Castle."

"Is that so?" He brightened, and Jade saw her sister had been accurate in her assessment of the earl. He was very good-looking with severely sculpted features that created interesting planes across his face.

"The town's church has the most interesting crypt. From the eleventh century."

"Will you tell me about it?"

Jade edged away, leaving them to their conversation. A pinch of envy dismayed her. She had had a chance to enjoy a handsome man's attentions on this trip to Lon-

don, so she should not begrudge her sister the opportunity. She hoped Sian's flirtation would lead somewhere
happier than where Jade had gone in hopes that Gideon
would love her, too.

She did not join in with the long conversation over
breakfast and another at midday where once again Lord
Lastingham chose a seat next to Sian's. Instead, she ex-
cused herself as quickly as she could. She did not want
to see anyone. She preferred to nurse her broken heart
in private.

She grew more despondent as the day went on. If her
sisters noticed, they kept that to themselves. Maybe they
knew that nothing they said or did would make her
feel better.

She could not help wondering if Gideon was sharing
her melancholy. Her lips tilted in derogatory humor. She
could not imagine him pining after any woman. Certainly
not Jade Nethercott who had lured him into his bed and
proven that he had been right when he said she would
come to him before the seven days passed. Maybe Gideon's silence when she left had been wise. There had
been nothing he needed to say, because once she walked
out of his house and his life, he was no longer a part
of hers.

If only it were that easy.

The light was not good for sketching, but Jade knew
it did not matter. Her skills were far inferior to Sian's.
Her attempt to sketch the scene from her window had
been a disaster. The garden arbor looked more like . . .
She added a few more lines, and she realized the drawing was evolving into a picture of *Perdition's Folly*. As
she added the windows of the long cabin, she sighed.

A week had passed. If Gideon missed her as she did
him, surely he would have called. Or was pride keeping
him away? That was a comforting thought, but she must
not soothe herself with what might be a lie. The rest of
their possessions had been delivered to the Duchess of
Northborough's house yesterday. There had been no
note, not even one from Tabor asking her to reconsider.

Light glared off the page, and Jade looked up. She sighed again. Every day, she had expected Sir Mitchell to appear. It was a confrontation she wanted over. Every day, there had been no sign of the ghost. She had begun to wonder if he would not appear again.

Now he was materializing.

Without a greeting, he asked, "What have you learned?"

"I have learned that there is nothing more I can do." She gathered up her art materials and, rising, set them on the table beside her chair. "I am sorry, Sir Mitchell, but I am finished."

"What do you mean that you are finished?" he asked. "You have not found the proof to send Bannatyne to hang."

"You will have to get someone else's help."

"You know that is impossible."

"Why?" She leaned back on the thick windowsill. "There is no reason on earth or in heaven why I would be the sole living person to see you. Find someone else!"

"Why have you changed your mind?"

"It is nothing I care to discuss."

He swore vehemently. "It is Bannatyne, isn't it?"

"I said it was nothing that I care to discuss. Please leave it at that."

"You *must* help me. You are the only one who can now."

"I am sorry, Sir Mitchell." She pushed away from the window. "I have done all I can to help you. I can do no more."

"If you do not, he will succeed in avoiding justice for my murder!"

"Will he?" She walked toward him, so vexed that she could disregard the fierce cold surrounding him. "Will he really, Sir Mitchell?"

"Are you questioning me?"

"Yes! You have given me information that is worthless, and I have believed you."

"You are defending him because he has wooed you to his side. He has taken you under his roof and probably into his bed, and you now are as blind to the truth as everyone else."

She laughed sharply. "Do you see where we are, Sir Mitchell? We are at the home of the Duchess of Northborough."

"We are?" His brow rutted. "Why?"

"The reasons are not important to the investigation of your murder. What is important is the truth, and I believe you have very little of that. You have said you were to meet Gideon and enjoy the company of some harlots."

"Yes."

"Then why was Lady Persis present when you were slain? Gideon would never bring his sister into such a situation."

He did not respond, shocking her because he always had a quick retort to any of her questions or comments.

"That is why," she said, pressing her point, "I believe you have confused the moment of your death with another. It is said that one's life passes before one's eyes just before life is over. That is why I think you think you see and hear Gideon and Lady Persis as you were dying. Your memories took you away from death's agonies to a better time when you were happy."

"Are you saying that I do not know the truth of my own death?"

"I am saying you are confused."

"You are a fool, Jade Nethercott! You have created a scenario that allows you to convince yourself that Bannatyne had no hand in my death. I have tried to warn you."

"No, you have tried to betwattle me by making the facts fit your assumption of who killed you and why. I will not listen any longer. Chase your theories, if you wish, but I will have no more part in it."

She was surprised the whole house did not tremble with his screech of rage. She put her hands up to cover her ears, but the ghost and his fury were gone. Lowering her arms slowly, she shuddered. The idea of having a ghost at daggers drawn with her was unsettling. What choice did she have? She had to be honest with him.

But I was snappish when Gideon was honest with me.

She ignored her conscience. She did not need to be dressed down again. China had already lectured her on the mistakes made during the past week. That had not been necessary, because Jade was aware of every single one.

And she was aware, too, that she had tossed aside her best and probably only chance to speak with her father again. Tears washed up into her eyes. She blinked them away. Even though she knew Father would want her to remain true to what she believed, she felt as if she had lost him anew.

What would she tell her sisters? They had hoped she would succeed in proving their father's hypotheses about ghosts. She was glad she had never revealed her true bargain with the baronet's ghost.

Sitting, she picked up the sketch. She started to work on it, then put it on the table. Wallowing in what could have been would add to her grief. That was not the way of the Nethercotts. It was time for her to remember that.

"Miss Nethercott?" asked a maid, poking her head around the bedroom door in the hour after the midday meal.

Jade looked up from the seam she was closing on a dress Sian had torn—when?—and which was ripped beyond Sian's skills with a needle. "Which one are you seeking?"

"Miss Jade Nethercott."

"Then you have found her."

The maid came in, her apron flapping around her legs. With a half curtsy, she held out a folded slip of paper.

Jade opened it and read the few words over Lady Persis's signature. "When did this arrive?"

"Only a few minutes ago," the maid said. "I was sent with it to find you as quickly as possible."

"Thank you." She smiled at the maid, who gave another quick curtsy and rushed out of the room.

Jade set the gown on another chair and rose. She could not sit while she read the note.

My dear Miss Nethercott,

I have learned that you are determined to prove my brother's innocence in the matter of Sir Mitchell Renshaw's murder. If you still are interested in doing so, I suggest you give a call at this house, which he frequents. I suspect you may find information there to assist you.

It included an address she did not recognize, but she knew little of London.

Jade was astonished. When she had called on the lady, Gideon's sister had been adamant in her belief that Gideon had slain her fiancé. The note suggested a complete change of heart. It might be a sign that Lady Persis was coming to terms with her loss and making a decision to move ahead with her life.

Gideon had been hurt by his sister's assumption of his guilt. To discover that she had changed her mind would be a great relief to him.

She refolded the letter and set it on the table. Going to the cupboard, she took out her reticule. She picked up the page and slipped it in. If she had half the wits she claimed to possess, she would find some paper and ink and write a note back to Lady Persis expressing her regrets that finding out the truth about Sir Mitchell's death was no longer her concern. If she had quarter of the wits she claimed to possess, she would call for a footman and have the letter delivered into Gideon's hand.

Instead, she picked up her paisley shawl and her bonnet. Opening the larger bag, she drew out her parasol. She would never forgive herself if she lost what might be her last opportunity to speak with Gideon. It might be the most foolish choice she had ever made, but she was willing to take that risk.

Gideon wiped his filthy hands on a rag and frowned at the steam engine. One of the seals had popped, and it had taken him all week to repair it. He could have left the repairs to someone else, but doing them himself allowed him to forget—for a few seconds—about Jade.

Dash it! She was a confounded woman, and she had failed to see the good sense of enjoying each other for as long as they both wanted. Instead she had stormed out like an overemoting actress in a bad play, denying them the pleasure that could have been theirs.

He had found it simpler to be here on *Perdition's Folly* where he could avoid questions about why she was no longer seen in his company. By now, the *ton* must be abuzz with rumors of why the Nethercott sisters had left his house in the middle of the night and had sought sanctuary at the home of the Duchess of Northborough.

Not that he cared what the Polite World thought. And what had he done other than accept Jade's invitation to make love with her?

"Dash it!" he repeated aloud.

Footfalls sounded on the deck beyond the cabin. He instantly recognized them, for he had been listening for them—even though he had not owned to that, not even to himself—for the past week. When a slender silhouette appeared in the doorway, he heard, "May I come in?"

How could he have forgotten—even for a moment—the warm huskiness of Jade's voice? He had thought he heard its echo through his dreams when he was able to sleep, but that sound had been a weak imitation of reality. He thrilled in the sight of her firm breasts beneath her sprigged linen gown, which followed the curves of her lithe body. She looked lovely in the simple gown, but he knew how much more beautiful she would be without it. Every muscle reacted to that thought, and he wanted to pull her into his arms.

"Please come in," he replied.

"Is something wrong with the engine?" she asked, looking past him.

"A minor problem, but I have fixed it." He motioned toward the bench. "Will you sit?"

"Thank you."

Their words belonged to strangers, polite and with as little emotion as possible. Yet when he sat beside her, he caught her gaze before she could avert her head, concealing her face with her bonnet. In her eyes were the fires that had melded them together in the bed across the cabin. He cupped her chin and tilted her mouth toward his like a starving man finally able to dine on his favorite sweet.

"No," she whispered.

"No?" He must have heard her wrong. She did not want him to kiss her? Then why had she returned to where they could be alone to share ecstasy?

"No." She lifted her chin out of his palm and turned away. She loosened the strings on her reticule and drew out a folded page. "You need to read this."

"Now?" He could not imagine anything that could not wait until after he had shared her wondrous body again.

"Yes."

He took the page. It was not one piece of paper, but two, he discovered when a second sheet dropped onto the bench. Picking it up, he opened it. "Is this drawing of *Perdition's Folly*?"

Her eyes grew round. "Oh, bother! I did not mean for you to see that." She held out her hand. "It is very amateur."

"Quite to the contrary. You have captured some of the boat's best lines." He folded the sheet and smiled. "I would like to keep it, if you don't mind."

"It is yours, if you want it."

In spite of her cool tone, he could tell she was pleased that he appreciated her simple sketch. "Thank you, Jade."

"You should read the other page."

He scanned it. "When did you receive this?"

"Are you suggesting that I have kept this from you?" She came to her feet, her voice icy. "The only delay in bringing it to you was that I first called at Bedford Square, thinking you might be there."

"You are looking for accusations where I intended none, sweetling."

She flinched at the endearment, and he dropped the letter on the bench before setting himself on his feet.

"I am very pleased to see that your sister has reconsidered her opinion of you. I thought you would be, too. I hope whoever is at that address can help you persuade your sister and everyone else of your innocence in the baronet's tragic death. I wish you the best of luck with that." She took a single step toward the door, then went on without looking at him, "Good afternoon."

"Good afternoon?" he roared, his temper fraying past the point of control. "Is that all you have to say? It has been over a week since you scurried away like a frightened child."

She did not answer as she walked away.

He stepped in front of her, blocking her path to the door. "Was delivering that letter the *only* reason you came here?"

"Yes." She refused to meet his eyes. "I know you think you are irresistible, but what you are offering is not what I want."

"No? You don't want *this*?" He pulled her to him and captured her mouth.

For a moment, she was rigid in his arms. Then, slowly as her bonnet fell back to hang by its ribbons, she returned his ravenous kiss. He heard her whisper his name as his mouth rediscovered the luscious flavors along her neck. He must have her now. He had never wanted any woman as he wanted her.

She pushed him away with a soft cry. Pulling her bonnet over her hair, she said, "No, Gideon, I will not let you seduce my good sense from me again."

"May I remind you that you seduced me?"

Color flashed up her face before her cheeks became ashen. "I do not believe that we have anything else to say to each other."

"So you will run away again?" The words once begun spilled out of his mouth before he could halt them. "You are like my sister, aren't you? Afraid to allow yourself to be happy again because you think that will be a betrayal to the grief you have worn like a royal cloak."

Her hand on his cheek made a sharp sound that resonated through the cabin. "I have endured enough of your arrogance, my lord. Good afternoon."

"Or do you mean good-bye?"

"Whichever you prefer it to be." She walked out of the cabin. He was about to give chase when he heard her say, "Good afternoon, Mr. Ward."

Ward? Why was the Bow Street Runner on the boat? Curiosity taunted him, but, even so, he still considered halting Jade and asking her to come back into the cabin. He had handled the conversation wrong from the start. So thrilled to see her, he had not imagined—until she left—that she had not returned to join him in his bed. She remained infuriated at him, but she had risked what could have been an even more acrimonious encounter to bring him Persis's letter because she had believed it would make him feel better.

Dash it! She had made every effort to help his dreary spirits, and he had done nothing but lower hers.

"Lord Bannatyne!" came a call from the doorway.

He focused his scowl on Ward. "What are you doing here?"

"I have information that I thought you would be interested in, my lord." He smiled broadly as he glanced around the cabin. "This is a very odd vessel. Do you think you can make the boat seaworthy?"

He was not going to discuss his plans for *Perdition's Folly* with the Bow Street Runner who already seemed to know too much. "What information do you have for me?"

"Very good information, but this information will not be free."

"Name your price."

Ward did, and Gideon pretended to be shocked. In truth, he was, but because the amount the Robin Redbreast wanted was far less than he had expected.

He went to a bench and opened the top. He drew out a portable writing desk and set it on the bench. Unstoppering an ink bottle stored inside, he took out a sheet of paper. He scribbled the amount Ward wanted along with his authorization to pay it. He signed it with a flourish before saying, "Take this to Mr. Heath the solicitor. He will arrange payment for you."

Ward reached for the page.

Gideon jerked it out of his reach. "The information, Ward, then the payment."

"How do I know if you will pay?"

"Are you calling me a cheat? Do you think I will bilk you out of your rightfully earned fee?" He smiled coolly. "May I emphasize *rightly earned*? I am not interested in purchasing information I already have."

"I doubt you are aware of this, my lord." Without asking permission, he sat on another section of the bench. He folded his arms in front of him, then smiled. "If you did, you would not be here."

"Where would I be?"

"Wherever Miss Nethercott is right now." He paused, clearly waiting for a reaction from Gideon. When Gideon kept his face blank, Ward continued, "Or maybe, after seeing her sorrowful face as she left the boat, you do not care any longer what happens to her. That would concur with what I have heard." Ward laughed. "Do you know that it is being said that she tossed you over because she found you in bed with her sister? Or both sisters? That your sister threw the whole lot of you out of the Bedford Square house because of your lewd behaviors? That—?"

"Enough!" he snarled. "I did not realize that Bow Street made it a habit to listen to ridiculous gossip."

"We Runners listen to everything, my lord. Even in the most ridiculous gossip, there can be an element of truth." He winked. "Sometimes a very pleasurable element of truth."

Gideon suppressed his fury at the insult to Jade and her sisters. If he already had Ward's information, he would have taken two handfuls of the man's waistcoat and hoisted him over the rail and dunked him in the Thames.

"You suggested," he said in a serene voice, "that I should be concerned about Miss Nethercott's welfare."

Ward could not hide his shock at Gideon's calm answer. He sputtered for a moment, then said, "It has come to our attention that your enemy intends to focus his attention on her."

"Tell me his specific words."

"He said that they intend to destroy her. That doing so would be the greatest injury they could do to you."

Gideon cursed. He knew his family's enemies were without honor, but he had not imagined that they would turn their focus on Jade. Until now, he had assumed the attacks had been solely aimed at him . . . even though the last two had been when she was with him. He had been an utter fool.

Chapter 18

Jade wished she had never taken Lady Persis's message to Gideon. She should have listened to her head, which told her to have it delivered. Instead, she had heeded her heart, and it had been broken anew.

She had not returned directly to the duchess's house. She had gone to Grosvenor Square to view the wreckage and see if repairs had begun. The Duchess of Northborough had urged her not to worry about the house, that the duchess would arrange to have it returned to its one-time beauty.

Yet, Jade had driven the simple cart into the square and watched as workmen carried debris out and piled it by the street. She was not sure how long she had sat there, but, when the workmen left at the end of their day, she turned the cart out of the square.

She did not want to return to the duchess's house. She wanted to go home. To go to Nethercott Castle and to the time before Father had died. How simple life had been when the greatest cause for concern was if she would be able to defend her opinion to her father in their next discussion.

As soon as she entered the duchess's house, she heard, "She is here! She is here! Finally!"

Almost instantly her sisters raced down the stairs and enveloped her in smothering embraces. She was almost knocked from her feet. Disentangling herself from her sisters, she gave an uneasy laugh.

"I know I am late," she said.

Instead of chiding her as she had expected, China cried, "Thank heavens you are safe!"

Sian hugged her again. "When you did not come home, we feared the worst. Are you all right?"

"I am fine," Jade said, confused. "I stopped at Grosvenor Square. I should not have lingered as long as I did, but I needed some time to think, and I am here in plenty of time to change and join everyone for the music."

Sian choked out, "She does not know."

"Know what?"

China took her arm and said, "Come with us. Nobody else needs to witness this."

"Witness what?"

Neither of her sisters answered as they hurried her into a small room off the front foyer. When Sian closed the double doors, she burst into tears.

"What is wrong?" Jade asked.

China dropped onto the closest chair. " 'Tis Lord Bannatyne."

Fear threatened to turn her to stone. Somehow, she pushed herself forward to kneel by her sister's chair. She had seen such a distraught expression on her sister's face only once before—when China had come to tell her sisters that their father was taking his last breaths.

"Is Gideon alive?" Jade whispered.

From by the door, Sian said through her sobs, "First we heard he was dead, and we feared you were, too, when we learned a message had been delivered here from Bedford Square and then you had the cart brought for you."

Jade sat back on her heels, gripping the chair so hard her nails cut into the upholstery. "But is he alive?" She did not want to believe that after so many failed attempts on his life, one had succeeded.

"The duchess received word that he is alive," China said, throwing her arms around Jade. "He is alive, but gravely injured. It is a miracle he survived."

"What happened?"

"His boat exploded."

Jade rocked back as if the detonation was right in front of her. "*Perdition's Folly* exploded?" She thought of Gideon working on the boat. He had been sure he had repaired whatever had been wrong.

"No one has said what caused the accident," China said.

Jade pushed herself to her feet. "I doubt it was an accident."

China glanced at Sian, then whispered, "Are you saying someone made the boat to explode?"

"Yes."

Sian put her arm around Jade's shoulders. "You are upset. You should rest. Such thoughts are sure to distress you more."

"I am not distressed. I am outraged! Can nobody else see the truth right in front of our faces? First Lord Derlan's death when he was mistaken for Gideon."

"You cannot be sure of that," China said.

Jade wanted to hug her sisters as they fell into the familiar pattern of questioning every assumption to whittle the facts down to the pure truth. "No, but there seems no other reason for his death, especially in light of the ambush in Hyde Park and the arranged accident where Gideon's carriage was wrecked."

"Why would anyone want to kill Gideon?" Sian tapped her chin as she began to pace the room. "He has a wicked reputation, but so do many other men. They are lauded, not stalked."

"There have been other deaths in his family, deaths that have brought the title to him."

"Which, of course, made him a suspect in the deaths, even though they, too, were deemed accidental." Sian's shoulders sagged as she sank into another chair. "Oh, my! Now I can see why you are questioning what made the boat explode."

Jade smiled at her younger sister. "I am glad you understand. I must go and learn the truth about Gideon's condition."

As she hurried toward the closed doors, she heard China call her name.

"I must find out the truth!" Jade insisted as she opened one of the doors.

China crossed the room to her. "Take someone with you. Someone burly who will make anyone think twice about attacking you."

"Yes." She hugged her sister again before running out in the hall. She shouted for a footman, hoping he would fit China's specifications. She wanted to believe she would not need such brawn, but she could not be sure of anything any longer.

Jade stepped out of the carriage in front of Gideon's house. She smiled when she saw the glow from the window she knew was in his private chamber. Then her smile faded. Such a light could mean he was being tended to.

The window below belonged to Lady Persis's room. The plants that usually sat on the sill were gone. As she stepped onto the walkway, she saw a small pile of dirt and some broken pottery. One of them must have fallen out of the window. It was firmly closed now, just as all the other windows were.

Climbing the four steps to the landing in front of the door, she reached up to knock. It opened before she could rap. A footman peered out as if he feared the murderer would appear at the front door.

He recovered himself and said, "Lord Bannatyne is not at home, Miss Nethercott." He looked over her head, and she guessed he was trying to hide that he was lying.

"The light is on in his chamber."

"I should have said that Lord Bannatyne is not at home for you, Miss Nethercott."

"But—"

"Lord Bannatyne is not at home *for you*. I was told to say exactly that if you were to call."

She recoiled as if he had hit her. The words were as much of a slap to the face as an open palm. "Did Lord Bannatyne himself give that order?"

"Yes."

His answer sent both pain and relief through her. If Gideon had been able to give that order, he must be well enough to speak.

"Will you take a message to him for me?" she asked.

"No, Miss Nethercott."

"Is there someone I can speak to?" She knew it was not likely, but asked anyhow. "May I speak with Lady Persis?"

"She is seeing no one now."

"Then may I speak with Tabor?"

The footman faltered, and she knew he had not been given specific orders to answer that question. "I must find out, Miss Nethercott."

When he started to close the door, she put her hand out to halt him. She suspected he would leave her standing on the doorstep and pretend that he never had spoken with her.

"Miss Nethercott, I cannot—"

"Leave me out here when there may be a murderer lurking nearby to finish what he started earlier?"

The footman's face turned almost as green as his livery. He did not open the door wider, but he did not try to shut it either.

As he rushed away to find Tabor, she let herself in. She considered, for the length of a single heartbeat, going up the stairs without waiting for an escort. If Gideon *was* badly hurt, her intrusion could lead to further damage. He would try to show her that he was hale, no matter how he suffered.

Someone coming down the stairs tore her out of her fearful thoughts. When she saw the footman, she waited anxiously for his first words.

"I am sorry, Miss Nethercott. I must ask you to leave immediately," he said.

"But—"

"Please, Miss Nethercott. I have never put my hands on a lady, and I do not wish to do so now."

She sighed. The young man's dismay showed her that he had tried to his utmost to arrange for Tabor to speak to her. When he opened the door wide, she thanked him quietly and went out. She looked up at Gideon's window.

The muscular footman appeared from around the back of the carriage to open the door for her. As she was about to step in, she heard a very quiet, "Miss Nethercott?"

Hope sprung up in her heart when she recognized Tabor's voice. She edged away from the carriage, motioning for the footman to close the door.

"Drive to the other side of the square," she ordered.

The footman looked puzzled, but nodded. He climbed up to sit beside the coachee, and, with a rattle of wheels and harness, the carriage drove away. She saw the footman looking back, watching her as he had promised.

Jade remained where she was until Tabor reached her. She guessed he had come around the end of the long terrace, exiting the house through the mews at the back. When he glanced up at the windows overlooking the square, he motioned for her to move closer to the house. She understood what he did not say. He wanted to speak to her where they would not be seen by a casual glance out of an upper window.

"Thank you, Tabor," she said with a weak smile as soon as they stood within the shadows just beyond the door. "How is Gideon?"

"He was not hurt in the explosion on *Perdition's Folly*. By some providence, he was not onboard. Nobody was. There was a fire on a nearby vessel just before the explosion. He went to help douse it." His mouth tilted in a wry smile. " 'Tis said that good deeds offer no escape from trouble, but my lord proved that wrong."

She sank down to the lowest step and put her face in her hands. Tears that she had kept in check along with her fear threatened to burst out of her now as tears of joy. Yet, even as she exulted in the tidings that Gideon had escaped unscathed, she could not keep from wondering why—if he was unhurt—he had forbidden the footman from giving her that information.

"Tabor, is it only me that he will not receive or everyone?"

"I don't know, Miss Nethercott. He has said nothing of you."

"All his thoughts are of the boat." She tried to keep the bitterness out of her voice, but failed.

"I cannot speak to the course of his thoughts." He looked at the door. "I should go in, for Lord Bannatyne will be looking for me. You should return to your sisters. It is not safe for a young woman to be out at this hour on her own."

She wanted to plead for him to take her to Gideon or to take a message to him on her behalf. She asked neither. Tabor was risking Gideon's anger by seeking her out to reassure her. She could not repay his kindness by asking him to do something that might risk him being given his congé.

Standing, she said, "He will not see me, but will you tell him that I called? That I was concerned for his well-being?"

"If the opportunity arises, I will." Guilt lengthened his face, and she knew he believed the opportunity would never come.

"Thank you." There was nothing else to say, so she turned to walk to where the carriage waited. As she stepped into it, she looked up at the window of Gideon's chamber. Even as she watched, the light went out along with the last remaining hope in her heart.

Gideon pushed back the chair in his office. The blueprints and designs for *Perdition's Folly* were nowhere in sight. He guessed Tabor or one of the other servants had placed them on an upper shelf, hidden in the shadows from the one lamp lit in the room. Did they think he would rend them to shreds or sit and weep over the loss of his boat?

Maybe he would have . . . a fortnight ago. Now the loss of the boat only added to his rage. If he had been aboard, he would be in as many pieces as the boat was. Where it had floated, only splinters and pieces of tortured metal remained. And if Jade had not left when she had . . .

Dash it! Ward's warning had almost come too late. But the warning *had* come, and Gideon could not disregard it, no matter how much he wanted to. His enemy had grown bolder and might not believe the rumors that Gideon had started himself that he was suffering gravely and might soon die. Already there had been callers at the house to express their sympathy at his passing, so he knew the rumors were warping and growing.

He intended to take advantage of the world's assumption that he needed to recover from his injuries. That would give him a chance to arrange an irresistible bait to draw his enemy into a trap. He would do that once he was sure those around him were safe. He hoped Jade would heed his request and leave with her sisters for their home in Yorkshire. If she refused, he would speak with her older sister. He had already made arrangements so that by week's end, Persis would be on her way to Cornwall.

Once they were safe, he could concentrate on running that bastard to ground. He looked forward to that moment, but first he must persuade Jade to return to Yorkshire.

He smiled as he picked up a handwritten invitation that had been left on his desk. He had been startled to receive it and, at the time, had sent his regrets. Maybe he should change his mind.

Blowing out the lamp, he went across the hallway to his bedchamber. He glanced once down the steps toward where Persis's door was closed as firmly as ever. When he had knocked on it earlier, he had been told that his sister was receiving no one. The maid who had come to the door would not even open it far enough for him to see his sister, but he had felt a breeze that must have come through an open window. He did not recall his sister having her window raised before, but he knew it was useless to ask questions. He would get no answers. Not that it mattered. He was sending Persis to the family estate, even if she traveled the whole way draped in a black cloak and speaking to no one but her maid.

He lit the lamp there and, picking up a book on the

table by the room's sole chair, he sat. He opened the book, knowing he needed to wait at least an hour before he acted, but his gaze kept drifting from the words to his bed. The scent from Jade's hair no longer lingered on the pillows. But in the short time that it had remained, he had breathed in the aroma until he could recreate it from his memories.

Tabor walked in. "Good evening, my lord." He set some clothes on the foot of the bed. "The final bits of the Nethercott ladies' laundry have been finished."

"You know what to do with it." He was astonished. He had thought the remaining clothing that had been soaked during the storm had been sent to the duchess's house days ago.

"I shall have it delivered in the morning."

"Good." He kept staring at the page.

"I suspect Miss Jade will be interested in the return of her dressing gown, too."

"Dressing gown?" His eyes flicked up but he forced his gaze back at the book.

"It is still hanging in the cupboard, my lord, if you did not notice."

He had noticed. He was not going to admit that to his valet. "Thank you, Tabor, for bringing that to my attention. I trust you will have all the clothing delivered on the morrow."

For a long moment, Tabor said nothing as he wandered around the room, drawing back the covers on the bed and preparing Gideon's clothes for the next day. The valet walked back toward the door, and Gideon thought he was leaving without another word. Quite unlike Tabor, who had never been tempted to keep his tongue between his teeth when he felt strongly about a matter.

"I thought you would want to know," Tabor said from beside the door, "that the Duchess of Northborough sent a servant to inquire on your health, my lord."

"I assume he was given the message I instructed."

"Yes." He cleared his throat. "How long will you allow Her Grace to assume you are at death's door?"

He glanced up at Tabor, then back at the book. "I had not realized that you had developed such an interest in Her Grace's state of mind."

"She was obviously worried, and she is very busy right now with her guests."

Gideon knew where the conversation was headed. "Her guests will keep her from thinking about me. That is what guests do. They create complications that wreck havoc on one's household."

"And when they leave, it becomes very quiet. You cannot be certain how your erstwhile guests fare." He cleared his throat. "You had one other caller."

"Who was sent away, I assume," he said without looking up from his book.

"Yes, but you should have received her. She was deeply worried about the rumors she has heard."

"She?"

"Miss Jade, of course."

"Jade called here?"

"And was turned away."

"Why didn't you tell me?"

"You said you did not want to be disturbed and that all callers were to be sent away." His mouth was set in a straight line. "It is not my place to argue . . ."

"But you intend to." He closed the book, hoping that his manservant did not ask what he was reading. He had no idea because the words had been nothing more than nonsense symbols on the pages. Dash it! He should have realized that Jade would rush to see how he was. Even in the midst of her anger and hurt, she would set aside her own feelings to ascertain how he fared.

If he had known she was calling . . . No, he could not let his longings weaken his resolve. He needed to keep her alive, even if that meant hardening her heart to him. Pain sliced through him like a heated blade as he thought of her leaving and never returning.

Tabor came to stand in front of him. Clasping his hands behind him, he said, "No, my lord. I have no intention of arguing with you. I do, however, wish to remind you of something."

"And what is that?" He hated the petulant sound of his voice.

"When you obtain the information you need to prove that your family members were murdered and you have the name of the person who is responsible, what then?"

"I will see the person is punished as the law provides."

"And what then?"

"He will hang."

"And what then?"

Pushing himself to his feet, Gideon said, "If I wanted a parrot, I would buy one."

Tabor did not move nor did he answer.

"I know what you are trying to do." Gideon tossed the book on his bed. "You are trying to get me to say that, without Jade, my life will return to the emptiness it had before."

"Your words, my lord, not mine."

"I have heard enough of your words tonight, Tabor." He took a deep breath and released it slowly. "Pardon me, old man. I am not angry at you. I am furious at myself for failing to stop my enemies."

"May I suggest, my lord, that you may be looking in the wrong place?"

"Excuse me?"

Tabor met his eyes steadily for the first time. "You have considered those who have a grudge against the Bannatynes. Your questions have gained you nothing. Maybe you should consider others."

"People who outwardly are the family's friends and allies." He laughed tersely. "I have looked into those people's motives and activities, as well. Again I have found nothing. The only ones who seem to have a connection to all the deaths are myself, my sister, and Renshaw. I had my suspicions about him, but he is as dead as the others. A victim rather than the perpetrator. And Persis has been with me when many of the deaths occurred."

"I did not mean to suggest the lady was involved."

Gideon clapped his valet on the shoulder. "I know. You were only trying to get me out of my dismals by drawing me into the investigation. You know I am fascinated by it."

"It is more than fascination."

"Yes. It is the need to find the answers before my enemy is, at last, successful and puts an end to my search at the same time he puts an end to me."

"Are you sure you are still the target?"

He laughed, again without humor. "Tabor, have you become a mind reader?"

"No, my lord, but I have looked at the facts. In every attack on you in recent days, there has been one commonality. Miss Jade."

"As you have figured that out, listen to what else I have been told." He quickly outlined the information Ward had given him.

Tabor pondered it, then asked, "May I ask you one thing, my lord?"

"You know you will whether I say yes or no."

"How will not seeing Miss Jade help safeguard her?"

"My enemy believes me to be nearly dead. That has gained me the past few hours to make some plans. Tabor, I will be going out tonight, so please get my best coat ready." As the valet went to obey, Gideon walked to the window and looked out at the rain. "The first step is to persuade Jade to leave London tomorrow at first light."

Tabor sighed deeply from by the closet door. "Giving your enemy another victory over you."

"At least for now. Once it is safe, I will find out if she wants to return here."

"That would be a worthy decision, my lord, if your enemy did not know you so well."

"Too well. Far too well." His own mouth grew taut as he said, "If all goes as I plan tonight, I will know my enemy very well soon."

Chapter 19

The duchess's ballroom was well lit. Music came softly from the orchestra set in one corner. Guests mingled in the room, which was becoming stuffy as more people crowded into it. Unlike her previous gathering, nobody left to go out into the garden. Many of the guests glanced up at the gallery where footmen stood at regular intervals, their eyes scanning the crowd, ready to react to the first sign of trouble. Her Grace was determined not to have another evening ruined by a corpse.

Jade sat with China to one side of the room as they both watched a country reel unfolding. At the last minute, the duchess had decided there must be dancing as well as listening to music. Lord Lastingham had asked Sian to stand up with him, and now they were laughing as they tried to follow the complicated pattern of the dance.

"You need not feel obligated to remain here with me," Jade said. "If you want to dance, please go ahead."

"Maybe the next set." China gave her a bolstering smile. "Mr. Sheldon asked me earlier if he and his brother could lead us into one dance."

She recalled Mr. Sheldon as a tall man with barely an ounce of flesh on his bones. She had not realized he had a brother. She might have if she had paid any attention to the duchess's other guests, but her thoughts continually wandered to Gideon. Why had he been willing to let her believe he was horribly wounded? If Tabor had not come to tell her the truth, she would be grief-stricken, unable to forget the last words they had shared had been in anger.

As the dancers whirled about, laughter rang through the room. The merriment just made her more aware of her sorrow. She should have protected her heart with more care. Gideon's reputation had been a warning. She had not listened. Not even to her own mind, which had urged her to take care. Rather, she had let her heart and her own cravings for his touch lead her into joy and then into a misery made all the worse for having known ecstasy in his arms.

When Mr. Sheldon came over to ask China to dance, her sister hesitated until Jade urged her to go. Mr. Sheldon's brother took one look at Jade's grim expression and asked Sian to be his partner.

The music started anew, and the dancers took their places. Jade watched quietly through the first repetition of the dance steps. As they began the next set, she stood and walked away. She considered going upstairs, but that might insult the duchess.

She passed the open French windows to the terrace overlooking the garden. Out there, she could be alone to regain her composure. She would not walk out of view of the other guests or so far that a single scream would not bring dozens running to her rescue.

"Why are you fretting?" she asked herself as she stepped out onto the stones that were damp with the rain that had ended just as the guests began to arrive. "You are not the focus of a murderer's rage."

Walking to the edge of the terrace, she put her hands on the wall that separated it from the garden. She gazed out into the darkness. Gideon was safe in his house. Or was he? He would not linger there in hopes of waiting until his enemy tired of the chase. He could be anywhere, trying to turn the hunter into the hunted.

"I wondered how long it would be before you did something stupid like coming out here alone," came a voice from the night.

She whirled as she gasped, "Gideon!"

He stepped from the shadows, even more vital and

enticing than in her most arousing dream. Dressed in
prime twig in a dark coat and cream breeches, he wore
boots that shone in the moonlight. As he crossed the
terrace, she took one step, then another toward him. She
halted herself before she could run to him and fling herself into his arms.

"It is good to see you alive and unharmed," she said,
her voice stiff.

"It is good to be alive and unharmed." A hint of a
smile played across his lips. He glanced toward the ballroom where the music was leading the dancers into the
next part of the quadrille.

"Did the person at the address in the note have any
information to help you in your search for the truth?"

"No."

"Oh. I am sorry." She hesitated, then said, "You did
not need to sneak in. I will not embarrass you by creating a scene."

"The thought that you might never crossed my mind.
You are too well mannered to do so."

"Thank you."

"However, I am not." He grasped her by the shoulders and pulled her to him.

His mouth captured hers before she had a chance to
answer. When his tongue brushed her lips, they parted,
welcoming him into her mouth. He deepened the kiss
with a low groan that she felt rather than heard, because
she shared his craving for what they had denied
themselves.

His hands swept up her back as his embrace gentled
to enfold her against his chest. She ran her fingers along
his sleeves and pressed even closer. The clothing between them was bothersome. She imagined tearing it
away until his skin was bare against her. The soft sound,
from deep within her throat, was a mixture of yearning
and regret.

"Jade?" he whispered. "That sounded sad."

"Why did you come here tonight?" she asked as
softly.

"Because I could not stay away."

Hope trilled through her heart. "Really?"

"Really." He framed her face with his hands. "Jade, if you do nothing else ever again for me, I beg you to do as I am asking now. Take your sisters and go back to Yorkshire tomorrow as soon as it is light enough to travel."

"You want me to go?" Her exultation was skewered and dropped heavily through her stomach.

"It is not safe for you here any longer. If you had remained on *Perdition's Folly* as I had asked, you could be dead now."

"You want me to go while you stay here? You want me to run away to Nethercott Castle and sit there, never knowing if you are alive or dead?" Her voice broke. "I do not want to spend days suffering what I did today until Tabor told me the truth."

"He did, did he?" He gave her a wry smile. "He did not mention that."

"I guess he did not have the opportunity." Hurrying on before he could ask what she meant, she asked, "Why do you think I will be safer in Yorkshire than here? Your family members were not in London when they were slain, were they?"

"Must you always be logical? I am asking you to go in hopes that my enemy will refocus his fury on a closer target."

"Your sister? Are you mad?"

"I am sending Persis to Cornwall, another long journey from Town. With both of you gone, he will have to aim his ire directly at me." His thumbs stroked her cheek. "Say you will go, so I know you are safe, sweetling. Promise me that you will—"

She put her finger to his lips. "Before you say more, you need to hear what I have to say."

"And what is that?" he asked, drawing her hand down away from his mouth. He laced his fingers through hers and chuckled. "As forthright as you are, Jade, I cannot imagine a single thing you have *not* said to me already."

"What I have not told you is the truth."

He rested his elbow on the wall, drawing her closer. "And what is the truth you have not told me?"

She almost blurted out that she loved him, but that would be the wrong thing to say. Not only had she spoken of love that magical night on *Perdition's Folly* and he had been upset, but she could not avoid revealing what she had hidden for so long.

"I have been using you to help me find the truth about Sir Mitchell's death," she said, steeling herself for his response. He had, she knew, every right to be furious with her.

"I suspected that." He took a deep breath, then released it. "And what did you discover?"

"That it is highly unlikely that you wielded the knife that slew the baronet."

"You thought I killed him?"

"At the beginning, yes."

He released her. Walking away a pair of steps, he put his hand on the rail beside the stairs leading down into the garden.

She waited, her teeth over her lower lip, for him to say something. Anything. She could not bear to have him shut her out of his life again. He had been honest with her, and she had to be the same with him, especially if the truth would offer him some clue to why there had been attempts on his life.

"Why did you believe I killed Renshaw?" he asked.

"That was what I was told." She went to stand beside him. What she had to say could not be spoken across a terrace where someone else might hear.

"By whom?"

She did not hesitate. To do so would suggest she was creating a tale to bamboozle him. "By Sir Mitchell."

"Jade, don't be ridiculous! How could a dead man tell you the identity of his murderer?"

Taking his hands in hers, she wove her fingers between his again. She stepped closer and drew his arms around her as she whispered, "Because he is a ghost."

"Jade! I thought you were going to be honest with me." He started to pull his arms from around her.

She tightened her hold on his hands. "I know it seems impossible, but it is the truth. Sir Mitchell's ghost appeared to me first at Nethercott Castle and sought my help to prove that you drove a knife into him. He asked me to come to London so I might uncover the truth."

"And you agreed to do as a . . . ghost . . ." He cursed. "I cannot even bring myself to say the word."

"Yes, I agreed to what a ghost asked me to do."

"Why?"

She sat on the stone bench. "My father spent his whole life trying to prove there is a spirit world that interacts with ours. No matter what he did, he could not find undeniable proof."

"And Renshaw was going to give that to you?"

"He offered to try."

Gideon shook his head. "You have a generous heart, Jade, but even you would not be willing to risk your life in exchange for a promise merely to try. As you have come to learn more about the baronet, you should have seen he was not a man who could be trusted to keep his word. Why did you continue?"

"Because he also agreed to try to bring my father's spirit back so we could speak to him one last time. You may think that is silly, Gideon, but the chance to see my father again means so much to me."

"I know." He sat beside her. "Who among us would not be willing to do almost anything to have the opportunity to speak again to someone who has been taken from us? And what about Violet? Is she real?"

"No, I created her in order to give you a reason for my interest in the demimonde where Sir Mitchell's ghost assured me that I would find the proof of your part in his death. My father was faithful to my mother, even after her death."

"And too lost in his studies to think of anything but proving that ghosts truly exist, a challenge his daughter has assumed upon his death."

"Please believe me." She brushed his hair back from his eyes. "Ask yourself how I could have known what I did about Mr. Heath if Sir Mitchell did not tell me."

"I had my suspicions."

"What were they?"

"They were proven to be false, so what do they matter now?"

"You thought I was part of the conspiracy surrounding your family."

"I hoped you were not." He stroked her cheek. "What you are telling me, it is too incredible to believe."

"Just as I knew Sir Mitchell's accusations were . . . once I met you."

He smiled. "Until then, you deemed me capable of such a crime."

"Why not? I knew nothing of you but what the baronet and gossip had whispered. After I met you, I changed my mind."

"Because of my undeniable charm?"

"Flattering yourself is a bad habit, Gideon. You should halt it immediately."

"Then I must leave that task to you." Coming to his feet, he held out his hand. "If you are leaving on the morrow, you should get to bed early tonight."

She put her hand on his and let him bring her to stand facing him. "I am ready, if you are."

"Jade . . ."

"Say nothing but yes. If we keep talking, we are certain to say something to upset each other."

"Why would I say anything else?" He took a single step toward the shadows.

"I must leave a note for my sisters, so they know I am safe."

His brows shot up. "If you leave them a note, they will know you are with me."

"I am ruined anyhow for being alone with you out here on the terrace."

"So you might as well make our ruin undeniable." He laughed. "Now you are getting the idea."

She locked her hands behind his nape. "Sweetheart, I have had *that* idea for a long time now."

As they went into the house by another door, Jade looked back at the ballroom. Her sisters were having a wondrous night. She hated to ruin it with the tidings that they must leave in the morning. It took her only seconds to dash off the note that she was fine and would explain everything when she returned to leave with them for Yorkshire. She placed the note on her pillow where her sisters would not fail to notice the slip of paper.

Gideon did not ask her what she had told her sisters about where she was going. He simply led her out of the house. When he swung into the saddle, he reached down and drew her up behind him. He undid his cloak and handed it to her. She hooked it around her own neck before wrapping her arms around his waist and leaning her cheek against the smooth wool of his coat. His cloak flew out behind them, hiding her to any curious eyes.

As soon as they reached the house on Bedford Square, a footman hurried out to take Gideon's horse. Gideon dismounted, then reached up for her to slide into his arms. He lowered her slowly to the ground, and her breath caught as she stroked his broad chest and firm thighs.

With a laugh, he lifted her in his arms and carried her up the steps. He thanked the footman there for opening the door, but did not pause as they went up the flight of stairs toward his bedchamber near the top of the house.

"You will exhaust yourself," she said with a laugh as he put his foot on the riser of the upper staircase.

"You are right." He set her on her feet. "I would rather you exhaust me in other ways." He laughed.

She said, "Shhh! We will disturb your sister."

"For the first time in weeks, I am glad that she is hiding behind her door."

"Shame on you, Gideon!"

"Yes, shame on me for not kissing you." He pulled her into his arms and demanded her lips cede themselves to him. She gladly returned the kiss with the same fervor.

He raised his mouth away, but kept his arm around her as they climbed the stairs. "Tonight, I will stay with you instead of in my office across the hall." He swung open the door and motioned for her to precede him.

She looked around the familiar room, amazed that it felt as if she were coming home. She saw something she had not expected, something that had not been in the room before. She went to the table where a piece of paper, that had been folded in half, was propped against a stack of books.

"It is the sketch I made of *Perdition's Folly*," she whispered. "I had no idea that you had kept it."

"Kept it close to me." He touched the drawing and then her lips. "It has been my sole comfort since."

"After your beautiful boat was destroyed."

He shook his head. "No, it is a reminder of the night when you were mine for what I had hoped was only the first time." Walking to the cupboard, he opened it and drew out her dressing gown. "You left this behind, Jade."

She took the silken garment and asked, "Would you like me to change?"

"Never."

"I mean into the dressing gown."

He plucked it from her fingers and tossed it onto the chair. "Maybe later. For now, I do not want to see it on you."

She loosened the cloak and let it fall to the floor behind her as she walked to him.

"You are so beautiful," he whispered.

Putting her finger to his lips as she had before, she shook her head. "Do not speak, Gideon. No words now, because I do not want to risk this moment with you. So forget about everything but you and me. Think of me touching you."

He drew her to the bed and lifted her to sit on it. As his lips captured hers, he leaned her into the pillows. His hand slid along her side, and he drew her over him. His fingers made short work of the hooks down the back of her gown, even as she was loosening his clothes. Eagerly they undressed each other, and he stretched out beside her. When he gazed at her, she ran a quivering finger along his jaw where the day's whiskers were a coarse caress.

She moaned softly into his mouth when he stroked her breast. Needing to touch him, she tried to escape from his tongue as it tantalized her neck. She wanted to kiss him, to touch him, to rediscover every pleasure and find more.

"Be mine, sweetling," he murmured.

She shook her head and sat. "No, tonight, I am making you mine."

He chuckled, but his eyes were aflame with dark fire. "How shall you do that?"

She leaned forward to tease his ear. His breath caught as he wrapped his arms around her, drawing her over his hard body once more. His hands edged down to curve over her bottom, pressing her closer to the hardness she ached to have within her.

She had to fight succumbing to the scintillating pleasure, for she wanted to offer him the bliss he had given her before. She let her tongue lave a meandering path along his chest, then lower. Her lips and fingertips sampled the sensual delights awaiting her.

He moaned as she tasted his firm, flat abdomen. Decorating his skin with moist whorls, she heard him gasp her name over the thunder of her pulse in her ears. She was thrilled that she could give him this pleasure.

Her tongue continued along him. When she ran it over his hard shaft, he writhed beneath her. She trembled as the longing threatened to overwhelm her. When he gasped, she looked toward him. With a growl, he tugged her over him and drove himself deep into her. His hands stroked her hips as she moved over him with the slow, undulating motion they had shared on his boat.

Then she forgot everything but the wanton need. She claimed his mouth as the motion escalated as he slid in and out of her. A heated tempest flowed over and around them. Then she quivered over him, aware in that one perfect moment of union that he had found ecstasy, too. She could not imagine anything more wondrous.

"Sweetling?"

Jade opened one eye. She did not want to move from

where she was lying curled up against Gideon. "Why do you call me that? I have never heard that word before."

"It was what my mother called my father." He chuckled. "When she was not threatening to throw something at his head. He had more than his share of the Bannatyne temper, and she learned to deal with it by improving her aim and holding her ground when he got angry."

"As I have with you."

"One of the things I love about you, Jade."

She opened both her eyes and sat up to look down at him. "You love me?" She hardly dared to speak the words aloud, afraid the sound of her own voice would shatter the enchantment.

"You need not sound so amazed."

"But I am. You said—"

"I know what I said, but I was a fool." He wrapped his arms around her and drew her down into the rumpled nest of pillows and covers. "I think I have loved you from the moment I saw you."

"And realized I was not Gwendolyn."

His laugh resonated through his chest beneath her ear. "You will not let me forget that mistake, will you?" He put his finger beneath her chin and tipped her head back so her gaze met his. "But it is the truth, Jade. I have loved you, I swear, from that moment. I did not want to own to the truth so I tried to drive a wedge between us by making you a salacious offer I never expected you to accept."

"Because you could not know how much I longed to see my father again."

"I was shocked when you accepted a place in my bed at the end of a week and agreed to attend Sharla's mistress school, but even more so when you agreed that, in exchange for my help, you would stay with me for a month."

"Maybe I knew—even then—that one night would never be enough."

He smiled, but grew somber as he said, "But we cannot have our thirty nights together now. You must leave with the morning, Jade. Leave with your sisters and do not come back until I can be certain you are safe."

"Your enemies—"

"Have become yours as well."

Jade listened in shock as he told her what the Bow Street Runner had revealed after she had left *Perdition's Folly*. When he had finished, she asked, "Are you sure that the warning was to me? A boat is called 'she,' and your steamboat was the next target of your enemies."

"I had not thought about that."

"So if there is no threat—"

"The threat remains, sweetling." He kissed her to silence her retort, then said, "I should have stayed away from you tonight, so you would stay safe, but I could not stay away. Without you in my life, it was so empty I might as well be dead. So go back to Yorkshire, Jade. I will send for you as soon as my enemy hangs."

"And then I will return and—"

"We will enjoy this." He rolled her onto her back and leaned across her. As his mouth found hers, she knew she wanted only this joy with him . . . for as long as she could.

A loud sound intruded into Gideon's dreams. Dash it! He did not want to awake. He wanted to stay in his dream of holding Jade as he had one almost perfect night.

The sound did not stop. He heard the muffled sound of his name.

Tabor!

Why was his valet banging on the door? Why didn't the man just come in and say whatever he felt he must?

"What is it?" came a melodic voice close to his ear.

Opening his eyes, he knew he would never hear the words "a dream come true" and not think of that moment when Jade gazed up at him. Her eyes were soft with sleep, and her hair was scattered across her pillow and his. Cupping her cheek, he leaned into a kiss that roused every inch of him.

The rapping on the door got more insistent. Through

the thick mahogany, he heard, "Lord Bannatyne! Lord Bannatyne, are you awake?"

Gideon raised his mouth reluctantly away from her beguiling lips. Tabor would not come into the room when he suspected Jade was here. An excellent servant, as always, but Gideon wished his valet had waited until dawn before coming to him with whatever matter had upset him.

"Wait here, sweetling," he murmured as he ran the back of his fingers across her cheek. "Let me see what has Tabor all on end, and then I shall return to you. Don't fall back to sleep . . . yet."

He was astonished when she nodded. It was not like Jade to accept any order meekly; then he realized she was as anxious as he was to find out what was causing Tabor to pound on the door like a drummer calling a company of soldiers to battle.

He was grateful for the faint moonlight, so he could step around their scattered clothes without ruining any of hers. He winced when he stubbed his toe against a chair. Picking up his shirt, he pulled it on. Tabor's rapping was becoming frantic, so there was no time to look for his breeches.

"I am coming," he growled at the door as he hit his other foot on the heel of his boot. Unlocking the door, he opened it and asked groggily, "What is it?"

The valet's face was an odd gray in the light from the candle he held. " 'Tis Lady Persis!"

"What about her?"

"She has been attacked, and I fear she is going to die."

Chapter 20

Jade jumped out of the bed, pulling on her dressing gown. She ran to the door. "Have you sent for a doctor, Tabor?"

"I came first to inform Lord Bannatyne."

"Go! Get the doctor," Gideon ordered as he turned to pull on his breeches.

Not waiting for him to button them in place, Jade ran down the stairs after the valet. He quickly explained how he had been awakened by odd thuds from the lower floor. When he had gone to investigate, he found the door open and Lady Persis injured. He had no time to add more as he continued down the lower stairs, shouting to the footman by the door to wake the rest of the household staff.

She went to Lady Persis's door. Not bothering to knock, she opened it. The light from a single lamp showed blood splattered on the floor and across the bed. Lady Persis was propped against the pillows as she had been the one time Jade had spoken with her. Her eyes were closed, and her hair in complete disarray. In the corner, her maid was lolling in a chair, obviously knocked senseless.

Hurrying to the bed, Jade picked up Lady Persis's hand and chafed her wrist gently. "Can you hear me?"

"Yes," came the lady's peevish answer. "Speak quietly. My head . . . Oh, my head . . ." She moaned piteously as the door came open and slammed against the wall. "Oh, my head . . ."

Jade set the lady's hand on the bed and went to Gideon. Putting her hands on his chest to keep him from rushing to the bed, she said in a near whisper, "She is alive, but she is obviously injured. Her head is paining her greatly."

He nodded, and she stepped aside to let him go to his sister. He went on tiptoe, she noticed and struggled not to smile at another sign of his kind heart. A heart he had offered her upstairs. No, she could not think of that now. She must focus on Lady Persis.

She went to where the maid had not moved. Tapping the woman's cheek gently, she tried to rouse her. The maid groaned, but her eyes did not open. Going out of the room, Jade motioned to two footmen.

They nodded to her request to find two more strong men and come to Lady Persis's chamber to take the maid to a guest room where she could be examined by the doctor.

"And carry her as if she is made of the most delicate porcelain, for she may have suffered injuries we cannot see," she added as they ran to obey.

As she came into the room, she heard Gideon ask, "Persis, why didn't you call out for help?"

His sister shifted on the bed and moaned. "Please lower your voice. You are making my head hurt even worse." Closing her eyes, she looked away from him. "Why is it hurting so bad?"

"Who did this to you, Persis?" he asked.

"Gideon, stop shouting."

"I am . . ." He lowered his voice even further. "Who struck you and your maid?"

She simply groaned, the sound growing louder when the footmen came into the room.

Jade pointed to the maid. As the footmen went to pick her up with care, Gideon came to where she stood.

"She seems barely aware of us past her pain," he said. "While she is lost in it, whoever attacked her and her maid could be making his escape."

"Someone must have seen something. Go and talk to your servants. I will sit here with her."

He shook his head. "You need to leave immediately. Whoever did this to my sister may still be in the house. I will not risk you being injured, too."

"I doubt her attacker has lingered in the house when everyone has been alerted."

"I am glad you are sensible now."

"Being logical was how I knew I loved you. What I felt could not have been anything else."

He smiled and curved his hand along her cheek. "All right. Let me see what I can learn before Tabor returns with the doctor. Promise me that you will call out as loudly as you can if there is even a hint of danger for you and Persis."

"I promise."

He brushed her lips with a quick kiss before he went into the hall.

As she started to close the door, she heard him calling to his housekeeper. She gasped as the door seemed to leap out of her hand and shut itself. She heard a click. As she reached for the knob again, an icy chill from her right made her edge away hastily. Why was Sir Mitchell making an appearance now?

She turned to face him and beg him to return later. The words never left her mouth as she stared at the most incredible sight. Lady Persis was leaping out of her bed and raising her fists to drive them into Sir Mitchell.

"Be careful!" cried Jade. "He is so cold he will—" She halted, then gasped, "You can see him!"

"Of course, I can see him." Lady Persis smiled.

"You are unhurt!"

The lady simply continued to smile.

"But the blood—" Jade was afraid her stomach would erupt and betray her. "It was your maid's!"

"She was tired of remaining in this room, so she threatened to leave. I could not allow that." She glanced at Sir Mitchell, who was beaming with pride. "I have suffered enough since I made that one small mistake."

"Yes, your dagger found the wrong target that night, my beloved," he crooned.

"*You* killed Sir Mitchell?" Jade stared at them in disbelief. "You killed your own fiancé?"

"You see, Miss Nethercott," he said, his voice hardening, "she thought I had broken off our betrothal. Instead, Bannatyne tried to halt it."

"He is lying!" Jade ran to Lady Persis and drew her away from the ghost. "Your brother had no respect for the baronet, and he could not understand why you wanted to marry an obvious fortune-hunter, but he would have done nothing to make you so unhappy."

Lady Persis pulled herself away. "My beloved Mitchell has never been false with me. He has helped me obtain what I deserve."

"Yet you killed him!"

"A small mistake. I thought he was another."

Jade reeled away. "You intended to kill your own brother!"

"Actually I thought my beloved was my cousin Derlan."

Jade continued backward, groping for the door. "So Lord Derlan's death was not an accident?"

"It was necessary," Sir Mitchell said with a smile as he moved between her and the door.

"Why? To put more suspicion on Gideon?"

"That was one reason." His smile was as icy as the cold emanating from him. "But you quickly showed us there was another way to destroy Bannatyne."

"Destroy him? Why would you want to destroy your own brother?" She tried to draw Lady Persis into the conversation, hoping to reach the part of Gideon's sister that remained from before her life became entangled with the baronet.

"To show that he was guilty of murder to obtain his title," answered the ghost.

"But he did not want the title!" she argued. "He was happy with his life and his boat."

Sir Mitchell acted as if she had not spoken. "How better to make him look an utterly depraved beast than to have him ruin the innocent daughter of a harmless, crazy old man?" He sneered in her direction. "And Miss Jade Nethercott played her role to perfection, letting Bannatyne ruin her first in the eyes of the *ton*. I have heard that Bannatyne will be called out by Miss Nethercott's cousin who now holds the family title. It seems, my beloved Persis, he has recently learned that your brother has acted as if his cousin Jade is a harlot."

"His Jade is a jade," Persis said with a laugh.

Jade paid her no attention, for the joke was a stale one. "How did he learn that Lord Nethercott wants to challenge Gideon to a duel?" She suspected she already knew the answer.

"I told you I was not limited where I could go."

"But, until now, no one else was able to see you."

"So you believed." Sir Mitchell chuckled. "You are so like the Professor. A challenge makes you work twice as hard. Why should I deny you the pleasure of scrambling about in an effort to help me find my murderer?"

"You are deranged! Both of you!" She whirled and ran to the door. She tried to turn the knob. It seemed frozen.

Frozen!

She turned when cold crept down her spine, both from within and from beyond her. She pressed her hands back against the wood as Sir Mitchell's ghost moved closer.

"You did not think we would allow you to leave so easily, did you, Miss Nethercott?" His smile warned he was not yet done tormenting her. "You have eluded us too many times. You will stay and answer our questions."

"What questions?"

Lady Persis gave a sniff as condescending as Sir Mitchell's had been. "Beloved, I do not know why you are continuing with this. She is nothing. Just my brother's latest whore."

Jade bit her lip to keep from retorting. If they got into a brangle, she might have a chance to escape. How? She did not know, but she would even try going out the window if that was her only choice. She edged in that direction, moving slowly past a dressing table.

"It is not simply that Bannatyne enjoys having her in his bed, my beloved Persis." Sir Mitchell crowed with another laugh. "He loves her."

"Gideon loves her?" Lady Persis laughed coldly. "He has never loved anything but the business that our great-grandfather built. He failed to realize that while it was acceptable for our great-grandfather to work, that was before our family was granted its first peerage. And then he started building that ludicrous boat in hopes of increasing our family's shipping business. All my life he shamed me with his low pursuits of commerce."

"But you loved—you *love* Sir Mitchell Renshaw." Jade closed her fingers around a silver hairbrush on the dressing table. It was heavy enough to knock Lady Persis senseless. That might enable her to flee. After all, if the ghost could have done her physical harm directly, other than touching her with his deathly cold hands, he would have already, not bothering to arrange this confrontation.

"I do love him, don't I, beloved?" she cooed to the ghost. When he moved toward her, she waved him away with a scowl. "You are as cold as a winter's Friday."

Not wanting to let either of them change the subject, Jade hurried to ask, "But, my lady, how can you love Sir Mitchell when he is as embroiled in business as your brother?"

"My beloved knows his place. He is a gentleman first and foremost."

"Undermining your family's business to shift as much of its profits into his purse as possible." She did not know if that was true, but she would say anything to drive a wedge between them.

"You are lying! Mitchell is a gentleman in every aspect of the word."

"Believe what you will." She gave an indifferent shrug. She hoped neither guessed how difficult it was for her to feign a complete lack of concern on the matter. "He lied to you about your brother's intrusion into your betrothal. About how many other matters has he lied to you?"

"He lied when he said you would be no problem. It would have been so much simpler if you had been on that absurd boat when it exploded yesterday." She frowned at the ghost. "I thought you said she would go there now that she was useless to us, and that would have put an end to them."

Jade stared in shock at the lady and her dead lover. Lady Persis's scold revealed the truth that Jade had failed to see because she had not imagined either of them capable of such avarice and hatred. When Jade had refused to help Sir Mitchell any longer, he must have come to the lady and arranged for her to write the note. They had known she would not recognize the address, but would, in spite of her heartbreak, want to help Gideon.

Who was on *Perdition's Folly* . . .

Which had been oddly damaged . . .

Which he was working on that day . . .

Where she would go to deliver the note . . .

Where they could be alone for the next few hours . . .

During which time the ship would have exploded, killing them both . . .

Barely able to believe her own words, Jade whispered, "You did not want to kill only me. You wanted to kill Gideon, didn't you? *You* were behind the attempts to kill him. Your own brother! You wanted him dead. Just as you arranged for the others to be killed so he could inherit the title and the Bannatyne family properties."

"I did it for Gideon," the lady said with another sniff. "And did he appreciate what he gained? No! He acted as he always had. A viscount should concern himself with more gentlemanly things than an appalling boat." She smiled at the ghost. "Not like my beloved. He was a man who deserved such a title for him and his descendants."

"Beloved, take care what you say," warned Sir Mitchell.

"Why? You told me that she is as silly as her witless father. She even believes that you can find a dead man and bring him back to talk to her."

Jade swallowed hard as she faced the most painful of Sir Mitchell's lies. He never had intended to help her fulfill her wish to speak to Father one more time.

She hid her pain, not wanting them to revel in it, as she held the brush behind her back. She crossed the room to stand an arm's length from Lady Persis. "My father was a respected scholar, a man with a facile mind. He was no fool, and he did not suffer fools lightly. Nor do I. You have said enough for me to realize you are in a delicate condition." As the lady opened her mouth to reply, Jade hurried to correct herself. "You *were* in a delicate condition. Once you and Sir Mitchell learned that, you hatched your hideous plan. You intended for your child to be heir once Gideon and his cousin were dead. You hired some assassins to kill your brother, giving them instructions on where he could be found. But three things happened that upset your plans. Not only were your assassins inept, but your betrothed was murdered by your own hand, and then you lost the baby. You did not shut yourself away because you were in mourning, but because you wanted nobody to know you were going to have a baby."

Sir Mitchell snarled a curse as Lady Persis dropped back into a chair, her face ashen.

"And your final mistake," Jade said, "was trying to use me to distract Gideon from his search. You misjudged him as thoroughly as you did my father. Gideon never suspected you, Lady Persis, of complicity in these crimes because he is not the beast you label him. He—"

A knock came at the door followed by Gideon calling, "Jade! Open the door! It seems to be locked."

She ran toward the door. "Gideon! Get out of here! Your sister is—" Her voice rose to a scream as a frigid palm clamped onto her shoulder. She dropped to her knees. She tried to call out another warning, but the pain was too strong.

"Jade! What is going on in there? Jade? Are you all right?"

She heard Gideon's desperate voice through the waves of pain crashing within her skull. The cold grew stronger as if it were sucking the heat of life out of her. From the other side of the room, Lady Persis was ordering Sir Mitchell to help her reach the knife she had hidden on top of her cupboard.

"He thinks only of her," the lady complained. "He should be worried about me, but listen to him."

Released from the ghost's agonizing grip as he went to do as the lady asked, Jade half crawled to the door. She grasped the knob to pull herself to her feet.

"You will never get it to turn to open!" crowed the ghost. "It is frozen shut."

"I was not planning on turning it." She raised the hairbrush and slammed it with every bit of her remaining strength on the knob.

Metal cracked, and the knob tumbled to the floor, leaving a broken shaft. A piece of the hairbrush sailed across the room. It bounced off the mirror. Glass shattered. Lady Persis screeched in horror.

Jade shouted, "Pull on the knob now, Gideon!"

He did. The shaft vanished.

She started to reach in through the hole to open it by manipulating the lock, but heard running steps behind her. She jumped aside as Lady Persis thrust a knife at her, then slashed at her again. Her sleeve was caught. Before she could react, the blade cut right through it. Agony flashed up to her shoulder. She did not dare to take her eyes off the insane woman, who was laughing wildly as she raised the dagger again. The blade was red with Jade's blood.

The door crashed open. Gideon ran in and choked out a curse as Sir Mitchell's ghost sped toward him. Dropping to the floor, he moaned as the ghost flowed over him. Before the ghost could turn, Gideon stretched out a hand and grasped his sister's ankle. He gave a sharp pull. She toppled to the floor.

Jade ran to him and pulled him to his feet, taking care not to touch the white patches where his skin had been frozen by Sir Mitchell. She knew how painful they must be.

"What is going on here?" he asked.

"They are the ones you have been seeking," she said, drawing him away from where the ghost was hovering near the lady who was pushing herself to her feet. "Your sister intended to kill you as she had the others in your family when she discovered she had conceived the baronet's child. They planned to have it inherit the family's title while they enjoyed the family's wealth."

"Is this true, Persis?" he asked.

"You believe *her*?"

"Yes." He took Jade's hand between his own, stroking it tenderly. "I believe everything she has ever told me, even when she was trying to protect me from my own foolishness."

"Then you are as stupid as she is! You believed I was happy for you when you got everything even though you did not appreciate it. All of it should have been mine." Her eyes, burning with insane fury, focused on the ghost. "You said it would be mine. She is right. You lied to me!"

"Beloved," Sir Mitchell said, "calm yourself. You know I wanted it all for you."

"No, you wanted it all for yourself." She waved the knife at him. "You said it would be mine! All of it would be mine! Now I have nothing."

She raised the knife and looked at her brother. Gideon gave Jade a fierce shove behind him. She stumbled back as he reached for the knife. He was too late. His sister plunged the knife into her own chest.

Gideon caught her before she could strike the floor. He dropped to his knees, cradling his sister as blood pooled beneath them. She gave one shuddering sigh and whispered, "Nothing . . ."

Jade put her hand on his shoulder, then knelt beside him. She was about to tell him how sorry she was when a flash exploded through the room. Next to the light from Sir Mitchell's ghost, there was now another glow, weak but growing stronger. Even before it gained form, she could hear Lady Persis's voice coming from it. She was still berating the baronet.

Then the two blobs of light merged and slowly faded.

Epilogue

Gideon twisted the knob on the bedroom door. "There. I think it is fixed."

Jade rose from the bench in the hallway. She put her hand on the knob and slowly closed the door, not sure when anyone would ever open it again. There might come a time—maybe—when someone would be willing to enter the room where a woman's mad greed and jealousy had destroyed her.

"Heath is arranging for the house to be sold," he said as he put the tools in the box that had been brought from the shed in the back garden. "There are enough people eager to live on Bedford Square that I doubt even the tale of a death here two months ago will halt them from vying to purchase it." He set the box on a nearby table and held out his hand. "Come with me. There is something I want to show you."

She put hers in it. Going with him down the stairs, she took her bonnet from the footman. She tied it under her chin and tucked her hand within Gideon's arm until he handed her into the new carriage that had been delivered only a few days before. It was a twin to the one that had been destroyed in the rampage to obtain Lady Persis everything she desired.

"Where are we going?" she asked when he sat beside her.

He stretched his arm along the back of the seat and smiled. "You never change, sweetling. You are just as impatient as the night I met you."

"I have changed. I have learned that one must never take happiness for granted. When I feared I would lose you to the hell swirling around us, I came to see that I must treasure every moment we have together."

"A lesson my sister and her fiancé never learned. They thought all that mattered were the possessions and prestige they could amass. We will never know how Renshaw persuaded my sister to embark on that deranged path with him. Not that it matters. She was as much at fault as he was. For all we know, *she* could have instituted the scheme."

"I hope we never know. Their ghosts have not returned."

"Nor did you get the proof you needed to show your father was right in his hypotheses."

"I know the truth, and now so do you."

He sighed. "I guess I should be satisfied with that, but it is not easy to imagine how things could have been quite different if they had not let greed poison them."

"And lead them to make promises they had no intention of keeping."

"Like the one that your father would return to speak with you."

"Yes." She blinked back the tears that came too easily each time she thought of her dashed hopes. "I know how silly I was to allow myself to be taken in by a lying specter. If I had not been so desperate to speak to Father—just one more time—I would have seen through Sir Mitchell's schemes. As I began to trust you and see you for the good man you truly are, I should have started to question what he had told me. Everything he told me was a lie, but I refused to admit that as long as I believed there was a chance I could speak with Father again."

"They discovered your weakness and exploited it." He gave a terse laugh. "I will never understand why they let the darkness in their souls consume them."

"You cannot let such questions . . ."

"Haunt me?" He smiled as he tapped her nose. "You are right, as you are way too often, Jade. You must do something about that before it becomes an intolerable habit."

"Must I?"

"I understand such a habit is most bothersome in a wife."

"Then—A wife? Are you asking me to marry you?"

"Patience, Jade." He wagged his finger at her. "Such bold questions from a young miss. You learned your lessons too well at Sharla's mistress school."

She slapped his arm playfully. "Answer me! Are you asking me to marry you?"

He did not answer, not even looking toward her until the carriage slowed to a stop. He opened the door. Stepping out, he held up his hand to her. She alighted and realized they stood on a walkway in Grosvenor Square. When she glanced toward the house where she had lived with her sisters for such a short time, she gasped.

"It is completely repaired," she said.

"Not completely." He went up the steps and opened the door. "There remains quite a bit of work to be done inside."

She walked with him up the stairs. There were still shredded strips of wall covering that had not been removed, but the sitting room's floor had been refinished. The furniture had been pushed to the center of the room, but, on a table were carefully stacked books from Nethercott Castle.

"Ask me," he said from by the settee that was covered with cloths to protect it from the work.

"Ask you?"

"Ask me again."

Her voice almost failed her, but she managed to whisper, "Are you asking me to be your wife?"

He held out his hand to her. She went to take it. When he knelt, he said, "Yes, I am asking you to be my wife."

"Here?"

"Yes." He smiled. "I have hoped that the first place I kissed you, sweetling, would also be the first place I kissed you as my betrothed. What do you say? Will you take responsibility for reforming this rake?"

"No."

"No?" he asked, shocked.

She dropped to her knees beside him. "No, I will not take responsibility for reforming you. I am afraid I am too late. You are no longer a rake, Gideon. You are an amazing man with a sense of honor that I admire. I love you exactly as you are now." She tapped his nose as he had hers so often. "On the other hand, yes, I will marry you."

When his mouth caressed hers, he leaned her back onto the cloths by the settee. His fingers settled on the hooks along the back of her dress.

"The workmen!" she gasped.

"I gave them the day off."

"You?"

"Didn't I mention that the duchess agreed to sell me this house? I suspect it is, in part, to assuage her guilt at believing the worst of me."

"All I am interested in right now is the best of you." She drew his mouth down to hers again.

Read on for an excerpt from the next book in
the Nethercott Tales series, coming soon from Signet.

China Nethercott did not guess, as she drove along the country lane, that she was being stalked.

Why should she? After all, she had driven three times in the past three days over this same road from Cropton to Nethercott Castle, her family's home at the edge of the North Yorkshire Moors. On those previous trips, her younger sister, Sian, had been with her. This afternoon, Sian had decided to remain at Mrs. Stone's house in Cropton and finish the quilt that the ladies had been sewing for the harvest festival that would be held in a month.

China did not enjoy sewing and listening to prattle about news that drifted north from York or inland from Whitby. She preferred being outside, wandering through the fields around the castle or going for a drive across the windblown moors. Each season brought a new vista, and she exulted in the changes.

She sighed. She had had little chance to drive across the moors since she and her younger sister returned from London. Her time was taken up by household matters and reviewing account books. That had been her life before she went to Town, but, since she had come home, she found herself chafing at the responsibilities she had accepted without complaint over the past few years. She tried not to think that she had been content with her life then because she had not known any better.

Now she could not help wishing her days contained

something more exciting than decisions about which
foods to order and how she could best serve the local
community. She knew many women envied her position
as chatelaine of Nethercott Castle, but she wanted more.

More what, she was not sure.

But she also knew how important it had been to work
on the quilts, which would help raise money for a new
roof for the ancient church in Lastingham. The parishio-
ners were accustomed to discovering pools of water on
the church floor and in the eight hundred-year-old crypt
beneath it. The new bell that had been installed several
years ago sounded lovely when it rang with the other
two bells, echoing across the valley and against the
moors, but she could not help worrying that all three
would tumble through the leaking roof.

China looked through a break in the trees edging the
narrow dirt lane. With the road following high Rawcliffe,
she had a splendid view of the valley below. The fields
were awash with August sunshine, but the light held little heat. The month had been as unseasonably cold as
July had been, more like March than summer. Most of
the farmers along the moors kept sheep, so they were
not as affected as the farms farther south, which struggled to bring crops to harvest. Word had reached Yorkshire that even the hardiest plants were failing because
summer seemed to have forgotten to come.

There had not been a single day when the sunshine
was too hot through her straw bonnet. On the moors,
the usually brilliant purple heather was sparse because
many plants had never shaken off their wintry brown.
The few that had blossomed were fading as the chill
stole their color. Oldsters said that there had never been
such a cold summer.

Trees closed in around the road again—tall and thin
trees set in not much undergrowth. A rustling sound
came from her left. She looked, hoping to espy some
roe deer in the shadows, then realized the sound came
from far above the ground. Odd, because there was no
breeze. The day was strangely still. Even birdsong had

vanished. The distant *baa*ing of sheep was gone. It was as if she alone were alive.

"Stop being fanciful," she chided herself. Letting her own imagination bamboozle her would be silly. She had spent most of her life trying to avoid that. There were enough rumors about the Nethercott family's peculiar ways. She did not want to add to them.

Suddenly her horse neighed and violently tugged the cart to the right. China groaned as the reins jerked her arm, straining her shoulder.

"What is wrong with you, Bayberry?" she asked. The horse was usually placid, not starting at a hare jumping from the grass or a bird rising with a squawk.

The horse whinnied again, more frantically. Again the cart pulled to the right.

Something stuck out of the hedgerow on her left. Sunlight flashed off metal. Something long and metal. A gun!

Her first instinct was to slap the reins and set the horse to a run. Instead, she drew back on the reins, halting Bayberry before the horse could panic.

Or the highwayman.

There had been rumors about a knight of the pad stopping carriages along the deserted roads of the moors, but those attacks had taken place on moonless nights. It was the afternoon! Had he grown more bold? Or—she gulped at the thought—more desperate?

She must not panic. It might be one of her neighbors hunting in the wood. And Squire Haywood, the local magistrate, had asked the men in the local parishes to help find the highwayman. Nobody had seen a hint of him, save for his victims. He obviously knew the moors well, which meant he must be a local resident. That was a horrifying thought.

"Stay where you are! Say nothing!" came a shout. The voice was oddly accented, but the words were clear and emphasized with a motion from the weapon.

China stared. The metal thing sticking out from the hedgerow was not a gun. Only the end was made of metal. The rest of it was a wooden shaft. A pike. No, a spear! Why was a highwayman using a *spear*?

The man stepped out from the concealing branches. He wore leggings that reached just below his knees and a long shirt with short sleeves. Both were faded red. A cloak with a cowl was draped over an armored waistcoat made in strips of metal, lashed together in the front. More pieces of metal hung over his shoulders and half-way down his upper arm. His shoes were leather, and as he stepped closer, she could see they were studded on the bottom. On his head, he wore a helmet that had a broad piece of metal to protect the back of his neck. A short sword in a scabbard was lashed to the armored waistcoat. In one hand, he carried the spear, which was almost seven feet long; in the other, he held a scarlet shield, which was rounded to offer him protection on three sides.

Sunlight glinted off the mail and spear, surrounding him with a cool glow. He wore a frown beneath his prominent nose. His eyes were pale blue and his dark hair closely cropped.

China stared at him, shocked. She had seen drawings of the odd clothing in her father's books about ancient Roman legionnaires who once held the area as part of their vast empire. She wanted to ask him why he was dressed so, but decided she would be wise to heed his request for silence. If she angered him, he might drive that spear through her.

But why was a highwayman dressed as a Roman soldier?

"Get out," he ordered, holding the spear inches from the center of her chest.

She obeyed, whispering a soft apology to the horse before saying, "If you are planning on stealing the cart, please treat my horse with kindness. There is no need to lay on the whip."

"I have no interest in your horse or cart."

Drawing her reticule out of the cart, she opened it and emptied a few coins into her hand. She held them out to him.

"I have no need for your money."

"Then what do you want?" She took a step toward the rear of the cart as his gaze swept over her. The road was deserted. Was her only choice her honor or her life? No! If she took the offensive . . . "I must warn you that I can scream very loudly. If you lay a single hand on me—"

"We have no time to waste. Will you be silent?"

China nodded, surprised at her own prattle.

"What is your name?" he asked.

"China Nethercott."

"From the priory—I mean, from the castle?"

"Yes, in Nethercott Castle. Not many people around here remember that it was a priory more than two hundred years ago." She hesitated, then asked, "Are you interested in many periods of history?"

"All of them."

"Excuse me?" She was ready to condemn the man as deranged, but it was an epithet she did not use easily. Too many people had labeled her sweet father crazy when he had simply chosen to live his life in his own manner and raise his three daughters to question what everyone else took for granted.

"I am interested in all the periods of Britannia's history, since I was sent here with other Menapian and Belgics when Carausius proclaimed himself emperor of Britannia while Diocletian was emperor in Rome."

"Excuse me?" she repeated. She had not recognized any of the names except Britannia and Rome.

He paused so long in answering that she wondered if he had gone into some barely conscious state. If he were truly mad, he might be unsettled by her questioning his fantasy, and was perhaps frozen in thought. She had read about such cases. No one comprehended why such a reaction occurred, and it was extremely rare.

Then he replied, "We are wasting time when . . . All right. Let me see if I can explain this with terms you will comprehend," he said in a calm voice that suggested she was the witless one. "I came here with members of my clan from the area you call the Low Countries. I served my emperors—both the one in Rome and the usurper who claimed to rule Britannia and western France. I served in Derventio—I mean, in Malton."

Another name she recognized. The town of Malton was about fifteen miles south of Nethercott Castle.

"And I trained troops here, at what is now known as Cawthorne Camp," he went on.

She knew that name, too. Beyond the trees, on the edge of a flat hilltop that dropped sharply into the valley, were the ruins of a Roman settlement. Her father had spent many pleasant afternoons digging among the earthwork ruins, always excited whenever he found an artifact, even if only a pottery shard.

"That camp has been abandoned for almost fifteen hundred years," she said, hoping she would not infuriate him by questioning his delusion.

"I realize that." He grimaced and shook his head. "Why is it always the same? Why must all of you pester me with the doubt, the questions, the attempt to pretend you believe me even though you think I am insane?"

"Are you asking me to answer those questions?"

"No!" He drew in a deep breath, then let it sift out past his clenched teeth. Glancing over his shoulder, he squared his shoulders. "I was talking to myself. Let us get this under way. *Tempus omnia revelat.*"

"Time reveals everything?" she asked, unsure because his odd accent was even more pronounced in Latin than in English.

"You know Latin?"

"Yes, my father taught my sisters and me so we could read his books and discuss them with him."

"It is about time that women were educated!" He smiled.

That smile altered everything about him. What had seemed threatening no longer did. Even though his spear was still aimed at her heart, she could hope—for the first time—that he had no intention of driving it through her.

"I agree," she said carefully.

"And you are educated enough that you cannot believe that a Roman centurion stands before you."

"It is unlikely."

His smile broadened, creasing his deeply tanned cheeks. "It would be, if I were still alive. However, more than a century before the camp in the trees was allowed to return to its natural state, I died here."

Also from
Jocelyn Kelley

MY LADY KNIGHT

Isabella de Montfort's talents lie not in the knightly arts, but in science and alchemy. So she's surprised when Queen Eleanor assigns her the task of retrieving something that could start a war—aided by Jordan le Courtenay, a knight who's lost his lust for battle. But soon Isabella inspires in Jordan a passion for the world around him—and a dangerous longing for her.

**Available wherever books are sold or at
penguin.com**

Jocelyn Kelley

A MOONLIT KNIGHT

In twelfth-century England, St. Jude's Abbey is no ordinary holy sanctuary: it trains young women in the knightly arts.

Summoned in the middle of the night, Mallory de Saint-Sebastian must leave the Abbey to protect Queen Eleanor's life as a revolt against King Henry rages. With a knight's sense of obligation, she is determined to not only sheild Eleanor but to find the enemies threatening her. Arriving at St. Jude's Abbey, Saxon Fitz-Juste is amazed by the Queen's choice of a female knight as her newest warrior. A troubadour in Eleanor's royal court, Saxon is ostensibly loyal to Her Majesty, but his true mission remains to be seen.

Available wherever books are sold or at
penguin.com